WILBUR SMITH

VICIOUS CIRCLE

MACMILLAN

First published 2013 by Macmillan
an imprint of Pan Macmillan, a division of Macmillan Publishers Limited
Pan Macmillan, 20 New Wharf Road, London N1 9RR
Basingstoke and Oxford
Associated companies throughout the world
www.panmacmillan.com

ISBN 978-0-230-75763-9 TPB
ISBN 978-1-4472-5012-8 HB

1 3 5 7 9 8 6 4 2

A CIP catalogue record for this book is available from the British Library.

Typeset by Ellipsis Digital Limited, Glasgow
Printed and bound in Australia by McPherson's Printing Group

Visit **www.panmacmillan.com** to read more about all our books
and to buy them. You will also find features, author interviews and
news of any author events, and you can sign up for e-newsletters
so that you're always first to hear about our new releases.

This book is for my wife

MOKHINISO

who is the best thing
that has ever happened to me

HE CAME FULLY AWAKE before he moved or opened his eyes. He lay for a second assessing his situation, checking for danger, his warrior instincts taking control. Then he smelled her delicate perfume and heard her breathing as softly and regularly as the dying surf running up a distant beach. All was well, and he smiled and opened his eyes. Gently he rolled his head so as not to awaken her.

The early sun had found a chink in the curtains and through it had laid a sliver of beaten gold across the ceiling. It cast an intriguing light on her face and form. She lay on her back. Her face was in repose and it was lovely. She had kicked off the sheet and she was naked. The golden curls covering her mons Veneris were a shade darker than the splendid tangle of the locks that had fallen over her face. Now, so far along in her pregnancy, her bosoms were swollen to almost twice their normal size. He let his gaze drift down to her belly. The skin was stretched tight and glossy by the precious cargo it contained. As he stared at it he saw the small movement as the child stirred within her womb and his breathing was stifled for an instant by the weight and strength of his love for them both, his woman and his child.

'Stop staring at my big fat belly and give me a kiss,' she said without opening her eyes. He chuckled and leaned over her. She reached up with both arms around his neck and as her lips parted he smelled her sweet breath. After a while she whispered into his open mouth, 'Can't you keep this monster of yours on a leash?' She reached down with one hand to his groin. 'Even he must know that at the moment there is no room at the inn.'

'Colour him brainless,' he said. 'But you have never been any great help in keeping him under control. Unhand me, you brazen wench!'

1

'Just wait a few weeks and I will show you the true meaning of the word brazen, Hector Cross,' she warned him. 'Now ring down to the kitchen for coffee.'

While they waited for the coffee to be delivered he left the bed and drew back the curtains, letting the sunlight burst into the room.

'The swans are in the Mill Pool,' he called to her. She struggled upright using both hands to cradle her belly. He came back to her immediately and helped her to her feet. She picked up her blue satin bed robe from the chair and slipped into it as they crossed to the picture window.

'I feel so ungainly!' she complained as she tied the belt. He stood behind her and with both hands reached around and gently cradled her belly.

'Somebody is kicking again,' Hector whispered into her ear and then took the lobe between his teeth and nibbled it lightly.

'Don't tell me. I feel like a ruddy football.' She reached back over her shoulder and lightly slapped his cheek. 'Don't do that. You know it gives me goose bumps all over.'

They looked down at the swans in silence. The cob and the pen were a dazzling white in the early sunlight, but the three cygnets were a grubby grey. The cob dipped his long sinuous neck into the green waters and reached down to feed on the aquatic plants at the bottom of the pool.

'Beautiful, aren't they?' he asked at last.

'They are just one of the many reasons I love England,' Hazel whispered. 'What a perfect scene. We should have a good artist paint it.'

The river spilled into the pool over a stone weir and the waters were limpid. They could look down ten feet and see the shadows of the big trout lying on the gravel bottom. Willows lined the banks and brushed the surface with their trailing fingers. The meadow beyond was a luscious green and the sheep grazing on it were as white as the swans.

'It's the perfect place to raise our little girl. You know that's why I bought it.' She sighed contentedly.

'I know that. You've told me often enough. What I don't know is what makes you so certain this is a girl.' He caressed her stomach. 'Don't you really want to know for certain the gender, instead of just guessing?'

'I am not guessing. I know,' she said smugly and covered his large brown hands with her slim white ones.

'We could ask Alan when we get up to London this morning,' he suggested. Alan Donnovan was her gynaecologist.

'You are an awful nag. But don't you dare ask Alan and spoil my fun. Now put on your dressing gown. You don't want to terrify poor Mary when she comes with the coffee,' she said fondly.

Moments later there was a discreet knock on the door. 'Come!' said Hector and the chambermaid carried in the coffee tray.

'Good morning to all! How are you and the baby, Mrs Cross?' she said in her cheerful Irish brogue, placing the tray on the table.

'All is well, Mary, but do I spy biscuits on that tray?' Hazel demanded.

'Only three small ones.'

'Take them away, please.'

'Two for Sir and just one for you. Plain oatmeal. No sugar,' Mary wheedled.

'Be a darling, Mary. Humour me. Take them away, please.'

'Poor little mite must be starving,' Mary grumbled but she picked up the biscuit dish and marched from the room. Hazel sat on the sofa and poured a single mug of coffee so black and strong that its aroma filled the room.

'God! It smells so good,' she said wistfully as she handed it to him. Then she poured warm unsweetened skimmed milk into her own porcelain cup.

'Ugh!' she exclaimed with disgust as she tasted it, but she drank it down like medicine. 'So how are you going to keep yourself busy while I am with Alan? You know he will take at least a couple of hours. He's very thorough.'

'I have to take my shotguns to Paul Roberts for storage, and then I have a suit fitting with my tailor.'

'You aren't going to drive my beautiful Ferrari around in the London morning traffic, are you? You'd probably give it a ding, same as you did to the Rolls.'

'Will you never forget that?' He spread his hands in mock outrage. 'The silly woman jumped the lights and drove into me.'

'You drive like a maniac, Cross, and you know it.'

'Okay, I'll take a cab to do my errands,' he promised. 'I don't want to look like a football player in that poncey machine of yours. Anyway, my new Range Rover is waiting for me. Stratstone's phoned me yesterday to let me know that it's ready. If you are a good girl, which we all know you are, I'll take you to lunch in it.'

'Talking about lunch, where are we going?' she demanded.

'I don't know why I bother. We can get lettuce leaves anywhere, but I reserved our usual table at Alfred's Club.'

'Now I know you really love me!'

'You had better believe it, skinny.'

'Compliments! Compliments!' She gave him a beatific smile.

Hazel's red Ferrari coupé was parked under the portico that sheltered the front door. It sparkled like an enormous ruby in the sunlight. Robert, her chauffeur, had polished it lovingly. It was his favourite amongst all the many cars parked in the underground garage. Hector made an arm for her down the front steps and helped her into the driver's seat. When she had wriggled her belly in behind the wheel he fussed over her, getting the adjustment of the seat just right and the safety belt comfortably looped under her bump.

'Are you sure you don't want me to drive?' he asked solicitously.

'Never,' she replied. 'Not after all the horrid things you said about her.' She patted the steering wheel. 'Get in and let's go.'

It was three-quarters of a mile from the manor house to the public highway, but the estate road was paved all the way. Where it looped into the approach to the bridge over the River Test there was a fine view back to the house. Hazel pulled over for a moment. She could seldom resist the temptation to gloat over what she humbly referred to as 'simply the finest Georgian building in existence'.

Brandon Hall had been built in 1752 by Sir William Chambers for the Earl of Brandon. He was the same architect who had built

Somerset House on The Strand. Brandon Hall had been shamefully neglected and rundown when Hazel acquired it. When Hector thought about how much money she had lavished upon the house to bring it to its present state of perfection he could barely suppress a shudder. However, he could never deny the beauty of its elegant and perfectly balanced lines. Last year Hazel had been placed seventh on *Forbes* magazine's list of the richest women in the world. She could afford it.

Still and all, what woman in her right mind needs sixteen bedrooms, for God's sake? But the hell with expense, the fishing in the river is truly great. Worth every dollar, he consoled himself silently. 'Come on, baby,' he said aloud. 'You can admire it on your way back, but right now you are going to be late for your appointment with Alan.'

'I do so enjoy a challenge,' she said sweetly, and pulled away leaving black rubber burns on the tarmac surface behind her and a pale blue cloud of smoke hanging in the air.

When she reversed effortlessly into the underground parking bay beneath the Harley Street building, from which Alan Donnovan had removed his own vehicle to make room for hers, she glanced at her wristwatch.

'One hour forty-eight minutes! I do believe that's my personal best time to date. Fifteen minutes ahead of my appointment. Would you like to retract that gibe about me being late, smarty-pants?'

'One day you are going to hit a radar trap and they are going to pull your driver's licence, my beloved.'

'Mine is a US licence. These sweet Brit cops can't touch it.'

Hector escorted her up to Alan's suite. As soon as he heard her voice, Alan came out of his consulting room to welcome her; a rare show of respect he generally accorded only to royalty. He paused in the doorway to admire her. Hazel's loose-fitting maternity gown in soft Sea Island cotton had been especially designed for her. Her eyes sparkled and her skin glowed. Alan bowed over her hand and touched it to his lips.

'If all my patients were as patently healthy as you I would be out of a job,' he murmured.

'How long are you going to keep her, Alan?' Hector shook hands with him.

'I can readily understand why you are so eager to have her back.'

Such levity was seldom Alan's style, but Hector chuckled and insisted, 'When?'

'I want to run some checks and possibly consult my associates. Give me two and a half hours, will you please, Hector?' He took Hazel's arm and led her into his inner chambers. Hector watched the door close. He stared after her. He was overwhelmed by a sudden premonition of impending loss such as he had seldom experienced before. He wanted to go after her, and bring her back and hold her close to his heart for ever. It took a long moment for him to recover himself.

'Don't be a bloody idiot. Take a hold of yourself, Cross.' He turned away and went out into the passage and headed towards the lifts.

Alan Donnovan's receptionist watched him go impassively. She was a pretty Afro-British girl with big sparkling dark eyes and a good figure under her white uniform. Her name was Victoria Vusamazulu and she was twenty-seven years old. She waited until she heard the elevator stop at the end of the passage and the doors open and close behind Hector as he stepped into it, then she brought her mobile phone out of her coat pocket. She had punched his phone number into her list of contacts under the name 'Him!' The phone rang once only and she heard the click on the line.

'Hello. Is that you, Aleutian?' she asked.

'I told you not to name names, bitch.' She shivered when he called her that. He was so masterful. He was unlike any man she had known before. Instinctively her hand went to her left breast. It was bruised and still tender where he had bitten her last night. She rubbed it and the nipple hardened.

'I'm sorry. I forgot.' Her voice was husky.

'Then don't forget to delete this call when we finish. Now tell me! Has she come?'

'Yes, she is here. But her husband has gone out. He told Doctor that he would return at one thirty.'

'Good!' he said, and the line went dead. The girl took the phone from her ear and stared at it. She found that she was breathing hard. She thought about him; how hard and thick he was when he was inside her. She looked down at herself and felt the warmth oozing through the crotch of her panties onto her thighs.

'Hot as a dirty little bitch in heat,' she whispered. That was what he had called her last night. Doctor would not need her for a while, he was busy with the Cross woman. She left the reception room and went down the passage to the toilet. She locked herself in one of the cubicles. Then she pulled her skirts up around her waist and dropped her panties around her ankles. She sat on the toilet seat and spread her knees. She put her hand down there. She wanted to make it last, but as soon as she touched her hot switch she could not hold back. It was so quick and so intense that it left her gasping and shaking.

Two hours later Hector returned and ensconced himself in a leather armchair in the waiting room facing Alan's door. He picked up a copy of the *Financial Times* from the side table and turned to the FTSE reports. He did not even glance up as the intercom rang on the receptionist's desk. She spoke softly into the receiver and then hung up.

'Mr Cross,' she called across to him. 'Mr Donnovan would like to have a few words with you. Please would you go through to his room?' Hector dropped the newspaper and jumped up from the armchair. Again he felt the quick stab of anxiety. He had learned over the years to trust his instincts. What dire news did Alan have for him? He hurried across the waiting room and knocked on the inner door. Alan's muffled voice bid him enter. The consulting room was panelled in oak and the shelves were lined with sets of leather-bound medical volumes. Alan sat behind a vast antique desk and Hazel faced him. She stood up as Hector entered and came to meet him, pushing her big belly ahead of her. She was smiling radiantly and that allayed Hector's premonitions of disaster. He embraced her.

'Everything all right?' he demanded, and looked at Alan over Hazel's shining blonde head.

'Tickety-boo! Calm seas and fair winds!' Alan assured him. 'Take a seat, both of you.' They sat side by side and stared at him with full attention. He removed his spectacles and polished them with a piece of chamois leather.

'Okay, shoot!' Hector encouraged him.

'The baby is doing just fine, but Hazel isn't so young any more.'

'None of us are,' Hector agreed. 'But ever so kind of you to mention it, Alan.'

'The baby is just about ready to make its move, but perhaps Hazel might need a little bit of a hand.'

'Caesarean?' she asked with alarm.

'Dear me, no!' Alan assured her. 'Nothing so extreme. What I have in mind is an induction of labour.'

'Explain please, Alan,' Hector insisted.

'Hazel is in her fortieth week of gestation. She will be good and ready by the end of this coming week. The two of you are stuck out in the wilds of darkest Hampshire. How long does it take you to get up to London?'

'Two and a half hours is good time,' Hector replied. 'Some drivers with heavy right feet do it in under two.'

Hazel pulled a face at him.

'I want you to move up to your town house in Belgravia immediately.' Alan had been a dinner guest there on more than one occasion. 'I am going to book Hazel into a private ward in the Portland Maternity Hospital in Great Portland Street for Thursday this week. It's one of the leading establishments in the country. If she goes into spontaneous labour before Thursday you will only be fifteen minutes away from it. If nothing happens by Friday I will give Hazel a little injection and pop goes the weasel, so to speak.'

Hector turned to her. 'How do you feel about that, my darling?'

'That suits me just fine. The sooner the quicker, as far as I am concerned. Everything is ready for us in the London house. I just need to pick up a few things, like the book I am reading, and we can move back into town tomorrow.'

'That's it, then,' said Alan briskly and stood up behind his desk. 'See you both on Friday at the latest.'

On their way through the waiting room Hazel stopped in front of the receptionist's desk and rummaged around in her handbag. She brought out a gift-wrapped bottle of Chanel perfume and placed it in front of the receptionist.

'Just a little thank you, Victoria. You have been so sweet.'

'Oh, you are too kind, Mrs Cross. But you really shouldn't have!'

As they rode down in the lift Hazel asked him, 'Did you get your Range Rover from Stratstone?'

'It's parked just across the street; I will take you to lunch in her and bring you back afterwards to pick up your old can of rust.' She punched his shoulder and led the way out of the building.

He took her arm crossing Harley Street and the taxi drivers coming from both directions, seeing how pretty and pregnant she was, braked sharply to a standstill. One of them leaned out of his window, grinning. He signalled at her to cross in front of his taxi and called out to her, 'Best of luck, luv! Bet it's a boy!'

Hazel waved back. 'I'll let you know.'

None of them noticed the motorcycle parked in a loading zone a hundred yards up the street behind them. Both the driver and his pillion passenger wore gloves and helmets with darkened perspex visors which hid their faces. As Hazel and Hector reached the parked Rover the motorcyclist jumped on the kick starter and the engine of the powerful Japanese machine under him burbled to life. The pillion passenger lifted his booted feet onto the footrests, ready to go. Hector opened the passenger door for Hazel and handed her up into the seat. Then he moved briskly around to the driver's side. He jumped in, started the engine and pulled out into the traffic stream. The motorcyclist waited until there were five vehicles separating them and then he followed. He maintained the separation discreetly. They went around Marble Arch and down to Berkeley Square. When the Rover drew up in front of No. 2 Davies Street the motorcyclist rode on past and turned left at the next road junction. He circled the block and stopped when he had a view of the front of Alfred's Club. He saw at once that the doorman had parked the Rover a little further up the street.

Mario, the restaurant manager, was waiting at the entrance to greet them, beaming with pleasure. 'Welcome, Mr and Mrs Cross, but it's been far too long.'

'Nonsense, Mario,' Hector contradicted him. 'We were here ten days ago with Lord Renwick.'

'That's far too long ago, sir,' Mario protested and led them to their favourite table.

The room went silent as they passed down it. All eyes followed them. Everybody knew who they were. Even in advanced pregnancy Hazel looked magnificent. The gossamer skirt billowed around her like a rose-coloured cloud, and the handbag she carried was one of those crocodile-skin creations which made every other woman in the room consider suicide.

Mario seated her and murmured, 'May I presume that it will be the grapefruit salad for madame, followed by the grilled St Jacques? And for you, Mr Cross, the steak tartare, followed by the lobster with Chardonnay sauce?'

'As usual, Mario,' Hector agreed seriously. 'To drink, Mrs Cross will have a small bottle of Perrier water with a bucket of ice. Please fetch a bottle of the Vosne-Romanée Aux Malconsorts 1993 from my personal wine keep for me.'

'I have already taken the liberty of doing so, Mr Cross. Fifteen minutes ago I checked that the temperature of the bottle is sixteen degrees centigrade. Shall I have the sommelier open it?'

'Thank you, Mario. I know I can always rely on you.'

'We try our best to please, sir.'

As the manager left them Hazel leaned across and placed her hand on Hector's forearm. 'I do so love your little rituals, Mr Cross. Somehow I find them very comforting.' She smiled. 'Cayla also used to find them amusing. Do you remember how we laughed when she imitated you?'

'Like mother, like daughter.' Hector smiled at her.

There had been a period when Hazel had not been able to say the name 'Cayla' out loud. That had been from the time of her daughter's brutal slaying and the mutilation of her corpse by her

10

killers until she had discovered that she was pregnant with Hector's child. That had been a catharsis and she had wept in his arms and blurted out the name. 'Cayla! It's going to be another little Cayla,' she'd sobbed. After that the wounds had healed swiftly until she could talk about Cayla easily and often.

She wanted to talk now and when the sommelier had brought her Perrier water she sipped it and asked, 'Do you suppose Catherine Cayla Cross will have blonde hair and blue eyes like her big sister did?' She had already chosen the new infant's name as a tribute to her dead first child.

'He will probably have black stubble on his chin like his father,' Hector teased her. He also had loved the murdered girl. Cayla had been the magnet that had first brought them together against all the odds. Hector had been head of security at Bannock Oil when Hazel had inherited control of the company from her late husband.

From the start Hazel had detested Hector, despite the fact that he had been appointed by her own beloved deceased husband. She knew Hector's record and reputation intimately and was repelled by the hard and sometimes brutal tactics he used to defend the company assets and personnel from any threat. He was a soldier and he fought like one. He showed no mercy. He flew in the face of all Hazel's gentler female instincts. At their very first meeting she warned him that she was looking for the slightest excuse to fire him.

Then Hazel's cosseted and privileged existence was plunged into chaos. The daughter who was the cornerstone of her solitary existence was kidnapped by African pirates. Hazel exerted all her vast fortune and her influence in high places to try to rescue her. No one could help her, not even the President of the United States of America with all his power. They could not even discover where her Cayla was being held. At her wits' end, she had cast aside her pride and gone back to the cruel, brutal and merciless soldier she so hated and despised: Hector Cross.

Hector had tracked down the kidnappers to their den in the fastness of the African deserts where Cayla was being held. She was being brutally tortured by her captors. Hector had gone in with his men and brought Cayla back to safety. In the process he had demonstrated to Hazel that he was a thoroughly decent person of high principles; somebody that she could trust without reserve. She had given in to the attraction she had so carefully suppressed at their first meeting and once she had got closer to him she discovered that under his armour-plated exterior he could be warm and gentle and loving.

She looked at him now and she reached across the table to take his hand. 'With you beside me and baby Catherine Cayla inside me, everything is perfect again.'

'It will be like this for ever,' he assured her and another tiny frisson of dread ran up his spine as he realized he was tempting the fates. Though he smiled tenderly at her, he was brooding on how the rescue of Cayla had not been the end of the affair either. The fanatics who had seized her had not given up. Their hired thugs had come back and murdered Cayla and sent her decapitated head to Hazel. Hector and Hazel had been forced to re-enter the fray and finally eradicate the monster who had ruined their lives.

Perhaps this time it is really over, he thought as he watched Hazel's face. She went on talking about Cayla.

'Do you remember how you taught her to fish?'

'She was a natural. With just a little coaching she could cast a salmon fly at least a hundred and fifty feet in most wind conditions and she instinctively knew how to read the waters.'

'What about the big salmon the two of you landed in Norway?'

'It was a monster. I was hanging on to her belt, and it almost pulled us both into the river.' He chuckled.

'I'll never forget the day she announced that she was not going to be an art dealer, the career I had planned for her, but that she had decided to become a veterinary surgeon. I nearly had a blue fit!'

'That was very naughty of her.' Hector pronounced judgement with a stern expression.

'Naughty? You were the naughty one. You backed her up all the way. The two of you talked me right into it.'

'Tut. Tut. She was such a bad influence on me,' Hector admitted.

'She loved you. You know that. She really loved you like her own father.'

'That's one of the nicest things anyone has ever said to me.'

'You are a good man, Hector Cross.' Tears welled up in her eyes.

'Catherine Cayla is going to love you also. All three of your girls love you.' She gasped suddenly and clutched her stomach. 'Oh my God! She gave me a mule kick. She obviously agrees with what I just said.' They both burst out laughing so that the guests at the other tables looked around at them, smiling in sympathy. However, they might just as well have been alone in the room. They were totally engrossed by each other.

They had so much to remember and discuss. Both of them had filled their lives with strivings and endeavour. They had both experienced soaring triumphs and shattering disasters, but Hazel's career had been by far the more spectacular. She had started out with little more than guts and determination. At the age of nineteen she had won her first Grand Slam tournament on the professional tennis tour. At twenty-one she had married the oil tycoon Henry Bannock and borne him a daughter. Henry had died when Hazel was almost thirty years old and left control of the Bannock Oil conglomerate to her.

The world of big business is an exclusive domain. Intruders and upstarts are not welcome there. Nobody wanted to bet on a some-time tennis-player-cum-society-glamour-girl-turned-oil-baroness. However none of them had taken into account Hazel's innate business acumen, nor the years of her tutelage under Henry Bannock, which were worth a hundred MBA degrees. Like the crowds at the Roman circus, her detractors and critics waited in grisly anticipation for her to be devoured by the lions. Then, to the chagrin of all, she brought in the Zara No. 8.

Hector remembered vividly how *Forbes* magazine had blazoned on its front cover the image of Hazel in her white tennis kit, holding a racquet in her right hand. The headline above the photograph read 'Hazel Bannock aces the opposition. Richest oil strike in thirty years.'

The story described how in the bleak hinterland of the godforsaken and impoverished little emirate named Abu Zara lay an oil concession once owned by the Shell Oil Company. In the period directly after World War II, Shell had pumped the reservoir dry and abandoned the exhausted concession. Since then it had lain forgotten. Then Hazel had picked it up for a few paltry millions of dollars and the pundits nudged each other and smirked. Ignoring the protests of her advisors, she spent many millions more in sinking a rotary cone drill into a tiny subterranean anomaly at the northern extremity of the field; an anomaly which with the more primitive exploration techniques of thirty years previously had been reckoned to be an ancillary of the main reservoir. The geologists of that time had agreed that any oil contained in this area had long ago drained into the main reservoir and been pumped to the surface, leaving the entire field dry and worthless.

However, when Hazel's drilling team pierced the impervious salt dome of the diapir, a vast subterranean chamber in which the principal oil deposits had been trapped, the gas overpressure roared up through the drill hole with such force that it ejected almost eight kilometres of steel drill string like toothpaste from the tube, and the hole blew out. High-grade crude oil spurted hundreds of feet into the air. At last it became evident that the old Zara 1 to 7 fields which Shell had abandoned were only a fraction of the total reserves.

Recalling all this seemed to draw them closer to each other over the lunch table, fascinated by the reminiscences they had repeated many times before but in which they still discovered things totally new and intriguing. At one point Hector shook his head in admiration. 'My God, woman! Have you never been daunted by anything or anybody in your life? You have done it all on your own, and you have done it the hard way.'

She slanted her startling eyes at him and smiled. 'Don't you see, life was never meant to be easy; if it was, we would place no real value on it. Now that's enough about me. Let's talk about you.'

'You already know everything there is to know about me. I have told you fifty times over.'

'Okay, let's make it fifty-one. Tell me about the day on which you took your lion. I want all the details again. Take care. I will know if you leave anything out.'

'Very well, here I go. I was born in Kenya, but my dad and mum were both Brits, so I am a genuine British citizen.' He paused.

'Their names were Bob and Sheila . . .' she prompted him.

'Their names were Bob and Sheila Cross. My father had almost twenty-five thousand hectares of prime grazing land abutting the

14

Maasai tribal reservation. On this he was running over two thousand head of prize Brahman cattle. So my boyhood companions were mostly Maasai boys of my own age.'

'And your little brother, of course,' said Hazel.

'Yes, my little brother, Teddy. He wanted to be a rancher, like our father. He would do anything to please the old man. On the other hand, I wanted to be a warrior like my uncle who had died in the war fighting Rommel at El Alamein in the North African desert. The day my father sent me to the Duke of York School for boys in Nairobi was the most devastating experience of my life to that date.'

'You hated it, didn't you?'

'I hated the rules and the restraint. I was accustomed to running wild and free,' he said.

'You were a rebel.'

'My father said I was a rebel and a bloody savage. But he said it with a smile. Nevertheless, I was third from top of my class and captain of the first fifteen rugby team in my final year at the Duke. That was good enough for me. That was when I was sixteen years of age.'

'The year of your lion!' She leaned forward across the table and took his hand, her eyes shining with anticipation. 'I love this part. The first part is a little tame. Not enough blood and guts, you know.'

'My Maasai companions were coming of age. So I went to the village and spoke to the chief. I told him I wanted to become a Morani with them. A warrior.'

She nodded.

'The chief listened to everything I asked for. Then he said that I was not a true Maasai because I had not been circumcised. He asked if I wanted to be cut by the witch doctor. I thought about it and then declined the offer.'

'And a good job too,' Hazel said. 'I prefer your whistle the way that God originally designed it.'

'What a kind thing to say. But to return to the story of my life; I discussed this rejection with my companions, and they were almost as distressed by it as I was. We argued about it for days and in the end they agreed that if I could not become a true Morani, at least I could take my lion, then I would be more than halfway a Morani.'

15

'But there was just one little problem, wasn't there?' she reminded him.

'The problem was that the Kenyan government, in which the Maasai tribe was poorly represented, had banned the lion ceremony of manhood. Lions were now strictly protected throughout the entire territory.'

'But then came some divine intervention,' she said, and he grinned at her.

'Straight from heaven!' he agreed. 'In the Masai Mara National Park, which adjoined the tribal lands, an old lion was driven out of his pride by a younger and stronger rival. Without his lionesses to drive the hunt he was forced to leave the protection of the park, and to seek easier prey than zebra and wildebeest. Firstly, he started on the Maasai cattle herds, which were the tribal store of wealth. This was bad enough, but then he killed a young woman as she came down to the waterhole to draw water for her family.

'Much to the joy and feverish excitement of my friends the Maasai, the Government Game Department was forced to issue a licence to eradicate the old rogue. Because of the links that I had forged with the tribe over the years, and because I was big and strong for my age and the elders knew just how hard I had trained with the fighting sticks and the war spear, they invited me to join the hunt with the other young Morani candidates.'

Hector paused as the sommelier added half an inch of red wine to his glass and then topped up the Perrier water in Hazel's. Hector murmured his thanks and then wet his lips with the Burgundy before he continued.

'The lion had not killed and eaten for almost a week and we all waited in an agony of suspense for his hunger to force him to kill again. Then on the sixth evening, as the light was fading, two little naked herdboys came racing back to the village with the glad tidings. As they were bringing the herd down to the waterhole the lion had waylaid them. He had been lying in ambush in the thick grass on the downwind side of the path, and he charged out at the herd from a range of only ten paces or so. Before the cattle had time to scatter he had leapt onto the back of a five-year-old cow that was heavy with calf. He sank his fangs into the base of her neck while he reached around with one great paw and sank his long yellow claws into her snout. Then he heaved back with all the massive strength of his forearm against the lock he had on the cow's neck. The neck vertebrae parted with a crack, killing her instantly. She went down nose first as her forelegs collapsed and she somersaulted in a cloud of dust. The lion jumped clear before he was crushed by her fifteen hundred pounds of dead weight.'

'I still can't believe he was strong enough to kill a huge animal so easily,' Hazel said in awed tones.

'Not only that, but he was able to lift her in his jaws and carry her into the grass, holding her so high that only her hooves dragged in the dust.'

'Go on!' she urged him. 'Don't mind my silly questions. Get on with the story!'

'Well, it was already dark, so we had to wait for the dawn. None of us slept much that night. We sat around the fires and the older men told us gleefully what to expect when we walked up to the old lion on his kill. There was not much laughter from any of us, and our chatter was subdued. It was still dark when we dressed in our black goatskin cloaks against the chill of dawn. We were naked under the cloaks. We armed ourselves with our rawhide shields and our short stabbing spears, which we had sharpened so that we were able to shave the hair off our forearms with the bright edge. There were thirty-two of us, a band of brothers. We went singing in the dawn to meet our lion.'

'You'd think that would have warned the lion and driven him away,' said Hazel.

'It would have taken much more than that to drive a lion off his kill,' Hector told her. 'We sang a challenge to him. We called him to battle. And of course, we bolstered our own courage. We sang and we danced to warm our blood. We stabbed at the air with our spears to loosen the muscles of our arms. The young unmarried girls followed us at a distance to see who would stand to the lion and who would break and run when he came in all his noble might to answer our challenge.'

Hazel had heard the story a dozen times already, but she watched his face so raptly that it might have been the very first telling of it.

17

'The sun came up and showed its upper rim above the horizon directly in front of us, bright as molten metal from the furnace. It shone into our faces to dazzle us. However, we knew where we would find our lion. We saw the tops of the grass move where there was no wind, and then we heard him growl. It was a terrible sound that struck into our hearts and into our bowels. Our legs turned to water and each dancing pace was a conscious effort as we went forward to meet him.

'Then the lion stood up from where he had lain flat behind the carcass of the heifer. His mane was fully erect. It formed a majestic corona around his head. It burned with a golden light, for he was vividly back-lit by the sun. It seemed to double his bulk. He roared. It was a gale of sound that swept over us and our own voices faltered for a moment. Then we rallied and shouted back at him, calling on him to pick his man and come against him. The flanks of our line started to curl in around him, surrounding him and leaving him no escape route. He swung his head slowly from side to side, surveying us as we closed in.'

'Oh God!' she breathed. 'I know already what is going to happen, but I can barely stand the tension.'

'Then his head stopped swinging and his tail began to lash from side to side, the black tuft on the end of it whipping his own flanks. I was in the middle of the line, the place of honour, and I was close enough to see his eyes clearly. They were yellow, bright burning yellow, and they were fastened upon me.'

'Why you, Hector? Why you, my darling?' She shook his hand urgently, her expression filled with dread as though it were happening before her very eyes.

'God alone knows,' he shrugged. 'Perhaps because I was in the middle of the line, but most likely because my pale body was shining out from amongst the darker bodies that flanked me.'

'Go on!' she begged. 'Tell me again how it ended.'

'The lion fell into a crouch as he gathered himself for the charge. His tail stopped lashing from side to side. He held it straight out behind him, rigid and slightly upwardly curled. Then it flicked twice and he came straight at me. He came snaking low along the ground, so fast that he was only a tawny streak of sunlight, ethereal but deadly.

18

'And in those microseconds I learned the true meaning of terror. Everything slowed down. The air around me seemed to grow dense and heavy, difficult to breathe. It was like being trapped in a thick mud swamp. Every movement required a deliberate effort. I knew I was shouting, but the sound seemed to come faintly from far away. I braced myself behind the rawhide shield and raised the point of my spear. The sunlight caught the burnished metal and sent a bright splinter of light into my eyes. The form of the lion swelled up before me until it filled all my vision. I aimed the point of my spear at the centre of his chest. His chest was pumping as he deafened me with his killing fury, mighty gusts of sound like those of a steam locomotive running at full throttle.

'I braced myself. Then at the final instant before his weight hurtled into my shield I leaned into him and caught him on the point of my spear. I let his own weight and speed drive the point so deeply into his chest that the spearhead and half of the shaft were swallowed up. He was dying as he bore me backwards to the earth and crouched on top of me raking the shield with his claws, bellowing his rage and agony into my upturned face.'

Hazel shuddered at the picture he had created for her. 'It's too horrible! I have goose flesh running down both my arms. But don't stop. Go on, Hector. Tell me the end of it.'

'Then suddenly the lion's whole body stiffened and he arched his back. With his jaws open wide he vomited a copious gout of his heart blood over me, drenching my head and my entire upper body before my companions could drag him off me and stab him a hundred times over with their own blades.'

'It terrifies me to think about how differently it could have ended,' she said. 'How we might never have met each other and shared all that we have now. Now, tell me what your father said when you returned to the ranch that day,' she demanded of him.

'I rode back to the big old thatched-roof ranch house, but it was afternoon before I reached it. My family were seated at the lunch table on the front stoep. I tethered my horse at the hitching rail and climbed the steps slowly. My euphoria evaporated as I saw my family's faces. I realized then that I had not bothered to wash. The lion's blood had dried thickly in my hair and on my skin. My face was a mask of dried blood. It had rubbed off on my clothing, and was black on my hands and under my fingernails.

'My little brother Teddy broke the horrified silence. He giggled like a schoolgirl. Teddy was a giggler. At that my mother burst into tears and hid her face in her hands; she knew what my father would have to say.

'He rose to his feet, all six foot two of him, and his face was dark and twisted with rage. He choked incoherently on it. Then slowly his expression cleared and he said ominously, "You have been with those black savages, your bosom chums, have you not, boy?"

'"Yes, sir," I admitted. My father was always "sir"; never "Dad", and especially never "Daddy".

'"Yes, sir," I repeated, and suddenly his expression changed.

'"You have been for your lion, just like a bloody Maasai Morani. That's it. Isn't it?"

'"Yes, sir," I admitted, and my mother burst into fresh gales of tears. My father went on staring at me with that odd expression for a long while and I stood to attention in front of him. Then he spoke again.

'"Did you stand or did you break?"

'"I stood, sir." Again his long silence, before he spoke again. "Go to your rondavel and get yourself cleaned up. Then I will see you in my study." This summons was usually the equivalent of a death sentence or a least a hundred lashes.'

'Then what happened?' Hazel demanded, although she knew full well.

'When I knocked at the door of his study a short while later, I was wearing my school blazer and tie with a clean white shirt. My shoes were polished and my damp hair was slicked down.

'"Come in!" he bellowed. I marched in and stood in front of his desk.

'"You are a bloody savage," he said firmly. "An utterly uncivilized savage. I see only one hope for you."

'"Yes, sir." Inwardly I quailed; I thought I knew what was coming.

'"Sit down, Hector." He indicated the armchair facing his desk. That rocked me. I had never sat in that chair, and I could not remember when last he called me Hector, and not boy.

'When I was seated bolt upright facing him he went on, "You will never make a rancher, Hector, will you?"

'"I doubt it, sir."

'"The ranch should have been yours, as the eldest son. But now I am going to leave it to Teddy."

'"I wish Teddy joy of it, sir," I said, and he actually smiled, but fleetingly.

'"Of course he will not have it too long," the old man said, and the smile was gone again. "In a very few years we will all be booted out of here by the former owners from whom we stole it in the first place. Africa always wins in the end." I was silent. There was no reply I could think of.

'"But you, young Hector. What shall we do with you?" Again I had no answer, and I kept my mouth shut. I had long ago learned that was the safest option. He went on speaking. "You will always be a savage at heart, Hector. But that is no serious drawback. Most of our revered British heroes, from Clive to Kitchener, from Wellington to Churchill, were savages. There would never have been a British Empire without them. But I want you to be a well-educated and cultivated English savage, so I am sending you to the Royal Military Academy at Sandhurst to learn to kick the living shit out of all the lesser peoples of this earth."'

Hazel burst out laughing and clapped her hands. 'What a remarkable man. He must have been completely outrageous.'

'He was full of bluster, but it was all an act. He wanted to be known as a hard man who never backed down, and who always called a spade a bloody shovel. But under the veneer he was a kind and decent man. I think he loved me, and I certainly worshipped him.'

'I wish I had known him,' Hazel said wistfully.

'Probably much better you didn't,' Hector assured her. Then he turned as Mario coughed politely at his elbow.

'Will there be anything further you need, Mr Cross?' Hector looked up at the restaurant manager as if he had never seen him before. Then he blinked and looked around the room that was now empty except for a couple of bored waiters standing by the doors to the kitchen.

'Good Lord, what is the time?'

'It is a few minutes past four o'clock, sir.'

'Why on earth did you not warn us?'

'You and Mrs Cross were enjoying yourselves so much I couldn't bring myself to it, sir.' Hector left a fifty-pound note on the table for him and took Hazel out to where the doorman had the Rover at the front entrance of the club with the engine running. When they reached Harley Street, Hector drove down the ramp into the underground garage of Alan's building and helped Hazel into her Ferrari.

'Now, my queen honey bee, remember that I am behind you and it isn't a race. Look in your rear-view mirror occasionally.'

'Do stop fussing, darling.'

'I won't stop until you give me a kiss.'

'Come and get it, greedy boy.'

While Hector waited for her to leave the garage ahead of him he drew on a pair of soft kid leather driving gloves, then he followed the Ferrari up the ramp. The motorcyclist following them kept well back, using other vehicles as stalking horses as they weaved their way through the streets of London and at last joined the M3 motorway. There was no need for him to press too closely and run the risk of alerting the quarry. He knew exactly where they were headed. Besides that, he had been warned that the man was a hectic dude; definitely not somebody to mess around with. He would only make his move much later after they had passed through Winchester. At intervals he spoke briefly into the hands-free microphone of the phone which was fitted into his crash helmet, reporting the progress of the two vehicles ahead of him. Each time the receiving station clicked the transmit button to acknowledge the transmission.

Two hundred yards ahead of the motorcyclist Hector drove with one finger tapping time to the music on the steering wheel. He was tuned to Magic radio, his preferred station. Don McLean was singing 'American Pie', and Hector sang along. He knew all the intricate lyrics by heart. However, he never relaxed his vigilance. Every few seconds his eyes darted up to the rear-view mirror, scanning the following traffic. The vehicles in his line of vision were constantly changing but each one was saved in his memory. 'Always watch your tail' was one of his aphorisms. Just before Basingstoke the traffic thinned out and Hazel opened up the Ferrari. Hector had to push the Rover up to nearly 120 mph to keep her in sight.

He called her on his hands-free mobile: 'Take it easy, lover. Remember you have a very important passenger riding with you.' She blew a loud raspberry back at him, but dropped the Ferrari back to just a little over the speed limit.

'What a good girl you can be when you really try,' he said and eased his speed to match hers.

'Approaching Junction 9. Red vehicle is still leading. She has taken the slip-road for Winchester. Black vehicle is tracking her.' Behind them the motorcyclist spoke into his concealed microphone and the receiving station clicked acknowledgement again.

Still in loose formation, Hazel led them into the bypass around the ancient cathedral city of Winchester, fifteen centuries old and once the capital and stronghold of King Alfred the Great. At intervals Hector could make out the cathedral spire rising above the other buildings of the city. They left it behind. Ahead of Hector the red Ferrari slowed for the turn-off signposted Smallbridge on Test and Brandon Hall. As he followed Hazel into the turning Hector noticed two workmen on the side of the road. Dressed in yellow high-visibility coats with BRITISH ROADS printed across their backs, they were unloading the components of a steel barrier from the back of a parked truck. Hector paid them little attention, but he looked ahead to where the Ferrari was dwindling in the distance. Apart from the red machine the narrow road was deserted as far ahead as Hector could see.

Less than a minute later the biker and his passenger followed them into the road to Smallbridge. As he passed the workmen the biker raised a gloved hand to them and they were galvanized into action by his signal. Quickly they dragged the sections of the steel barrier into the road and set it up, blocking both lanes. Then they raised a large yellow and black road sign which read, ROAD CLOSED. NO ENTRY. DIVERSION.

A large black arrow directed traffic to continue up the main road, effectively isolating both Hazel and Hector and the motorcycle that followed them. The pseudo workmen jumped back into their truck and drove away. They had been paid and their job was done.

So close to home, Hector drove relaxed. Once he glanced up at the rear-view mirror and he noticed only a motorbike that was two hundred yards further back. He switched his attention to the road ahead. There was rolling green countryside on both sides of it, interrupted by copses of darker trees. Some of these pressed up close against the road as it twisted and undulated over the gentle hillsides. The road had shrunk to two narrow lanes. Even Hazel was obliged to reduce her speed.

'Both vehicles entering demarcated zone,' said the motorcyclist crisply, and this time he was answered by the other station.

'Roger that, Station One. I have you and the chase both visible.'

Suddenly between the motorcycle and Hector's Rover another vehicle turned out of a muddy farm track onto the tarmac road. It had stayed concealed behind a clump of trees until Hector had driven past. It was a large left-hand drive Mercedes Benz van with French registration plates. Apart from those, it showed no other markings. The motorcyclist accelerated until he was positioned twenty feet off the van's rear bumper.

Ahead of them Hector's Rover disappeared over another rise. When the Mercedes and the motorbike reached the same crest they saw that the road ahead of them descended into a shallow valley where it crossed a raised embankment with boggy ground on either side. Hector was just driving out onto the embankment while in the distance the red Ferrari was already climbing the low hill on the far side of the valley. The driver of the Mercedes van smiled with satisfaction. The trap was perfectly set. He floored his accelerator, roared down the slope and out onto the embankment. As he came up swiftly behind Hector he blew a piercing blast on his horn. Hector glanced up at his rear-view mirror.

'Now where did this cheeky bastard spring from?' He was startled. The van had not been there when he had last checked the mirror.

Nevertheless he judged that, despite the fact that the embankment was so narrow, there was just enough room for the two vehicles side by side. Instinctively Hector slowed and eased off onto the verge to let the bigger vehicle pass. It barged by him with only inches separating them.

Hector was level with the van of the cab for only a fraction of a second. As he had expected from the French number plates, it was left-hand drive. The van driver looked directly down at him. Hector was startled by the bizarre fact that he was wearing a rubber Halloween mask depicting the grinning face of President Richard Nixon. His left arm rested on the sill of the van's open side window. It was a muscular arm, with a small design in red tattooed on the very dark skin.

Close behind the van, its front wheel almost touching the rear bumper, a black Honda Crossrunner motorcycle with two riders crouched on the double seat flew past Hector. Both riders wore crash helmets with full-face dark visors and complete black leather motor-cycle gear.

On the far side of the boggy hollow Hazel's Ferrari was just topping the crest of the hill. Hector realized that they had been neatly cut off from each other by the alien van and bike.

'Hazel!' Hector shouted her name as all his feral instincts kicked in at full force. 'They are after Hazel!' He grabbed his mobile phone and punched in her number.

A disembodied voice answered the call: 'The person you have called is presently unavailable. Please try again later.'

'Shit!' he swore. The reception was always intermittent along this stretch of the road. He dropped the phone.

The van and the bike were already pulling rapidly away from him. He rammed the accelerator to the floor and roared in pursuit of them. As he stared ahead he saw Hazel's Ferrari disappear over the crest of the rise, so he switched his full attention to the vehicles he was pursuing. The engine of his Range Rover was new and freshly tuned and he gained rapidly on them. Instinctively he thrust his right hand into the front of his jacket to where the Beretta 9mm automatic was usually concealed in its armpit holster. Of course, it wasn't there. Carrying handguns is strictly prohibited in Jolly Old England.

'Bloody politicians!' he snarled. It was a fleeting thought and his full attention never deviated from the menace on the road ahead. He decided he would ram the lumbering Mercedes van first. It was the easier target. If he could get up alongside he would use the old police tactic of swinging into it at the level of its rear wheels. That would spin it off the road. The bike would be more elusive, but once the van was taken out of the way he would be able to concentrate on running it down.

He was closing rapidly on the van. The Honda swerved out of his way and pulled up level with the cab of the van. Now Hector was right on its tail. The van driver began to weave from side to side, frustrating Hector's attempts to force his way past.

'Shit!' Hector swore as the rear doors of the van swung open above him. 'What now?'

He looked up through the open doors into the cargo hold. There was a massive builder's pallet packed with large concrete building blocks wrapped in transparent plastic sheeting looming over him. The pallet was mounted on rollers. There must have been another thug in the hold pushing it. It trundled back towards him. Hector saw what was about to happen, and he hit his brakes hard. Even then he was only just quick enough.

The pallet toppled out of the open rear doors of the van. It crashed into the roadway directly in front of Hector's Rover. The plastic wrapper burst on impact and tons of the huge blocks cascaded across the narrow road, piling up in a barrier that sealed it from verge to verge; an obstacle that would challenge even his powerful machine. He just managed to stop with the car's nose almost touching the tumbled wall of blocks. Over the top of the barrier he saw that the van had dropped two more pallets further on, sealing off the road for fifty yards. Far ahead, the van and the bike were starting up the rise over which Hazel's Ferrari had already disappeared.

He studied the pile of blocks briefly. It was a formidable obstacle; almost impossible to scale. Nevertheless, he had to try. He hit the gear lever and slammed the Rover into extra low. Then he revved the engine and flew at the barrier. He began to climb it torturously, the chassis banging and scraping over the jumbled blocks which shifted under the Rover's weight, denying the wheels traction. His speed bled off until he was stranded and high-centred halfway up

26

the barrier with three of his wheels spinning futilely in the air and the offside front wheel jammed between two of the concrete blocks.

Ahead of him the van and its escort disappeared over the rise. Truly desperate by now, Hector slammed the gears into reverse. He gunned the motor again and the vehicle rocked and slewed sideways, threatening to topple over and roll back down the pile. Gravity took hold at last and it bounced back onto the level road, regaining its equilibrium. He opened the door and jumped out onto the footboard. He looked about desperately, trying to find a passable way around the heap of blocks.

He saw that hard up against the road on each side ran barbed-wire fences, obviously to keep livestock off the embankment. Below each fence ran a drainage ditch. The mud in the ditches was shiny black and glutinous, but there was no other way round.

'They set this up cunningly. Narrow road, cargo of bricks to block it, bog, fence and ditch on each side. Crafty bastards!' he fumed as he slipped back behind the wheel, snapped on his seat belt again and performed a quick three-point turn. He lined up the Rover on a section of the fence in which two of the wire strands had rusted almost through. He drew a deep breath and muttered, 'Here goes nothing!' The Rover flew off the verge into the fence. The weakened strands of wire snapped like a double whiplash, and he plunged through into the ditch beyond. He was flung up against the seat belt so violently that he thought his collar bone had broken. He ignored the pain and wrestled with the steering wheel that kicked and spun in his grip. Painfully the Rover dragged itself out of the muddy ditch, and into the open meadow beyond. He turned and ran parallel to the tarmac road. The going was muddy and treacherous. Twice he nearly bogged down, but the Rover ploughed on with mud and clods of turf thrown high from the spinning wheels. Mud splattered the windscreen until he could hardly see through it. He switched on the window washer. He passed the piles of concrete blocks on the road above him. He eased the Rover back towards the embankment, making no sudden movement of the wheel. The Rover increased speed slowly as the ground firmed. He saw that the drainage ditch was shallower here. He drove straight into it. The Rover bucked and her nose slewed from side to side but she struggled out of the far side of the ditch. Here the embankment was lower and its slope gentler. He charged up it and hit the fence above it. The barbed wire checked the Rover for a heart-stopping moment but then the fence pole snapped and the fence itself was flattened. The Rover rolled over it, and lurched onto the paved roadway. Hector spun the wheel to point her up the hill and with a grunt of relief raced for the crest over which Hazel and her pursuit had disappeared.

Hazel was only three miles from the turn-off onto the estate road that led to Brandon Hall, and with the same anticipation of a horse smelling its stable she quickened her pace. Without realizing it she began to pull away from the Mercedes van coming up behind her. She was unaware of its presence. It was her habit to use the mirror above her head more for touching up her make-up rather than for any other purpose.

The driver in his Richard Nixon mask was at the limit of his speed, but abruptly he saw the Ferrari begin to pull away from him. He knew he had to catch her before she reached the turn-off onto the Brandon Hall Estate. He opened his side window and stuck his upper body out of it. He flashed his headlights and waved one arm wildly above his head while with his other hand he blew a long blast on his horn. He saw the red brake lights on the Ferrari ahead of him glow brightly. Once again the van began to overhaul the sports car, but the van driver kept his hand on the horn and his headlights flashing.

Hazel was startled by these antics, until she realized that he was signalling her to stop . . . but why would he do that? Then she saw that the road behind the van was empty. There was no sign of Hector's Range Rover and her face paled with shock.

Something terrible has happened to Hector. The van driver is trying to warn me. Maybe Hector has crashed. Perhaps he has been hurt or . . . She could not finish the thought, it was too horrible. She hit her brakes hard and swerved onto the narrow grass verge. The van raced up behind her, still hooting and flashing its headlights. The driver grinned behind his mask as he saw that his ploy had worked, and that the woman in the red sports car was confused and alarmed by his erratic behaviour. The red car was ideally positioned for his purpose on the lip of the ditch. The barbed-wire fence had ended some distance back but the drainage ditch still ran beside the road.

At that moment the Range Rover appeared on the crest of the rise behind them. Hector took in the scene at a glance.

'Don't stop for the bastard!' he screamed despairingly. 'Keep going as fast as you can, my darling. Don't stop, for Chrissake!' He had his foot flat on the accelerator and as the Rover felt the downwards slope it spurted forward, picking up speed rapidly. But he was still a quarter of a mile back, a helpless spectator to the developing tragedy being played out ahead of him.

The Mercedes van never slowed as it came up to the stationary Ferrari, but as it drew level the driver spun his steering wheel hard over and broadsided into her. There was a clash of steel on steel and a shower of sparks. The lighter sports car was flung over the lip into the drainage ditch; the entire right-hand side of the bodywork was deeply scored and buckled. It came to rest in the bottom of the ditch. It lay on its side with its two nearside wheels high in the air. The Mercedes van rocked wildly, swaying and skidding away from the impact back towards the opposite verge. The driver skilfully countered its gyrations and, as he regained control, opened the throttle and raced away with barely any reduction in his speed.

The motorbike had been following the van closely, but now it skidded to a stop in the roadway, level with the Ferrari in the ditch. The driver remained astride the saddle holding the Honda poised for a getaway, but the passenger sprang off the pillion and raced towards the upended Ferrari. The man was quick and agile as an ape. He leapt from the lip of the ditch onto the battered right-hand side of the sports car and stood poised over the driver's window, balancing there with both arms lifted high above his head. Only then did Hector realize that he was wielding a four-pound lump hammer. Even the shatterproof glass window could not resist the tremendous blow that he delivered from on high. The glass starred and sagged in its frame. The helmeted man lifted the hammer and swung again. This time the glass exploded into thousands of sparkling chips that showered down over Hazel. She was still in the driver's seat, held by the safety belt around her bloated waist. She threw up her hands to protect her face from the flying glass. The man above her hurled the hammer aside and in the same movement reached for something in the cargo pocket of his leather jacket.

Hector was close enough now to the scene of the crash to see exactly what it was he pulled from his pocket. It was a Smith & Wesson pistol chambered in .22 Long Rifle and fitted with a nine-inch silencer. This was the weapon of choice of the Israeli Mossad executioners. With his free hand the gunman raised the perspex visor from his face, and he aimed the elongated barrel down through the window.

Hazel looked up at him. She saw that he was young and black. Then she realized the menace of the pistol pointed at her face and she looked over the barrel into her attacker's eyes. His stare was flat and merciless.

'No!' she whispered. 'Please. I am having a baby. You mustn't do this. My baby . . .' She raised her hands to protect her face. The man's expression did not change and he fired. The silenced weapon made almost no sound. It was just a soft, almost polite pop. Then the man looked up and saw Hector's Range Rover bearing down on him. There was no time for a second shot, but he was a pro, and he knew the first had done the business. He spun round and jumped down off the battered bodywork of the Ferrari. As he landed, the Range Rover hit him squarely in his back. The sound of the impact was a meaty thump. His body was hurled back over the roof of the Rover. Hector never reduced his speed. He drove straight on, aiming for the man on the front seat of the Honda.

The biker tried to avoid his rush by dropping his machine hard over and opening the hand throttle wide to bring the Honda around in a tight skidding turn. He almost succeeded in avoiding the Rover's charge. But Hector was too quick for him. He wrenched the steering sharply and managed to catch the Honda's spinning rear wheel with the point of his front bumper. The bike cartwheeled end over end and the rider was thrown from the saddle, under the front wheels of the Rover. Both the front and the back wheels of the heavy vehicle bumped over his body. In his rear-view mirror Hector saw him lying sprawled in the roadway. His crash helmet must have protected him, for he sat up groggily. Hector slammed on his brakes and crash changed the Rover into reverse. He shot backwards and his victim saw the big vehicle coming back at him and tried to get to his feet. Hector hit him again. He went down under the body of the Rover and Hector felt him bumping and thumping along under the chassis until he rolled out from under the front end and lay face down on the tarmac surface of the road. Hector jumped out of the Rover and ran to him. He stooped over him and in one quick motion he flicked open the buckle of his helmet, ripped it from his head and dropped it aside. Then he placed his knee between the man's shoulder blades to anchor him, pinned the back of his neck with one hand and reached around with the other to cup his chin. With one quick wrench he twisted his head almost fully around. The vertebrae snapped with a sound like the breaking of a stick of dry firewood. There was a spluttering noise from the man's black leather breeches and a sharp fetid stink as his bowels voided. Hector snatched up the helmet, crammed it back on his head and buckled it in place. Then he carefully opened the visor of the helmet to expose the man's face. The police were going to ask questions. He was not going to blindside himself. He did not have to worry about leaving fingerprints; he was still wearing his leather gloves. He was desperate to get to Hazel, dreading what had happened to her, but he dared not leave a living enemy behind him. He had to clear his back. That was one of the vital laws of survival.

The gunman who had fired at Hazel was dragging his paralysed lower body along on his elbows. Obviously either his spine or his pelvis had been smashed when Hector had knocked him down, but he was still armed. Hector had to make sure of him. The hammer lay on the verge of the road where the gunman had thrown it. Hector scooped it up on the run. He hefted it as he came up behind the gunman. The man had his chin lowered onto his chest so that the helmet on his head was cocked forward. The lower part of his neck, just above the level of the C4 vertebra, was exposed. Accuracy rather than brute force were necessary to finish the job. Hector swung the hammer no more than eighteen inches but he whipped his wrist into the blow. The force of the steel head on bone jarred his grip and he heard the vertebrae break. The gunman's head dropped forward and he lay still. Hector dropped on one knee and flipped the gunman over onto his back. His visor was lifted. His eyes were wide open but unfocussed. There was a look of mild surprise on his dark Nilotic features. Hector slipped off his glove and touched the man's throat, feeling for the carotid artery. There was no pulse. Hector grunted with satisfaction, and pulled on his glove again.

'No doubt where you come from, laddie. I've seen your ilk before,' he said grimly as he glanced at the face of the corpse. He deliberately left the helmet visor open. He took a moment longer to place the shaft of the sledgehammer in the man's dead hand and squeeze his fingers closed around it. When the police studied the scene they would be unlikely to conclude that he had used the hammer to break his own neck.

Waste no more time looking for his pistol. Leave that for the police to find, he decided as he jumped to his feet and ran to the overturned Ferrari. He scrambled up onto it. He stood over the shattered window and looked down on Hazel. She was slumped over the steering wheel. He knelt quickly and reached down to cup her head in both his hands. Gently he rolled it back so he was able to see her face. With a huge lift of relief he saw that no sign of a bullet wound marred her lovely features. Her eyes were open, but they stared ahead blankly.

Concussion. He tried to rationalize her lack of reaction. *She must have hit her head when the car went over.* Then he spoke aloud. 'You are going to be okay, my baby. We'll have you out of there in a jiffy.' But still he used his teeth to pull off one of his gloves, then slipped his bare fingers down under her chin and felt for her carotid just to make certain.

'Thank you, Lord.' He felt the artery pulsing, softly but steadily under his fingers. He had to wriggle the upper half of his own body into the empty window frame to reach down to the buckle of her seat belt. He steadied her with one arm round her shoulders as he clicked open the buckle, and then with both hands under her armpits he lifted her. She was big with the child in her and his stance on the body of the wreck was insecure, but he used all his strength to lift her dead weight. He growled with the effort, but slowly he brought her head out of the window. Her chin was lolling forward on her chest.

'That's my girl,' he gasped. 'We are nearly there. Hold tight.' With another convulsion of every muscle in his upper body he lifted her high enough to get her swollen belly clear of the windowsill. Then he eased her into a sitting position and slipped her left arm over his own shoulders to prevent her flopping over backwards. He recovered his breath quickly, for he was still in very good physical condition despite the soft life he had lived recently. He turned his head to kiss her cheek and whisper close to her ear, 'That's my good brave girl.' As he shifted his grip on her arm he saw with a jump of his own heart that her left hand was bleeding. He stared at it in trepidation until he realized that the heavy gold wedding ring on her third finger had been beaten or knocked out of shape by some powerful force. The metal had cut into her flesh and the blood oozed from the wound.

'The bullet!' he breathed. She must have covered her face with her hands as that swine aimed at her. The bullet must have hit the ring. It was only a light .22 calibre and it had been deflected from her face. He exulted. 'She's going to live. It's all going to be all right.'

His strength came flooding back. He swung his legs over the side of the Ferrari and once he was in a sitting position he was able to work her legs out of the window and swivel her whole body round until he held her on his lap with her head cushioned against his shoulder. Then he lowered his feet to the ground and ran to the Range Rover, carrying Hazel in his arms like a sleeping child. He opened the back door and carefully laid her on the seat. He wedged the travelling blanket and the seat cushions around her to prevent her slipping onto the floor. He stood back and smiled at her, but it was a thin and desperate smile which never reached his eyes.

'You will never know how much I love you,' he told her, and was about to close the door when he saw something which brought his fear flooding back. A thin glistening snake of blood crawled out from under her blonde hairline and ran down her cheek, onto her chin and neck.

'No!' he blurted. 'Oh God, no!' He reached out one hand to her, but he was reluctant to touch her and discover the worst. He forced himself to do it, and he parted the golden waves of her hair. The bullet hole had been hidden beneath them. Hector brought his face close to hers and studied the wound. He was a soldier, and he had seen countless bullet wounds. His first estimate of the situation was confirmed. The light bullet must have been deflected by the heavy gold ring, but it had also been tumbled. The deflection had not been sufficient to leave Hazel untouched. The bullet had hit her high in the front of the skull. The entry wound was not a neat circular puncture but an elongated tear in her scalp. The bullet had rolled in flight and hit her sideways on.

Gently he ran his fingers back through her hair, examining her scalp. There was no sign of any exit wound. The bullet was still inside her skull; inside her brain.

He closed his eyes tightly. Yes, he was a soldier and he had seen many good men go down. But not this, never the one woman he had ever truly loved. He had thought he was tough and he had thought he could take it. But he discovered now he was not and he couldn't. His soul quailed. His universe reeled. He braced himself. It took an enormous physical effort, but he spoke aloud to himself. 'You stupid bastard! Standing here moping while her life bleeds away. Move! Damn you, move!'

He closed the door and ran round to the driver's side. He clambered into the seat. The engine had stalled. He started it again. His mind was racing now. The nearest general hospital was the Royal Hampshire in Winchester. The road behind him was blocked and impassable. He calculated the quickest alternative route to reach it. It would put an extra eight miles on the journey.

Nothing else for it, he told himself grimly and gunned the Rover. He drove fast, very fast. He took chances passing other vehicles in dangerous situations. This was nearly his downfall, but also his ultimate salvation. He shot past a heavily laden lorry that was lumbering up a blind rise. In doing so he avoided by mere inches a head-on collision with an oncoming police car. The driver made an immediate U-turn and came after him with the siren blaring. Hector saw in the rear-view mirror the vivid blue and yellow reflective markings of the vehicle, and the peaked cap of the police driver chasing him.

'Thank you, God!' he breathed and pulled over immediately. The police car parked in front of him and two uniformed officers jumped out and came back to him with grim expressions. Hector lowered his window and stuck his head out. Before either of the traffic officers could speak he shouted at them.

'My wife has been shot in the head. She is dying. You must give me an escort to Winchester Hospital A & E.' They both paused with their grim expressions changing to consternation. 'Here! Take a look. She is on the back seat,' Hector insisted. The man with sergeant's chevrons on his sleeve ran to the rear window and peered in.

'Jesus!' he said. 'There is blood all over the place.' He straightened up and looked at Hector. 'Okay! Follow me, sir.'

'Let your mate ride in the back with my wife. He can cushion her head from being thrown about.'

'Peter, you heard the man,' the sergeant snapped, and the younger man scrambled into the back seat of the Rover.

Gently Hector helped him settle Hazel's head onto his lap. Then he shouted to the sergeant, 'All set. Let's go.' The patrol car raced away with its siren howling and Hector's Range Rover close on its tail.

There was an ambulance parked outside the main doors to the emergency room at the hospital, but the sergeant gave it a blast with the siren and it moved off the stand hurriedly as Hector drove up. The sergeant jumped out and ran into the building. He came back almost at once leading a white-coated orderly pushing a theatre trolley. Hector helped the orderly lift Hazel's limp body onto the trolley and cover her with a sheet.

'Go with your wife, sir,' the sergeant told him. 'I'll wait here to take your statement later. You will have to tell us how this happened.'

'Thank you, officer.' Hector turned and followed the trolley into the entrance. A young female doctor accosted him.

'What happened to this lady?'

'She was shot in the head. There is a bullet in her brain.'

'Take the patient to X-ray,' the doctor snapped at the orderly. 'Tell them, I want front and side plates of the head.' Then she glanced at Hector. 'Are you related to the patient?'

'She is my wife.'

35

'You're in the best place, sir. The consulting neurosurgeon from London is here today. I will ask him to come to examine your wife as soon as he can.'

'Can I stay with her?'

'I am afraid I have to ask you to wait until she has been to X-ray and until the neurosurgeon has examined her.'

'I understand,' Hector said. 'You will be able to find me outside with the police. They want to take a statement from me.'

Hector spent the next half-hour with the police sergeant sitting in the front seat of the police car. The officer's name was Evan Evans. Hector gave him directions to the scene, and a brief description of the nature of the attack.

'I was trying to defend my wife from the assailants,' Hector explained, but he was careful not to give too many details. As far as the law was concerned he had committed a double murder. He had to have time to think his cover story through. 'I drove my Range Rover into their motorcycle and I think both the riders were injured. I did not have time to attend to them. I was most anxious to get my wife under proper medical care.'

'I can understand that, sir. I will phone my headquarters immediately and have them send a vehicle to the scene. I am afraid they will have to impound your wife's car for a full forensic examination.' Hector nodded his understanding, and the sergeant went on, 'I know you will want to be with your wife now, but we shall require a full written and signed statement from you as soon as possible.'

'You have my home address and my mobile phone number.' Hector opened the car door. 'I will be available any time you need me. Thank you, Sergeant Evans. When my wife recovers, a great deal of the credit for that will go to you.'

As he walked back into the hospital the young doctor hurried to meet him.

'Mr Cross, the neurosurgeon has examined your wife and her X-ray plates. He would like to speak to you. He is still with Mrs Cross. Come with me, please.'

The neurosurgeon was in a screened examination cubicle bending over Hazel's supine figure, which was still on the trolley. He straightened up as Hector entered the cubicle and came to meet him. He was a handsome middle-aged man. He had the self-assured air of one both intelligent and highly competent; a master of his craft.

'I am Trevor Irving, Mr . . . ?'

'Cross. Hector Cross. How is my wife, Mr Irving?' Hector cut across the pleasantries.

'The bullet has not exited.' Irving was just as business-like. 'It's lying in an extremely delicate position, and there is bleeding. It must be removed, and at once.' He pointed to the backlit X-ray plate on the scanner beside Hazel's bed. The dark shadow of the tiny round-nosed projectile stood out boldly against the soft billows of brain tissue that surrounded it.

'I understand.' Hector averted his eyes. He didn't want to look at that terrible harbinger of her death.

'There is a complication in that your wife is pregnant. How far along is she?'

'Forty weeks. She was examined by her gynaecologist this morning.'

'I thought it might be that far advanced,' Irving said. 'The foetus will be dangerously distressed by the mother's surgery. If we lose her, we might lose her child with her.'

'You have to save my wife at all costs. She is the one who bloody counts.' Hector's tone was savage. Irving blinked.

'They both bloody count, Mr Cross. And don't you bloody forget that.' His tone matched Hector's.

'I apologize unreservedly, Mr Irving. Of course I did not mean that. My only excuse is that I am distraught.'

Irving recognized in Hector Cross a man who did not back down easily. 'I am going to do my utmost to save both of them, mother and child. However, we will need your permission for Doctor Naidoo here to immediately remove the child by Caesarean section using a spinal block anaesthetic. Only then can I proceed to remove the bullet.'

He turned to the other physician in the cubicle, who came forward to shake Hector's hand. He was a young Indian man but there was almost no trace of an accent as he said, 'The baby is still in very good condition. Caesarean section is a very simple procedure. There is almost no danger involved and neither your wife nor your child will be traumatized.'

'All right, then. Do it. I'll sign any piece of paper you need,' Hector said. He felt as cold as his voice sounded in his own ears.

Anurse conducted Hector to a hospital waiting room. There were half a dozen other people there before him. They all looked up expectantly as Hector entered, but then slumped with disappointment and resignation. Hector helped himself to a cup of coffee from the communal urn. He saw his hands were shaking and the cup chattered against the saucer. With an effort he controlled them, and found a seat in a corner of the large room.

He was accustomed to being in complete command of any situation, but now he felt helpless. There was nothing for him to do but wait. And not allow despair to overtake him.

He had not had a chance to think things through since the dreadful moment that the Mercedes van with the masked driver had roared past him on the narrow road. From that moment he had been driven only by adrenalin and the instincts of survival towards himself and his loved ones, Hazel and the infant. This was his first chance to evaluate the situation soberly and calmly.

One thing was certain; he was in a war to the knife. He had to shore up his mental defences and prepare for the next assault from a faceless and hidden enemy. He could only guess whence it would come. All he was really certain of was that it would come.

However, his mind was still playing tricks with him. His despair returned in full force; this feeling of confusion and uncertainty, this overpowering sense of dread. All he was able to concentrate on was the picture in his mind of the trickle of blood running down Hazel's face and the nothingness in her staring eyes.

He took a gulp from the coffee mug and pressed the fingers of his free hand into his eye sockets until it hurt; trying to rally his resources. It took a while, but at last he had himself under control.

'Okay. So what have we learned about the nature of the beast?' he asked himself. He reached into the inside pocket of his suit and found his small moleskin notebook. 'The van was almost certainly stolen, but I have the registration number.' He scribbled it down. 'Next, the driver of the Mercedes. Very little there. Face covered by the mask.' He replayed the brief sighting in his mind and scanned it for details. 'Blue denim work shirt, probably fifteen quid at Primark.' He paused for a moment, and then went on. 'Left arm bare. Very dark skin. Good muscle tone. Young and fit.' He wrote it down in his own personal shorthand. 'Impression of a wristwatch on his skin, but no watch. Careful bastard, then. Stripping for action. Red tattoo on back of the hand. Heart? Scorpion? Coiled snake? Not sure.' He paused. 'Nothing else there. What about the two dearly departed? Police forensics will check their fingerprints and will milk every other detail from their cadavers. Though there is little doubt about their tribal origins. I had a good look at them both, post culling. Those Nilotic features are unmistakable. Thin nose and lips. Prominent front teeth. High cheekbones. Handsome. Tall, lean bodies. Almost certainly Somalis.' Then he smiled grimly at his own naïvety. 'Or Maasai, or Ethiopian, or Samburu or any one of the other Nilotic tribes. But Somali still makes the most sense to me. The dynasty of Tippoo Tip, the great warlord. They were the original Beast. They were the ones who hijacked Hazel's yacht; who kidnapped Cayla; who hacked off her head and sent it to us in a bottle. This is very much their style. I thought that I had culled most of that clan. I thought that I had got them all, but a nest of scorpions breeds up again quickly. Could easily be that some of them escaped us to carry on the blood feud.'

Hector had often tried to fathom the tradition of these honour killings. The blood feud was one of the concepts of Sharia law most alien to the Western mind. The aim of the blood feud was neither punishment nor retribution. If it were, then the killing would be of the original perpetrator of the crime, and once that had been achieved the matter would come to an end. It is rather the cleansing of the family honour by the slaying of any member of the offender's family. Of course, the spilled blood of that victim cries out to the opposite family for purification. Circle without end.

Hector sighed. 'Time to call up some help here.' He did not have to ponder that question. There was only one answer: Paddy O'Quinn. Good old Paddy and his merry men.

When Hector and Hazel had first met, Hector had been the owner and operator of Cross Bow Security. Cross Bow's only client was Bannock Oil, the enormous oil conglomerate that Hazel still headed as CEO. Once the two of them had united, Hazel had wanted Hector close to her at all times. She had persuaded him to take up a position on the board of directors of Bannock Oil, and to sell all his holdings in Cross Bow to Bannock Oil so that he would be free to join her. The price Bannock Oil paid to buy Hector out was substantial but completely fair. It was a sum sufficient to make him financially independent and the master of his own destiny. This was Hazel's way of ensuring that Hector was a free man, and that they could always be equal partners in their marriage. She did not want him to be subservient to her by reason of her own vast wealth. She knew he was an alpha male and would not, could not, have tolerated any other arrangement for long. It was a gesture so typical of her.

'Smart as new paint and twice as beautiful!' His mood lightened for a moment as he thought of her, but almost immediately the dark clouds closed over him again.

Paddy O'Quinn had been Hector's second in command at Cross Bow. He had helped Hector build up the company from the earliest days. There was no man Hector trusted more. He was solid as a mountain, he was savvy and quick, but over all his other virtues he had the fighting man's instinct for danger almost as strongly as did Hector himself. Hector took comfort in the fact that Paddy was only a phone call away.

His reverie was interrupted by a hospital nurse who entered the waiting room and called out his name. He jumped to his feet.

'I am Hector Cross.'

'Please come with me, Mr Cross.' As he hurried after her, Hector glanced at his wristwatch. He had been waiting a little over an hour and a half. He caught up with the nurse in the passage.

'Is everything all right?' he demanded to know.

'Yes indeed.' She smiled at him.

'My wife?'

'She is in theatre. Mr Irving is still operating on her. But I have somebody else for you to meet.' She led him through a labyrinth of passages to a door marked Maternity Observation Room.

When they entered, Hector found that there were chairs arranged along one wall facing a large glass panel that looked into a room beyond. The nurse spoke into a microphone on the table below the window.

'Hi there, Bonnie! Mr Cross is here.'

To which a disembodied voice replied, 'Be with you in a sec.'

Hector stood close to the window and minutes later another nurse, in the uniform of a ward sister, entered the observation room on the far side of the glass. She was possibly thirty years of age; young to carry such high rank, Hector thought. She was plump and pretty with a round, jovial face. She carried in her arms a small bundle wrapped in a blue blanket which was embroidered with the initials RHCH in red, Royal Hampshire County Hospital. She came to the opposite side of the window and gave Hector a beaming pink smile. It was contagious and Hector smiled back at her, although it was not indicative of his true feelings.

'Hello, Mr Cross. My name is Bonnie. May I have the pleasure of introducing you to somebody?' She opened the blankets to reveal a ruddy and wrinkled little face with tightly closed slits for eyes. 'Say hello to your daughter.'

'Good God! She's got no hair.' Hector came out with the first thing that sprang to mind, and immediately realized how inane it sounded, even to him.

'She's very beautiful!' said the nurse sternly.

'In a funny sort of way, I suppose she is.'

'In every possible way she is,' she corrected him. 'She weighs exactly six pounds. Isn't she a clever girl? What are you going to call her?'

'Catherine Cayla. Her mother chose those names.' Surely he should feel more than this when he looked at his firstborn child, but instead he thought of Hazel lying somewhere nearby with a bullet in her brain. He was on the verge of tears and he coughed and blinked them back. The last time he had cried openly was at the age of six when his pony had thrown him and he had broken his arm in three places on landing.

Catherine Cayla opened her mouth in a wide yawn which exposed her toothless gums. Hector smiled and this time the smile was genuine. He felt a small flame flare in his heart.

'She is beautiful,' he said softly. 'She's bloody gorgeous. Just like her mother.'

'Oh! Look at the little darling,' said Bonnie. 'She's already hungry. I am going to take her for her first feed. Say bye-bye, Daddy.'

'Bye-bye,' said Hector dutifully. No one had ever called him Daddy before. He watched the nurse carry his daughter away. For a short while that tiny soul had shone for him like a candle in the darkness of a winter's night. Now she was gone the arctic cold of despair descended upon him once more. He turned away from the window and went back to the main waiting room.

He sat hunched in a corner chair. The darkness broke over him in waves. He searched his soul for the courage to endure it, and found instead anger.

Anger is a better cure than resignation. He squared his shoulders, and stood up straight. He left the waiting room and went out into the passage. He found the men's toilet and locked himself in a cubicle and sat on the seat. He took his mobile phone from the leather pouch on his belt. Paddy O'Quinn's number was in his contact list.

The phone rang three times and then Paddy said, 'O'Quinn.'

'Paddy. Where are you?' Hector spoke into the mouthpiece. His tone was crisp and sharp again.

'Sweet Jesus! I thought you had dropped off the end of the world, Hector.' They had not spoken to each other in months.

'They got Hazel.'

Paddy was stunned into silence. Hector could hear him breathing hoarsely. Then he said, 'Who? How?' His voice rang like a sabre being drawn from its scabbard.

'Four hours ago we ran into an ambush. It's bad. Hazel took a .22 calibre bullet in her brain. She's in theatre now. The medico is going for the bullet. We don't know yet if she's going to make it.'

'She's a great lady, Heck. You know how I feel.'

'I know, Paddy.' They were warriors, they didn't wail and bleat.

'She was pregnant, wasn't she? What about her baby?' Paddy growled.

'They saved her. We have a girl. She seems to be doing well.'

'Thank God for that, at least.' Paddy paused and then he asked, 'Do you have any leads?'

'I cancelled two of the bastards. They were Somalis, I think.'

'It has to be the Beast again!' Paddy said. 'I thought we had got all of them.'

'That's what I thought. We were wrong.'

'What do you want me to do?' Paddy asked.

'Find them for me, Paddy. Some of the Tippoo Tip brood must have survived. Find them.'

Hector had built up Cross Bow Security into a formidable operation on the principle that offence was more effective than defence and that good intelligence was the most powerful offensive asset. When Paddy took over from him he had built on those precepts. As one of the directors of Bannock Oil, Hector still had access to the accounts of Cross Bow. He knew just how much Paddy was spending on his intelligence arm. If it had been good before, now it had to be that much better. Hector went on speaking.

'Is Tariq Hakam still with you?'

'He is one of my main men.'

'Send him back into Puntland to search for any survivors of the family of Hadji Sheikh Mohammed Khan Tippoo Tip. Nobody knows that terrain better than Tariq. He was born there.'

'After what we did to them in Puntland, any of them that got away are almost certainly dispersed across the Middle East.'

'Wherever they are, just find them. Tariq must draw up a list of every male descendant of Khan Tippoo Tip over the age of fifteen years. Then we will hunt them down; every last one of them.'

'I hear you, Heck. In the meantime I'll be pulling for Hazel. If anybody can make it, she is the one. All my money is on her.'

'Thanks, Paddy.' Hector broke the contact and went back to the waiting room.

An hour dragged by like a cripple, and then another passed even more painfully before a theatre sister came for him. She wore a plastic cap over her hair. A surgical mask dangled around her neck and she had theatre slippers on her feet.

'How is my wife?' Hector demanded as he sprang to his feet.

'Mr Irving will answer all your questions,' she told him. 'Please, follow me.'

She led him to one of the post-operative recovery rooms adjoining the operating theatres. The sister opened the door and stood aside for him to enter. Hector found himself in a room with green painted walls. Against the far wall was a single hospital bed. Beside it a heart-monitoring machine stood on its trolley and peeped softly. Across its electronic screen bounced the glowing green electronic point of light keeping time to the heartbeats of the patient on the bed below. It left a vivid green sawtooth trail across the screen. In the few seconds that Hector stood in the doorway he realized the trail was not regular. A rapid series of heartbeats was followed by a distinct pause, then an almost hesitant beat, another pause and then three or four rapid beats.

Irving was leaning over the patient on the bed, screening the supine body. He stood aside as he sensed Hector behind him, enabling Hector to see Hazel's face.

Her head was bound up in a tight turban of white bandages, which extended under her chin and covered her ears. The lower half of her body was covered with a sheet. She still wore the green theatre gown. There were IV needles in the veins of her arms and the backs of both her hands. Plastic tubes dangled down from the sacs of liquid that were suspended above her on a moveable stand.

Irving came to meet Hector.

'How is she?' Hector managed to keep his voice level. Irving hesitated. The heart monitor beeped twice before he replied.

'I have removed the bullet. But there was more soft tissue damage than we anticipated. It did not show up on the X-ray plates.'

Hector walked slowly to the side of the bed and looked down at her. Her face was white as pastry. Her eyes were slightly open. Only the whites showed between her long curling lashes. There was a tube up her left nostril connected to the oxygen machine standing on the floor. Her breathing was so light that he had to bring his face down an inch from hers to catch it. He kissed her lips with a butterfly touch. He straightened up and looked at Irving.

'What are her chances?' he asked. 'Don't lie to me.'

Again Irving hesitated, and then he shrugged almost impercep-
tibly.

'Fifty–fifty, or perhaps a little less.'

'If she does recover, will she regain full brain function?'

Irving frowned before replying. Then he said, 'That is unlikely.'

'Thank you for your honesty,' Hector said. 'May I wait here with
her?'

'Of course. That chair is for you.' He indicated a seat on the other
side of the bed. 'I have done all I can, now I must hand your wife
over to Mr Daly, the hospital's resident neurosurgical specialist. He
has already seen her. His room is just down the corridor. He can be
here in a few seconds if Sister Palmer here summons him.' He nodded
at the theatre sister who was adjusting the taps on Hazel's IV drips.

'Goodbye, Mr Cross. God bless you and your lovely wife.'

'Goodbye and thank you, Mr Irving. I know that nobody could
have done more for her.'

When he was gone, Hector spoke to Sister Palmer.

'I am her husband.'

'I know. Sit down, Mr Cross. We may have a long wait.' Hector
moved the chair closer to the bed and sat.

'May I hold her hand?' he asked.

'Yes, but please be careful not to disturb any of the IV tubes.'
Hector reached out gingerly and took three of Hazel's fingers. They
were very cold, but not as cold as his heart. He studied her face.
Her eyelids were almost closed. The eyes themselves were rolled back
in their sockets. He could not see their pupils. Only a sliver of iris
was visible. They had lost their sapphire-blue lustre. They were dull
and lifeless. He moved his chair again so that when she opened her
eyes he would be sitting directly in her line of sight. He would be
the first thing she saw when she regained consciousness; he carefully
prevented himself from even thinking the conjunction 'If'.

He listened to the irregular peep of the heart monitor and every
once in a while he glanced at the rise and fall of the bellows of the
oxygen apparatus. The only other sounds were the tap of Sister
Palmer's heels on the floor tiles and the rustle of her skirts as she
moved around the room. He glanced down at his wristwatch. It was
his gift from Hazel on his last birthday. It was the platinum model

with the Rolex signature blue dial. The time was twenty minutes to two in the morning. He had been awake since sunrise. His chin dropped onto his chest and, still holding her hand, he dozed just below the level of consciousness, but any change in the rhythm of the heart monitor brought him back again with a jerk.

He dreamed that he and Hazel were climbing the hill on the Colorado ranch. Hand in hand they were following the path through the forest that led to Henry Bannock's mausoleum. Cayla was running ahead of them.

'I want to see Daddy!' She was laughing, looking back over her shoulder. The likeness of daughter to mother was astounding.

'Wait for me!' Hazel called after her. 'I am going with you.' Dread overwhelmed Hector. He hardened his grip on her hand.

'No!' he said. 'Stay with me. You mustn't leave me. You must never leave me.' Then he felt a hand on his shoulder and heard another voice speaking.

'Mr Cross, are you all right?' He opened his eyes and Sister Palmer was standing over him. Her expression was concerned. 'You were shouting in your sleep.' It took a few moments for Hector to gather his wits. Then he knew where he was. He looked into Hazel's face. She had not changed the position of her head, but her eyes were open. The lustre of cerulean blue glowed in them again. She was seeing him.

'Hazel!' he whispered urgently. 'Squeeze my hand!' There was no reaction. Her fingers were limp and cold. He passed his left hand across her face. Her eyes did not move. They stared out at him.

'It's Hector,' he whispered. 'I love you. I thought I had lost you.' He stared into her eyes and thought that he saw her pupils contract minimally; or perhaps it was merely vain hope that engendered the thought. Then he heard the beat of the heart monitor. It was rapid and regular.

'She can see me,' he said. 'She can hear me.' His voice was rising.

'Calm yourself, Mr Cross,' Sister Palmer said. 'We must not race ahead of ourselves. The cerebral damage . . .' He did not want to hear her say it.

'I tell you she can see me and hear me.' He reached out and touched Hazel's pale cold cheek. He felt his courage and determination rushing back.

'Sister Palmer,' he said crisply. 'Please go down to Maternity and tell the duty nurse to bring my daughter here.'

'We can't do that, sir. Your wife is very ill and—'

'Sister, do you have children of your own?' He cut her short.

She hesitated, then her voice and tone changed. 'I have a son of six.'

'So you can imagine what it would have meant to die without ever laying eyes on him?'

'There are rules,' she said weakly. 'Babies born by Caesarean section must remain in the unit for—'

'I don't give a good stuff for the rules. My wife may die. Go down to Maternity and bring her daughter to her. Do it now!'

Sister Palmer hesitated a moment longer then she whispered, 'At this time of night there will be very few people around.' She straightened her back and turned to the door. She closed it quietly behind her as she went out into the passage.

Hector brought his lips close to Hazel's ear and whispered to her, 'You were right, Hazel my darling! Our baby is a girl. Her name is Catherine Cayla, just the way you planned it.' He stared into her eyes, searching for signs of life. It was like looking into two fathomless blue pools. 'They are going to bring Catherine to you. You will see how beautiful she is. Her hair is going to be golden just like her big sister's. She weighs six pounds.' He stroked her cheek softly as he whispered encouragement and endearments.

The heart monitor beeped to a steady beat. The sawtooth pattern across the screen was regular and even.

It seemed to Hector like an age of waiting, and then the door behind him opened and Sister Palmer entered. She was smiling. Close behind her came Bonnie, the maternity nurse. Hector was surprised to see her still on duty. In her arms she carried the blue-blanketed bundle. Hector leapt to his feet and went to her. Without a word, the nurse offered the bundle to him.

Hector reached out uncertainly, and then took a step back and muttered, 'Which end must I take? I don't want to drop her.'

'Make an arm for her,' Bonnie ordered, and when he obeyed she laid Catherine in the resulting cradle. Hector looked as apprehensive as if he was holding a ticking bomb.

'I have never done this before.'

'She won't break,' Bonnie reassured him. 'Babies are pretty tough little customers. Hold her as though you love her.'

Slowly Hector began to relax. He smiled. 'She smells good.' His smile turned into a wide grin. 'She's so warm and soft.'

'Yep!' Bonnie said. 'That's the way babies are.'

Hector turned back to the bed, still holding the infant. He leaned over Hazel until he could bring Catherine's face down level with hers.

'Just look at her! Isn't she the most magical little thing?' he murmured.

Nothing moved in Hazel's face, her expression was impassive and her eyes expressionless. He brought their two faces closer together.

'I think your daughter needs a kiss, Mrs Cross,' he said, and touched Catherine's lips to those of Hazel. Immediately the infant's lips started making suckling motions, instinctively seeking the teat. She began to move her head from side to side, brushing against her mother's face. Still Hazel's face was stony and pale as chalk.

When Catherine was unable to find what she was looking for she squawked. Almost at once her frustration turned to anger and she let out a series of grunts and muted bellows; the most evocative sounds to any mother's ears. But Hazel's features remained blank.

Crestfallen, Hector lifted Catherine back into the cradle of his arms. He had hoped for something, for anything. Just a sign that she had known this was her own child nuzzling her cheek.

Then a small miracle was enacted before him. A tear welled up from the blue depths of Hazel's left eye. It was the size of a seed pearl, and it shone with the same opalescence.

'She is weeping,' Hector said in a small, awed voice. 'She sees. She knows. She understands.'

Bonnie took the child from him. 'We must go now. I dare not stay any longer. It's more than my job is worth.' She went quickly to the door and from there looked back at him with a smile. 'It was a hell of a risk, but I'm glad I took it.'

'So am I.' Hector's voice was gruff. 'I owe you one,' he said to Bonnie. 'I owe you a very big one.' Then she and Catherine were gone.

Hector looked at Sister Palmer. 'You too, a very big one!' he told her.

Hector went back to his station beside the bed. He took Hazel's fingers and tried to rub some warmth into them. He whispered to her a little longer, and then weariness and emotional burnout overtook him again and sleep dropped over him like a dark fog.

Something woke him. He was not certain what it was. He looked around him groggily. Then two things registered with him in quick succession: the sound of the beeper was wildly erratic and the trace on the screen of the heart monitor was dancing and skipping chaotically. In panic he came to his feet and stood over Hazel. Her chest was heaving and a rasping sound came from her open mouth.

'Hazel,' he said with rising anger. 'Fight, my darling. Fight the bastard.' He knew the black angel had come for her. 'Don't let him take you!'

Sister Palmer hurried in, alerted by the tone of his voice. She went to the far side of the bed, took one long look and said, 'I will call the duty doctor.' She rushed from the room. Hector did not watch her go. He was shaking Hazel's hand.

'Listen to me!' he pleaded with her. 'Stay with us. We need you. Catherine and I need you. Don't go! Please don't go with him.'

The wild cacophony of the heart monitor slowed. The peaks of the pattern on the screen drew further apart.

'Fight with that great heart of yours, Hazel. Don't give in,' he told her, and the tears streamed down his face. He had seen this happen so often on the battlefield but he had never wept before. 'Think of us. You never give in. Fight him off with your warrior's heart.'

Hazel expelled the air from her lungs in a long and whispering sigh. Then she breathed no more. The monitor beeped one last time and then went silent. The trace levelled out into a flat green line at the bottom of the screen.

Hector stood over her and his tears dropped onto her face as he seized her shoulders and shook her.

'Come back!' he cried. 'I won't let you go!'

The door opened behind him and the young duty doctor strode up behind him and took his arm, leading him away from the bed.

'Please, Mr Cross. Stand back and let me do my job.' The doctor worked quickly. He placed his stethoscope on her chest, listened a few seconds and frowned. Then he felt for a pulse at her wrist and said softly, 'I am sorry, Mr Cross.'

Gently, he passed his hand over Hazel's face, closing her staring blue eyes. Then he reached down for the bed sheet and drew it up to cover her face.

'No!' Hector caught his wrist. 'Don't cover her. I want to remember her face for ever. Please leave us alone for a while.' He looked at Sister Palmer who was hovering at the foot of the bed. 'You too, Sister. There is nothing more you can do here.' The two of them left quietly.

Hector knelt beside the bed. He had not prayed in a long while but he prayed now. Then he stood up and wiped his eyes.

'This is not goodbye, Hazel. Wherever you have gone, wait for me. One day we will be together again. Wait for me, my darling.' He kissed her on the mouth. Her lips were already cooling. He drew the sheet over her face and went to the door.

On the way to the exit he stopped at the maternity wards and knocked on the door of the nurses' room. A sister appeared. 'May I help you, Mr Cross?' Hector was mildly surprised that she knew his name. He had no idea of the flutter he had created in the staff room. The word had spread.

'I am looking for a nurse called Bonnie.'

'Bonnie Hepworth? She went off duty an hour ago.'

'What time will she come on again?'

'Six o'clock this evening.'

'Thank you. May I see my daughter now? She was born last night.'

'Yes, I know.' She glanced at her clipboard and found the name. 'Catherine. Okay. Let's go to the observation room.'

When they arrived, Hector pressed close against the glass. 'She looks more human than a few hours ago.' The nurse looked disapproving. He had learned that they didn't like derogatory remarks about their babies, and hurried on. 'When will she be discharged?'

'Well . . .' The sister looked doubtful. 'She is a Caesarean and her mother . . .'

'When can I come and fetch her?' Hector insisted.

'Probably three or four days if all goes well, but of course it's up to Doctor Naidoo.'

'I'll be back this evening to visit her,' he promised.

He went out to where the Range Rover stood in the car park. He walked around it to check the damage. It was filthy with dried mud and the front offside bumper was buckled. He climbed in and started the engine, and then drove back towards Brandon Hall.

He was on the direct road from Winchester, which took him past the scene of the ambush. Police Crime Scene tape cordoned off the area, but Hazel's Ferrari had been towed away. Three police officers were still taking measurements and working the site for further evidence.

Hector slowed for the road block, but one of the officers waved him through.

Reynolds, the butler, opened the door for him. 'It's very good to see you, sir. We were very worried when you and Mrs Cross did not return yesterday evening. Mrs Cross is not with you?' He looked over Hector's shoulder. Hector ignored the question.

'Please have Mary bring a pot of coffee up to my study. Then this afternoon at two o'clock I want the entire staff assembled in the blue drawing room.'

Hector went upstairs. He set out his shaving kit, but then on an impulse decided to let his beard grow as a tribute of mourning for Hazel. Instead he showered and went through to his dressing room in a bathrobe. Mary brought the coffee tray.

'Have you and Mrs Cross had breakfast, sir?'

'Don't worry about breakfast. Did Mr Reynolds tell you about the staff meeting?'

'Yes, he did, sir.'

Hector dressed in casual country cords and brogues and went to his study at the end of the passage. He sat at his desk and reached for the phone. Paddy answered on the fourth ring.

'Paddy, it's a crying bastard to have to tell you this. Hazel didn't make it. She died at five o'clock this morning.'

There was an echoing silence as Paddy weighed his reply, then he said hoarsely, 'My condolences, Heck. We are going to get the sons of bitches that did this. You have my oath on that. What about the funeral? Nastiya and I would want to be there.'

Nastiya was Paddy's KGB-trained wife, a magnificent Russian blonde who had doubled for Hazel in the Trojan Horse operation that had wiped the pirate stronghold in Somalia from the face of the earth.

'Private cremation. No fuss. That's what she always wanted. However, if you can get here, Hazel would have wanted you two, of all people, to be there. Where are you?'

'Abu Zara.'

'The cremation won't take place for a while. The police will want a forensic autopsy. But come anyway as soon as you can. We need to talk. Make some plans.'

'What about your baby, Heck? Did the poor little mite make it?'

'She was delivered by Caesarean before Hazel . . .' Hector checked. He didn't want to say the word. It was too final. He hurried on. 'Her name is Catherine. She's gorgeous.'

'Takes after Hazel, then. Not you.' Hector's laugh was more like a croak, and Paddy went on. 'We'll have to hide her, Heck. If the Beast finds out about her they'll come back for the both of you.'

'That's something that has been worrying me, Paddy. They were not after me. They were targeting Hazel only.'

'Tell me,' Paddy encouraged him.

'They had a clear shot at me, but they didn't take it. They deliberately fenced me off from the action. They dropped a load of bricks in the road to block my way to her.' Hector and Paddy were both silent, pondering the conundrum.

'I don't know the answer to that. It doesn't make sense,' Paddy admitted at last. 'Maybe they had been warned not to tangle with you. I just don't know. It will become clearer as we work through the rest of it. But we dare not take any chances with your Catherine. We have to hide her away where they can't find her.'

'Okay, Paddy, before you leave Abu Zara I want you to set up a safe house there for Catherine. Try to get the top floor of one of the new skyscrapers the Emir is building on the waterfront; something that we can defend easily.'

'I'll talk to Prince Mohammed himself. No problem. But it might take some time. Perhaps even a couple of weeks.' The prince was the brother-in-law of the Emir and he controlled not only the treasury, the army and the police force but the state building programme as well. He was indebted to Bannock Oil, the company which had drilled the hole that made Abu Zara one of the most prosperous of the smaller states on the globe.

'Good man, Paddy! Let me know what you can find for us. I'll meet you.' He rang off and pressed the intercom button. In the office at the end of the long passage Agatha, Hazel's secretary, answered at once.

'Agatha, please come to my office.'

'Is Mrs Cross with you, sir? I have some letters for her to sign.'

'Come to my office, and I will explain everything.'

When Agatha knocked, Hector pressed the electrical release for the door under the panel beside his knee and the door clicked open. Agatha entered. She was dressed in a sober grey business suit. Her grey hair was neatly coiffured. She had worked for Hazel since her marriage to Henry Bannock.

'Take a chair, please,' said Hector.

She sat in the chair facing him and smoothed her skirt over her knees.

'I have tragic news, Agatha.'

She half rose from the chair, her face distorting with dread. 'It's Mrs Cross, isn't it? Something terrible . . .'

'Sit down, Agatha. I rely on you to be calm and strong, as you always are.' He drew a deep breath and said the fateful words. 'My wife is dead.'

She began to weep silently and softly. 'How did she die? She was so young and vital. It doesn't seem possible.'

'She was murdered,' he said, and she stood up abruptly.

53

'May I use your toilet please, Mr Cross? I think I am going to be sick.'

'Take as long as you need.' He listened to the soft sounds of her distress. Then at last the toilet flushed and she came out. Her eyes were red, but every hair on her head was in place.

She sat down on the chair and looked at him. 'You have been crying also.' He inclined his head in assent, and she went on. 'What about your baby?'

'It's a girl,' he replied, and she smiled sadly.

'Yes, Hazel and I knew that. Is she well?'

'She is very well. But we have to be extremely careful not to let the fact of her birth and survival become public. If that happens she will be in as great a danger as Hazel was. We have to hide her. I will need your help.'

'You shall have it, of course.'

'First things first. I want you to find a firm of undertakers in Winchester. As soon as the police have conducted their investigations and released her body, the undertakers must take my wife from the mortuary at the RHCH and prepare her for cremation. Then they must make arrangements at the crematorium for it to be done as soon as possible.'

'What else?'

'There is a large buff envelope with red wax seals in my wife's safe. Please bring it to me.'

'Very well. I know the envelope you are talking about.' She stood up and looked at him steadily. 'We must both be brave,' she said. 'She would have expected that of us.'

Agatha left the room but returned within a few minutes and laid the buff envelope on Hector's desk.

'Thank you, Agatha. Now, one other thing. We must inform all those who need to know of what has happened to my wife. Please go through Hazel's contact book and make a list of their names for me. I will compose a message to go out to all of them.'

Hector waited until she had left the room before he studied the envelope. It was addressed to him in her hand. He turned it over and made sure the seals were intact.

Hazel had written on the back of the envelope in her bold script: *To Be Opened Only In The Event Of My Death.*

Then he split the flap of the envelope with the curved Arabian dagger he used as a paper knife. He slid out a thick sheaf of documents. To the top of this pile a letter was appended by a paper clip. He recognized her handwriting and felt a sharp pang as he read the salutation:

> *My darling Hector,*
> *I hope you will never read this, because if you do it will*
> *mean that the unthinkable has happened and you and I will*
> *be parted for ever . . .*

Then the tone of the letter became more business-like. She was detailing for him the extent and the disposition of her estate.

> *. . . Most of the property that has been at my disposal*
> *during my lifetime is in fact owned by the Henry Bannock*
> *Family Trust. This includes the ranch in Houston as well*
> *as the one in Colorado, the apartments in Washington and*
> *San Francisco, the house in Belgravia and Brandon Hall*
> *in Hampshire. All of these will revert to the trust on my*
> *death . . .*

Hector grunted. None of this surprised him. He would never have contemplated continuing to live in any of those grand homes. Not with Hazel's ghost walking beside him through the empty rooms.

> *All I truly hold in my own name is the island in the*
> *Seychelles and 4.75% of the market capitalization of*
> *Bannock Oil. In terms of Henry's will I administered and*
> *voted the other 48%, but those stocks also revert to the*
> *Trust on my death.*
> *If you and I have any children of our own they will be*
> *generously taken care of by the Trust. Henry was a good*

and saintly man. He knew he would almost certainly go first, and that I would probably marry again. He did not want me and my still unborn children to be punished for that. I am certain he has made arrangements for any of my children, whether he is the father or not.

You are really and truly going to love dealing with the trustees, but you will have to do so on our children's behalf. I will use your own idiom to describe these gentlemen to you.

A bunch of tight-assed lawyers with faces like piss-pots.

Please be gentle with them, darling, even if they drive you mad with frustration. Henry bound them to a vow of silence. They can't and won't tell you anything about the Trust. They won't tell you the names of the other beneficiaries or what assets the Trust owns. Henry deliberately chose the Cayman Islands as a base for the Trust, because that little state enforces a non-disclosure rule. Not even an order from the Supreme Court of the USA will make them budge.

However, you can rest assured that our children will get everything they need and a lot they don't really need, without a quibble from the trustees. Henry was always very generous. One of his stipulations is that every dollar earned by a beneficiary will be supplemented by the Trust with three dollars. So when Cayla earned $100 baby-sitting for a neighbour the Trust paid her out another $300. When I collected a few million dollars in director's fees from Bannock Oil . . . Well, need I say more?

The chief trustee of the Henry Bannock Family Trust is Ronald Bunter of Bunter and Theobald Inc., a law firm in Houston, Texas. Agatha will be able to give you his address and telephone numbers.

What else is there? Oh yes! In addition to the above I have a few roubles and shekels and other loose change placed with sundry investment banks and financial institutions in various parts of the world. I am not entirely

certain how much there is, but at the last count it was
roughly five or six hundred million dollars. There is a list
of these banks attached to this letter together with the
names of the officials that handle my accounts and the
appropriate passwords to give you access. These are all
numbered accounts so you will have access to them
immediately without having to jump through any hoops.
Nor will you have to pay any taxes on them, unless you
want to. If I know you as I think I do, my silly darling,
you will want to do just that.

What was the Gospel according to St Hector that you
preached to me?

'Pay all the taxes that you owe. Not a penny less and
not a penny more. That is the only way you will sleep well
at night.'

You always knew how to make me laugh.

The G5 belongs to Bannock Oil, and the Boeing
Business Jet belongs to the Trust. But as you are a director
of Bannock Oil you will always have one of the other
company jets at your disposal. Okay, I know you prefer
flying commercial, plebeian that you are. All the cars and
race horses are mine. So drive them carefully and bet on
them wisely. Sadly, the paintings belong to the Trust; all
those lovely Gauguins and Monets (Sigh!). The clothes,
shoes and handbags, the furs and all the jewellery are
mine; as are all the other odds and ends lying around.
That's just about it.

I leave all of this to you in my will, to which this epistle
is attached.

Goodbye, Hector, my true love. I really didn't want to
leave you; I was having so much fun.

I will love you through eternity,

Hazel

One last thought, my dearest darling. Do not pine too long
over my departure. Remember me with joy, but find

yourself another companion. A man like you was never
designed to live like a monk. However, make sure she is
a good woman, or else I will come back and haunt her.

He jumped up from his desk and went through the double doors
onto the balcony. He leaned on the parapet and looked down on
the river, but the lovely view was blurred by the tears in his eyes.

'I never wanted any of that. It's far too much. Four and three-
quarter per cent of all the issued stock of Bannock Oil? My God!
That's an obscene amount of money. All I ever really wanted was
you.'

In the study behind him the intercom chirped and he went back
to his desk and picked up the receiver. 'Yes, Agatha?'

'I have the list you asked for, Mr Cross.'

'Thank you. Please bring it through to me.'

The list that Agatha had prepared comprised over five hundred
names, all Hazel's friends and business associates. With a ballpoint
in hand, Hector pruned it down to four hundred and ten. Then he
circled a number of the names.

'These are the ones that must know immediately. These people
must be the first to know ahead of all the others and before the
media storm bursts. You can send the others tomorrow.' Amongst
the urgent messages were those for John Nelson in South Africa,
brother of Hazel's mother Grace, and John Bigelow in Houston, the
former Republican senator, who was the vice-president of Bannock
Oil under Hazel, who was the president and CEO. Another name
he had circled was Ronald Bunter's.

Hector flipped over a leaf in his notepad and wrote on a clean
sheet, 'It distresses me to have to inform you of the death of my
beloved wife Hazel Bannock-Cross in tragic circumstances. Invitations
to her Memorial Service will follow shortly. Hector Cross.'

Agatha took the amended list and the draft message from him,
and then reminded him, 'It's almost two o'clock. The staff are already
waiting for you in the blue drawing room, sir.'

All the employees of Brandon Hall, from the butler to the gamekeepers and water bailiffs, and from the matron to the chambermaids, were gathered in the blue drawing room. The men stood along the wall while the women were seated awkwardly and self-consciously on the sofas and chairs.

Hector wanted very much to get it over with. These were all fine people and had rendered excellent service. He did not want to turn them out into a job market that was already glutted by the economic recession. He steeled himself and told them about Hazel. There were gasps of shock and exclamations of disbelief. Some of the women began to weep.

'Brandon Hall will probably have to be sold. I will do my utmost to see that you are re-employed by whoever takes over here. But whatever happens you will all receive two years' severance pay.' He went on to thank them for their loyalty and hard work, and then invited all of them to pay their last respects to Hazel at the funeral service in the crematorium. Finally he warned them, 'There are going to be swarms of reporters buzzing around here like flies, trying to get you to reveal details of our private lives and my wife's death. Please don't speak to them. If they offer you money tell me, and I will pay you double to keep quiet. Thank you.'

When they began to file from the room Hector asked the two nursemaids, that Hazel had hired, to remain behind.

'Termination of employment does not apply to you two ladies. My wife gave birth to a little girl before she passed away. I shall need both of you to take care of her.' They perked up immediately.

'A girl! How wonderful. What's her name, sir?'

'Her name is Catherine. But please remember. You must not talk about this to any strangers. Now I want to have a quick look at the nursery to make sure everything is ready for the baby when she comes home from the hospital.'

The nursery suite was directly across the corridor from the master bedroom suite. It was entirely Hazel's creation. Hector had kept well out of the way while she was planning and building it. It comprised five rooms, including the two bedrooms for the nurses. The colour scheme was baby pink. Hector was reminded of a throne room when he walked into the baby's bedroom. In the centre of the floor was a large white and gold cot with a tented pink canopy spread over it. The walls were lined with shelves on which reposed an array of soft cuddly toys, a menagerie of bunnies, giraffes and zebras, lions and tigers. This was a display to outdo Hamleys toy shop at Christmas time.

The two nursemaids were young and deeply respectful. As they led him on a conducted tour, Hector looked wise and said little. In the end he gave his measured judgement: 'Well, it seems that you have everything you need here.' Silently he added, *Except a more mature and experienced hand on the tiller*. He thanked them and escaped back to his study.

As he sank into his swivel chair he saw on his computer screen that there was already a reply to his email from John Nelson, Hazel's uncle in South Africa. He opened it. There was no salutation and the text was stark and bitter.

> You are directly responsible for the deaths of the three people in my life that I have truly loved: my sister Grace, Cayla Bannock, my great-niece, and now Hazel herself.

> The stench of death follows you, Hector Cross. You are as loathsome as a great black hyena. I curse you to your grave, and I shall spit upon it when at last they lay you in it.

Hector rocked back in his chair. 'Poor John, you are really hurting. I understand. So am I.' He deleted the message from his inbox. It took him a while to recover his equilibrium.

'Keep busy!' he urged himself. 'Don't brood. Move on. Keep moving.' He swivelled his chair and reached for the telephone. He dialled the mobile number that Sergeant Evans had given him at the hospital and Evans answered almost immediately.

'I am pleased you called me, Mr Cross. I am very sorry to hear about your wife, sir. The two perpetrators of the attack were dead when my colleagues reached the scene. At this stage we presume they were killed in the collision with your vehicle. The case is being handled by Detective Inspector Harlow at police headquarters in Winchester. I know he is anxious to take a statement from you. Please give him a call to arrange a time and place.' Hector hung up and dialled 101, which took him through to the police non-emergency centre. From there he was passed up the chain of command until he reached Detective Inspector Harlow. They arranged to meet at police headquarters later that evening. He hung up and checked his wristwatch.

He rang down to the underground garage and told the chauffeur, 'Please bring the Bentley around to the front door as soon as you can. I am going into town.'

'Will you need me to drive you, sir?' the chauffeur asked hopefully. He was clearly feeling underemployed.

'Not today, Robert. But by the way, you can take the Range Rover to the panel beaters in town and have them repair the damage to the front end.' Hector grabbed his coat off the hat stand as he left his study. He shrugged it on as he ran down the stairs, taking them two at a time. He was breathing hard as he reached the entrance lobby.

'Puffing like an old man. You'll have to sharpen up if you are going to survive this shit storm,' he told himself. The butler had heard him coming and held the front door open for him.

'Will you be home for dinner, sir?' he asked.

'Give my apologies to Chef. I will be eating out,' Hector told him. The huge house and the empty rooms were already becoming oppressive. He would find his dinner in a pub somewhere. Maybe meet up with a local gamekeeper or a water bailiff with whom he could discuss fishing and shooting, and shake off the dark clouds of sorrow for a short while. The chauffeur already had the Bentley waiting for him.

He drove to the hospital first, and spent half an hour in the registrar's office going through all the procedures for the issue of Hazel's death certificate and Catherine's birth certificate, which entailed the production of his own passport. From what Hazel had written in her last letter to him, he was going to need these documents if he were to get the full attention of the trustees of the Henry Bannock Family Trust.

From the registrar's office he returned to the maternity section, where already the nurses knew him and his tragic circumstances well. Between themselves they had given him the nickname of 'Daddy Heart Throb', or DHT for short.

'It's not visiting hour yet,' one of them told him sternly, and then her tone mellowed. 'But for you we can make an exception, Mr Cross.'

She led him through a door marked 'No Entry. Strictly Private.' Then she fitted him with a gauze mask that covered his mouth and nose and took him into the nursery proper. Only three of the cots were occupied. From the middle cot she lifted a blanket-wrapped bundle and placed it in his arms.

'Ten minutes, no more. Then I am coming back to evict you,' she warned him.

His conversation with Catherine was predictably one-sided. He tried out his own version of baby talk on her, to which she responded by blowing bubbles and falling asleep. He rocked her in his arms and studied her face while she slept. When the nurse returned he relinquished her reluctantly.

At ten minutes to six he went out into the car park and waited until Sister Bonnie Hepworth drove up in an elderly Mini Cooper with faded British racing green paintwork and Formula One stripes. As she parked he opened the car door for her. She looked startled, until she recognized him.

'May I talk to you for a few minutes, Sister?' he asked.

'My pleasure I'm sure, Mr Cross.'

'Do you have children of your own to look after?' he asked seriously.

'I wish I did, but I don't.'

'Then perhaps we can arrange that. I want to offer you a job,' he said.

'I already have a job,' she replied, and then she back-tracked. 'What job?'

'Head nurse to my daughter, Catherine. I know you are very experienced and good with babies. I think my Catherine likes you already. You will have two other younger nurses working under you.'

'But, but I already have a job,' she repeated. She flapped her hands in confusion.

'How much are they paying you here?' he insisted.

'Forty thousand a year.'

'I'll make that one hundred and twenty thousand,' he said, and she gulped.

'I don't know,' she mumbled. 'What about my pension?'

'How much is it?'

'Around about one hundred thou paid up with twenty-three years to term.'

'I'll double that and make it open ended. No retrenchment because of age. You can stay with us as long as you like. Think about it, Bonnie. You can tell me your decision tomorrow when I come to visit Catherine.'

He turned away and walked to his silver Bentley parked at the end of the row. He sensed Bonnie's eyes on him as he opened the door.

'Mr Cross,' she called after him urgently, 'I've thought about it.'

He looked back at her over his shoulder. 'And?' he asked.

'You have got yourself a deal.'

He turned back to face her. 'You had better give me your number.' She recited the number and he committed it to memory. 'I'll call you,' he said. 'We can work out the details. In the meantime you had best give in your notice here.' He gave her a quick firm handshake. 'Welcome on board, Sister Bonnie.' He went back to the Bentley and drove down to police headquarters.

Detective Inspector Harlow was fortyish, overweight and balding. His eyes behind the steel-rimmed spectacles were a washed-out brown, world weary and wise. He stood up and came around his desk to shake Hector's hand.

'My commiserations on your loss, sir. Please be seated. Can I get you a cup of tea or coffee?'

'Coffee. Black. No sugar.'

Harlow obliged and Hector sipped the foul-tasting brew.

'Are you ready to begin?' Harlow asked. Hector set the mug aside and Harlow led him through a detailed description of the events leading up to the murderous attack on Hazel, his own efforts to ward off the assailants and his subsequent actions up until the chance meeting with Sergeant Evans in the patrol car.

Hector omitted only a detailed description of the driver of the French van that had dropped bricks on the road to head him off. When Harlow pressed him, Hector told him, 'He was wearing a rubber mask, and I only saw him for a second as he drove past me.'

'You couldn't tell his nationality?'

'His bare arm was black. That is all I could be sure of. Sorry, but it was just a fleeting glance.' To himself he mused, *If anybody gets to question that buckaroo it's going to be me and Paddy O'Quinn. There'll be no due process, nor reading him his rights when we begin to take him apart.*

At last Harlow was satisfied. 'Yes. That all fits in with what we found at the scene.'

Hector read through the statement Harlow handed him and signed it. 'I heard from Sergeant Evans that the two perpetrators were dead when you found them,' he said.

'That is correct, Mr Cross,' Harlow confirmed.

'Have you managed to identify them, Inspector?'

'Yes. We had an immediate match on their fingerprints. Both of them have criminal records.' He opened a drawer in his desk and brought out a thin sheaf of papers. He passed them one at a time across the desk to Hector. The first was a police mugshot. Hector recognized it at once.

'Yes! He was the driver of the motorcycle.'

Harlow dropped his eyes to the papers in his hand and read aloud. 'His name was Victor Emmanuel Dadu. Twenty-four years old. British citizen. Born in Birmingham. Both parents emigrated from Kenya in 1981. No fixed address. Three criminal convictions. Served six months in 2004 in Feltham Young Offenders Institution for car theft; three months in 2009 for aggravated robbery; three months in 2011 for public violence, mixed up in the 2011 summer riots. In all other respects a nice sweet boy.' He turned over the next sheet of paper and passed it to Hector.

'Yes.' Hector glanced at the photograph. 'That's the shooter, the filthy little swine who murdered my wife.'

Harlow frowned at the outburst but went on reading from the papers in his hand. 'He was Ayan Brightboy Daimar. Age twenty-three years. Born in Mogadishu, Somalia. Illegal immigrant. Served one year in 2009 for housebreaking and burglary. Appealed against deportation and was granted refugee status in 2010.'

Hector nodded noncommittally, pleased that his first appraisal had been confirmed. *Somalia. Another pointer towards the Tippoo Tip clan. It's starting to come together neatly*, he thought, and looked across at Harlow.

'Is there anything else I can do to assist you?' he asked.

'Thank you for your time, Mr Cross. If I need to speak to you again I have your contact details. If we are able to apprehend the driver of the French van we will need you to give evidence at his trial. Once again, my deepest condolences on the death of your wife. Please rest assured that we will leave no stone unturned to find all those involved in this dreadful business.'

On the way back to Brandon Hall Hector stopped at the Flag and Bear at Smallbridge. He finished half a serving of greasy cottage pie and less than half a pint of warm draught beer before the bold stares and pointed remarks of two heavily made-up young ladies seated at the bar began to annoy him. He drove back to the Hall, took a couple of Melatonin and fell into the big double bed.

He woke in the dawn to the sense of something terribly wrong. He lay and listened for her breathing. The silence was complete. Without opening his eyes, he reached for her but the sheets on her side of the bed were cold. He opened his eyes and turned his head and saw that she was truly gone. Then the pain began again, like a deep-rooted cancer, unrelenting and scarcely endurable.

He had to have a focus for his anger and his hatred. He jumped out of the bed and went to the bathroom. As soon as he had showered he went down to his study. He switched on his desktop computer. Even though he knew it was much too soon, he hoped that Paddy had something for him already. However, as soon as he opened his email account he saw that his inbox was overloaded. He skimmed through the first few email messages and saw they were all messages of condolence. He realized what had happened.

The rabid dogs of the press had the story. How had they got on to it so quickly?

Against his better judgement, he opened the home page of the *Sun*, one of Rupert Murdoch's notorious rags. Above a photograph of Hazel in furs and diamonds descending from her Rolls with Hector in the background the headline blared out at him: 'Billionairess gunned down on country road – Kills two of her attackers before she dies.'

It was a mangled piece of reportage. The only part of it that was correct was that Hazel was dead. There was no mention of Catherine's birth.

'Give thanks for small mercies.' He worked through all the other websites. Every major paper had the story. *The Times*' report was dignified and reserved, those of the *Mail* and the *Telegraph* were less so, but none of them reported Catherine's birth. He was mightily relieved.

I have to get her out of that bloody hospital sharpish. The news hounds obviously have it staked out. His blood was up again, and he was ready to take on the day. There was nothing from Paddy, but he knew it was too soon to expect anything.

John Bigelow had sent a long email. On behalf of all the other directors of Bannock Oil he expressed his shock and horror at Hazel's murder. He had already made arrangements for a memorial service to be held for her in Houston, and he went on,

> I would like to have your permission to arrange a
> similar service in London, where Hazel had so many

friends and business associates. I have asked the
US Ambassador to the Court of St James, who is an
old friend of mine, to use his good offices to reserve
the Church of St Martin-in-the-Fields in Trafalgar
Square for the purpose. I have suggested a date two
weeks from now to give those who wish to attend,
and there will be many of these, the opportunity to
arrange their travel plans.

I do hope that you are not contemplating resigning
from the board of Bannock Oil because of this tragic
business. You are highly thought of by all your
fellow directors, and your contributions are valuable
and important.

'You are not going to get rid of me that easily, Biggles. I need you
as much as you say you need me,' he said to himself. The Bannock
infrastructure would give him the clout and wherewithal to enable
him to take down all the bastards who'd done this to Hazel.

He replied to the company vice-president thanking him, accepting
his offer and assuring him of his wish to remain on the Bannock Oil
board. He told him that he considered it his duty to the memory of
Hazel to continue the work that she had devoted so much of her
life to.

He worked quickly down the column of emails and deleted great
swathes of them. Then one caught his eye, and he opened it. It was
from Ronald Bunter, the chief trustee of the Henry Bannock Family
Trust.

Dear Mr Cross,

I was deeply saddened to receive your email. I would
like you to accept my condolences on the death of
your wife, Mrs Hazel Bannock-Cross. She was a
beautiful lady of great presence and stature. She
was also highly intelligent. I personally held her
in the utmost respect and admiration.

Most fortunately, I happen to be in London on business at this very time. I am staying at the Ritz Hotel in Piccadilly until Saturday. The telephone number of the switchboard is 0207 493 8181 and my suite number is 1101.

As you are the executor of your wife's last will and testament, I believe it is of the utmost importance that we should meet at your very earliest convenience. Please telephone me to arrange a meeting.

Yours very sincerely,

Ronald Bunter

Hector reached for the telephone and dialled the number. The switchboard operator answered him almost immediately and transferred him to Suite 1101. His call was answered by a woman's voice.

'Good morning. This is Jo Stanley, legal assistant to Mr Ronald Bunter. How may I assist you?' The accent was mid-Atlantic, the modulation was crisp and controlled.

'May I speak to Mr Ronald Bunter, please?'

'Who may I say is calling?'

'My name is Hector Cross.'

'Oh, goodness gracious. Mr Bunter is expecting your call. Please hold on.'

He smiled at the old-fashioned expression 'Goodness gracious!' The only other person he had ever heard use it was his own mother.

Within a minute Bunter came on the line. His voice was thin and precise; a priggish old maid's voice.

'Mr Cross, it's so good of you to call.'

'Mr Bunter, when and where can we meet?'

'I will be free after six o'clock this afternoon. I understand that you live out of town. Unfortunately I am without transport . . .'

'I can come to you at the Ritz.'

'Yes, that would be very convenient.'

He worked all the rest of the day, making phone calls and receiving them; clearing up all the paperwork on his desk. A few minutes after one o'clock he went down to the wet room and slipped on his waders, then picked up his fly rod from the rack and went out to the river. There was a good fish rising under the trailing willow branches in Honeymoon Pool, which Hazel had named while they sat on the bank holding hands.

The fish was in a difficult position to reach with a cast from this bank. But Hector tied on a Daddy Longlegs dry, and with his third cast he achieved a perfect drift over the trout's lie. It came up in a flashing roll, all silver and crimson, and he set the hook. For fifteen minutes he thought of nothing but the fish as it charged wildly about the pool. When at last he had it laid out on the bank he knelt over it for a moment admiring its elegant lines and shimmering beauty, then he put it to rest with a sharp blow of the priest, the small staghorn club with which the angler administers the last rites. The chef grilled it with wild mushrooms, and Hector ate lunch on the terrace.

After he had eaten he changed into a dark business suit and ordered the Bentley again. He liked driving it. It handled sweetly. He stopped over at the hospital and spent a stolen hour with Catherine.

She was getting more beautiful every day, he decided. When he was finally evicted from Maternity he went to see Doctor Naidoo.

'When will you be able to discharge my daughter, Doctor?'

The doctor studied Catherine's file. 'She is doing very well. Have you made arrangements for her to be cared for, Mr Cross?'

'Yes, I have.'

'Yes, you have indeed. I understand you have hijacked one of my best nurses.'

'Guilty as charged,' Hector admitted.

The doctor looked sorrowful. 'Okay. I am going to discharge your daughter tomorrow morning after my ward rounds. You can sign for her and take her away.' As he walked out into the car park, Hector felt strangely elated at the prospect of having that tiny scrap of humanity being given into his care. Catherine was all he had left that was truly part of Hazel.

He took the London road.

Hector handed over the Bentley to the doorman at the side entrance to the Ritz and he ran up the steps to the hotel lobby. He paused in front of the concierge's desk. There were three or four guests ahead of him waiting to see the concierge and he took his place at the back of the line. He glanced casually around the grand lobby and into the lounge.

The sacrosanct ritual of British afternoon tea was in full swing and the tables in the hotel lounge were almost all taken. Sitting on her own at a table facing the lobby was a woman. As his eyes passed over her, she stood up and looked directly at him. His gaze darted back to her. She was tall and strikingly beautiful. Her hair was glossy black, with russet highlights. Her eyes were wide set in a heart-shaped face. Even across the lounge he could see that they were green, sea-green, and serene. She walked towards him on long slim legs. Her pencil skirt was an inch above her knees. Her high heels accentuated the fine lines of her calves. Her hips were narrow but rounded. Her breasts were high and full under the tailored grey suit. She stopped in front of him and smiled. It was a reserved and guarded smile, but enough to reveal that her teeth were even and sparkling white. She held out her hand.

'Mr Cross?' she asked. 'I am Jo Stanley.' Her voice was soft and gently modulated, but her enunciation was clear and compelling. He took her hand.

'Yes, I am Hector Cross. I am pleased to meet you, Miss Stanley.'

'Mr Bunter is expecting you. May I show you up to the suite?'

There were others sharing the lift as they rode up, so they did not speak again until they stopped at the top floor. However, as they walked down the corridor and reached the double doors at the far end she touched his arm to detain him for a second and said quietly, 'I am so very sorry about your wife. I knew her quite well. She was a wonderful person, so honest and strong. My heart bleeds for you.'

Hector saw that she meant every word and he was deeply touched. 'Thank you. You are very kind.'

Ronald Bunter stood up from the sofa at the far end of the sitting room as they entered the suite. He was a small neat man with silver hair and gold-rimmed reading glasses. He was in shirtsleeves and he wore a pair of bright scarlet braces that were at odds with the rest of his sober attire. His expression was forbidding. Hector could barely suppress a smile as he recalled Hazel's description: *A bunch of tight-assed lawyers with faces like piss-pots*. They shook hands and Hector caught the twinkle in Bunter's pale eyes. Perhaps the dashing scarlet braces were indicative of his true nature.

'Allow me once more to tender my condolences. These are tragic circumstances in which we meet, Mr Cross.' He indicated the tabloid newspapers scattered on the table in front of him. Hazel's photograph was on every front page. 'And a grim business you and I have to deal with.'

'Very kind and thoughtful of you, Mr Bunter.'

'But before we proceed, first let me offer you some refreshment. Will it be tea or coffee?'

'Coffee for me, please.'

'For me too.' Bunter glanced at his assistant. 'Will you see to it please, Jo.' While she phoned the order through to room service Bunter indicated the easy chair opposite him and Hector placed his briefcase on the table and sank into it.

'I hope you will not object to my assistant being present during our meeting. I rely on her to keep accurate records of all that is discussed.'

'Not at all.'

While they waited for the arrival of the room butler with the tea trolley they discussed the weather, which they agreed was very pleasant for this time of the year, and the run-up to the American presidential elections. Bunter was a solid Republican and Hector inclined more towards him. Jo poured the coffee and when they all had their bone-china cups Bunter looked across the table at Hector.

'Shall we continue, Mr Cross?' Bunter went on without waiting for his reply. 'You are aware that I am the senior trustee of the Henry Bannock Family Trust in as much as I have the casting vote on the board?'

'Yes, my wife explained that to me.'

'Your wife was one of the beneficiaries of the Trust.'

71

'How many other beneficiaries are there?' Hector fired a ranging shot, and Bunter ducked it.

'I am not at liberty to disclose that information.' The twinkle was gone from his eyes and his expression was stony. Hazel had told him this would happen but he had to test it for himself. Bunter went on. 'Your wife had the lifetime use of some of the Trust assets. Those do not form part of her estate. They must be returned to the control of the Board of Trustees.'

'Yes, she warned me about that also. You will have my full co-operation.'

Bunter's expression lightened slightly. 'Thank you, Mr Cross. Would you also be able to provide us with a copy of Mrs Bannock-Cross's death certificate? It would save a great deal of trouble.'

'Yes, I can do that immediately.' Hector opened his briefcase and took from it a transparent plastic folder. He extracted the document and slipped it across the table. Bunter perused it briefly.

'You are very efficient, Mr Cross.'

'I think you will also require the birth certificate of my wife's daughter?' Hector took another document from the plastic folder.

'Thank you, but we do have originals of both Cayla Bannock's birth certificate and her death certificate on file.'

'No. I was not referring to Cayla Bannock. I was talking about Catherine Cayla Bannock-Cross.'

Bunter looked startled.

Score one to me, sir, Hector thought with satisfaction. He guessed that it was not easy to win a point from this little man.

Bunter recovered swiftly. 'I beg your pardon, but I do not follow you, Mr Cross. Your wife had only one daughter, surely?'

Hector enjoyed his discomfort for a few moments. Then he told him, 'Five hours before my wife's death she gave birth, by Caesarean section, to a baby girl. She wanted this child to be named Catherine Cayla. Here is Catherine's birth certificate.'

Bunter reached across the table and took the document from his hand. He studied it avidly, muttering to himself. 'Extraordinary. What a remarkable turn of events. A spark of beauty lighting for an instant the dun and gloomy clouds of tragedy.' Then he looked up at Hector, and he actually smiled. 'I do congratulate you as the father, Mr Cross.'

'Thank you, Mr Bunter.' Hector returned his smile, and then he felt a light touch on his arm. He looked down and saw that Jo Stanley had leaned forward and placed a hand on his forearm. 'I am so very happy for you. I know that Catherine will be a great consolation for you,' she said as if she truly meant it.

Bunter went on speaking. 'This is of the greatest significance to the Trust. Catherine will be a full beneficiary.'

'Even if she is not a blood relative of Henry Bannock's?' Hector was drawing him out again.

'No doubt about it,' Bunter said. 'Henry was a remarkable man. One of the finest men I have ever known. There was nothing small or mean about him. From now on until the end of her days the Trust will be fully responsible for all your daughter's needs, no matter how large or how small. You must send the invoices to us, and if you are unable to provide invoices then brief descriptions of her needs and an estimate of the cost will suffice. The Trust will reimburse you immediately. When she grows old enough to seek paid employment of any kind, the Trust will quadruple her earnings. This will apply for her entire lifetime.'

'Yes, Henry Bannock was an impressive man. I met him on a few occasions in the line of duty. He gave me the job as head of security at Bannock Oil,' Hector agreed.

'Yes, I know. He mentioned your name. He liked you,' Bunter replied.

'That is truly gratifying,' Hector said.

Bunter glanced at his wristwatch. 'Twenty after six. I suppose it is still rather early, but shouldn't we wet your daughter's head to welcome her into this wicked world?' He did not wait for a reply but turned to Jo Stanley. 'Jo, my dear, I think I saw a bottle of Dom Pérignon in the minibar.'

Hector drank the flute of champagne slowly. The company was pleasing and he was reluctant to return to the empty hall. He was surprised when Bunter invited him to stay for dinner. The three of them dined in the splendour of the Ritz restaurant. Bunter was a gracious host; Jo Stanley was a good listener. It was not an occasion for merriment, but once she laughed at something Hector said, and her laughter was even more musical than her speaking voice. When

73

Hector left, they both walked with him to the front door of the hotel. Although it had been a friendly dinner they were not yet on first-name terms. It was still Mr Cross, Mr Bunter and Miss Stanley.

When they shook hands Bunter told Hector, 'Jo and I are flying back to Houston tomorrow, but remember I am always just a phone call away if Catherine Cayla should require anything.'

When Hector offered Jo Stanley his hand in farewell she took it without hesitation. Once again her beauty registered fleetingly in the recesses of his mind. But there was nothing subjective in it. It was like noticing a passing cloud or a blooming rose. The doorman was holding open the door of the Bentley for him. He turned away from her, slipped behind the wheel and drove away without looking back in the rear-view mirror.

The next morning Hector had with him Bonnie Hepworth and both the junior nurses when he arrived at the hospital in the Range Rover. They were fully equipped with carry cot, feeding bottles, packets of spare nappies and all the other paraphernalia necessary to support a single infant.

There was a small reception committee waiting for them in the maternity department. All the duty nurses had turned out to see Catherine off and to catch a last glimpse of her father. Hector carried his daughter out to the car with the rest of Catherine's entourage trailing behind him. When they arrived back at Brandon Hall the entire household staff headed by Agatha and Reynolds were lined up under the portico to welcome them.

With appropriate ceremony Catherine was displayed to the company, and she immediately puked up half her bottle over her embroidered nightdress and the lapel of her father's jacket. Hector was thoroughly alarmed and wanted to rush her back to the hospital. Nurse Bonnie managed to dissuade him.

'That's what babies do, Mr Cross.'

'Well then, I wish she didn't have to do it over me.'

Once Catherine was installed in her new quarters the big house came to life again with the constant excited bustle and the sound of female laughter. However, Hector seemed to stand apart from it all.

In her will Hazel had stipulated that in the event of her death she wished to be cremated as expeditiously as was possible. But the coroner would not release her body until the results of the post mortem examination were known. Hector lay awake at night tortured by images of the indignity and mutilation being perpetrated on the corpse of the lovely woman he would love for the rest of his life. It seemed an interminable wait, but eventually her remains were returned into his keeping.

Hector had wanted the cremation to be a very private ceremony but during the delay the news of her death had spread far and wide. Several hundred people had flown in from around the world to pay their last respects to her. In addition, the entire household staffs of both Brandon Hall and the Belgravia home wished to attend. The chapel was almost full. However, Hector was still trying to keep private the fact of the birth of Catherine Cayla. He left her in the care of her nurses.

Hazel's coffin was closed. Hector had visited her in the funeral home the previous evening and he did not want her cold pale face exposed to all those curious eyes. He sat alone in the first row of pews. The chapel was filled with white arum lilies. A priest Hector had never met before read the service. Hector's face remained expressionless as the clergyman pressed the button to send her coffin trundling along the conveyor and through the doors that slid aside to receive her. When the doors closed he stood up and walked back down the aisle. He looked straight ahead without acknowledging any other person in the crowded chapel.

That night he sat alone at the long dining-room table in Brandon Hall and drank two bottles of claret, seeking a state of oblivion. He remained sober but with every glass of wine he consumed his anger burned higher until it became a raging inferno that threatened to consume him.

When he awoke the next morning he was sober and he had his anger under control. He took three aspirin and cleaned his teeth vigorously, his cure for a hangover. He showered and dressed. Then he went down to his study. The maid had left *The Times* on his desk. It was lying face-up so he could read the front-page headline from across the room. For a moment he was frozen with horror, then he roused himself and crossed the study with a few quick strides. He snatched up the paper.

Murdered Woman Gives Birth On Her Deathbed

It has emerged that mortally wounded billionaire heiress Hazel Bannock-Cross gave birth to a daughter five hours before she died from an assassin's bullet. The infant is in good health and was discharged last Thursday from the Royal Hampshire County Hospital in Winchester into the care of her father, Mr Hector Cross of Brandon Hall near Smallbridge in Hampshire . . .

Hector's eyes darted down the page. The story was all there, and the facts were essentially correct. He crumpled the news-sheet into a ball and hurled it against the wall.

'Bastards!' he snarled. 'Bloody bastards!' He turned and ran back into the passage and up the stairs two at a time to the next floor. He burst into the nursery and then checked himself in the doorway. Catherine lay stark naked and tummy down on the table. She was waving her legs in the air as Bonnie stooped over her, sprinkling her pink bottom with white talcum powder.

'Mr Cross!' she gasped with shock. 'Whatever is the matter?'

'Nothing.' Hector backed away. 'I just wanted to check on something. Is everything all right?'

Bonnie smiled. 'Oh, yes. We have just finished up our entire bottle and done a lovely big poo.' Her use of the plural conjured up a macabre image in Hector's mind.

'That's good. That's very good. Now listen to me, Bonnie. I want you to pack up everything here. We are moving up to the London house right away.' The press had broadcast Catherine's birth to the world. The Beast would know exactly where to find them.

'Pack everything?' Bonnie stared at him incredulously. 'But we only just got here! Do you really want us to do that, sir?'

'Yes, I really want you to do that. Just make sure you are ready to leave by one o'clock this afternoon.'

Hector left them and went back to his study. He picked up the internal phone and called the head gamekeeper's cottage. 'Paul, I want all the gates to the estate closed and locked. Put one of your underkeepers on guard at every entrance. They must all carry their shotguns. No stranger is allowed onto the estate. Do you understand?'

'What about deliveries from the village, Mr Cross? We are expecting a van from Farnham's with feed for the pheasant chicks.'

'Make sure they know the driver by sight. No strangers.' He dropped the phone back on its hook and looked around the room, making a list of the few items that he wanted to take up with him to London. There was not much. With her usual attention to detail, Hazel had duplicated most of the contents of the two houses. In most instances it was a case of walk out and walk in. Even Catherine had her own nursery waiting for her there. If only they had stayed in London on the fatal day, they would never have run into the ambush and perhaps she might still be alive. He wondered bitterly what was the title of the book she had wanted to collect from Brandon Hall that day.

He picked up the phone and dialled the number of the Belgravia house in London. The butler answered. 'You have reached the Cross residence. How may I assist you?'

'Morning, Stephen.'

'Ah, Mr Cross! How are you, sir? We have all been so distressed about Mrs Cross. Thank you for inviting us to the service.'

'Thank you, Stephen,' Hector replied gruffly. 'I will be arriving this afternoon with the new baby and her nurses. We will be staying for an indefinite period. Please have everything ready for our arrival.'

When they left Brandon Hall the gates to the estate were locked and Paul Stowe, the head keeper, was on guard with his shotgun under his arm. Hector rolled down the side window of the Range Rover to speak to him. Paul had served with the SAS, which was Hector's old regiment. In Afghanistan he had been badly wounded in a firefight with the Taliban and after leaving hospital he was discharged from the army. Hector had not hesitated when Paul applied for the gamekeeper's job, and he had never had any reason to regret the decision. Hector reinforced his instructions to keep the gates locked and allow no strangers into the grounds. Then they drove on and in the rear-view mirror he watched Paul close the heavy steel barred gates behind them. He drove into the underground parking garage at No. 11 in Belgravia three hours later. Hector had moderated his speed to give Catherine a smooth ride.

When Hector visited the nursery an hour after their arrival he found Catherine fed, burped and tucked up in her cot fast asleep. He relaxed for the first time that day.

One of the items he had brought with him from Brandon Hall was his favourite portrait of Hazel. He hung it on its hook facing his desk in the study before he even switched on his desktop computer.

As soon as the computer booted he logged on to his Gmail account. Near the top of the column of incoming messages was the one he had been keenly anticipating.

> Nastiya and I arrive Emirates flight EK 005 at 1800 hours GMT this Thursday. Heathrow Terminal 3. Can you meet please? I have news. Paddy.

Twenty-four hours later when the two of them came through the arrivals gate Hector was waiting for them. Paddy's craggy face was tanned cocoa brown. Nastiya's face and bare arms were a glowing shade between copper and gold. They both looked fit and vital. Hector embraced each of them in turn. Their bodies were hard and lithe as those of trained athletes, which of course they were.

'You are staying with me at Number Eleven,' he told them.

'I hoped you would say that,' Nastiya replied. 'It's good to be treated like a duchess for a change.'

'You are no duchess, Nazzy. You are a tsarina.'

'What kind of bullshit you must speak all times, Hector Cross?' She tried to look haughty, but she failed. Hector knew she secretly loved it when he called her that. She kissed both his cheeks.

They piled their luggage into the Range Rover. Paddy sat in the front passenger seat and Nastiya took the seat behind him. Hector suppressed a smile as he thought about how when Nastiya was not kicking the guts out of somebody who had annoyed her, she was convincingly playing the role of a subservient wife.

As soon as they were alone, both Paddy and Nastiya reiterated their commiserations on Hazel's murder and spoke of their determination to revenge her. Hector responded awkwardly, maintaining a brave face with difficulty. It was a relief to all three of them when their conversation became more relaxed and commonplace. They had not been with each other for a while and so they exchanged news of their mutual friends and acquaintances and Paddy brought Hector up to date with the activities of Cross Bow Security.

Once they hit the motorway the traffic was light and Hector could give his full attention to the important issues.

'So you say that you have news for me, Paddy? Good or bad?'

'Good and bad. I'll give you the good gen first. Nazzy has found a perfect safe house for your Catherine. As you suggested, it's the entire top floor of one of Prince Mohammed's new beachfront developments in Abu Zara. It is served by a private lift. It also has a helicopter landing pad and a swimming pool on the roof. There is plenty of space for a good security team on the site. We can make it impregnable. That's the good gen.'

'And the bad?' Hector raised an eyebrow.

'Princey wants one hundred and twenty million US for an outright sale, cash on signature of contract.'

'Jesus!' Hector exclaimed, and Paddy shook his head in disagreement.

'Jesus isn't involved in this deal. Princey doesn't believe in him.'

'Will he rent it to us?'

'Yes, he will. But that's not much of an improvement. He wants fifteen mill for a one-year rental. That's his best price for good friends, or so he says.'

Hector thought quickly.

'He has got us by the testicles,' he said at last.

'Not me, he hasn't,' Nastiya said smugly.

'Can't you keep that woman of yours under control, Paddy?' Hector asked and relapsed into silence again while he pondered the problem. Ronald Bunter had assured him that the Bannock Trust would foot all Catherine's expenses. This wasn't a luxury, it was a necessity. It was for Catherine's safety; probably her very survival was at stake. Now was the time to put old Ronnie's word to the test. If Bunter refused, Hector was determined that he would pick up the tab himself. God knows, Hazel had left him enough 'small change' to do the job, and then some. Catherine had to be moved to the safe house, and price didn't come into the reckoning.

'We have to take it. One year should see us running free. How soon can we move in?' he asked Paddy.

'Pretty much right away. Furnishings and fittings are included in Princey's price. The property is highly liveable as it stands. You can add the finishing touches once we get Catherine safely installed. How long will it take you to get her down to Abu Zara?'

'The sooner the quicker,' Hector told him. 'Every day increases the risk exponentially. Excuse me for a few minutes. I have to speak to a friend.' He checked his wristwatch. Houston was six hours behind.

He had Ronald Bunter's private number on his phone.

'Bunter here.' The unmistakable old maid's voice broke his train of thought.

'Good afternoon, Mr Bunter. It's Hector Cross.'

'It's good to hear from you, Mr Cross. How can I help you?'

Hector told him, and Bunter listened silently until he had finished. Then he asked quietly, 'What other options are there for safeguarding Catherine, Mr Cross?'

'There are no other options, Mr Bunter. You know what they did to Catherine's mother.'

'I must speak to my fellow trustees. I'll call you back before close of business today, Mr Cross.'

80

'Thank you, Mr Bunter.'

He broke the connection and glanced across at Paddy. 'Okay, what else have you got to tell me? You have that look on your face. You are holding an ace in the hole.'

'We are almost at Number Eleven,' Paddy demurred. 'It'll keep until we get there.'

'Very well,' Hector agreed reluctantly. 'Your usual suite is ready for you two. But first I'll take you to say hello to Catherine. Then I'll give you half an hour to primp and preen. Hazel made it a rule of the house that gentlemen dress for dinner.'

'I see no gentlemen around here,' said Nastiya.

'Don't encourage her,' Paddy said sadly. 'Russian jokes are like Russian snipers; well camouflaged and difficult to see.'

When Nastiya laid eyes on Catherine for the first time a strange transformation came over her. She seemed to melt like a glittering sheet of titanium steel in the glow of an electric furnace. She took Catherine in her arms and spoke to her in Russian. Catherine's milky blue eyes rolled around in their sockets short-sightedly as she tried to locate the source of these extraordinarily barbaric sounds. Then Nastiya looked up at Paddy accusingly.

'Why don't you give me one of these?'

'Be fair!' Paddy responded indignantly. 'I'm trying my best, aren't I?' When he could drag Nastiya away from the nursery, Paddy led her up to their suite.

An hour later when they came downstairs again to Hector's den, Paddy was wearing black tie and decorations, and Nastiya had her blonde hair up and her décolleté down.

'My God, Paddy! You know how to pick them.' Hector looked at her with exaggerated awe. 'You've got a very fine-looking lady, there.' Nastiya blew him a kiss. Hector had a vodka and lime juice ready for Nastiya and a large Jameson whiskey for Paddy.

'Okay,' he told them. 'Sit. Drink. Then talk.'

Paddy took a sip from his glass and exhaled noisily. 'You'll no' find anything to match that, this side of Dublin,' he said in his broadest brogue.

'Tell me something more interesting.'

'Tariq has come up with a lead on somebody we missed when we thinned out Tippoo Tip's brood.'

Hector sat up straight in his high-backed chair and set his own glass aside. 'I'm listening,' he said quietly.

'As we agreed, I sent Tariq back into Puntland. It's his homeland and he blends in. He has family and friends there. He travelled by bus. First he went down to the old pirate base at Gandanga Bay. He found it completely deserted.'

'That doesn't surprise me.' Hector gave a grim smile. 'We worked it over pretty thoroughly.'

'Scorched earth,' Paddy agreed. 'After that, Tariq returned to Tippoo Tip's stronghold at the Oasis of the Miracle where you rescued Cayla from the Beast. There were a few survivors living in the ruins. One of them had been a concubine of the Khan. Tariq says she is an ancient crone, blind as a bat and starving. Tariq fed her and jollied her along. Her name was Almas and although she couldn't remember what she had eaten for breakfast she could remember everything from twenty years ago with absolute clarity. She knew the Tippoo Tip family tree by heart, back for two centuries. She claimed that she had borne the Khan twins: a boy and a girl. She told Tariq that her son was Kamal, who commanded the Khan's fleet of pirate attack boats. That's the same likely lad you shot dead on board the *Golden Goose*.'

'Never forget him.' Hector smiled. 'It took five nine-millimetre rounds to quieten him down.'

'He was a tough bastard,' Paddy agreed.

'Not so tough.' Nastiya spoke for the first time. 'He squealed like a baby when I bit his finger off.'

Hector laughed out loud. 'Which reminds me never to make your wife mad.'

'Actually, she's a soft-hearted little thing when you get to know her.' Paddy looked at Nastiya fondly. 'However, I digress. According to the old woman who claimed to be Kamal's mother, Kamal's twin sister gave birth to a son when she was sixteen years of age. So this child would be the grandson of Tippoo Tip.'

'Do tell!' Hector urged him. 'Did Tariq get his name? What happened to him? Is he still alive?'

'His name was and is Aazim Muktar Tippoo Tip. He left Africa as a young man of twenty or so and he came here to London to study Islamic Law at the Great Mosque in Regent's Park.'

'Is he still here in London? Does his grandmother know?' Hector demanded.

'No, she doesn't know. In fact she knows very little about anything that recent. She lives with the fairies most of the time. She doesn't know where she is herself, let alone where her grandson is. However, I phoned the London mosque and spoke to one of the mullahs there. He knew Aazim Muktar well. He has become an important cleric, highly regarded across the Middle East; a man with influence and power.'

'All right, but where can we find him?'

'Just across the Gulf from Abu Zara. He is now one of the senior mullahs at the Masjid Ibn Baaz Mosque, in Mecca. I sent Tariq to do a recce of the mosque. That's why it took so long for me to come back to you. Tariq attended prayers there a number of times. He saw Aazim Muktar in the flesh and heard him preach. Apparently the mosque was packed. Aazim Muktar had the congregation eating out of his hand. The faithful come from all over the Middle East to listen to him. Even Tariq was seriously impressed. He says Aazim Muktar is a very holy man.'

'I am pleased to hear that. So when I have finished with him Aazim Muktar will have a place to go where Allah will welcome him,' Hector said grimly. 'How easy will it be to pick him up, Paddy?'

Paddy considered the question and then asked his own. 'I take it you're not considering a long-range sniper shot when he leaves the mosque?'

'Correct,' Hector agreed. 'I want to look in his eyes and search his soul. I want him to know who I am and I want him to know what he has to pay for. I want to tell him about Hazel. Then I want him to see the black angel coming for him. I want him to die slowly and I want to hear his screams.'

Even Paddy was shaken by the force of Hector's anger. It took him a while to consider his reply. 'I am not saying it's impossible, but snatching him will have its problems. At least we won't have to parachute into a desert fortress the way we had to do to get at his grandfather. After one prayer ritual Tariq followed him and his entourage to where he lives in the temple compound only a kilometre or so from the mosque. He could not get close to the building without attracting undue attention to himself. But he says it's a large building surrounded by a fairly substantial wall. It is a difficult place to approach; many eyes watching. There are armed guards at the gate. On the terms you have stipulated it might not be as easy as I, for one, would have liked.'

Hector picked up his glass and stared into it, swirling the golden whiskey in its depths. Before he could speak the phone in the pouch on his belt played the opening bars of 'American Pie'.

'Sorry, I'll have to take this one.' He lifted the phone to his ear. 'Cross speaking! Thanks for calling back, Mr Bunter. Do you have news for me?'

'I have spoken to my colleagues and we are all agreed that the safe house for Catherine is a legitimate charge to the Trust, together with the costs of all the other security arrangements. Furthermore, at the moment the Trust's Boeing Business Jet is hangared at Farnborough airport. The crew has been instructed to stand by to fly you and Catherine down to Abu Zara. Obviously the sooner we can get her out of harm's way the better.'

'I am very grateful to you and your fellow trustees, Mr Bunter.'

'We can do no less, Mr Cross. Please feel free to call on us for anything further Catherine may require. Goodbye, sir.' Hector returned the phone to its pouch.

'Good man, Bunter,' he said, and then looked back at Paddy. 'Thank you, Paddy. You have given me plenty to think about.' He glanced at his wristwatch. 'But right this minute I am hungry. Shall we go through to the dining room and see what Chef has got for us?'

The first course was grilled Fine de Claire oysters on the half-shell, dressed in a heavenly mantle of Tabasco-tinted hollandaise sauce and accompanied by an ice-cold Chablis. Hector had just slipped the first oyster into his mouth and was rolling his eyes with pleasure when his iPhone rang again. He cursed around the oyster.

'Who the hell rings at a time like this?' He glanced at the illuminated screen on the phone. 'It's my gamekeeper at Brandon Hall. I don't need to speak to him in the middle of dinner. Excuse me, while I switch off this infernal machine.'

'*Nyet*, Hector,' Nastiya told him. 'That is not weary vice at a time like this.' Hector knew she meant 'not very wise', and he hesitated. He had learned to respect Nastiya's advice. She had the warrior's instinct finely developed. Then he lifted the phone to his ear.

'Paul, whatever it is, make it short. We are in the middle of dinner,' he said and Paul Stowe's voice was so raised and agitated that all of them seated at the dining room table could hear him clearly.

'Sir, the Hall is on fire. At least four of our people are trapped in the flames.'

'Oh my God, Paul! What started it?'

'Incendiary grenades, sir.' Paul was an old soldier. 'I would know the smell of burning white phosphorus anywhere. There were two of them in quick succession. I heard the explosions and the next second the whole hall went up like a bonfire.'

'Which part of the house did they hit?' Hector demanded.

'The bedroom wing. It looks like one grenade went in through your study windows below the master bedroom, and the other through the library window under the new nursery area.'

Swiftly Hector digested that information. The attackers must have known the layout of the house. They had made a very focussed attack. Hector had a vivid mental picture of what might have been the consequences if he and Catherine had been sleeping in the Hall this very evening. Thermate in an incendiary grenade burns at 2,200 degrees centigrade. It can melt steel almost instantaneously.

'Did anyone get a look at the attackers? Do you have any idea who they are?'

'Two scumbags got into the estate late this evening, probably around about dusk.' Paul's voice rang with certainty and outrage.

'How do you know that, Paul?'

'I found their car, a new Vauxhall Zafira, where they'd hidden it on the other side of our boundary wall opposite the Corner Stone Drive. I was on my way home when I noticed something that hadn't been there yesterday, a pile of green branches. Because you had warned me to be on the lookout, I went to take a butcher's and found the car hidden under the branches. Then I tracked the two thugs from there and found where they had climbed over our wall. It took me almost half an hour to get back to the Hall because I had to circle around to the stone bridge to cross the river. By that time it was dark and I was just crossing the lower meadow when I heard the grenades go off and saw the flames. It was no good trying to track them because it was too dark. Anyway, my first priority was to rescue any of our people who were trapped in the Hall. It's a racing certainty that those thugs headed straight back to where they left their car. But of course the car won't start, will it? I took care of that.'

'How?' Hector demanded.

'Well, I had my Leatherman tool with me. So first thing I did when I found it was I pulled all the spark plugs out of the engine and tossed them in the river. The only way they are going to be going anywhere tonight is on foot.'

'What are you doing now, Paul?'

'I am trying to save some of those poor devils who are trapped in the fire. But I don't think there is much hope. The flames are so fierce we can't even get close. Already the entire roof is starting to collapse.'

'You've done the right thing, Paul. I am coming down to give you a hand. This time of night there won't be much traffic; I should be there in less than two hours.' He cut the connection and looked at Paddy.

'It's the Beast again,' Paddy said. 'No question about it. They read the newspapers, so they know about Catherine and they think she is at Brandon Hall. They are after her.' He paused and then added, 'And you also, Hector.'

'Get changed and let's go,' Hector said. They left the remains of the oysters and the wine untouched. They rushed up the main staircase and ran to their bedrooms. Only minutes later all three of them met on the staircase again, dressed in rough clothing. Hector was carrying an Irish fighting club made from blackthorn wood, a shillelagh. He tossed it onto the back seat when they reached the Rover in the underground garage.

Driving very fast along the almost deserted motorway, it took just under an hour and twenty minutes to reach Winchester. As they passed the town, Hector called Paul Stowe again.

'Fill me in with what's happening, Paul.'

'The Fire Brigade have got the fire under control now, but it had just about burned itself out anyway. They have found two bodies. But it's impossible to tell who they are. They are too badly burnt.'

'Poor devils! Leave the firemen to their job. We must try and catch those bastards that put the grenades in. If they are trying to walk out they must still be on the road. We are coming through Winchester right now. We will search the road from here to Brandon Hall. But they might not have come this way. They might have gone south towards Southampton. Take one of the Land Rovers and cover that stretch of road. Have a couple of your underkeepers with you and make sure you are carrying shotguns. These are murderous swine we are dealing with.' Hector cut the connection and spoke over his shoulder to Nastiya on the back seat.

'There is a spotlight in the locker behind you. Get it out and plug it into the lighter socket next to the ashtray between the seats. Then open the sun roof. If you stand on the seat, even a little short-ass like you will be able to stick your head and shoulders out through the opening. Sweep both sides of the road with the spotlight. It's fairly open ground from here to the turn-off to Brandon Hall, but they might hide in the trees when they see us coming.'

The road was still deserted as they sped along it. Country folk don't keep late hours, so they did not see another vehicle for the next five miles. Then they came around a sharp turn through a stretch of woodland and ahead of them the road descended through open fields on both sides. Only two hundred yards ahead, full in the beam of the powerful spotlight that Nastiya was wielding, they picked up a pair of dark masculine figures trudging towards them down the white line in the centre of the road.

The woodland had screened the approaching lights until the Range Rover was close upon them, and now they were taken by surprise. For a few critical seconds they stood frozen as the Range Rover bore down on them.

Their faces were concealed, for they both wore hoodie jackets. Swiftly they recovered their wits, and they turned and ran. They were stupid enough to let themselves get caught out in the open, and dumb enough to run for it and confirm their guilt, but they were smart enough not to stay together. They split up as if by prior agreement. One of them left the road, scrambled over the fence and ran up the gentle slope through a freshly planted field of winter wheat, heading for the dark patch of trees that just showed against the stars near the crest.

The other man went in the opposite direction, over the fence and through the open field down towards what looked like a small stream running parallel to the road at the bottom of the hill.

When Hector reached the spot where they had left the road he slammed on the brakes and flung the door open. As he reached back to the seat behind him where the blackthorn shillelagh lay, he shouted, 'Paddy, you and Nazzy take the one on your side. I'll get the other bastard.'

Nastiya wriggled out onto the roof of the Rover, jumped and landed lightly in perfect balance on the verge. She reached the fence before Paddy was out of the side door. She used the slope of the embankment to gather momentum and she ran at the fence. She leapt at it and placed one hand on the top of a fence pole, jack-knifed her body and dropped over the far side. The sprouting wheat in the field was no more than a foot high and didn't impede her at all. She gained on the fleeing figure as swiftly as a whippet running down a hare. She caught him long before he reached the tree line and while Paddy was still twenty yards behind them.

The man heard her light footsteps rustling the wheat stalks close behind him and he turned at bay. When he saw it was a skinny little girl pursuing him, he reached into his pocket. He brought out a flick knife and snapped open the blade. He dropped into a defensive crouch, and he presented the point of the weapon to her.

'Come then, bitch,' he panted at her. 'I'm going to cut your stinking cunt out of you and stuff it up your arse.' Nastiya never checked her charge. She went in fast and at the very last instant she dived feet-first under his guard, taking her weight on her shoulders as she hit the ground. Then she rebounded and at the same time shot out both legs with the speed and power of an arrow from a longbow.

Taken by surprise, the man was slow to react. He shouted with pain as Nastiya slammed the soles of her feet into his right wrist. Even above the sound of his agony, the crackle of his carpus bones breaking was sharp and clear. The knife flew from his hand in a high spinning arc. Nastiya used the impetus of her rush to flip back onto her feet. She caught the knife neatly by the handle as it dropped.

Nursing his shattered wrist, the man backed away from her but she followed him remorselessly, slashing the blade of the flick knife back and forth only inches from his face.

'Down!' she ordered him. 'Get down on your knees, you dirty-mouth son of a Satan, before I cut out your stinking balls and make you eat them.'

'Wait!' he whimpered. 'I'm doing it. I'll do anything you say.' He dropped to his knees, nursing his damaged wrist, setting himself up perfectly for her next kick. It caught him under his chin and he went over backwards and lay choking and bubbling blood from his half-severed tongue that he had bitten.

Paddy came up beside Nastiya and looked down at the writhing figure in the wheat.

'Jesus and Maria, woman! You haven't left much for me, have you?'

On the lower side of the road Hector was closing the gap on the man he was pursuing. He seemed much younger than Hector, but Hector was faster and fitter.

Hector wanted to avoid a hand-to-hand with somebody who would almost certainly be carrying a knife. When he was only a dozen paces behind his quarry, he swung the shillelagh back over his shoulder, and then whipped it forward again. Hector had spent his childhood in Africa and his small indigenous companions had all been experts with throwing sticks. Even the youngest of them could bring down a flying spurfowl at twenty paces. They had taught Hector well. The shillelagh cartwheeled into the back of the man's legs and he went down in a heap with a cry of surprise.

Hector snatched up the shillelagh on the run and as he came up behind his fallen victim he made a quick calculation. If he broke the man's leg that would certainly anchor him, but he would have to carry him back up the hill to where he had parked the car. On the other hand, a broken arm would anchor him almost as effectively, but he would still be able to hobble back to the Range Rover, especially if Hector gave him a little encouragement with the blunt end of the club. He stood over the man, who instinctively lifted both hands to shield his face. Hector hit him on the point of the elbow with a full swing of the shillelagh, and the man screamed as his elbow joint shattered.

Hector seized the wrist of his injured arm and twisted it. The man howled again and Hector levered him to his feet.

'Christ, man, you're hurting me,' he blubbered.

'You mustn't say that,' Hector told him. 'You're breaking my heart.' He twisted the injured arm up between the man's shoulder blades and frog-marched him back up the hill. When he reached the Range Rover he saw Nastiya and Paddy coming down the hill to join him. Paddy was carrying their captive over his shoulder in a fireman's lift.

When he reached the fence he dumped his burden over the wire and called to Hector, 'Have you had a good sniff of your nice young friend?'

'I certainly have,' Hector replied. 'Mine smells of garlic. How about your beauty?'

'Reeks of the stuff.' Paddy looked stern.

'What else smells like garlic? Please remind me,' Hector asked.

'Could it be burning white phosphorus from an incendiary grenade?' Paddy asked.

Hector snapped his fingers. 'That's it!' He gave the man's broken arm a firm twist. 'Now, we haven't been burning down any houses recently, have we?' His victim squealed shrilly. 'I'll take that as an affirmative,' Hector said, and bundled him through the open rear door of the vehicle.

Paddy jumped over the fence and dragged the second man out of the ditch by his heels, picked him up bodily and threw him into the back of the Rover on top of his mate, and then Hector slammed the door and locked it from the outside.

'Nazzy, please keep your new knife handy just in case one of these lovely lads gets a bit obstreperous,' Hector warned her as they all climbed aboard. Before he started the engine Hector called Paul Stowe.

'Okay, Paul. You can call it a day and come home. We have picked up both of the runners.'

He started the Rover and drove sedately back to the Brandon Hall Estate. When he crossed the bridge over the River Test and entered the main gates of the estate he did not drive directly to the Hall, but turned left and took the dirt road down to the Old Barn. This renovated building was used as a luncheon venue on shooting days. It was almost half a mile from the Hall, concealed from it by trees. Hector parked on the side of the building furthest from the main road. Nobody would be able to see or hear what was happening inside.

While Nastiya went ahead to unlock the front door and switch on the lights in the barn, Hector and Paddy dragged the two captives out of the back of the vehicle and followed her into the commodious building.

'Keep an eye on our hostages, Paddy,' Hector said, even though he could see there was no fight left in either of them. He went to the row of cupboards on the rear wall of the barn and came back with a large reel of yellow electrical cable and a pair of wire cutters. One at a time he trussed the two captives into a pair of straight-backed chairs at the dining table, leaving only their injured arms free. It was a neat and expert job. They were pinioned help-lessly.

'Okay, put your free arms on the table in front of you,' he ordered. When they hesitated, Hector reached across the table and grabbed one of them by the wrist. He twisted it sharply. The man screamed and his face in the hood of his jacket went chalky white. Sweat burst out on his chin and forehead.

'Do it!' Hector insisted.

'Okay! Okay! Just take it easy, man.' The fellow mumbled around his lacerated tongue which had swollen to fill his mouth. Gingerly he stretched out his arm towards Nastiya, who was leaning across the table towards him. She slipped a loop of the yellow cable around his swollen wrist and tugged it tight.

'Shit, man!' he whined. 'Do you want to kill me?'

'A few things you need to know, comrade,' she told him. 'Firstly, I still don't like your dirty speaking. Secondly, I am not a man. Thirdly, yes, I would like very much to enjoy killing you. Please give me an excuse to do that.'

The second captive had watched what had happened to his companion and he cooperated with alacrity, offering his injured arm to Paddy across the table without a quibble. Paddy slipped a loop of the cable over his wrist.

Hector stood behind the two prisoners and yanked the hoods down over their shoulders, leaving both their heads bare. Then he walked to the other side of the table and stood between Paddy and Nastiya. For a while he studied the two captives in front of him.

They were both in their twenties or early thirties; both white. He had expected them to be the same colour as the men who had killed Hazel.

Colour meant nothing, Hector reminded himself. Some of the worst swine he knew were white; and some of the best men were black.

He studied the man that Nastiya had caught. He was thickset; dark unruly hair; flat Slavic features; yellow pustules and bright acne scars on his chin and cheeks. He was sweating heavily with pain. He could not take his eyes off Nastiya, who was holding him on the end of the cable. She stared back at him coldly.

The second man was lanky in build and sallow in complexion. His sandy-coloured hair was already thinning. His eyes were a pale gingery brown and his teeth were twisted and discoloured. Hector could smell his breath from across the table.

'Very well, gentlemen. Now please pay attention. My name is Hector Cross. I am the person who you tried to burn to death. My daughter is Catherine. She is still an infant. You also tried to kill her. Thus, I am not very well disposed towards either of you.' He gave them a few seconds to digest that, and then he continued, 'Like it or not, you are going to answer some questions. If you answer them truthfully you get ten Brownie points. If you tell me a porky pie you get your sore arm twisted.' He smiled at the one with acne scars. 'Do you know what a porky pie is, lover boy?'

'A lie,' the man mumbled. A little trickle of blood oozed from the corner of his mouth. He licked at it. His tongue was deeply gouged by his own teeth, swollen and turning blue.

'That's correct. Now, shall we play the game?' He did not wait for a reply. He took the ends of the yellow cables from Paddy and Nastiya and held one in each hand.

'First question is for you.' He looked at the one with bad teeth. 'Do you know that your breath stinks?'

'It doesn't stink.'

'Wrong answer,' Hector told him and yanked his cable. The broken bones in his elbow clicked like dice, and he screamed. He struggled wildly to break out of his bonds. At last he subsided, panting and sobbing.

Hector repeated the question quietly. 'Let's get it clear, does it stink or not?'

'Yes! Yes! It stinks.'

'Excellent. So I'm going to call you Spots, which is short for Leopard Breath.' He turned to the other one. 'Do you know that you have pimples?'

'Yah. Okay. I got a few pimples.'

'*Beaucoup* rather than just a few. Anyway that's your new name. So tell me, Pimples. Where did you get the incendiary grenades?'

His dark eyes shifted. Hector raised his left hand holding the tag end of the cable.

'Quickly,' he warned.

'The nigger gave them to me.'

'Very interesting reply, even though it offends my political conscience.' Hector smiled, and it was more menacing than any scowl. 'Shall we rather refer to your grenade supplier as the Worthy African Gentleman, or WAG for short?'

'Whatever.' Pimples shrugged, and then winced at the pain the movement afforded him.

'What was his name, this WAG?'

'I don't know.'

'Careful!' Hector said, and showed him his end of the cable.

'I swear on my mother's grave. I don't know his name. I didn't ask and he didn't tell.'

'How did you meet him?'

'Someone I worked for one time before gave him my name.'

'What kind of work did you do before? Was it wet work?'

'Yeah, we snuffed an old guy who owed some money and didn't pay. Kind of an example for others.'

'What was the old guy's name and where did you do him?'

'His name was Charley Bean, I think, but I don't remember the address; somewhere in Croydon.' He twisted his head around to look across at his companion. 'Where was it, Bonzo?'

'Sixteen Pulson Street,' Spots muttered.

'The two of you are doing just fine.' Hector applauded their performance. 'What did you use to dish Charley Bean? Knife, was it?'

'Nah. Golf club.'

'Where did you find a golf club?'

'In a bag hanging behind his bedroom door.'

'Wedge or five iron? How many strokes?' Hector asked. Pimples looked blank.

'Never mind. I was just having a little fun with you,' Hector consoled him. 'Who gave you the contract on Charley Bean and put the WAG onto you?'

'Can't remember.' Hector gave the yellow cable a firm tug, and Pimples howled and burst out in a fresh sweat.

'Think!' Hector encouraged him.

'Bookmaker named Aaron Herbstein,' he sobbed. 'He runs a book on the dogs at Romford and Sunderland stadiums.'

'Thank you, Pimples. How did Herbstein the bookie set up a rendezvous with you and your WAG?'

'A runday what?' Pimples looked bewildered.

'A meeting. Where and how did you meet?'

'We waited outside the tube station on Brixton Road at nine o'clock last Sunday morning and he came past in a car and picked us up.'

'What car?'

'A black Ford.'

'Did you get the registration number?'

'Didn't bother.'

'Why?' Hector asked and Pimples shrugged.

'It was nicked, wasn't it?'

'Of course it was. So you got in the back of this Ford and you looked at the driver. Tell me what you saw.'

'I saw a black guy in a funny mask,' Pimples said.

'A Richard Nixon mask?'

'Nah, it was a Dolly Parton mask.'

'How did you know he was black?'

'I was looking at the back of his neck. It was black, wasn't it?'

'What else did you notice about him?'

'Well, he was a Muzzie.'

'A Muzzie? What's that?'

'A Muslim. A Hadji.'

'You could tell that by looking at the back of his neck?'

'Nah, he had a Maalik tattoo.'

'What is a Maalik?'

'An Angel. A Muzzie Angel. They are a gang that call themselves Maaliks because they think they are the warriors of Allah, or some shit like that. They tattoo the sign on themselves and they think it makes them some kind of big deal. But they're just a gang of street soldiers trying to make a little bread like the rest of us. Usually we fight them for territory. But this time we were doing business. This Maalik guy offered five K for us to torch a big old house in the sticks.'

'My house,' Hector said.

'Sorry, guv. If I had only known I would have told him to stuff his five K really deep.' Pimples hurried on. 'I knew he was sub-contracting to us. That's what these shit-face Maaliks do. Someone offers them ten K for a job so they offer us the same job for five. They are shit, I tell you.'

'So you agreed to take on the job?'

'I wish I hadn't,' Pimples muttered ruefully. 'I didn't know about you and your daughter. But, after all, five K is still money. It buys a few tokes. This Maalik told me the house belonged to an old guy who couldn't fight back for pussy.'

'And, baby, look at you now.' Hector gave the yellow cable a double jerk. Pimples wailed, his voice broke and he began to blubber.

'Please stop. I am telling you everything. Please don't do that again.' Tears ran down his cheeks, weaving their way slowly between the pustules. He had no free hand to wipe them away and they dripped onto the front of his hoodie.

'No, you haven't told me everything yet, Pimples. Tell me more about this Maalik tattoo. Describe it to me.'

'It was on the back of his left hand, about the size of a ten-pence coin. It looks like a worm crawling out of a lump of shit; all sort of twisted up. I think it's some sort of Muzzie writing. Not all of them are allowed to wear it, only the top tomatoes in each chapter.'

'What colour is the tattoo?'

'Different colours for each chapter.'

'Your man. The one who gave you five K. What colour was his mark?'

'He's American, isn't he?'

'How do you know that?'

'For starters he talked with a Yankee accent. For seconds his tattoo is red. Bonzo and me checked on it before we took the contract. Red means the California chapter.'

'What's he doing over this side of the Atlantic?'

'Dunno! Must be one of their Capo de Capos, like Robert de Niro in the flicks, or something.'

'You don't know his name?' Hector insisted, and Pimples shook his head vehemently.

'No! That's all I know.'

'Where is the five thousand pounds they gave you for the job?'

'Not here, I ain't got it here.'

'I asked you where it is, not where it isn't.'

'Gave it to my girlfriend to keep for me.'

'You've got a girlfriend? I can hardly applaud her taste in men.

Anyway, this is her lucky day. She's got five grand and she never has to look at your revolting face again. Why? Because if we don't kill you, the boys in blue are going to lock you away for twenty or thirty years, maybe more. You know? Arson and multiple murders, innit,' he said, imitating the man's accent. 'You gentlemen are in between a rock and a very hard place.' They stared at him in dull resignation.

Hector turned to Nastiya. 'They haven't got much more to tell us that we need to hear. What do you think we should do with them, Nazzy my dear? As if I couldn't guess.'

'I think to kill them. Let me do the one with the pimples. He said some very bad things to me. I am still very, very cross.'

'That should be a lot of fun to watch.' Hector turned to Paddy. 'What's your vote?'

'We haven't got time to waste on this dungheap. Let's do what Nazzy suggests and get on with it.' Hector pretended to ponder the position. Both the captives watched his face anxiously. At last, Hector sighed.

'It is definitely a most attractive proposition. But it would leave us with a lot of cleaning up. A brace of human carcasses is not easy to dispose of. I think we should be charitable and give them a little time to think it all over and repent their sins, something like twenty or thirty years enjoying the hospitality of Her Majesty. That should do the trick.' He took out his phone and dialled 999. Two cars despatched from Winchester police headquarters arrived at the Hall within forty minutes.

The police officers were very polite and deferential towards Hector. They were well aware of his standing in the community, and of Hazel's murder. They tried to smooth the whole arrest process, so as not to exacerbate the burden of his bereavement. Nonetheless, it was a long night. Firstly, Hector insisted on staying on at Brandon Hall until all his employees had been accounted for. It was after midnight before the firemen found the fourth and last corpse amongst the ashes.

It was Reynolds, the butler, who had been trapped by the flames in his own pantry. In the final moments before the smoke over-whelmed him he had covered his head with a fire blanket from the emergency kit. His face was only superficially scorched and still recognizable, but from the neck down he was a blackened and wizened stump of charcoal.

After the firemen zipped his corpse into a green body bag, Hector turned away and went to the Range Rover. They followed the police cars to Winchester to make their sworn statements.

The two prisoners were cautioned, charged and locked in the holding cells. Then Hector, Paddy, Nastiya and Paul Stowe were taken to separate interview rooms to make their statements.

This was a tedious chore, but they had rehearsed their version of events and it all went smoothly. Hector was even able to place on the record what the perpetrators had confessed to concerning the previous contract killing of a certain Charles Bean at 16 Pulson Street. The detective sergeant who was interviewing Hector excused himself and went back to the computer in his own office. He returned after only ten minutes or so. As he took the seat facing Hector again his expression was grim.

'It ties in with Central Records. Same name and same address; fifth of March two years ago. Unsolved murder.'

In addition Nastiya handed over the flick knife she had captured, and testified as to how the accused had attacked her with it and how she had been obliged to defend herself by disarming him. The officer who was taking her testimony looked at her with an awed expression.

'You did that to his wrist with only one kick?'

'I was careful not to use undue force,' Nastiya explained.

'I meant that you are so small and he is so big!' Few men were able to resist the little Russian when she batted her eyelids and assumed an attitude of childlike innocence.

It was two o'clock in the morning before they were able to leave the police station. None of them had eaten or slept for hours, but they were still driven by a surfeit of adrenalin. Hector stopped at the first McDonald's along the road and brought back a large bag full of double cheeseburgers and cardboard beakers of coffee. Thus fortified, their conversation on the way home to No. 11 was lively as they tried to make some sense of the two attacks on Hector and his family, and the part that the mysterious masked Californian gang leader had played in both assassination attempts.

'It sounds as though he was the one driving the van. Obviously he is the next one up the chain of command. The two on the motorcycle who killed Hazel and now these two we put away tonight are merely grunts. They had no idea why they were doing what they did. They did not know who was giving the orders. They just followed them blindly. This in itself is significant,' Hector postulated.

'In what way?' Paddy asked.

'Okay; on their first attempt they had the drop on me. They might have taken me out pretty easily; but they passed up on the chance. They fenced me off from the action, or at least they tried to. Clearly, their orders were only to get Hazel. They weren't interested in me. Why? Tell me why, will you? It worries me.'

'It's a tough one,' Paddy admitted.

'If they were acting logically I should have been the prime target, not Hazel. I killed the head of the clan, Khan Tippoo Tip. I also took out at least five of his sons, including Kamal and Adam, his favourites. I was the one who set up the Trojan Horse operation that destroyed their fleet of pirate boats. I should have been number one on their shopping list.'

'Hazel was as responsible as you were; more so, even. She had the cheque book. You were simply her hired gun. What's more, she was the one who actually pulled the trigger at Adam's execution,' Paddy pointed out.

'That's true,' Hector countered. 'But those yobbos never knew that. Even if they did, they should have taken both of us. Why were they after her exclusively?'

'Hector is right, *Muslaki*.' It always amused Hector when Nastiya called Paddy 'Sugar Baby'. He was neither of those. 'And what about last night? Who were they really after with their fire bombs? Hector or our little Catherine?'

'You have married a pretty smart cookie,' Hector remarked. 'She's absolutely right. Why did the Beast suddenly change its mind last night and decide that it wanted me after all?'

'Why is it as soon as the newspapers blurt out about our Catherine they make another attack?' Nastiya looked smug.

'You are saying that last night they were after Catherine, and not Heck?' Paddy's tone was sceptical. 'That doesn't make sense to me. What could they possibly gain by torching a newly born infant?'

The argument lasted all the way back to London. They went round in circles; they picked nits and shot down one another's theories, and at last agreed that none of it added up. The Beast had acted irrationally, and that in itself did not compute. The Beast never acted irrationally.

As they ran through the West End, Hector summed up. 'All I am sure of is that we have to get Catherine out of England. Only when we have her tucked away on the top floor of Seascape Mansions in Abu Zara with a platoon of Paddy's top men to watch over her will I be prepared to leave her.'

'To go where and do what?' Paddy demanded. 'What are your plans, Heck?'

'To go with Tariq Hakam to Mecca; to find this last remaining sprig of the Tippoo Tip clan; to capture him and take him to a safe place where I can question and evaluate him. Then, if I find him guilty, I will consign him to burn in the flames of hell from which he has sprung.'

It would not take more than a few days to pack up and prepare for the move to Abu Zara. Hector's personal needs were easily catered for, not much more than a toothbrush and a change of underpants. Cross Bow Security had all the equipment he could possibly need for Phase Two of the operation stored in the Bannock Oil installation out in the desert a hundred miles south of Abu Zara City.

What concerned him most was what he knew least about: the supply train and logistics for the support of an infant. He called in his resident expert, Bonnie Hepworth. Despite the late hour, she answered his call with alacrity, and stood in front of his desk in her dressing gown, with an expectant expression not unlike a puppy waiting for a bone.

'You want me, Mr Cross?'

'I wanted to see you.' Cautiously Hector modified her question. 'Bonnie, do you know where Abu Zara is?'

'Is that a hotel, Mr Cross?'

'That wasn't even close. Let's try again. Do you know where the United Arab Emirates are?'

'Well, sort of. I have heard of it, but I have never been there.' She looked dubious. 'Somewhere between Egypt and India, I think.'

'Pretty close,' he commended her. 'Well, that's where we are all going, you and Catherine also.'

'Goodness! Working for you is such jolly good fun. One never knows what's going to happen next.'

'What is going to happen next is you are going to draw up a list of everything that you and Catherine might possibly need or want over the next six months. Bear in mind that antibiotics are not easy to obtain in the Emirates, so if you need a prescription for anything here is my GP's card.' He handed it over to her. 'Order everything that you need, pack it and have it ready to go in three days from now.' He paused and then went on. 'Do you have a valid passport?'

'Oh yes, sir. I went to Paris last Easter with some of the other girls from the hospital; I had to get one.'

'Excellent. Don't forget to pack that also.' He knew that the two junior nursemaids already had travel documents. Hazel had made sure of that before she employed them.

He slid his black Harrods credit card across the desk to Bonnie. 'Pay for everything with this. Have them deliver all of it here.' She fled for the door, but he called her back. 'I have decided that we are going to move Catherine into my bedroom until we leave for Abu Zara.'

'Oh dear!' Bonnie looked distraught. 'Who will give her her bottle, and change her nappy?'

'I will,' Hector assured her.

'I could stay with the two of you, just to help. I wouldn't mind at all,' she offered.

'Thank you, Bonnie. But I am sure the two of us will be able to cope well enough on our own.'

Hector expected to find the self-appointed task of night-nurse onerous, but it turned out to be a delight rather than a chore. He adjusted the reading lamp on his bedside table to throw a soft light

101

on Catherine's face when he held her on his lap. As she sucked away at the teat of the bottle he revelled in the smell and the feel of her tiny body. He searched her face for vestiges of Hazel and was convinced that he found them in the shape of her mouth and the set of her little chin. Somehow it lessened his sense of loss and loneliness.

Know your enemy. Study him long and hard, and then strike him down with the speed and venom of a king cobra; that was Hector Cross's principle of action.

Before sunrise the next morning Hector rose and showered. Then he donned a dressing gown and rang down to the nursery and called for Bonnie.

As he handed Catherine over to the nurse he told her, 'I have arranged for Mrs O'Quinn to spend the day with you and Catherine.' Nastiya had accepted the role of baby guard with a contented little smile. With Catherine in the care of these two women Hector could go about his other business without a qualm. 'I will be going out for a while; however, Mr O'Quinn will be here to make certain that everything is safe and secure in my absence. You will have nothing to worry about.'

Still in his gown, he went down to his study. There was a big marble fireplace facing his desk, with a decorated frieze of five lion heads running just below the mantle. He pressed the central head and when he heard the muted click of the concealed mechanism he rotated it in a clockwise direction. There was another click and a pause, and then silently and smoothly the bookcase on one side of the fireplace rotated to reveal a narrow steel door beyond. He punched his password into the keypad of the electronic lock. The door swung open and he stepped into the small room beyond. Row upon row of open shelves climbed the facing wall from floor level to the ceiling. Each shelf held a tidy row of cardboard boxes, each box with a cryptic label describing the contents stencilled on its side. Most held weapons or other sensitive items; everything from knives and nightsticks to his favourite 9mm Beretta automatic pistol, with two hundred rounds of ammunition. Possession of nearly all these was

strictly banned under British law. There was even a box marked
'Passports' which contained over thirty such documents from diverse
countries with his photograph but with names ranging from Abraham
to Zakariyya. He reached up to the top shelf and brought down the
box marked 'Arab costume'.

He left the other boxes undisturbed. He closed and relocked the
door, and then he activated the mechanism to rotate the bookshelf
back into place. He carried the cardboard box to his dressing room.
He stripped down to his underwear and spent the next few minutes
using a tube of make-up to subtly darken his already swarthy features
to a Middle Eastern tone. His beard had grown out in a dense, dark
stubble, which gave him a convincing Middle Eastern air.

He donned the full-length white dishdasha from the box and tied
the keffiya round his head so that the tail of the scarf draped over
his shoulders. He changed his platinum Rolex for a plain stainless-
steel Seiko, slipped into a pair of open leather sandals, placed a pair
of dark aviator glasses on his nose, and checked himself in the mirror.

You'll do, he decided. His Arabic was fluent and colloquial. His
inherent sense of Eastern mores and manners was impeccable. He
could pass readily as a native-born Muslim either in relaxed social
situations or when performing the traditional religious rituals.

He took his private lift down to the underground garage. One of
the vehicles parked in the second row there was a small, slightly
battered and neglected-looking saloon. Appearances were deliberately misleading. Hector had fitted it with tinted windows, racing
suspension and a powerful new engine that was capable of a startling turn of speed. He used it on special occasions such as this when
he did not want to draw attention to himself. He called it his
Q-car, after the Q-ships that the Royal Navy used to lure the Nazi
U-boats into range during World War II.

Hector started it up and for a few seconds listened with satisfaction to the deep growl of the engine, then drove up the ramp past
the roller shutter doors into the street. It was a Friday so even this
early the traffic was heavy and frenetic. Friday is also the day on
which all Muslims have a sacred duty to attend prayers. He found
a parking slot in Regent's Park a few hundred metres from the great
mosque. He left the car and headed towards it. There was a steady

stream of the faithful hurrying in the same direction. They were all dressed in traditional garb. Hector was one of a multitude as he entered the precincts of the mosque. This was not his first visit so he knew his way around the building. He went firstly to sit with the other men on the long concrete bench, facing the row of taps, to perform the ablutions. He washed his hands and feet and then his face. He rinsed out his mouth.

It was well in advance of the appointed hour, but already the demarcated area of the prayer hall, the masjid, was crowded with row upon row of kneeling white-clad figures. However, there were still a few open slots nearer the rear. He knelt on the piled prayer rugs with his shoulders almost touching his neighbours on each side.

The prayers began and Hector entered into the lulling sequence of prostrations and responses. Hector was not an atheist; he had been close to death so many times as to know how fleeting and inconsequential life really is. He believed deeply that there had to be some controlling force behind the wondrous working of the universe, and the unfolding of infinity. In this respect he was a believer; however, he was not committed to any single creed. He wanted to be free to select the best from the doctrines of each of the faiths that attracted him and to adapt those to his own particular view of God and the universe. To him both Christianity and Islam were studded with priceless diamonds of beauty and truth. Many of these were identical. He valued both religions equally for that. He prayed now with complete sincerity, and he found himself praying especially for Hazel, wherever she had gone. He felt rejuvenated when the prayers came to an end.

He left the main precinct and wandered down the adjoining cloisters. He passed a few of the cubicles in which the temple mullahs waited to meet any members of the congregation who were seeking spiritual guidance and counsel. He found the man he was looking for near the end of the second colonnade, one whose eyes in a setting of fine wrinkles were sharp and intelligent and whose beard was white under the ginger dye. He had the look of permanence about him, as though he had been in place for a long time. Hector entered the cubicle and bowed.

'As-salamu alaykum!'

'And on you be peace!'

They exchanged greetings, then the mullah indicated the rug spread in front of his low table on which lay a well-thumbed copy of the Koran and other religious texts and commentaries. Hector sat cross-legged in front of him and they chatted informally for a while. The mullah recognized his accent almost at once.

'You are from the East Africa, from Somalia, I suspect?' Hector spread his hands in acquiescence. His Arabic had been honed by Tariq Hakam, who was from Puntland, and Hector had picked up the accent from him.

'Is it so obvious, Sheikh?' He used the term of respect. 'I have lived in this country many years.'

The mullah smiled knowingly. 'So how can I help you, my son?'

'Father, I am planning to make the pilgrimage to Mecca soon. *Inshallah!*'

'*Mashallah!* Let it be so,' the old man intoned.

'I have heard men speak of a mullah in that country who once preached in this very mosque where we now sit. People who have heard him have told me that, despite his youth, this mullah is a man of great holiness and wisdom. I want you to tell me if you knew this man when he was here, and if you believe the time and expense of extending my sojourn in Mecca to listen to him would be justified. I want to know also if what he preaches accords with the teachings of the Prophet Muhammad.'

'My son, who is this mullah? Please tell me his name.'

'His name is Aazim Muktar—'

Before Hector could complete the sentence the old man's face lit with delight. He clapped his hands and exclaimed, 'In the name of Allah and his blessed Prophet, may they be praised for ever. You speak of none other than Aazim Muktar Tippoo Tip.'

Hector was surprised by the fervour of his reaction. 'You know him?' he asked.

'I know him as I know one of my own sons, and verily I wish he were my own son.'

'You admire him then, Old Father?'

'It is as though Aazim Muktar has been touched by the hand of

Gabriel, the chief of all the angels of Allah.' The mullah lowered his voice reverently. 'He has been given the sight to see far beyond where other men can see. He has the wisdom to understand clearly what is hidden from others. His heart is filled with the love of Allah and with the love of his fellow man.'

'Then you think I should take pains to hear him speak?'

'If you miss that opportunity you will regret it to the end of your days. His voice is like the sounding of the finest musical instrument, like the sighing of the wind in the branches of the cedar trees on Mount Horeb, the one mountain of the one God.'

'Describe his appearance to me, Old Father, that I might recognize him when first I see him.'

The mullah placed his fingertips together and pursed his lips as he considered the question, and then he began to speak. 'He is tall but not overly tall. He is lean and he moves with the grace of a leopard. His brow is wide and deep. His beard is not yet touched with the frosting of age. He has a good nose, strong as the beak of an eagle. His gaze is keen but gentle and without guile. In short he is handsome but not pretty.'

Suddenly, and to Hector's surprise, the mullah looked about in a conspiratorial manner, then leaned forward and lowered his voice. 'There are many who believe this man is the Mhadi; the Messiah who is prophesied to appear at the world's end; the Redeemer who will establish a reign of peace and righteousness. Perhaps once you have listened to him you might agree with them. If so, when you return to London you must come to speak with me again.'

Hector stared at him. Slowly his vision of the way forward changed dramatically.

Nothing about this was as straightforward as he had at first imagined. It contained many layers and hidden depths.

That evening Hector, Paddy and Nastiya gathered in the sitting room before dinner. As usual the men were in mess kit with decorations while Nastiya had her diamond necklace nestling in the cleavage of her high tight bosoms, a sparkle in her eyes and colour in her cheeks. While Hector was pouring Dom Pérignon into a tall flute glass for her she announced, 'Babies are wonderful. I truly never understood that before.'

'All babies?' Paddy teased her. 'Or just one baby in particular?'

'Don't be silly. I know only one baby. She is wonderful. I fed her with a bottle today and I even changed her nappy. I never thought I would be able to do that, but her nurse showed me how. I thought it would make me want to throw up. But you know something? It hardly smells at all.'

'Do you mind, my love! We are just about to enjoy one of Heck's legendary dinners. Can we not find a more appropriate subject to discuss than baby droppings?' Paddy protested and moved the conversation on hurriedly. 'I spoke to Prince Mohammed this afternoon about the lease of the Seascape Mansion apartment. Of course Princey felt it necessary to tell me that he had another tenant interested and that there was a better price on the table. We did a bit of toing and froing but in the end I nudged him down ten per cent on his asking price, and we did a deal. The apartment is yours, Heck. The other good news is that there are only twelve other tenants in the entire building and they are all either members of the royal family or senior ministers of the Abu Zara government, or both. He claims that the security is airtight and waterproof.'

'Can we take his word for that?'

'No, Heck. We take nobody's word for that. Immediately after I hung up on Princey, I called Dave Imbiss.' Dave was Paddy's right-hand man and the electronics expert at Cross Bow Security.

'Dave has promised to go in with his team at first light tomorrow. They are going to sweep every last centimetre of the apartment for electronic bugs and any other nasty surprises that might have been left behind by somebody with evil in mind. Dave will install movement and pressure sensors with silent alarms, closed-circuit cameras, iris scanners and all the other state-of-the-art stuff. No living thing will be able to move on the top floor of Seascape Mansions, or anywhere in the rest of the building for that matter, without Dave being aware of it. By the time we arrive in Abu Zara the apartment will be a virtual electronic fortress.' He accepted the glass of Jamesons whiskey that Hector offered him and took a swallow. He exhaled the fumes before he asked, 'So what did you find up at Regent's Park today to gladden our hearts?'

'Very little for your comfort or mine, I am afraid. It seems that our target is a religious demagogue who has the power to whip up the emotions of his listeners with his impassioned oratory. Some, or most, of them think he is the Mhadi.'

They stared at Hector, their expressions concerned and alarmed. Paddy spoke for both of them: 'In the name of all that's holy, Heck! You don't believe that bullshit, do you?'

'It matters not at all what I believe, my dear Padraig. What is crucial is that there is a vast multitude who do believe. The coming of the Messiah is a common belief that runs through Judaism, Islam and Christianity. The only divergence is about who he will be and when he will come, or if has already come and gone. In this particular case Aazim Muktar has sequestered himself in the holiest religious site in Islam. The birthplace of the Prophet Muhammad himself, no less. The city is guarded by a great multitude of the faithful and devout. Only true believers in Islam are allowed to enter the city, under pain of death. It seems now that many of these also believe with fanatic intensity that Aazim Muktar is the Mahdi. They will protect him with their own lives. With their bare hands they will tear the arms and legs off whoever raises a finger to him.'

He paused and sipped at his own glass as he composed his thoughts.

'What I originally had in mind was to go into Mecca disguised as a pilgrim and, concealed in the throng of worshippers, listen and watch Aazim. Then from what I saw and heard, I would evaluate the likelihood of him being the Beast who is perpetuating the blood feud. If he were patently innocent I would leave him there and seek out the true enemy. On the other hand, if there was any doubt at all in my mind as to his innocence we would snatch him and bring him out to stand trial before his accusers. Now we do not have the option of bringing him out. It would be just too chancy. That city is a death trap for the infidel. I must weigh up the odds against him being innocent, and if the balance swings against him then I must execute him on the spot and leave his corpse to rot in Mecca.'

'If I were you, Hector, I would go straight in and cancel him out without all this fussing and soul searching, which I'd just like to say is not your usual style,' Nastiya opined. 'But I ask you with tears in my eyes, why take a chance? If you kill him and later it turns out he was the wrong man and he was innocent then it will be a great pity and we can all shed a tear for him or burn a candle, but at least it means that there are no more Tippoo Tips left in this world. That is not truly such a great loss, is it?'

'Of course I agree with you, Flower of my Heart.' Paddy smiled at her fondly. 'But you know that sometimes Hector can be very silly and stubborn.'

'He is a man.' Nastiya shrugged and gave a sigh of resignation. 'And all men can be very silly and stubborn.'

'Nazzy, you know of the deep affection, nay, the deep veneration in which I hold you, but—' Hector started, but she cut him off with a groan.

'Spare me the bullshit, Hector Cross. Okay, so you want to play pussy foot? Good! Paddy and I go along with your decision, like always. But don't blame us if this Great Redeemer turns round and bites you in the balls.'

It was another forty-eight hours before Hector was satisfied that they were ready to make the transfer from London to Abu Zara. After dark the baggage train comprising two large hired trucks was sent from the Belgravia house to Farnborough airport, where Bannock Oil's Boeing jet was waiting to receive their cargo.

Hector and his guests dined in the comfort of home, and only after they had eaten did they change into comfortable travel attire. Hector returned to the secret room behind the bookshelf in his study. Firstly he took down the 9mm automatic pistol with two spare magazines and an additional hundred rounds of ammunition. He slipped the pistol into its quick-draw shoulder holster. He patted it and smiled. It felt good and comforting. Next he took down the box marked 'Passports' and from it chose three booklets of Saudi, Iraqi and Abu Zarian denomination. He closed and locked the secret room and went down to where the chauffeur had the Rolls waiting with engine running.

There was a bit of power play between Nastiya and Hector as to who would hold Catherine for the short run out to the airport. Nastiya played her trump with a snide remark regarding the fact that real English men never dandled infants. She sat up in front next to the chauffeur with the child on her lap and sang her soft Russian lullabies. Catherine emitted not a squeak for the entire duration of the journey. Bonnie and the other nursemaids followed the Rolls in a separate vehicle.

The convoy drove out onto the tarmac and parked under the wing of the Boeing Business Jet. There was a young Anglo-Indian woman from the UK Border Agency waiting on board who completed the immigration formalities with rapid efficiency and within minutes they were taxiing out onto the main runway. As soon as they were airborne Catherine was laid down to sleep in her cot by Nastiya with every other female on board in attendance.

When Nastiya returned to the lounge to join the men in a nightcap she curled catlike into the seat beside Paddy and vamped him extravagantly. 'You know how I detest standing in airport queues, husband who I worship?' she whispered in his ear. 'So if you really love me you will buy one of these things.'

'A Boeing Business Jet, right? They probably cost around two hundred million dollars. Do you still want one?'

'I've changed my mind. You can take me to our cabin and prove your love for me some other way.'

A little over seven hours later they touched down in Abu Zara, where an airport tender met them on the runway and with flashing beacons led them to the Royal aircraft hangar. They parked alongside the Emir's new 747–8. The lesser Boeings belonging to his wives were lined up behind the aircraft. Bannock Oil and anybody associated with the company enjoyed highly favoured status in Abu Zara.

There was a small reception committee from Cross Bow Security waiting to welcome them at the bottom of the boarding ladder. It was headed by Dave Imbiss and Tariq Hakam in the smart new tan uniforms that Nastiya had designed. Tariq was barely able to conceal his delight as he watched Hector coming lithely down the steps.

A long time ago, when Hector was still a major in the British Special Air Services, Tariq Hakam had been attached to Hector's unit in Iraq as his interpreter and local guide. He and Hector had taken to each other from the first day when they ran into an ambush and had to fight their way out. Later he had been at Hector's side on the dreadful day of the roadside bomb. When Hector opened up on the three Arab insurgents who had laid the bomb, and who seemed to be about to deploy a suicide device, Tariq had backed Hector's fire and taken down one of the enemy. When Hector resigned his commission in the SAS, Tariq had come to him, and told him, 'You are my father. Where you go I will go also.' Now he stood at attention in front of Hector and bowed deeply, with his hands clasped over his heart. 'May Allah love and protect you from all danger, My Father,' he said softly in Arabic.

Against all protocol, Hector took him in a bear hug, and his voice choked a little as he replied in English. 'Tariq, you old rogue you! God, how I have missed you.'

Having heard the salutation 'You old rogue' from Hector's lips on so many occasions over the years, Tariq understood that it was one of the highest words of praise in the English language. He beamed with pleasure and returned Hector's embrace, then he stepped back to let the other members of Cross Bow Security come forward to greet Hector. Hector knew all of them well. He had led some of them deep into Puntland to rescue Hazel's elder daughter and, in the furnace of combat, strong links had been forged.

Now Dave Imbiss was second in command of Cross Bow under Paddy O'Quinn. Dave gave the illusion of youth and innocence, but he had served two tours of duty in the US Marines and had a row of medal ribbons on his chest to show for it. Back in the early days of Cross Bow, Hector, with his eye for a winner, had picked him out of the pack. Dave was shrewd and tough. What appeared to be puppy fat was in fact hard muscle. Dave had seen men die and had personally sent a number of them off on the long one-way trip. He and Hector owed each other a number of their nine lives. As they shook hands Hector demanded, 'So is this safe house of yours really safe, Dave?'

'Iron clad, boss.'

'Don't tell me, show me.'

All of them found seats in Dave's sand-camouflaged Hummer and he drove them out of the airport complex into the open desert with the two trucks carrying the baggage following close behind. The road was four lanes wide, straight and glassy smooth. Like the ethereal city which loomed in the milky haze of distance far ahead, it had been built with the oil that lay far beneath the desert sands; the oil on which Hazel Bannock had staked her fortune and reputation when she stood at the helm of Bannock Oil.

Dave drove fast along the shore of the Gulf. The beach was white as sun-bleached bone and the waters beyond were a startling blend of blues and greens, changing as the seabed dropped away under them. The sky over it all was cloudless and a shade of blue so lustrous that it pained the eye.

The closer they came to Abu Zara City the higher the buildings seemed to climb into the sky; towers of creamy-coloured concrete and glass. Dave Imbiss pointed out one that stood well isolated from the others.

'There it is! Seascape Mansions, little Catherine's new fairy castle,' he told Hector. He turned off the main highway at the next junction.

'Pull over and park for a minute please, Dave,' Hector instructed him. There was a pair of binoculars in the tray below the windscreen. 'May I borrow these?'

'Help yourself, Heck.' As soon as the Hummer stopped, Hector stepped out and stretched over the engine compartment, focussing the binoculars on the towering building. He studied the external layout of the structure, and then swept the surroundings. The main building itself was encircled with extensive landscaped gardens; manicured lawns and fountains; stands of date palms and other exotic plants. The perimeter was guarded by a double palisade of razor wire. Beyond these gardens there was a separate complex of utility buildings and servants' quarters discreetly tucked away in their own gated and guarded compound.

'It looks okay from here,' Hector admitted. He climbed back on board the Hummer and they drove down to the main gates of Seascape

Mansions. The guards at the checkpoint were courteous but thorough. They even studied Catherine's baby passport carefully. After they were admitted to the grounds Dave stopped again in the middle of the gardens and they all craned their necks to look up at the building. Dave pointed out to Hector the discreet steel baffles that his workmen had already placed over the windows of the topmost floor. These were designed to deflect any RPG or other explosive device fired from the grounds or the beach below. Hector had warned Dave about the incendiary grenades that the Beast had deployed at Brandon Hall, and he was taking no chances of a repeat performance.

There was another guard posted at the entrance to the underground car park. He checked the registration plates on the Hummer that had been phoned to him from the main gates. They rode up from the basement in the elevator dedicated exclusively to the top floor. When Hector stepped out of the elevator into the lobby of the apartment he saw at once why Prince Mohammed had come up with such an extravagant rental demand, and he realized that it had not been grossly inflated by wishful thinking.

There were a dozen house servants in white robes and scarlet fezzes with dangling black tassels drawn up in a file facing the doors to the elevator. They greeted Hector with respectful obeisance and then disappeared silently into the nether regions of the vast apartment.

'I know what you are going to ask, boss,' Dave Imbiss told him. 'They have all been thoroughly checked and vetted. I personally vouch for every man jack of them.'

The interior décor of the apartment had been designed by a celebrated Italian studio. There were twelve bedroom suites, two dining rooms with their own kitchens, three lounges, a lavishly equipped gymnasium, two playrooms and a cinema. In addition, Dave Imbiss explained, there was accommodation for up to twenty-five servants provided in the separate gated compound.

Catherine had her own large nursery with an attendant nursemaid as her neighbour on either side, poised to rush to do her bidding at the first wail. On the roof there was a helipad, a swimming pool and a sun garden and entertainment area with bar and barbecue. There was a view across the bay to the centre of Abu Zara City. In the other direction lay the open waters of the Gulf with the white triangles of dhow sails scattered like daisy blossoms on the blue expanse.

'If we must pig it, then I suppose this sty will just about do.' Hector gave his opinion and called an immediate council of war in the cinema.

Hector set out his plan of action for Paddy and Nastiya, Dave Imbiss and Tariq. This was on a need-to-know basis; only those directly involved were briefed, not even the other senior and trusted Cross Bow operatives were involved.

The first stage of the operation was for Hector and Tariq in the guise of pilgrims to fly into Mecca on one of the many commercial flights. Tariq had already made the reservations, posing as an individual with no connection to Bannock Oil. He paid with Saudi riyals so he had left no credit-card traces. The two of them would fly directly from Dubai to Jeddah and from there take a public bus up to the sacred city itself. They were approaching the Islamic month of Dhu al-Hijjah, the high season of pilgrimage. During that period Mecca would be packed with hundreds of thousands of worshippers. Hector and Tariq would be swallowed up by the multitudes; hidden in plain sight.

Tariq had also taken the precaution of booking accommodation in one of the cheapest caravanserai in the city, where for under $20 a night they would be sharing a common dormitory with other pilgrims. The Beast would never suspect that Hector Cross would be holed up in a flea circus of that order.

These plans left Hector a little under three months to prepare himself before they left Abu Zara for the journey to Mecca. He knew his Arabic had become slightly stilted and rusty and would not convince a shrewd interrogator. The tanned skin of his face and arms had faded and the use of make-up would not withstand close scrutiny.

More importantly, his physical condition had deteriorated a little and he knew he was no longer battle fit. It was essential that he toughened himself up. Dave Imbiss and Tariq had planned to help him correct all these deficiencies.

Hector spent one night in the heady and rarefied luxury of Seascape Mansions. The next morning he kissed Catherine goodbye and he and Tariq went to join the labour force of a Saudi Arabian building contractor whose company was erecting yet another skyscraper on the Abu Zara beachfront.

The Abu Zara government had frowned upon the formation of trade unions in the emirate. The Emir in particular wished to dictate his own terms, and not to be beholden to his employees. With this example from on high, the foremen of Khidash Construction were not overly concerned with the rights of their labourers, human or otherwise.

The accommodation was primitive, the work brutal: sixteen to eighteen hours a day for seven days a week in the broiling sun, lugging sacks of concrete or crushed stone aggregate hundreds of feet up steep scaffolding, or working with pick and shovel in the deep foundations until their muscles burned and Hector's face and arms turned a dark bronze from the sun. Their fellow workers were the dregs of humanity. Their social graces were totally devoid of couth. Their turn of phrase was colourful and colloquial. Hector soon regained his lost fluency. Stoically he endured three weeks on the Khidash site before he and Tariq moved a hundred miles south into the desert to the main Bannock Oil installation. Here they spent three or four hours a day on the firing range, honing their marksmanship with pistol and rifle.

With his contacts in the US military and his genius for weapons procurement, Dave Imbiss had located an M110 Semi-Automatic Sniper System. Hector had pulled rank as a director to send the Bannock Oil jet to pick it up from the main US Marine base in Afghanistan. After only a few hours' practice Hector was able to set up a line of half a dozen yellow tennis balls atop a sand dune. Hector reckoned that a tennis ball was a little smaller than a human brain, a fair target. From a measured range of three hundred and fifty metres he could explode every single one of the balls with six successive rapid-fire shots.

The M110 SASS, including its miraculously accurate optics,

weighed only twenty-five pounds. Once it was broken down into its component parts it could be concealed effectively and carried by two men. Directly across the road from the mosque in Mecca where Aazim Muktar preached was a small public park, about two or three acres in extent. Tariq had reconnoitred an ideal stand in these gardens that overlooked the route the mullah took daily to walk from his home to the mosque and back. Tariq had paced out the range at 210 metres. Even on a moving target, that was a certain head-shot kill for Hector.

Of course, the most difficult part would be to smuggle the SASS into Mecca. Tariq had cultivated a contact in a transport company that, during the season of pilgrimage, carried thousands of tons of cargo every day from Jeddah airport into the city of Mecca. This was mostly in the form of perishable food items. However, Tariq was confident that he could get the sniper rifle through, once it was broken down into its separate parts. It could be labelled as spare parts for heavier machinery such as air conditioning or elevator units. Dave Imbiss was working closely with him on the project. He also had numerous contacts in Saudi Arabia who could be bribed or cajoled into assisting them. All this was merely long-range planning. There was plenty of time to work out a foolproof scheme. The final plan would only emerge after Hector had made the kill decision.

The last thirty days before they set out on the journey to Mecca were spent in the final toughening-up process that Hector had imposed upon himself and Tariq. Dave Imbiss sent one of his karate trainers out to the base. This creature was more machine than human. He took Hector to his limits and then pushed him even further, showing scant concern for either his rank or his status, nor for the fact that Hector was almost twice his age. In the end Hector earned his respect the hard way, teaching the young wolf to walk wide and wary of the leader of the pack.

Each evening, Hector had the helicopter fly the three of them out into the desert, in full battle gear. They parachuted to ground from low altitude and then ran twenty miles back to the base, still in full gear and lugging their parachutes.

In the beginning of the training it was harder for Hector than the two younger men. However, as he returned rapidly to his top form he began to revel in the brutal physical routine. He slept deeply and dreamlessly. The dreadful aching void left by Hazel began to close. At last he could remember her with joy rather than hopeless despair. He knew that he was going to avenge her death, and that maybe she would be able to rest more peaceably once he had accomplished that.

As his body regained its strength so too did his relationship with Tariq strengthen. The two of them were drawn as close as they had been many years ago. They had shared so much and together they had endured so much. They had stood shoulder to shoulder on the battlefield. Each of them had lost a beloved wife to the insensate cruelty of the Beast. Tariq's wife Daliyah had been burned to death with her infant son in the ashes of their home. Shared tragedy was a strong bond between them.

Hector found that he was able to speak to Tariq about Hazel's death as he could to nobody else, not even Paddy or Nastiya. Hazel had been with them on the expedition into Puntland to rescue her daughter Cayla from the fortress of Khan Tippoo Tip. Tariq had witnessed her courage and her physical stamina that matched that of even the toughest Cross Bow men. Tariq had developed a deep respect and admiration for Hazel. He wanted to know every detail of the ambush that the Beast had set for her. He listened intently while Hector explained how the attack had been carried out. At the end of Hector's description Tariq inclined his head gravely and was silent for a while, gazing out across the desert from the top of the dune on which they were resting. Then he coughed, hawked and spat a yellow globule of phlegm. It hit the sand and rolled down the dune like a tiny ball of sand. They watched its progress in silence until it reached the foot of the dune, and then Tariq asked, 'So, how did they know you were coming?'

The question took Hector by surprise. 'The two swine on the motorcycle must have followed us when we left Harley Street. They probably called ahead to the masked truck driver,' he explained.

'Yes, I understand that; but how did the bikers know that you and Hazel would be with her doctor that morning? Who else knew that she had an appointment with him?'

Hector stared at him for a few seconds and then he swore softly.

'Shit! You're right. Nobody knew; except Hazel, her secretary and me.'

'Can you trust the secretary?'

'She has worked for Hazel for years. It couldn't have been her. I would take strychnine on that!'

'Somebody knew,' Tariq said firmly. 'It's the only explanation for what happened.'

'I haven't been thinking straight.' Hector's face was grim. 'Of course you are right. Somebody must have known. I should have jumped on that right away. Am I getting old, my friend?'

'Not you, Hector. You had just been hit really hard by losing Hazel. When they killed my Daliyah and our baby I went mad as a rabid dog for almost a year. So I understand what happened to you. I have been there before you.'

'When I get back to London, somebody is going to die the hard way,' Hector said softly.

'But before that, you and I have to go to Mecca to follow the blood trail that leads us there.' He laid his hand on Hector's arm. 'One thing at a time. But in the end you will find the one who did this terrible thing to you. I know this in my heart. I would like to be with you when you find him.'

They sat in silence for a while and Hector thought about the bond between them that had grown strong as spun silk over the years, and he was reminded that the platonic love of one man for another is truly one of life's nobler experiences.

Here is another person I can trust with my very life, he thought with utter certainty, and it helped him to endure.

Six days later when Hector and Tariq boarded the crowded flight from Dubai to Jeddah they were both in top physical condition and Hector's skin was sun darkened and his beard black and curling. They were travelling light, carrying neither weapons nor any electronic gizmos, not even mobile phones. All they had with them were their return air tickets, their passports and a handful of crumpled and grubby banknotes in the money belt that each of them had strapped around his waist under the robes. Their basic toiletries and clothing were wrapped in small cloth bundles.

The aircraft was a pilgrim special: an ancient prop-engined Fokker operating out of a secondary domestic airport. The air conditioning was parlous and the odour of unwashed bodies in the cabin was eye-watering. The seats were narrow and unpadded. The legroom was so limited that Hector's knees were forced up under his chin. The child in the row in front of him urinated on the floor during take-off and the stream ran back under Hector's feet. The flight lasted three hours that seemed like thirty.

After they had passed through immigration and airport formalities in Jeddah they waited for seven hours before they could find standing room on a public bus up to Mecca. The bus broke down twice before it reached the Sacred City well after midnight. The hotel that Tariq had arranged for them was far from the painted marble splendours in the central areas of the city. It was hidden away in a muddle of narrow twisting streets. They shared a common dormitory with twelve other pilgrims. Not even the sounds of snoring and farting could keep Hector awake for very long. The room was astir before sunrise.

Hector took his turn at the single squat-pan toilet, and afterwards washed himself with scoops of cold water in a tin dish that was chained to the base of the only tap. As soon as they had donned fresh robes they went down into the noisome and narrow street, carrying the meagre bundles of their possessions.

They ate a breakfast of heavily spiced flatbread at one of the road-side stalls, and then they trudged into the centre of the city.

The Saudi royal family ploughs billions of oil dollars into the glorification of this most holy place in Islam. In the middle of it stands a mighty agglomeration of marble and gold-leaf clad spires, domes, minarets, buildings and squares. All this surrounds the most venerated mosque in Islam, the Masjid al-Haram and the Kaaba shrine, which were first erected fourteen hundred years ago by the very hand of the Prophet. Every true Muslim faces towards these monuments when he prays five times a day.

However, there are hundreds of less revered mosques in Mecca alone, many of them dating back to pagan times. It was in one of these lesser mosques that Aazim Muktar preached. This was the Masjid Ibn Baaz, lying on the western edge of the Azeeziyyah district. It looked very modern from the outside, though Tariq assured Hector that it was over a thousand years old and was widely venerated for the number of famously holy men who had prayed and preached within its precincts.

They entered the public park across the street from the mosque. It was a few acres of bare and sun-parched ground, but already many hundreds of pilgrims had gathered here waiting to visit the mosque on the far side of the road to attend dhuhr, the noon prayers.

Tariq led Hector to the slightly elevated knoll in the centre of the park on which grew a thicket of thorny desert euphorbia. They squatted close together on the brown grass among the clusters of waiting worshippers. The two of them shared a parcel of hummus and falafel wrapped in a round of unleavened bread. Then they drank from the same litre bottle of cold milky tea that Tariq had bought at a roadside stall. Tariq carefully wiped the neck of the bottle on the hem of his robe before passing it to Hector.

While they ate, Tariq pointed out the killing ground that stretched out ahead of them and Hector assessed it with a marksman's eye.

'I thought that you and I could take our stance amongst those bushes,' said Tariq. He turned his head and with his chin indicated the euphorbia plants. 'They are thick enough to conceal both of us and the weapon. In the early morning very few people come into these gardens. At about six a.m. Aazim Muktar leaves his home in its compound four hundred metres up the road.' He pointed out the flat-roofed building to Hector. 'He walks down the far side of the road with many of his disciples surrounding him.'

'Will I be able to pick him out from amongst his followers? I certainly don't want to waste the first steady shot on the wrong man.'

'You will see him today. Once you have seen him you will never forget him. He stands out in any crowd,' Tariq assured him.

'It will be a moving target,' Hector mused, but Tariq did not agree.

'If you are patient, that need not be so. There are always peti- tioners waiting for him along the road there. They prostrate them- selves in his path and beg for his blessing, others hold out their sick children for him to touch and cure. He turns none of them away, but stops for all of them. It will be a stationary target, impossible for a man like you to miss.' Tariq looked back over his shoulder. 'When Aazim Muktar goes down, there will be great confusion and pandemonium; you need only leave the rifle and walk away through the rear gate of the garden. There is a bus stop outside the gate, and always many tuk-tuks in the street waiting for fares. One of these will take you away from here very quickly.'

'I can see that. The report of the shot should echo off those high buildings on the far side of the street. Nobody will be able to tell for certain the direction it came from. That will win me a good start for a clean getaway.'

'Let us deal with one thing at a time. All this will only happen once you have seen and listened to Aazim Muktar today, and if you decide that he is the Beast that gave the order to kill Hazel.' Tariq spoke very softly, for there were many strangers squatting within easy earshot of them.

'Where is Aazim Muktar likely to be right now? You say he comes to the mosque every day in the early morning?' Hector asked.

'He comes every morning of every day at six o'clock, without fail. He remains there all day. He leads the prayers five times a day, as is laid down in the Second Pillar of Islam,' Tariq explained. 'He preaches twice a day; once after the dhuhr prayers at noon and then again after the isha prayers in the evening. Then at about nine o'clock in the evening he returns to his home and family. Many of his followers go with him.'

'So he should be in the mosque right now?'

'He is there, certainly.' Tariq checked his wristwatch. 'It is forty minutes from noon, so we are in good time. We can wait and rest here.'

The sun was warm and the murmur of the voices of the people crowded around them was lulling. Hector let himself doze off. Suddenly he jerked back awake. He was not certain how long he had slept and he looked around quickly. Tariq was gone. He felt a stab of anxiety, but then he saw him. Tariq was coming towards him, weaving his way through the clusters of other pilgrims scattered on the dusty earth.

'Where have you been?' Hector asked as Tariq squatted down beside him.

'There.' Tariq pointed out the public toilet at the entrance to the park. 'I went to make water.'

'You should have told me.' Hector was annoyed. They were in the den of the Beast. They were at risk. They should cover each other at all times, that was a basic principle.

'I am sorry. You were sleeping.' Tariq was hurt by the reprimand, but he deserved it. Hector reined back his irritation. Perhaps he was being too touchy. Besides which he was in equal blame; he shouldn't have fallen asleep. Tariq sat down at his side and Hector touched his shoulder lightly, a gesture of reconciliation.

At last the high-pitched chanting of the muezzin reciting the adhan, the call to pray, rang out from the minaret of the mosque at the bottom of the hill. Tariq stood up immediately.

'It is time for us to go down to pray,' he said and there was an eager tone in his voice that he could not conceal. Hector rose with him and they joined the flood of men headed down towards the mosque. They left their sandals in the courtyard outside the main doors to the masjid and went to perform the ablutions with all the other worshippers. Then at last, barefooted and ritually cleansed, they walked with the multitude into the masjid and knelt side by side on a woollen prayer rug facing the direction of the Kaaba.

There was a palpable sense of expectation which seemed to grip every one of the kneeling congregation. It was almost as though every person present was holding his breath. When Mullah Aazim Muktar Tippoo Tip entered the masjid Hector found himself exhaling and relaxing with all the others.

Tariq had spoken the truth. Hector was in no doubt whatsoever. He knew it was Aazim Muktar. The man had a presence that seemed to resonate through the great hall of the mosque. He emanated an internal force. Hector was not certain whether it was evil or benign, but it was powerful.

He was as he had been described to Hector: tall, lean and handsome, with strong almost ferocious features. This man could be a killer, Hector judged, but then again there was much else that cast doubt on that assumption. His mouth was generous but not soft. His gaze was searching and direct but not cruel. Hector realized almost at once that this man was an enigma.

Aazim Muktar mounted to the minbar, the pulpit that overlooked the congregation. He moved with grace; his body beneath the flowing robe was supple as that of some beautiful predator. When he called the congregation to pray his voice reached to every corner of the vast hall and echoed from the dome above them. Hector watched him with fascination as he led them through the ritual prostrations and devotions. He found himself riddled by uncertainty. At one moment he knew that this was the man he must kill, and then only seconds later doubts assailed him and eroded his determination. The waves of deep reverence that emanated from the worshippers that surrounded him coloured his judgement and swayed him back and forth like a river reed in a fitful breeze.

He knew it was not possible, but still he longed for an opportunity to confront this man face to face, to be able to peel back the layers which concealed his true identity, to reach down to his core and know for certain whether he was saint or demon. He realized that it would cheapen and belittle them both if he lay in ambuscade and shot him down from afar. He longed for proof positive, either that this was an enemy worthy of his steel or that he was a fine and honest man who deserved his respect.

The formal prayers ended. The worshippers rose from the final prostration and rocked back on their heels. A fresh tide of expectancy washed over their packed ranks and every one of their faces was raised to the imposing figure in the minbar above them.

Aazim Muktar sat before them. He raised his right hand and began to speak. The impelling and sonorous tones of his voice riveted them all, even Hector Cross the sceptic.

'I wish to speak to you of the Law of Al-Qisas, the Law of Retaliation, as it was first set out in the Torah in the twenty-first chapter of Exodus and subsequently endorsed by the Prophet Muhammad in the fifth sura of the Koran.

'Al-Qisas is the right of an injured party to claim a life for a life, an eye for an eye, a tooth for a tooth, a hand for a hand, a foot for a foot, a burn for a burn, a wound for a wound and a bruise for a bruise.'

Hector felt an arctic wind blow down his spine. Perhaps the text that Aazim had chosen was too close to his own intent to be purely coincidental. He was sitting well back in the crowded hall so he did not have a perfect view of the mullah's face. He could read neither his expression nor the light in his eyes.

'We know that this sura of the Koran was received by the Prophet directly from on high. We know that in the Hadith there are records of Muhammad putting into practice this aspect of Sharia law. In one instance when the aunt of Anas, one of his companions, broke the tooth of a serving maid and her family demanded recompense, Anas went to the Prophet and asked him to intervene. "Beloved Master," he cried. "Surely she will not lose a tooth?" But Muhammad replied, "It is the law of Allah."'

'*Inshallah!*' chorused the listeners.

'However, is it the will of Allah and his Prophet that we should conceal our lust for vengeance in the cloak of divine law?' Aazim Muktar demanded remorselessly. 'Is that why Allah the All Seeing, the All Powerful, had offered us a second choice? That is blood wit or Al-Qisas. The victim may choose to accept payment in cash or kind to discharge the offender's guilt. No blood need be spilled. Death need not be paid for by death, and the wrath of Allah is appeased.'

'*Mashallah!*' the congregation rejoiced.

'However, is greed a nobler motive than revenge? There are some that would say this is not the case. Once again Allah has offered us a third course of action. That choice is forgiveness.'

'*Allahu Akbar!* God is great!' They called out to heaven.

'Yet again, if we forgive the murderer, is it justice that he should walk away from his crime, perhaps to murder again? What nobility of mind is required for a man to let the killer of his beloved wife survive?'

'No! He must die,' they shouted out angrily. Skilfully Aazim Muktar was toying with them in the Socratic elenctic style, refuting argument by proving the error of its conclusion. Hector could only admire his subtlety.

'Then if the murderer is killed, will his brother have the right to revenge him also? Will he return and murder the dead woman's son? Does this not plunge mankind into a vicious circle of death begetting death?'

The congregation fell to muttering amongst themselves, confused and uncertain. Aazim Muktar let them wrestle with their own consciences for a while, before he took pity on them.

'Is it possible that each new age finds its own morality? Perhaps what was right and just fifteen hundred years ago is no longer so today.' He held up both hands and went on in a lighter and more joyous tone. 'It is one of the precepts of not only the Holy Koran, but of the Jewish Torah and the Christian Bible as well, that in the end days before the world that we know perishes and is gone for ever the Redeemer will be sent down to us by God. The Koran tells us that he will reign over us for nine years in a time of peace and love and righteousness when there will be no more cruelty and evil, and wrongdoing will vanish from the face of earth.'

'*Inshallah!*'

'There are many who believe that this blessed time of forgiveness and righteousness has come and the Redeemer is already amongst us.'

'*Allahu Akbar!*'

Aazim rose to his feet and made a sign of blessing over them and then he descended to the marble floor, and disappeared through the door behind the minbar.

The worshippers rose to their feet and moved towards the exit doors. Their collective mood was buoyant. They were excited and obviously moved by all they had heard. They were so densely packed that Hector was carried along bodily by the throng. The closer they came to the exit doors the more tightly Hector was hemmed in. The men closest to him were all big and tall, many of them as tall as Hector himself. It was almost as though they had been chosen for these attributes.

He looked around for Tariq but could not see him. He must have been carried away in the flood of humanity. Hector was not particularly concerned. He knew that he and Tariq would find each other in the courtyard beyond the doors. However, by now he could hardly breathe and the press of bodies around him was solid. The face of the man on his right side was only inches from his, and his lips were almost touching Hector's ear.

'Effendi,' he said quietly, and Hector started at the use of the Arabic term of respect. 'Please do not be alarmed. We mean you no harm and you are in no danger. However, I must insist that you are

125

to come with us, please.' His use of the plural instantly clarified Hector's situation for him. It must be that all the men surrounding him were working together. He estimated that there were twenty of them at the very least. He was their prisoner just as certainly as if he already wore manacles and leg irons. He tried to judge the odds set against him. He might take down two, three or even ten of them, but in the end their numbers would be decisive. Even if he managed to break free of the pack, he would not have any idea of the escape route from the unfamiliar maze of the mosque. He was unarmed in a strange city in a foreign land. The hand of every man would be turned against him. He knew he would not get very far. This was not the time to take it on the run. He must bide his chance until the odds turned more favourably towards him.

'Where are you taking me?' It was a fatuous question, but he asked it to buy time. He was thinking quickly. Where the hell was Tariq? Tariq was his best chance. Tariq was resourceful and brave. Tariq was on familiar ground. Most of all, Tariq was loyal and devoted.

'The Mullah Aazim Muktar Tippoo Tip wants you to know that it is of the utmost importance that you visit him as his honoured guest. He wishes to speak with you. He has ordered us to bring you to his home.'

'I think you are mistaking me for somebody else,' Hector protested.

'There is no mistake, effendi. We know who you are.' Hector lapsed into silence; as a form of defence it was a last futile effort. He had to hope that Tariq had realized the predicament they were in and he could work out some sort of solution.

Then he heard one of the men close behind him warn his companions quietly, 'Take care. He may be armed.'

'No. They were both unarmed.' The reply from one of the other Arabs was confident, containing not a shadow of doubt.

Hector was stunned as the full purport of that simple statement dawned upon him. The man had used the plural, which meant Tariq and himself. Only Tariq knew they were both unarmed, which meant Tariq had told them.

Tariq! It was a silent scream of despair from the depths of his soul. *Tariq has spoken to them. He has helped them set me up. Tariq is a traitor.* He stopped dead in his tracks. Immediately he was thrust forward again, not brutally but firmly. His captors closed up even more tightly around him.

When did he do it? He was with me at all times, when? Then he remembered. Tariq had left him while he was asleep. *Traitor! He has fed me to the Beast.*

He knew then with utter certainty that he was going to kill Tariq; Tariq who once he had loved like a brother. Tariq was going to die and the thought sustained him. Now he was coldly determined. He was going to kill them, Tariq and Aazim Muktar Tippoo Tip both. If he died with them he would welcome it, for there was nothing left in this world he could truly believe in.

They left the mosque through the main gate and turned up the road towards the walled residential compound that Tariq had pointed out to him earlier as the home of Aazim Muktar. They moved swiftly, with almost military precision, in a tight-packed ruck with Hector in their midst. When they reached the gates of the compound they were opened from within and they marched through into a paved courtyard. In the centre of it grew a large banyan tree with spreading branches. In its shade sat a small group of veiled women and young children. They looked on with interest as Hector was marched to the set of steps that led up to the veranda of a flat-roofed bungalow.

It was a modest and unpretentious building, not the home that one might expect belonged to a high-ranking cleric or important government functionary. Most of Hector's escort stopped at the bottom of the stairs, but two of them flanked him and took hold of his arms from either side to lead him up the steps onto the veranda. Hector shrugged their hands away irritably, and they did not insist. He went up the stairs two at a time and paused as he reached the porch. The door facing him was open and he crossed to it with long determined strides and paused in the doorway while his eyes adjusted to the gloomy interior after the brilliant sunlight of the courtyard.

The room was large but sparsely furnished in Arabic style. The furniture was aligned with the walls and the centre of the room was left bare and uncluttered. Aazim Muktar was the only person in the room. He was seated cross-legged on a pile of green velvet cushions, before a low table. He rose to his feet in one lithe movement and bowed as he touched his forehead, lips and heart. Then he straightened up and spoke quietly.

'You are very welcome in my home, Mr Cross.'

'It is very kind of you to invite me, Sheikh Tippoo Tip.' Hector returned his bow, and Aazim Muktar grimaced slightly at his ironical tone.

'It might be best if we speak freely and openly, Mr Cross. I do not wish to detain you longer than is absolutely necessary.' His English was perfect, educated and cultivated as that of any high-born Englishman.

'I would expect nothing less from you, Mullah Aazim Muktar.'

'Please be seated, sir.' He indicated a high-backed chair that had obviously been prepared for Hector. Hector went to it without hesitation and sat down. He was at a severe disadvantage, so it was essential that he maintained a hard expression and a stern resolve.

Aazim Muktar sat facing him, cross-legged on his cushions. They regarded each other steadily, until Aazim Muktar broke the silence.

'Did you know that I met your wife some years ago at a reception in the London residence of the American ambassador? Hazel Bannock-Cross was a very beautiful and superior lady. I liked and admired her immensely.'

Hector took a long slow breath. He did not want his voice to shake with the rage that flooded every cell in his body. When he replied it was in a low and level tone.

'So why, then, did you have her murdered?'

Aazim Muktar's eyes were dark and expressive. His lashes were long and almost feminine, incongruous when set in such powerful masculine features. Slowly they filled with stark shadows of pain and sorrow. He leaned towards Hector and for a moment it seemed he might reach out and touch him, but he restrained himself. He sat upright again and held Hector's angry gaze.

'I call on Allah and his Prophet to hear me when I tell you that is not true, sir. I was not involved in any way in the murder of your wife.'

'And I tell you, sir, that words trip glibly across the tongue of one who deals in them.'

'Is there no way I can convince you?' he asked quietly. 'I grieve for her almost as deeply as you do.'

'I cannot imagine anything that might convince me of that,' Hector told him. 'There is nobody else who had any motive, except you. The creed of retaliation and revenge killing is deeply embedded in your religion, your culture and your psyche.'

'That is not true, Mr Cross. There is also the light of forgiveness that leads us on. Did you take no account of the plea that I addressed to you personally in the mosque today? I pleaded with you to call a halt to this vicious circle of kill and kill again.'

'I heard what you said,' Hector replied, 'but I did not believe a word of it.'

'It seems I am left with only one other recourse.'

'What is that? Are you going to kill me also?'

'No, sir. I did not kill your lovely wife and I am not going to kill you. You are a guest in my home. You are under my protection. Will you bear with me for just a short while, Mr Cross?' Hector did not reply and Aazim Muktar stood up and left the room. Hector jumped up from the chair and moved quickly around the room. His eyes darted from side to side searching for an escape route, seeking a weapon with which to defend himself. He found nothing except books and scrolls, and when he glanced through the window he saw that the courtyard was still filled with Aazim Muktar's followers. He was trapped helplessly.

Within minutes the mullah returned. 'Forgive me, Mr Cross, but I had to make the final arrangements to get you out of the city. You may not know that it is a very serious offence for any person who is not of the Islamic faith to enter the holy places of Medina and Mecca. The penalty is death by beheading. I have a car and driver waiting at the gates of the compound to drive you down to the airport at Jeddah. I have made a reservation in the first-class section of an Emirates flight from Jeddah to Abu Zara which departs at ten p.m. this evening. Once you are airborne your people at Cross Bow Security will be alerted to your arrival. However, you must leave Mecca at once.'

Hector stared at him in astonishment and total disbelief. They were not going to set him free. This was another ruse, he knew that. He tried to see beyond the mullah's open gaze and his sincere expression.

'Please, Mr Cross. This is a matter of life and death. You must leave at once. I will follow you in a separate vehicle. We will have another opportunity to talk at Jeddah airport, in a VIP room that I have reserved.'

Hector inclined his head slightly, feigning acquiescence. He knew that the driver would take him out into the desert where there would be an execution squad of religious zealots waiting to receive him. They had probably already dug his grave.

No matter how heavy the odds this devious bastard has stacked up against me, my chances are better out there in the desert than bottled up here, he decided.

'You are very generous—' he began, but Aazim Muktar cut him short.

'Here is your air ticket.' He handed Hector an envelope with an Emirates crest stamped on the flap. Hector opened the envelope and checked the name on the ticket. It was the same as the false name in the Abu Zarian passport on which he was travelling. Of course, Tariq the traitor had given them that information.

Hector looked up. 'This seems to be in order.'

'Good! Now go, at once. I will meet you again in Jeddah.' He held the door open and Hector crossed to it and ran down the steps into the courtyard. Immediately a black Mercedes saloon drove in through the gate from the street. It parked in front of Hector. A bearded chauffeur in a black turban jumped out of the driver's seat and opened the rear passenger door for him. As soon as Hector had settled himself into the seat the chauffeur slammed the door and slipped back behind the wheel. The ranks of the disciples opened to allow the Mercedes through and they drove out through the gates of the compound into the street. Hector looked back through the rear window. Aazim Muktar was standing on the veranda of the bungalow and watching him leave.

Hector spent the entire journey down to Jeddah airport in a turmoil of indecision. It would have been so easy to reach over the back of the seat, take the chauffeur in a head lock and break his neck. Then he could take the Mercedes and make a run for the Abu Zarian border. However, that was over a thousand miles away and the fuel gauge on the dashboard of the Mercedes was indicating under half full. He did not have more than a few dollars with him, certainly not enough to refill the tank. The chauffeur might be carrying cash, but he doubted it. The man probably had a fuel card or some other type of debit card. Without cash he would never make it. Of course, once the alarm went out the Saudi police would have an APB on every road. He wouldn't go a hundred miles, let alone a thousand, before they had him. He abandoned that idea.

Then he thought about Aazim Muktar Tippoo Tip, and weighed the chance of his innocence against that of his guilt; could he believe and trust him? When he had listened to him speak in the mosque he had almost been convinced. But conversely, now that he had been set free Hector was certain that it had to be trickery. He knew that there had to be another shock in store for him.

There was a telephone in the rear armrest of the Mercedes and he picked up the receiver and held it to his ear. There was a dialling tone. He opened the envelope that Aazim Muktar had given him and found the phone number of Emirates check-in desk at Jeddah airport. He dialled it and a woman answered on the third ring. He gave her his ticket details.

'Can you confirm that my booking is correct, please?'

'Hold on please, sir.' There was a short delay and then she came back. 'Yes, sir. We are expecting you. You have already been checked in online. Your flight is running to schedule. Departure is at twenty-two hundred hours.'

He replaced the receiver in its cradle. It all added up neatly, perhaps too neatly. What finally decided him was the thought of Hazel. He owed it to her memory to confront Aazim Muktar and see it through to the end, no matter what risk that involved. He could almost hear her voice. *You have to do it, my darling. You have to do it or you and I will never be able to rest again.*

So he sat in the back seat and let the chauffeur drive him down to Jeddah.

At the first-class entrance to the UAE Airlines terminal at Jeddah airport a doorman in traditional robes opened the door of the Mercedes for him and with elaborate respect escorted him to the private room that had been reserved in his name. As soon as he was alone Hector tried the door and found it unlocked. He opened it an inch and glanced out through the crack. There was no guard outside. By now he was more intrigued than fearful. He closed the door and looked around the luxuriously furnished waiting room. His mouth was parched by the rancid taste of danger.

I would give my virginity for a decent Scotch, he decided, but of course there was no hard liquor on display in this Islamic stronghold. He drank a glass of Perrier water, poured another and carried it to one of the leather easy chairs. As he settled into it there was a knock on the door.

'Come in,' he called and Aazim Muktar entered. He must have followed Hector's Mercedes closely on the journey down from Mecca. However, Hector was astonished when the mullah was followed by a heavily veiled woman. She was weeping softly behind the veil. She led by the hand a brown-skinned lad aged six or seven years. He was a lovely little fellow, with curling black locks and huge dark eyes. He was sucking his thumb, looking unhappy and perplexed. Aazim Muktar gestured at the woman and she scurried to a corner of the room and squatted on the floor, hugging the child to her breast. Hector saw the glint of her eyes behind the burqa as she studied him, and then she began to sob again. Aazim Muktar cautioned her to silence with a sharp word, then he seated himself in the easy chair facing Hector.

'They will be calling your flight for boarding in forty-five minutes,' he said to Hector. 'That is all the time I have to convince you that I was not responsible in any way for the assassination of your wife. But first let me say that I know almost every detail of the tragic involvement of your family and mine. There were many deaths on both sides. I accept that you were a serving army officer and on occasion you were justified in killing in the line of your duty. But that was not always the case. There were times when you took the law into your own hands.' He paused and looked keenly into Hector's eyes.

'Go on!' Hector invited him expressionlessly.

'I accept the fact that my father and most of my brothers were pirates, acting in direct contravention of international law. They seized merchant ships on the high seas and held the crews to ransom. As a very young man I disassociated myself from these crimes committed by my family and I went to England to be as far as was possible from them. I have never considered that I had any right of retaliation against you or your family. I have told you that I met your wife and admired her. I was utterly devastated when I heard of her murder. It was against all the laws of man and God. However, I knew that after her death you would hunt me down to appease the sins of my clan.'

'You have my full attention.'

'I have dreaded this day of our meeting, but I have planned for it.'

'I am sure you have,' Hector retorted, and now his expression was grim.

'Not in your way, for you are a hard warrior, Mr Cross, and yours is the way of the sword.'

'Tell me then, Mullah Tippoo Tip. What is your way?'

'My way is the way of Allah. My way is mutual forgiveness. My way is Al-Qisas. I offer you a life for a life.' He stood up and went to the little huddle of abject humanity that cowered in the corner of the room. He took the child's hand and led him to stand in front of Hector.

'This is my son. He is six years old. His name is Kurrum, which means happiness.' The little boy thrust his thumb back into his mouth and stared at Hector.

'He is a beautiful boy,' Hector conceded.

'He is yours,' Aazim Muktar said in Arabic, and he pushed the child gently forward.

Hector jumped up from his chair in consternation. 'In God's name, what must I do with him?'

'In Allah's name, you must take him and hold him as a hostage against my good faith. If you find irrefutable proof that I killed your wife you must kill him as is your right in terms of the law of Al-Qisas, and I shall forgive you.'

The woman screamed and threw herself across the floor.

'He is my son. He is my only son. Kill me if you must, effendi. But do not kill my son.' She tore off her veil and clawed at her own face, raking both her cheeks with her long nails. The blood welled from the long wounds and dripped from her chin. She crawled to Hector's feet. 'Kill me, but let my son live, I implore you.'

'Be silent, wife.' Her husband used a kindly tone. He placed a hand on her shoulder and drew her away. Then he came back to face Hector. From the folds of his white robe he drew out a leather wallet, and proffered it.

'This is all the documentation you need in order to take Kurrum with you: his air ticket on today's flight, his certificate of birth, his passport and the papers that name you as his legal guardian. What is your decision, Mr Cross?'

Still Hector stood dumbstruck. This was the very last thing he had expected. He looked down at the child. He shook his head, as if to deny what was happening. He reached out and touched the boy's head. His curls were crisp and springing under his fingers. Kurrum made no attempt to pull away. He lifted his head and looked at Hector. His eyes were dark and wise far beyond his years. He spoke softly. 'My father says I must go with you, effendi. My father says I am now a man and I must behave like a man. It is the will of Allah.'

Still Hector could not speak. His throat was dry and the pulse beating in his temples echoed through his skull like a drum. He stooped and picked up the child and held him on his hip. Kurrum did not struggle. Hector touched his cheek. Hector turned his head and looked back at the boy's father.

At last he was able to see through to his very core, and what he saw there was good. He knew at last with certainty that this man was not the Beast he was hunting.

Hector turned back to the child on his hip. 'You are my hostage, Kurrum.' His mother heard him. She moaned. Hector ignored her and went on addressing the child. 'Do you know what that means, Kurrum?'

The boy shook his head, and Hector went on. 'It means you are brave and good, as your father is brave and good.' He replaced Kurrum on his feet, turned him towards his mother and gave him a gentle push. 'Go back to your mother, Kurrum, and take good care of her, for now you are a man as your father was a man before you.'

The woman held out both arms to him, and Kurrum ran into them. She swept him up and turned for the door. She paused when she reached it and looked back at Hector with tears and blood from the scratches streaming down her face.

'Master . . .' she started and then her voice failed.

'Go!' Hector ordered her. 'Take your son, and go with Allah.' She went and closed the door softly behind her. She left Hector and Aazim Muktar facing each other across the room.

'Are you sure?' Aazim asked.

'I am as sure as I have ever been of anything in my life.'

'There are no words that can express the extent of my gratitude.' Aazim bowed. 'You have given me a gift beyond any other I can imagine. I can never repay you.'

'I am paid in full. Simply knowing a man of your sanctity has enriched my own life.'

'I am still in your debt. My son's life outweighs all else,' Aazim told him sincerely. 'I understand that you actually saw the man who murdered your wife, and that he wore a gang tattoo.'

'Tariq Hakam told you that!' Hector's fury flared again. 'That man is a traitor. He betrayed my friendship. One day I will kill him.'

'No, Mr Cross. He is not your enemy.' Hector shook his head adamantly, but Aazim held up a hand to restrain him. 'One day you will realize that. Tariq Hakam asked me to give you a message. I promised to do so. May I tell you what he said?'

'If you wish.'

'He says that there was no other way to persuade you that you were looking in the wrong direction for your enemy. He said that you and I had to meet to understand each other.'

'I will never take him back, no matter what he says. I can never trust him again.'

'Tariq knows that.'

'What will he do now?'

'He is determined to turn aside from the warrior way. From now onwards he will follow the road that leads to the feet of Allah.'

'So, he has discovered God and become one of your disciples, has he? Good for him, the old rogue.'

'Old rogue. He told me that you would say that.' Aazim smiled. 'However—'

He broke off as he was interrupted by a woman's voice echoing over the airport's public address system. *This is a final call for all passengers travelling on Emirates Flight EK 805 to Abu Zara. This flight is closing at Gate A26. Passengers must proceed at once to Gate A26 for immediate boarding.*

'Our time together has come to an end, Mr Cross. When I lived in London I worked with a man there who devotes his life to helping rehabilitate young Muslim boys who had been caught up in the criminal street gangs of the UK's major cities. I will send a message to him to contact you. Perhaps he will be able to help you trace this killer with the Maalik tattoo. Perhaps that way you might be able to identify with certainty your hidden enemy.'

'How will you send this man of yours to me, Aazim Tippoo Tip? You do not know where I live.'

'Since Brandon Hall was burnt to the ground you have made your principal London home at Number Eleven, Conrad Road in Belgravia. Your primary email address is cross@crossbow.com, but you have many others. Is that not correct, Mr Cross?'

Hector inclined his head in wry acquiescence. 'Tariq has told you so much about me. It would not surprise me if you even know my shoe size.'

'US size eleven and a half,' Aazim replied without smiling, but Hector laughed out loud.

'Goodbye, Aazim Tippoo Tip. I shall never forget you.'

'Nor I you, Mr Hector Cross. May I shake your hand?'

Hector took his hand and they looked into each other's eyes.

'Go with Allah, Mr Hector Cross.'

'Pray for me, Sheikh Tippoo Tip.' Hector turned and without looking back strode out through the door, headed towards Gate A26.

Although it was after midnight when Hector arrived back at the penthouse of Seascape Mansions in Abu Zara, he called a council of war in the private cinema.

As the team assembled they greeted Hector enthusiastically but then looked around for Tariq Hakam. Hector made no effort to allay their curiosity until they were all seated on the tiers of seats facing him on the podium.

'So where is Tariq, then?' Nastiya asked the question for all of them.

'It's a long story,' Hector hedged.

'Okay. Then make it a short one,' Nastiya suggested.

'He is still in Mecca.' Nobody moved. Nobody spoke. Hector was forced to continue. He made it short and he stripped away all detail and commentary. The tension in the room rose steadily as he spoke. He told them everything except the final parting at Jeddah airport and Aazim's offer of a hostage. When he finished they all stared at him in grim silence. Nastiya broke the spell of their collective horror. She was the only one in the room who was not afraid of Hector Cross.

'So Tariq Hakam was the traitor all along. He betrayed you and he betrayed all of us. Why did you not kill him, Hector?'

Hector had prepared for this interrogation on the flight back from Mecca. They hammered at him with their questions and their doubts for almost another thirty minutes. He described in detail Aazim Muktar's sermon in the mosque, repeating it almost word for word.

'And you believed him, did you, Hector?'

'He was very convincing. But I did not truly, deeply, believe him. Not then. Not until he offered me his six-year-old son as a hostage. Then I believed him. He bared his soul to me and gave me his son. Then I knew he was on the side of the angels. I knew that he had not masterminded Hazel's murder.'

'If he gave you this hostage, Hector, then where is the boy now?'

'I accepted him, and then I returned him to his mother.'

'Are you crazy mad in the head, Hector Cross?' Nastiya demanded.

'Some may say so.' Hector smiled and went on. 'But then Aazim Muktar Tippoo Tip gave me the final proof of his innocence.'

'What was that, you silly man?'

'Although I was completely in his power, he allowed me to walk away and climb on the aircraft and return here to Abu Zara unscathed.'

Paddy O'Quinn let out a roar of laughter and slapped his wife's knee. 'Hector is right, my darling. There is no stronger proof than that. Now even I believe in Aazim Tippoo Tip.'

The tension in the room broke and they exchanged sheepish nods and grins. Only Nastiya removed Paddy's hand from her knee and challenged Hector one last time. 'And I am sure that, like the true blue Englishman you are, you even shook this murdering mullah's hand and I am sure that you are not even going to kill Tariq Hakam?'

'I can hide nothing from you, tsarina. I shook Aazim Tippoo Tip's hand and found no blood on it. Then I allowed Tariq Hakam to go with his God,' Hector conceded and stood up. 'To tell you the truth, I feel better for those two things. Now I need a few hours of sleep. We will all meet here after breakfast in the morning, to consider where we now stand.'

'I can tell you, for free, exactly where you now stand, Hector Cross. You are back at square one and lucky to be there.' Nastiya tried to sound stern, but there was a tiny spark of blue in her eye.

Hector held Catherine on his lap as he fed her the bottle. She made small grunting sounds of appreciation as she attacked the teat with gusto, totally oblivious of the interested audience seated on the rising tiers of seats confronting them in the cinema.

'Only man I know who can plot mayhem and death and at the same time feed an infant,' Paddy O'Quinn remarked and Nastiya punched his arm.

'You know nothing about babies, husband. Watch Hector and shut up your mouth.'

'That's enough, my children. Cut the squabbling and settle down. We have work to do,' Hector admonished them. 'I did not argue with Nastiya last night when she said we were back to square one. However, this is not entirely true. We do still have a tenuous lead to work on. This was suggested to me by Tariq Hakam. I give him full credit for that. We were discussing how the Beast set up the ambush for Hazel, and Tariq asked a simple question. He said, "How did they know?"'

Hector paused and let that sink in. Then he repeated, 'How did the Beast know that Hazel was coming up to London that day to see her gynaecologist?' They stirred and murmured agreement.

'The only ones that knew on our side were Hazel and me and Agatha, her PA, who set up the appointment. I phoned Agatha yesterday evening and she was absolutely adamant that she had told nobody. She was extremely distressed that I even made the suggestion. She has worked for Hazel for fifteen years and she is completely reliable.'

'Hazel's gynae knew,' Nastiya volunteered.

'Yes, you are right. Mr Donnovan knew. I am returning to London this afternoon to speak to him, but it's going to be a little embarrassing to suggest to him that he broke patient confidentiality. I want Paddy and Nastiya to come with me, and yes okay, Dave, I saw you looking anxious. You can come along. There is a good chance that we will need you.' Dave Imbiss smiled with relief. Hector went on. 'For the time being, Catherine will be safe and well cared for here at Seascape with Bonnie and all her back-up team.' He glanced at his wristwatch. 'Time is nine thirteen. There is a flight at eleven thirty for London Heathrow. If you all move arse we can make it.'

The four of them dined that night at Number Eleven. From the head of the table Hector raised his glass to them. 'I have just realized that exactly four months have passed since Hazel left me. It seems like a much shorter time. I still walk into every room in this house and expect her to be there. I want you to join me in wishing her Godspeed.'

Hours later, when Paddy and Nastiya went up to their own room, Nastiya sat before the dressing-table mirror in a pink satin robe and brushed out her hair. She watched Paddy in the mirror as he lay on the bed with the evening paper. 'Do you know what Hector needs?' she asked him.

'Tell me,' he grunted as he turned the page.

'He needs a good woman in his bed to help him forget.'

Paddy sat bolt upright and crumpled the news-sheet with alarm.

'Don't you dare suggest that to him! He will kill you, you callous Russian tart.'

'Callous I don't know. Tart I do know, and it's good and sweet. I can give you a little taste if you like.'

Early the next morning Hector found parking in Harley Street, and he walked half a block to Alan Donnovan's clinic. He climbed the stairs rather than take the lift and when he entered the reception area it was empty. He stood at the desk for only a few minutes before the receptionist returned from Alan's room carrying an armful of patients' files.

'I am so sorry to keep you waiting, Mr Cross.'

'That's all right, Victoria.' She seemed a little flustered to see him, but he put that down to the pressure of working for a man like Alan.

'Mr Donnovan is running quite a bit late. Do you have something else you need to do?'

'That's all right. I am in no hurry. I can wait,' Hector told her.

She stacked the files on her desk. In her free hand she held an iPhone S4, and now she laid it down beside the pile of files as the intercom rang.

'Excuse me, Mr Cross. Everything seems to be happening at once this morning.' She picked up the intercom and spoke into it. 'Yes, Mr Donnovan. Yes, at once.' She dropped the intercom in its cradle. 'Please excuse me again, Mr Cross.'

She started towards the inner rooms. She left her iPhone lying beside the files. Hector noticed that the device was identical to his own. It triggered something in his mind and suddenly it all seemed to drop into place. The answer to the conundrum had been staring him in the face all along. He had overlooked Victoria as though she was a piece of furniture. He was chagrined by the fact that he had not worked it out long before.

'Listen, Victoria,' he called after her. 'I have just remembered something else I should do. It wasn't really important that I see Mr Donnovan today anyway. Please cancel my appointment, and I will call you again next week to make another.'

'Oh, are you sure? All right, but I am so sorry for this, Mr Cross.' She fled for Alan's door.

As it closed, Hector leaned across the desk and scooped up the girl's iPhone. He slipped his own out of its pouch on his belt and switched them. He hoped that it might be some time before she tumbled to the exchange. He was not worried that he might have left vital information in the girl's hands. Dave Imbiss had taught him how to keep his phone impregnable and squeaky clean. He left the clinic and went down to where he had parked. He drove back to No. 11, where he found the other three members of his team in the library.

'That didn't take you too long, boss. We didn't expect you back so soon,' Dave Imbiss told him.

'I went to get you a little present. Here you go.' He tossed him Victoria's iPhone.

'Thanks a thousand.' Dave caught it neatly. 'But I already have one.'

'One like this you ain't got,' Hector assured him. 'What I want you to do is take it down to the workshop and strip every bit of information out of it. I want the full list of its contact numbers. All the messages received and sent, either in voice or SMS. I want copies of all the videos in memory. I want you to look particularly hard at everything dated from the week of Hazel's death up to the present time.'

'Where did you get this, boss?' Dave examined the iPhone with sudden keen attention, turning it over in his hands, not even glancing at Hector as he asked the questions. 'Who does it belong to? How did you get your hands on it?'

'I stole it from the receptionist at Alan Donnovan's clinic. Alan is Hazel's gynaecologist. The receptionist's name is Victoria Vusamazulu. She is a cute little African number and her name in Zulu is a political war-cry meaning "Rouse the Zulu Nation". I am not sure about the nation, but with her physical assets I have little doubt she could rouse a few of the dead. She has probably woken up to my switch of her phone already, but I can stall her until tomorrow. You have got until then to suck her iPhone dry. Apart from her boss, Victoria is the only one who knew that Hazel was coming up to London on the day of the ambush.'

Dave grinned with delight at the challenge. 'It won't take that long. This little Zulu number will soon have no secrets from me. Excuse me, folks.'

Hector resisted the urge to follow Dave down to the workshop in the basement. Dave was one of the best in the business but he would work even better without unsolicited advice and chivvying. Hector left him to get on with it, and he went up to his study.

Agatha had digitized all Hazel's information from the time she first came to work as her PA. On Hector's desk she had left an external hard drive that contained all of it; many hundreds of giga-bytes.

Now that the trail of Hazel's killer had gone cold in Mecca, Hector was determined to go right back to the beginning of Hazel's dazzling career, and search out all the rivals she had left along the road. As dearly as he loved her, Hector never once doubted Hazel's capacity for making enemies. She had kicked and clawed her way to the top of a tall heap, and she had never backed away from a fight.

If you spend your entire life shaking the mountains, churning the oceans and beating the jungles, as Hazel had done, you are bound to flush out some pretty scary creatures. Hector began a fresh search for one of these. The most vicious and vindictive of them all; the enemy who would make a great white shark seem like a toothless Chihuahua.

He had been at work for only a couple of hours when the intercom rang. It was Agatha.

'Good morning, Mr Cross. I have the receptionist from Mister Donnovan's clinic on the line. I tried to put her off, but she is most insistent. Will you take the call?'

'Thank you, Agatha. I'll take it.' He made a mental note to have a serious talk to Agatha. He badly needed a personal assistant, and she would be perfect in the job. Hazel had been her whole life. Perhaps now she might transfer that loyalty to him. A side benefit in the arrangement was the fact that there would be no danger of any emotional entanglements. He put that thought aside, and spoke into the handset. 'Cross.'

'I am sorry to bother you, Mr Cross. This is Vicky Vusamazulu. There seems to have been a mix-up. I noticed on your first visit to the clinic that you have an iPhone S4, exactly like mine . . .'

'Yes, I have,' Hector replied, and then he groaned. 'Oh, damn it to hell. Now I understand what must have happened. I have been unable to open my phone. It's been refusing to accept my password. I was standing at your desk this morning when you left the room. I was going to make a call, and then I changed my mind. Instead I went to the toilet. Then I realized I had left my phone in your office. I returned to your reception. You weren't in the room, but I saw an iPhone lying on the desk. I thought it was mine and I took it. I do apologize, Vicky. It was very stupid of me. You don't have my phone, by any chance, do you?'

'That is why I am calling you, sir. I do have yours. I know it's yours because you have written your number inside the back cover. Mine has a lot of very personal information on it. Can I come to your house after work this evening to exchange phones with you?'

'Please forgive me, Victoria. I am going out in the next few minutes, and I won't return until late tonight. But I will take your phone with me, if it has very sensitive information in it. Can't trust anybody these days. I will stop by your office first thing in the morning to make the exchange.'

'Oh dear! You can't make it any time today? It really is inconvenient for me.'

'Sorry, Victoria. Tomorrow before ten a.m., I promise you.' He hung up before the girl could protest further.

Dave Imbiss called him on the intercom a few minutes after five that afternoon.

'Sorry, boss. It took longer than I thought. Miss Vusamazulu is a cunning little vixen. She put a whole bunch of booby traps into her machine. But I have got it all out for you at last.'

'Good man. Tell me about it.'

'Better you come and have a look and a listen for yourself. We will need to use the cinema. I have got about an hour of videos to show you. Before you come, you should take a calm pill, or maybe even two. What I have for you is going to blow your mind, boss.'

'I'll be down in five. Give Paddy and Nastiya a call to join us for this gala performance.'

Paddy and Nastiya were sitting in the centre of the second row of seats when Hector entered the theatre. Dave was fiddling with the electronic equipment. He looked up as Hector swung one long leg over the first row and dropped into the seat beside Nastiya.

'Sorry to disappoint, folks. We ain't got no commercials. So, I'll go straight to the main features,' Dave told them. 'Firstly, some selected conversations. A fact that most iPhone owners do not know is that nothing is ever lost; no matter how many times you delete it we can always get it back. Miss Vusamazulu had two shots at deleting this particular conversation, but here it comes again, recorded on the day that Hazel had her final consultation with Alan Donnovan.' Dave started the audio machine. The first sound was the single ring tone of a mobile phone and immediately afterwards there was click as the receiver was lifted. There was a pause and then a woman's voice.

'Hello. Is that you, Aleutian?'

The answer came immediately.

'I told you not to name names, bitch.' The cadence was American hip-hop. The delivery was arrogant. The woman's soft gasp of contrition was barely audible. Then her voice took on a submissive pleading tone.

'I'm sorry. I forgot.'

'Then don't forget to delete this call when we finish. Now tell me! Has she come?'

'Yes, she is here. But her husband has gone out. He told Doctor that he would return at one thirty.'

'Good!' said the male voice, and the line went dead. Dave switched off the audio. They were all silent for a while.

Then Hector said, 'Aleutian. Was that the name she used?'

'That's what it sounds like. Anyway, it's probably a gangland handle; a *nom de guerre*. Not his passport name, if you know what I mean.'

'Play the call again.'

Dave ran it back and started it again. They all leaned forward to listen. When it ended Paddy agreed. 'Aleutian. Definitely Aleutian. So at least we have some sort of name to work with now.'

'The time and date are right. I dropped Hazel at Donnovan's clinic and went to run a few errands around town,' Hector agreed. 'What else is there, Dave?'

'The next call was at nine forty-five the same evening,' Dave told them. 'This is Aleutian calling Victoria.'

He started the recorder. There were four ring tones, and then the girl's unmistakable voice and intonation.

'Hello. This is Victoria.'

'I'll be there to pick you up in ten minutes. Wait for me down-stairs, outside the tobacconist. I am driving a rented blue VW.'

'You are late. You said seven.'

'Okay. Forget it. I'll get another ho for tonight. Pussy stacked up knee deep around here.'

'No! I didn't mean that. I am sorry. Please forgive me. I'll make it up to you. I promise.'

'You had better. I have a hard-on here that will blow the glass out of all the windows in the street when it bursts.'

Victoria giggled. 'You are so funny. Come here and blow my window out, lover boy.'

Hector intervened softly. 'At the time that cultured conversation was in progress, Hazel was lying in a coma with a bullet in her brain and just a few hours away from dying.'

Paddy looked down and shuffled his feet. Nastiya took Hector's hand that lay on the bench between them. She squeezed it hard, but remained silent. There was nothing that any of them could say for his comfort.

Dave coughed and broke the silence. 'There are four more conver-sations between the two of them but it's all the same sort of dismal stuff. It's just threats and boasts of sexual prowess from him and a few recriminations from the girl. However, there's not been a call from Aleutian for the past few weeks. I've tried the number, but it's unobtainable.'

'Either he dumped her, or he left the country a few weeks back,' Hector suggested.

'He just dropped her,' Nastiya said with certainty. 'Men like Aleutian don't stick around more than a few weeks. They move on once they have had a good taste of the tart.' Significantly she raised a perfectly groomed eyebrow at Paddy.

'No private jokes here, please,' Dave cautioned her. 'Let's keep it serious and on the ball. So that's the end of the phone calls but they have given us some good stuff.' He looked at Hector. 'If you are ready, I can run the videos for you, boss?'

'Go ahead please, Dave.'

Dave dimmed the lights and turned on the first video that he had copied from the iPhone. There was immediately a cacophony of background noise over the audio speakers, men's raised voices and women's high-pitched shrieks of laughter, loud music and the clatter of bottles and glasses. On the screen the images were jumbled and confused, as the camera panned wildly from ceiling to floor, over a table of beer bottles and half-empty glasses, down onto close-ups of human feet and legs. Then it steadied. The scene was obviously the interior of a squalid nightclub. The tables were crowded together around a tiny dance floor. Victoria's unmistakable voice rose above the hubbub.

'Be cool, everybody! Remember, this is your audition for *The X Factor*.' The lens pulled back and focussed onto a group of young people sitting around a table laden with drinks and overflowing ashtrays. Some of them leered at the camera and raised their glasses in salute, others held hand-rolled joints at jaunty angles in the corners of their mouths and blew puffs of smoke, and one thrust his finger down his throat and made vomit noises.

The camera zoomed in on a pretty blonde girl sitting on a boy's lap at the far side of the table, and Victoria's voice instructed her, 'Come on, Angie. Do some magic trick.'

Angie hooked her thumbs in the top of her dress and pulled it down to her waist. Both her large white breasts popped out and she took one in each hand and pointed her nipples at the camera. 'Bang! Bang! You're dead!' she squealed. The camera shook with laughter, then moved on to the next reveller in the circle.

'Here we go!' Dave Imbiss told them and froze the frame. They were looking at the image of a dark-skinned male. Hector guessed he might be thirty or a little older. His hair was gelled into a quiff and he wore a hoodie jacket with the sleeves rolled up above the elbows and the hood thrown back. His forearms were muscular and toned as though from gym work. He was good-looking in a brutal fashion, with a cruel cynical mouth. His expression was studiedly nonchalant.

Dave let them scrutinize the image for a little longer. 'I think we have here the missing link in the puzzle; the mover and shaker who set up the hit. This, boys and girls, is Aleutian.'

Hector straightened up in his seat and leaned forward like a hound with the scent of the quarry in his nostrils. 'Do we have any more footage of this beauty?' he asked in a deadly quiet tone.

'Plenty, boss. Plenty. Victoria obviously has the big-time hots for him. She just can't get enough.'

'Neither can I,' Hector murmured. 'I want him very badly. Let's move on, Dave.'

The video started again and Victoria's voice picked up the commentary. 'Ladies and gentlemen. They don't come any cooler than this. This is Mr Cool in person. Give your fans a wave, Mr Cool.'

Mr Cool lifted two fingers in a V sign and placed his thumb between them. Without a change of expression he prodded it towards the lens in a grossly lewd gesture. Victoria hooted and she sang, 'Do that to me one more time!'

The man in the frame leaned back in his chair and locked both his hands behind his head. He winked at the camera. Dave froze the frame again.

'Okay, folks, check his left hand,' he told them and zoomed in on it. 'Is that the red tattoo, boss?'

'That's the one, Dave. The Maalik tattoo. But are we sure this one is Aleutian? She hasn't used that name in this shot. Go on running the footage.'

Dave started the video again, but the camera panned off the subject and Dave apologized. 'Nothing more on this one. But not to worry too much. There is plenty more on three of the others; enough to make a strong man throw up.'

'Let's see them, please,' Hector ordered.

The next video was a wide shot of the same nightclub dance floor.

The camera operator must have been standing on a table to achieve such a high-angle view. On the closest edge of the dance floor Victoria Vusamazulu was dancing with the man with the Maalik tattoo. She was oscillating her hips, throwing her head from side to side so that her long false hairpiece whipped across her face. Her partner towered over her. He had shed the hoodie jacket and the sleeves of his sweat-shirt were cut away to expose the full length of his heavily muscled arms. Hector was able to judge his size by comparing him to Victoria. He stood head and shoulders taller than her.

He was big, very big, and he moved well. He was balanced and coordinated. He was quick on his feet. Hector judged that he would be a dangerous man in a fight. Suddenly the man snatched the hair-piece off Victoria's head and he circled her, lashing her with the hairpiece across her back and buttocks as though he was her slave driver. She writhed in feigned agony. He reached out to the zip fastener running down the back of her dress and pulled it down to the cleft of her buttocks. She held the front of the dress to her breasts but her back was naked and shiny black with sweat.

The other dancers crowded around them, clapping time to the music and to their primitive gyrations, urging them on with shrill screams and yips of excitation.

The man closed in behind Victoria, grabbed her hips and pulled her towards him, pounding his loins into her buttocks in a graphic parody of anal intercourse. She pushed back at him just as vigor-ously, meeting each of his thrusts, riding out his assault.

Suddenly the screen went black and the noise cut off into complete silence. Dave switched on the overhead lights.

'Sorry for that,' he said cheerfully. 'End of video. We will never know how that story ends.'

'And a good thing too. No nice girl would be safe in bed with a husband who watched that kind of thing.' Nastiya gave her opinion and prodded Paddy in the ribs.

'If you thought that was a little over the top, Nastiya, you had better leave the room now before I run the last one,' Dave warned her. She shook her head and moved closer to Paddy. She took a firm grip of his arm.

'I can trust this man to protect me,' she said. 'It is my duty to stay here. One day it may be my duty to kill that nasty Aleutian animal.'

'How do we know this is Aleutian?' Hector cut in. 'Come on, Dave, give us the name please.'

'Your wish is my command, boss. His name is coming right up!' He switched off the lights and started the last video.

Once again there was a rapid series of fuzzy, out-of-focus shots of the floor and ceiling of what was clearly a woman's bedroom, with pink bedclothes on the queen-size bed and a dressing table crowded with toiletries and perfume bottles. There was also a menagerie of fluffy animal toys arranged on the single chair standing beside the bed. Then the frame steadied as if the camera had been placed on a tripod. Focus pulled in on the bed. Now the man from the night-club sequence lay on the bed on his back. He was naked. He stared into the lens with that same enigmatic expression. He had one hand behind his head and the tattoo was in clear focus. With his other hand he was stroking himself.

'Come on,' he said to the person behind the camera. 'What are you waiting for? Does Mr Big frighten you, bitch?'

Vicky Vusamazulu sashayed into the shot. She also was naked. She undulated her glossy black buttocks as she went to the man on the bed. She swung one leg over him and straddled him.

No one in the theatre spoke again for a while. Twice more Victoria stood up from the bed and came back behind the camera to change the angle and the focus, from wide angle to tight close-up, and then she ran back to the bed and launched herself into the action once more.

'Isn't it strange?' Hector asked at last.

'Isn't what strange?' Paddy demanded without taking his eyes from the screen.

'Isn't it strange how boring it is to watch other people doing this, when it's such great fun to do it yourself?'

Nastiya laughed delightedly. 'I love you, Hector Cross! You can be so wise and funny.'

'Fast forward please, Dave,' Hector insisted, and Dave shrugged.

'Okay, but I warn you that you are going to miss a load of good stuff.'

The movements of the couple on the screen became as jerky and frantically rapid as those in a Charlie Chaplin black-and-white movie from the 1920s. The sound was squeaky and unintelligible.

Nastiya started giggling and that set them all off. At last Dave Imbiss controlled his laughter sufficiently to warn them, 'Okay, quiet please, the lot of you! Here comes the moment we have all been waiting for!'

The action calmed down into real time and Aleutian spoke out clearly.

'Brace yourself, you little beauty! Here comes the deadly African black snake!'

'Oh yes, Aleutian! Give it all to me, Aleutian, you dirty bastard, you!'

'There you are!' Dave Imbiss said smugly. 'Ask for the name and Imbiss gives it to you not once but twice. That's what I call real service.' He reached across and switched off the video.

Hector broke the silence that followed. 'That girl hasn't been very well brought up.' He gave his opinion gravely. 'Did you notice that at the end there she didn't even say please?' He stood up and went to the podium. He thrust his hands into his pockets and turned to face them.

'Great work, Dave. You never let me down. Right now you have made Victoria Vusamazulu the hottest property in town. She is our only conduit to Aleutian. We have to keep her on the boil.' He looked at Nastiya. 'Your job, I'm afraid, Nazzy.'

'Me?' She looked surprised. 'It doesn't seem to me that Victoria shows any signs of lesbian tendencies.'

'You know as well as I do that a woman is much more open to a friendly approach from another woman than from a man. She doesn't expect a pass. I want you and Vicky to become soul sisters. That way we stay close to Aleutian.'

'Okay.' Nastiya shrugged. 'What do you want me to do?'

Hector turned to Dave. 'Give me the girl's iPhone, please.'

Dave passed it to him and Hector switched it on and dialled in a number.

'I am dialling my own iPhone,' he explained. As soon as the ring tone sounded he switched on the speaker, and cautioned the others to silence.

'Hello. Hector Cross's phone. Victoria Vusamazulu speaking.'

'This is Hector Cross, Vicky. Do you still need your iPhone this evening rather than tomorrow? I think I can arrange that.'

'Oh, yes please, Mr Cross,' she exclaimed enthusiastically. 'That would be wonderful. I am totally lost without it.'

'Good. My secretary is going off duty now. I will put her in a taxi and send her to you. She will deliver it to you.'

'Thank you. Thank you so very much, sir.'

'I take it that you are at home by now. What is your address?'

'Yes, I am in my flat in Richmond. The address is Forty-seven Gardens Lane and the postcode is TW9 5LA. Tell the cabby it's on the corner with Kew Gardens Road. It's about three hundred yards down the road from the Kew Gardens tube station.'

'That's fine. My secretary's name is Natasha Voronov. She is a blonde Russian lady. She should be with you in thirty or forty minutes.'

He broke the connection and handed the iPhone to Nastiya. 'Off you go, tsarina. Victoria is waiting for you. Take your time. We'll keep dinner for you.' He paused a moment and then went on. 'I tell you what; stop at an off-licence on your way. Get Vicky a decent bottle of wine. Tell her that it's a present from me. A big apology for stealing her phone. She might invite you to share the bottle with her. She is probably lonely now that Aleutian has vanished from the scene. Get chummy with her, get her to share her girlie secrets with you. Most likely she will want to complain about Aleutian, and tell you what an utter bastard he is. You can complain about Paddy and tell her what an utter bastard he is. The two of you should have a great time.'

'I like that suggestion,' Nazzy agreed.

Nastiya returned from her visit to Victoria's flat an hour late for dinner. The three men were dressed in mess kit and waiting for her in the living room. All three of them were on their second whiskies. They stood up as she appeared in the doorway.

'So, how did it go, my lovely?' Paddy beat the others to the question.

'Let me go up and change first. I won't be a minute and then I will come down and tell you the full story.'

When she came down the staircase again they all realized it had been worth the wait. She was wearing her diamonds and she was gorgeous. As the host, Hector took her hand and led her into the dining room. The first course was grilled Dover sole served off the bone with wild girolles from Provence smothered in saffron sauce.

The food held them in respectful silence for another few minutes, then Nastiya sighed with pleasure and dabbed her lips with her napkin before she spoke.

'She is a sweet child, this Victoria. I like her. Of course she is very naïve and crazy about men, like every healthy girl of her age. But she is not really bad. She drank two glasses of the wine and she thinks that now I am her new best friend. She is lonely like Hector says. She wants someone to talk to. In the end it was not easy for me to get away from her. She thinks this Aleutian character is going to come back from America and marry her.'

'So that's where he has disappeared to. It fits in with his accent and his tattoo. Does she know that he was involved in Hazel's murder?'

Nastiya was firm and certain in her reply. 'I am sure she does not. Of course, I could not press her on the subject, but knowing I work for Hector, she brought up the subject herself. She knew all about the murder of Hazel from the TV and papers. But she never made the connection to Aleutian. Aleutian told her that he is a big wheel in the oil business in California. He asked her to help him set up a meeting with Hazel. He wanted to interest Bannock Oil and Hazel in some kind of deal he is brewing up. He asked Victoria to let him know when Hazel left Doctor Donnovan's clinic that day so he could wait to meet her, accidentally on purpose. I told you, Vicky is very naïve and a little bit stupid. But I like her.'

'So I suppose we are not going to snatch Vicky and make her warble?' Paddy looked at Hector. 'I am disappointed. That could have been fun.'

Hector smiled and replied, 'I am pretty damn sure Nastiya is correct. This girl is a patsy. She isn't very bright and she knows nothing. But there is a chance that Aleutian might come back for another taste of the good stuff she dishes out so freely. That is about the only use she is to him or to us now. Do you know if Vicky has his current telephone number or any other contact details?'

'I asked her, but she only has the number we got from her iPhone. She says he never answers her calls. She thinks that's only because he does not have roaming on his phone in the USA. All she knows is that he promised he would come back and then they would shack up together. She trusts him to keep his word.'

'Keep in contact with her please, Nazzy. It might just happen.'

'So what do we do until then, boss?' Dave Imbiss asked. 'Have we hit another dead end, or what?' They all looked at him but Hector did not answer at once. He took a sip from his wine glass and rolled it around his tongue.

'This Chablis really goes so well with the sole.'

'We all know that you are a great connoisseur, but that does not really answer David's question,' Nastiya pointed out.

Hector was saved by the reappearance of Stephen, his butler, and he turned to him with mild relief. 'What is it, Stephen?'

'I am sorry to bother you, sir. But there is a gentleman at the front door. Well, to be truthful, sir, I think he is more a scruffy youth than a gentleman. I tried to send him away but he is very insistent. He says that he has been sent to you by somebody named Sam Mucker. He said you would know who he means. He says it's a matter of life and death; those were his exact words.' Hector thought about it for a moment.

'Sam Mucker? I do not have the faintest idea what he is talking about. It's after ten o'clock and we are in the middle of dinner. Please, Stephen, tell the fellow to kindly piss off.'

'It will be a pleasure, Mr Cross.' Stephen smothered a grin and headed back to the door with a firm and determined step. As he closed the door behind him Hector suddenly leapt from his chair at the head of the table.

'Shit!' he cried. 'He means Aazim Muktar! Stephen, come back here at once!'

The door reopened and Stephen stood to attention in the doorway. 'You called, sir?'

'I did indeed. Change of plan; please take the gentleman to the library and offer him a drink. Treat him like a gentleman no matter what. Be kind to him. Tell him I will be with him right away.' Hector turned back to Dave. 'No, young David, my lad. I don't think we have hit another dead end. In fact, I think the real fun may just be about to begin.' He rang for the footman and told him, 'Ask Chef to keep the rest of this excellent meal in the warmer for me.' Then he stood up and told the others, 'Don't wait for me, I might be a little while.' And he left the dining room and went to the library.

The fewer people who got a look at Aazim Muktar's agent, the better for all of them.

T he visitor stood in front of the fireplace warming his back. He had a Coke can in one hand and Hector saw at once why Stephen had taken exception to him. He was unshaven and his hair was matted and greasy. His jeans were tattered and had probably never seen the interior of a washing machine. His mouth was sullen and his manner hangdog. Everything about him proclaimed that here was one of life's rejects, one of the losers.

Hector went to him and offered his hand. 'Hello, I am Hector Cross.' The boy took Hector's hand without hesitation. His eyes were light brown, friendly and intelligent, completely at odds with the rest of his appearance.

'I know. I googled you, Mr Cross. Very impressive you are too. I am Yaf Said, but I used to be Rupert Marsh before I found Allah.' His voice was pleasant and decisive.

'So what do I call you?'

'Take your pick, sir.'

'Yaf means friend. I'll call you that, okay?'

'Okay, I would like that, sir.'

'Take a seat, Yaf,' Hector invited him and he set an example by sinking into one of the leather armchairs.

'The fire is good, sir.' Yaf declined. 'It was cold on my bike. Besides, I prefer to stand in the presence of my elders and betters.'

Hector blinked with surprise. *This kid has got class*, he thought, and Yaf seemed to read his mind.

'Please excuse my hair and beard, and my general turn-out. This is my working kit.'

'Aazim Muktar told me that you help other kids find the road they've lost.'

Yaf's face lit up at the name. 'Just the same as Aazim Muktar did for me. When I wandered into his mosque I was a wreck, a total wreck. I was sick of life, sick of myself and full of drugs. He showed me the way and turned me around. He is a truly great man. A great and holy man.' He grinned sheepishly. 'Hey! Sorry, Mr Cross. I sound like a TV commercial!'

'I know how you feel. I am also one of his fans.'

'Aazim Muktar tells me you are looking for a man. He didn't tell me why, and I am not going to ask.'

'For what it's worth, the name of the person I want is Aleutian,' Hector said, and Yaf smiled.

'Out there in the netherworld, names mean either not much or nothing at all. Do you know what he looks like, sir?'

'I have pictures of him,' Hector confirmed.

'You have made my day, sir. Pics will make the job a cinch. May I see them, please?'

'I will get them for you. It may take a little time.' Hector stood up. 'When did you last eat, Yaf? You look pretty skinny to me.'

'I don't get much time to eat out there.'

'Well, you've got time now. I'll have the cook send you a stack of sandwiches and a bowl of chips with ketchup.'

'Thank you, sir. That sounds great. But please, no meat. I am a veggie.'

'Eggs and cheese?'

'Both those are good.'

Within an hour Dave had printed a dozen stills from Vicky's videos and Hector took them back to the library where Yaf had just demolished a platter of cheese, tomato and Marmite sandwiches and was busy with the hard-boiled eggs and the bowl of chips. He sprang to his feet when Hector walked into the library again.

'Those were the best sandwiches I have eaten in the fifteen years since my mum died and I took to the streets.' To Hector he did not look much older than twenty-five. So he must have been living rough since he was ten.

'What about your dad?' he asked, and Yaf smiled ruefully.

'Never knew him. I don't think even my mum knew much about him either. Maybe I am one of those lucky guys who have only one mother but twenty-five putative fathers. I just don't know.'

Hector smiled at this brave little jest and handed the prints to him. 'Take a look at these, and see what you make of them. But do me a favour and sit down, will you? You're making me nervous, Yaf.'

Yaf sat on the edge of the chair facing Hector and thumbed through Dave's prints, examining each of them carefully.

'You see the tattoo he is wearing?' Hector asked.

'Yeah, that's a Maalik gang mark. He must be a made man.' At last he looked up at Hector and said, 'I am sorry, sir. I don't know this guy but he looks like bad news.'

Then he saw Hector's disappointment and he hurried on. 'But please don't worry about it, sir. If he is within fifty miles of London I will find him. I will have a lot of eyes on the street looking out for him. Can you give me a number where I can call you in a hurry? Guys like this move around fast, like cruising tiger sharks.'

'When you do have a contact, you can call me on this number.' Hector went to his desk and scribbled his iPhone number on a blank card. 'You can get me wherever I am on the globe. Call me reverse charges.' He handed the card to Yaf.

Hector walked to the front door with Yaf and watched him climb onto his BWs 125cc scooter and putter away out of the gates.

'Probably never see him again, but you never know.'

He tried to put the lad out of his mind. However, over the next few days Yaf kept wheedling his way back into Hector's thoughts; even when he was trying to concentrate on reading through Hazel's documentation.

'This is a cocked-up society when the bankers pull in multi-million-pound bonuses and good kids can't find a job and so they rot on the streets and turn bad. We have a shit storm brewing up out there,' he observed to Paddy one day.

It made him think about Catherine Cayla and what the world had in store for her further down the line. He realized how much he had missed his daughter and how desperately he needed to see her again. So a few days later he took Paddy, Nastiya and Dave Imbiss and they all flew back to Abu Zara.

'We have been a very good little girl, Daddy. We have put on almost a whole pound since you went away.' Bonnie placed Catherine in his arms the moment he entered the lobby of the Seascape penthouse. 'But we have missed our daddy so much, haven't we, baby?'

Hector's ear was slightly out of tune to this variety of nursery talk and he was not quite sure who had missed whom, but he hoped it was not the way Bonnie made it sound.

Hector's arrival was just in time to allow him to give Catherine her bottle and put her into her cot. The next morning he placed her in a modern version of the papoose, a cocoon made of nylon on an aluminium frame, ergonomically designed to protect and cosset an infant. Dave Imbiss had obtained from somewhere this high-tech baby carrier for him. When it was strapped to his chest Hector could watch Catherine's face as he ran. Or he could strap it on his back so Catherine could look over his shoulder.

He took her for a ten-mile run along the beachfront. She seemed to enjoy the rocking motion, at least she made no audible protest; rather she slept the whole way and only woke up when they returned home with an appetite like a lion cub. She had missed her feed, as Bonnie announced to the world in stentorian and disapproving tones.

The days settled into a quiet but not unpleasant routine. Of course Paddy and Nastiya had their own apartment in Abu Zara City. They both worked out of Cross Bow headquarters in the same building, although days might pass without them meeting. However, Paddy phoned Hector every evening to discuss developments; but there were few of these and none of any great significance.

At least twice a week Nastiya invited Hector to dinner at their apartment or at one of the many five-star restaurants in the city. Always there would be one of Nastiya's guests in the company: young, female, nubile and unmarried. It was amazing where she found so many of them. She must have trawled the cabin crews of all the airlines, the offices of the secretarial staff of the British and American embassies and the major global companies operating in the city. Even when Hector adroitly side-stepped these obvious man traps, Nastiya never gave up trying. It became a friendly game between them. Paddy looked on with an amused air.

Dave Imbiss spent many hours each day at the Seascape penthouse checking and improving the security arrangements surrounding Catherine Cayla, and making certain that his men stayed alert and at the top of their game. Baby Catherine was never left alone. One of her three nursemaids was by her side every minute of the day and night. There was always an armed guard outside the nursery door, and another Cross Bow team in the CCTV monitor room down the passage watching all the entrances to the apartments and the interior of the nursery on the screens.

Hector ate breakfast with Catherine at six every morning. He waded into the bacon and eggs but she stayed with her bottle. Afterwards he took her for their constitutional run along the beachfront. When they returned to the penthouse he handed her over to her nurses and spent the rest of the morning perusing the poignant records of Hazel's life.

For Hector, the principal and most fascinating of these were her diaries. These were the only documents of Hazel's that Agatha had not digitized. Hazel had started writing them up from her fourteenth birthday. There were over twenty identical black booklets in her collection, one for each year of her life after puberty.

The diaries were written in a minute script, and strewn with her codes and secret writing. It took all of his imagination and ingenuity to break some of her codes. She had recorded every detail of her life, both trivial and apocalyptic. Hector was enthralled. He had already learned as much about her as he had ever dreamed was feasible. But here were her boasts and her confessions written in her own hand. She even described with relish the loss of her virginity on her fifteenth birthday, to her tennis coach on the back seat of his old Ford. This gave Hector a stab of jealousy.

'The randy bastard was almost thirty years older than my innocent little baby. He should have been locked up for what he did to her. Bloody paedophile!' Then he consoled himself with the thought that the bloody paedophile was probably fat, bald and impotent by now, and that Hazel had patently enjoyed the experience. He shuffled through the diaries, skipping the intervening years until he came to the day of their first meeting.

This was one of the pivotal points in his own existence. He could never forget a single detail of it. It had taken place at the Bannock Oil installation here in the Abu Zarian desert. With the other top brass of Bannock Oil he had waited for her arrival in a blustering sandstorm. Her helicopter had appeared out of the looming dun sand clouds. He recalled how when it landed and she appeared in the door of the fuselage he had been unprepared for the jolt of lightning that flashed up his spine. She had been so goddamned magnificent.

On that first day she had treated him in an off-handed manner, which made him furious. He was unaccustomed to being spurned. Hated? Yes, but never so casually dismissed.

Now at last he was able to read her own thoughts on that fateful day.

She had described him as *all attitude, testosterone and muscles. I pray to God that one day he will forgive me for finding such an obnoxious oaf to be quite cute and very sexy.*

Six weeks after his arrival in Abu Zara Hector was awoken by the ringing of his iPhone. He rolled over and switched on the bedside light, and then he glanced at the alarm clock. It was ten minutes to four in the morning. He picked up the phone.

'Cross,' he spoke into the mouthpiece.

'It's me. Yaf!'

Hector sat up quickly. 'Tell me!' he said.

'He is here. But you better come quickly. He is moving about a lot. No telling when he will disappear again.'

'What is your time in London?'

'Just before midnight,' Yaf replied. Hector made a quick calculation.

'Okay!' he said. 'I'll be there around about eleven a.m. your time tomorrow. Go to my home in the morning and wait for me. I will tell my butler to let you in and my chef will give you a slap-up breakfast.' He rang off and called Paddy's apartment. Nastiya's sleepy voice answered.

'This can only be Hector Cross!' she said.

'Good guess,' he commended her. 'Aleutian has shown up in London. Tell that lover boy in bed with you to get his pants on. Tell him to requisition the Bannock Oil G5 for an immediate and urgent to Farnborough. Tell them to rouse the pilots out of bed if needs be. We are going after the murderous bastard.'

Hector left Dave Imbiss at Seascape Mansions to command Catherine's guards. The rest of them in the G5 took off from Abu Zara at 0843 and touched down at Farnborough five hours later. Hector's chauffeur drove out onto the tarmac to pick them up. A little over an hour later they parked in the underground garage of No. 11. Yaf Said was waiting in the kitchens where he had struck up a friendship with Cynthia, the chef. She was fattening him up on her famous chocolate pudding and ice cream. He dropped his spoon and rushed up the stairs when he heard Hector's voice.

Hector introduced him to Paddy and Nastiya, and then called an immediate council of war in the library. At Hector's invitation Yaf outlined what had taken place in their absence.

'I had been getting reports about Aleutian for the last couple of weeks; mostly from nightclubs in the central London area. But every time I followed it up it turned out to be a false sighting or the mark had disappeared by the time I reached the scene. Then I scored a positive hit in a place called Fusion Fire. It's a pretty flash dive, strobe lighting and mirrors, lots of dealers and whores lurking about, but the music is wild. I got up real close to Aleutian at the bar. He was drinking with three other black guys, and I checked out his tattoo. It was the guy you want, no question about it. But his pals were calling him Oscar, not Aleutian.'

'When was that?' Hector asked.

'Friday two weeks ago. I didn't want to call you right away. It might have been a one-off appearance. I waited for him there for the next four nights. But he didn't show again. So I put my people into all the clubs in the area. We found him hanging out in two other joints over the next week, and then he popped up at Fusion again, two days in a row. That's when I called you. My thinking is that he is moving around, changing his digs every day. There is no pattern to his movements. You should stake out all the clubs where he has been spotted recently. He seems to be a creature of habit. I think that's your best chance of catching up with him.'

'Makes sense,' Hector agreed. 'But what about you, Yaf?'

Yaf looked uncomfortable, and it took him a little time to gather his courage and speak out.

'I was happy to tell you where you may be able to find this fellow, but I don't want to be there when you do find him. I gave up all that rough stuff a long time ago when Allah took me under his wing. No offence, Mr Cross. It's been a great pleasure to meet a man like you, but now I think I should leave you to go about your own busi-ness and I'll go about mine.'

'Thank you again, Yaf. It's probably a wise decision you are making. It has also been a pleasure for me to meet you. You reaffirm my faith in the younger generation. If ever I can help you in any way you know where to find me. In the meantime, can I pay you for your time and trouble?'

Yaf held up both hands in alarm. 'No, please. I didn't do this for money. I did it for a great and holy man.'

'Very well, Yaf. But there must be some charity run by your mosque to which I can make a contribution.'

'Well, sir, to tell the truth we do get a lot of our funding from the Muslim Youthwork Foundation,' Yaf replied diffidently. 'You could make a contribution online. You don't have to give your name.'

'I will do that in your name,' Hector assured him.

'Thank you, sir. It isn't necessary, but I assure you that the money will be very well spent.' Yaf reached into the pocket of his hoodie jacket and brought out a slip of paper. 'Here's a list of all the joints where we have spotted Aleutian. He usually shows up in one of them around midnight if he shows up at all, but then he stays until dawn. I hope you find what you are looking for, sir.'

Hector walked with him to the front door and told him, 'I hope our friendship does not end here, Yaf. Any time you are passing, please drop in. If I am not here then Cynthia, in the kitchen, will always rustle you up a cup of coffee and a bite. I'll tell her you are always welcome.'

'That's kind of you, sir. Goodbye and *ma'a salama*.' They shook hands and then Hector watched him straddle his motor scooter and ride away. He knew he would never see him again. Yaf was his own man, too proud to come around begging.

'Okay, the three clubs on Yaf Said's list are Fusion Fire, the Rabid Dog and the Portals of Paradise, all in the central London area, from Soho to Elephant and Castle. I don't know any of these joints, do either of you?' Hector looked at Nastiya first.

'No, not quite my style,' she retorted primly.

'What about you, Paddy?'

'No, but they sound like a great deal of fun.'

'Here is how we should go about this. I have checked the location of all three clubs on the internet. They are scattered over quite a large area; a good few miles apart. We will have to split up to cover all three of them. As Yaf has told us, it's no use starting the search before midnight. We have to go on the late-night shift. If one of us makes a positive ID then he or she calls the team together. We keep Aleutian under observation and follow him when he leaves the club. One of us will be driving the Q-car. At that time of the morning the streets should be pretty much empty. As soon as we get him alone and unobserved we slip him the Hypnos.'

The Hypnos was a tiny self-contained hypodermic syringe which could be palmed in one hand, or concealed in the seam of a jacket sleeve. It was made of a type of PVC which could not be detected by X-ray or any other screening device. The barrel was green in colour. The non-metallic needle was primed by flicking off the protective cover with a thumb. The needle was a mere 2cm in length and needed only to pierce the skin to deliver 2cc of a powerful knock-down drug which almost instantly rendered the subject totally paralysed. It was named for the Greek goddess of sleep.

It was impossible to obtain supplies of these weapons unless, like Dave Imbiss, you had contacts in the Chemical Warfare Division of the US Military.

'Then as soon as Aleutian goes down we bundle him into the Q-car and bring him back here,' Hector went on outlining the plan. 'By the way, the basement is soundproof and there is a room down there where I clean my fishing tackle, but it will make a very good interrogation room. We will have all the right equipment on hand. The walls and the floor are tiled and easy to hose down. If the water-board does not convince him, we might have to make a bit of a mess before Aleutian feels the urge to speak out, and give us the name of his employer. When we have finished with him we pack what's left of him into an airtight and waterproof fish box and export him to Abu Zara in the G5. If we choose the right take-off slot there shouldn't be any worries about customs wanting to look inside the box. At the other end Dave Imbiss will take Aleutian out to one of the oil-exploration teams that are drilling in the new Zara Number Twelve concession. Aleutian goes down the drill hole that presently is at the sixteen-thousand-foot mark, and then he comes up again in the slurry minced into a fine paste by the rotary diamond drill bit.'

He gave them a wolfish grin and went on. 'I know that it is a fairly sketchy battle plan, but I also know that you two are pretty damn good at improvising according to changing circumstances.'

He checked his wristwatch and stood up. 'We have an hour to change for dinner. I know Chef has something special lined up for us, but tragically there will be no wine served with it. We want to be bright and razor sharp for later in the evening. After dinner I plan a couple of hours' shut-eye. Then we will reassemble around eleven p.m. It will take an hour or more to get into our positions. I think Nastiya should go to the Portals of Paradise, for obvious reasons. Paddy will take the Rabid Dog for equally obvious reasons. I will stake out Fusion Fire, for no good reason that I can think of.'

'I imagine there are a few dolly-birds from your flaming past who could supply us with ample reasons,' Nastiya suggested.

Hector went up to his dressing room and opened the secret door behind the fireplace. From one of the open shelves he took down the box which contained his pistol, already in its shoulder holster. He pulled on a pair of surgical rubber gloves and wiped the weapon down carefully to remove his own fingerprints. Then he reloaded the magazine with the special ammunition that Dave had supplied. Finally, he wiped the pistol down a second time, just to be sure it was clean. He had calculated the odds for and against carrying the weapon tonight. It was a serious offence if the authorities found it on him, but he might be taking an even greater risk to go up against someone of the calibre of Aleutian with just his bare hands.

They dropped Nastiya at the Portals of Paradise a few minutes after midnight. The entrance was discreetly set in a narrow mews. There was a small crowd of excited young people grouped around the door. A pair of large and aggressive doormen barred their entrance to the premises, while an urbane door manager in dinner jacket and black tie made his selection of those he deemed worthy to enter such hallowed premises.

Hector parked the Q-car at the entrance to the mews, and he and Paddy watched Nastiya alight and head towards the club entrance.

The door manager spotted Nastiya as soon as she entered the mews. She was wearing a crimson sheath that clung to all her protuberances, and six-inch stiletto heels that put the fine muscles in her calves under tension. Her appearance stilled the clamour of the throng at the entrance to the club pleading to be allowed in. Their ranks parted and they watched in awed silence as she passed through. The door manager rushed forward to greet her and took her arm with an unctuous smile of welcome. He escorted her to the entrance, handed her over the threshold and told the girl at the box office, 'The lady is a guest of the house. Make sure she gets the best available table.'

Watching from the back seat of the Q-car, Paddy O'Quinn worried, 'I hope she is going to be all right. There is some queasy-making trash in that mob.'

Hector burst out laughing. 'You have to be kidding, Paddy. The only person I feel sorry for is any bloke who tries to mess with that lady of yours.'

He started the engine and drove on another two miles to the Rabid Dog.

'Okay, Paddy, this is your kennel. Keep your legs crossed and don't take any rubber cheques.' He watched Paddy slip the doorman a ten-pound note and disappear through the dark curtains that covered the entrance.

It was another mile back to the Fusion Fire. The club extended over two levels. Its façade was all floor-to-ceiling plate-glass windows facing the road. Through the windows he could see that the interiors were brightly lit by revolving towers of myriad-colour strobe lights. The ceilings were clad with mirrored tiles that reflected the flashing lights and the figures of the dancers on the floors below. The dancers were packed as tightly as shoals of glittering tropical fish, driven by the booming pulse of the music into a savage frenzy.

He drove past slowly, parked on the next corner and walked back to the entrance of the club. He was wearing dark aviator glasses and a gold brocade Nehru jacket with cut-out sleeves that Nastiya had chosen for him. They had deliberately chosen outlandish costume to make themselves appear kinky and effete. Nobody would think they were storm-troopers and take fright. Hector paid a hundred pounds for a VIP table.

He sat at the table and looked around the huge room. He recognized it immediately as the background to one of the videos that Vicky Vusamazulu had shot of Aleutian on her iPhone. That gave him encouragement. If Aleutian had hung out here before, there was a stronger possibility that he might return here again.

Within twenty minutes he had five different young ladies approach him one after the other, to offer everything from a fifty-pound under-the-table blow job to a five-hundred-pound all-nighter. All of which he declined with thanks.

By five twenty in the morning the crowds on the dance floor had thinned, and there was still no sign of anyone who even vaguely resembled Aleutian. So he went down to the Q-car and drove to the Rabid Dog to pick up Paddy.

'How did it go, old son?' he asked as Paddy climbed into the seat beside him.

'If I had smoked, sniffed and swallowed everything I was offered tonight I would be flying higher than the morning star up there.'

They drove on to the Portals of Paradise and when Nastiya appeared she looked as though she had spent the time in a beauty salon.

'No luck, Queen of my Heart?' Paddy enquired anxiously.

'I could have made a fortune. One dear old man of about ninety offered me ten thousand pounds for just a look and no touch.'

'You should have taken the offer,' Paddy told her, and she gave him a level stare through eyes that were as frosty blue as a tundra sky. When they got back to No. 11 all three of them slept until noon.

The next night was a repetition of the first. Only the clientele in the clubs had changed.

On the third night Hector strolled into the bedlam of Fusion Fire a little after midnight. It was Saturday night and it was shoulder to shoulder on the dance floor. The volume of the music numbed the senses. The huge mirrored light balls suspended from the ceiling bounced in time to the pounding feet of the dancers below.

So as to blend into the scenery, Hector was wearing a black satin Spanish bolero jacket over a frilled white shirt and a black string tie. His toreador sequinned pants were skin tight. Once again this costume had been assembled for him by Nastiya. He seated himself at his usual table and a girl in a mini-skirt with a pretty pixie face and pouting lips, who he had never seen before, immediately plumped herself down on his lap.

'You are so gorgeous I want to marry you,' she told him. 'You are rich, aren't you?'

'I am a multimillionaire,' he told her gravely.

'Oh my God!' she said breathlessly. 'I swear to God that you've just made me come.'

He found her really quite amusing. He laughed and glanced over her shoulder and looked straight at the dark sullen face that he remembered so well from Victoria Vusamazulu's videos.

Aleutian was standing on the far side of the dance floor, at the top of the stairs that led down to the entrance lobby. He was with a girl who was looking up at him but her face was turned away from Hector. Aleutian was looking down at her patronizingly. Although the crowd swirled around the pair he stood a full head above any of them. This was how Hector had picked him out so readily. He stared at him for a few seconds only, making utterly certain he had the right man, but even that was too long.

If you stare intently at a wild animal in the jungle it will often sense your gaze and react to it. Aleutian was just that, a savage predator in his own domain. His eyes flashed up from the girl's face and his gaze locked with Hector's. He recognized Hector instantly. He whirled and darted away down the staircase.

Hector jumped to his feet, dumping the girl from his lap in a heap at his feet. He jumped over her and ran onto the dance floor and fought his way through the dancers to the head of the stairs down which Aleutian had disappeared.

The stairs were almost as crowded as the dance floor. When Hector reached the entrance door and burst through it into the street there was no sign of him. Hector checked the blind instinct to rush through the dark streets searching at random.

He thought of the girl Aleutian had been with. Perhaps he could find her. Perhaps she could point him to where Aleutian was holing up. He abandoned that idea in the same instant as it came to him. Fusion Fire was overflowing with dollies like her. He had not even seen her face. He would never recognize her in the pack. Anyway, she was probably a hooker that Aleutian had picked up this very same evening.

How did Aleutian get here? Car? Taxi? If so, he is already long gone. He was thinking furiously. *Underground? Yes, of course!*

He knew from his online research that the north bank entrance to Blackfriars station was perhaps four hundred yards from where he now stood. He started to run. He raced to the first corner and saw the entrance to the station at the end of the block ahead. The street was almost deserted at this hour. There was only a handful of late-night revellers making their way homeward. One of these was Aleutian. He was sprinting away from Hector towards the tube station. As Hector started in pursuit Aleutian reached the entrance and disappeared like a jack rabbit into its warren. Hector followed him into the entrance. He went down the stairs three at a time with his footsteps echoing in an empty tunnel. He reached the T-junction at the bottom. The left-hand tunnel was signposted Richmond and the right was signed Upminster. He had no way of telling which one Aleutian had chosen. At random, he started down the right-hand tunnel and then he heard a train rumbling in on the Richmond line. He spun around and raced in that direction. He came out on the landing and looked down on the platform. The train was already standing stationary and the doors were open. There was a small crowd of late-night commuters and revellers climbing aboard. Hector saw at once that his hunch had been good. Aleutian was pushing his way through the other passengers. Hector watched him clamber into one of the carriages.

Hector started down the last flight of stairs, but before he was halfway to the platform the doors closed and the train pulled away. As the carriages slid by, Hector saw Aleutian standing at one of the windows looking up at him. Hector reached for the pistol in its concealed shoulder holster. Then he checked himself. The angle and the range were extreme. Aleutian was closely surrounded by other passengers. Hector dared not take the risk of hitting one of them as the train accelerated away.

Aleutian knew he was safe. He grinned up at Hector. It was a sardonic grimace, filled with menace. Hector's skin crawled. He was looking into the eyes of Hazel's murderer. His legs trembled under him with the strength of his emotions. It took him a few seconds after the train had disappeared into the mouth of the tunnel before he could force himself to think dispassionately again.

He spun around and raced back the way he had come, but he knew that it would take at least ten minutes to reach the parked Q-car. The train was carrying Aleutian away at forty miles an hour.

Aleutian's lead was far too great for him to ever catch up, even in the Q-car. He had to phone ahead and get Paddy or Nastiya to head him off. But there were a dozen or more stops where Aleutian could jump off the train before it reached the terminal at Richmond. It wasn't possible to cover them all.

But, he was missing something. He knew he was missing something as he stormed back up the tunnel to ground level.

Think! he exhorted himself. *Lead with your brain and not your balls. Where is the bastard heading for?*

He burst out of the tunnel and into the street before it hit him. It stopped him in his tracks. Then he reached for his phone and punched in Nastiya's number. It rang interminably, but he held it to his ear as he raced on at top speed.

Vicky Vusamazulu is the key. He knew it with crystal clarity. *I could almost see Aleutian making the connection. With the instinct of a fox he sensed immediately that he had been betrayed. He knew that the odds of me stumbling onto him in Fusion Fire by blind chance were astronomical. He knows that someone had put me onto him. He knows that Vicky is the only one who knew both of us. She was the only one who knew that he frequented Fusion Fire. It didn't take much for him to work out that she is the only one who could have given me the lead. The odds are ten to one on that he is on his way to revenge himself on Vicky right this minute. Come on, Nazzy sweetheart. Answer your bloody phone.*

'Hector, where are you?' Nastiya asked suddenly.

'I have spooked Aleutian. He made a break, and got clean away from me. My best bet is he's on his way to Vicky. You remember Vicky's address, don't you?'

'Forty-seven Gardens Lane and the postcode is TW9 5LA. It's about three hundred yards down the road from the Kew Gardens tube station.' Nastiya's reply was quick and sharp. She was a pro.

'At this moment Aleutian is on a train heading directly for Kew Gardens. You are much closer than we are. You can get to Vicky long before we will ever make it. Take a cab. Paddy and I will back you up as soon as we can. Just make it fast, Nazzy. Your pal Vicky is a sitting duck, and that bastard is a killer.' The phone went dead against his ear. Nastiya was always sparing with her words.

He dialled Paddy and spoke to him while he ran for the Q-car.

'Paddy, wait for me outside the Rabid Dog. I'll be there in twenty minutes, maybe less.'

'What's going on?'

'Aleutian showed up, but I made a right royal balls-up. He's bolted and he's running. Tell you more when I see you.'

Fifteen minutes later, Paddy whipped open the front door of the Q-car and jumped into the passenger seat before Hector came to a full halt. Hector hit the accelerator and powered away again.

'Forty-seven Gardens Lane, TW9 5LA. That's Vicky's address. Punch it into the satnav, Paddy. I am damned sure that's where Aleutian is headed.'

The insistent chimes of the front door of her apartment woke Vicky Vusamazulu. She sat up in bed groggily. She had taken a sleeping tablet. She glanced at the luminous dial of the bedside clock. It was almost two o'clock in the morning.

Thank God that Mrs Church is stone deaf. Vicky tried to knuckle the sleep out of her eyes. Mrs Church was her landlady. She lived upstairs and Vicky knew from experience that she switched off her hearing aid when she went to bed. She was such a strict and mean old harridan that Vicky was her only tenant.

The doorbell rang again. Vicky switched on the lights, threw back the bedclothes, swung her legs over the side of the bed and stood up. She was wearing short pyjamas in a bright floral pattern. She stumbled into the passage and went down to the door at the end.

She checked that the two safety chains were fastened securely before she went up on tip toe to peer through the peephole. The visitor outside was standing with his back to her.

'Who is it?' she called irritably. He turned back to face her and she recognized him.

She gasped with shock and delight and she came fully awake. She had not even known that Aleutian was back in town.

'Open the door, bitch,' he said.

'Aleutian! Oh God! Is it really you? I thought you were never coming back.' She was so excited that she fumbled with the safety chains. 'Wait! Don't go away. It won't take me a second. Wait, Aleutian, my darling.'

She got it open at last and ran out to embrace him, but he pushed her aside and strode into her apartment. He walked down the passage towards her bedroom without looking back at her. She shut the front door but did not waste time re-securing the safety chains. Then she ran after him.

'I thought you were never coming back. I should never have doubted you. I knew you would keep your word. I missed you. I missed you so very much.' She was babbling with excitement.

He was sitting on the bed. He was watching her with a strange expression on his face.

'Have you been good while I was away?'

'Oh yes, yes. I stayed at home every night waiting for you. I never even looked at another man. I love you so much.'

'You are lying to me,' he said in that special soft and deadly tone of his that made her tremble. 'I think you have been a bad little bitch. I think that I am going to have to punish you.'

She knew this game so well that her nipples came erect under the thin stuff of her pyjama top.

'Take off your pyjamas!' he commanded and she pulled the top off over her head, bundled it and threw it onto the bed beside where he was sitting. Then she pulled her short panties down over her hips and let them fall around her ankles. She kicked them away, and stood naked before him.

'Are you going to beat me, Aleutian?' she asked fearfully and covered her pubes with cupped hands.

'Take your hands away and come here.' He crooked one finger at her and she came and stood close in front of him. 'Open your legs, bitch.'

She moved her feet apart. He leaned forward and put his hand between her thighs. 'Open wider!' he ordered.

She could feel his finger wriggling into her and she wanted it so badly. She thrust her hips towards him and she felt him touch the mouth of her womb.

'You are as slimy as a bucket of eels down there, you dirty bitch,' he said. 'But do you understand that I have to punish you, because you have been so bad?'

'Yes, I understand.'

'Master. You call me Master. Or have you forgotten?' He did something with his finger that was so painful it made her whimper. It felt as though he had torn something inside her. Her eyes opened wide with the pain. But the pain felt so good that she was already close to the point of her first orgasm.

'Yes, I understand, Master.'

He slid his finger out of her and held it up in front of her face. 'Now, look what you have done, you dirty little whore. You have made my nice clean finger dirty with your filthy pussy.'

'I am sorry, Master. I didn't mean to do that.'

'Get down on your knees,' he ordered and she dropped down in front of him. He held out his finger towards her. 'Suck it clean.' She took it into her mouth. He forced it down her throat; so far that her shoulders heaved with the gagging reflex.

'Admit it; you have been really bad while I was away, haven't you?'

She made incoherent sounds of denial. Her face was swelling as she suffocated. He leaned back and pulled his finger out of her throat. She sobbed with relief, and her whole body convulsed with the effort as she struggled for air. She looked up at him and her eyes were bloodshot and streaming with tears.

He took his hand out from behind his back and she realized that he held a flick knife. He pressed the release button and the blade snapped out under her nose. It was seven inches long and bright as a sunbeam.

This was something new. He had never shown her this knife before. She tried to back away on her knees, but he picked up her pyjama top from the bed beside him and wound it around her neck and held her like a puppy on a leash.

'You have been talking to people about me, haven't you, bitch?'

'No!' she whispered and shook her head vehemently.

'Don't lie to me, you cow!' He pricked her cheek with the point of the knife and she squealed with shock and pain.

'Please don't hurt me any more. I don't like these games any more. I don't want to play any more. Put that knife away please, Aleutian.'

'This isn't a game. You told Hector Cross about me, bitch.'

'No, I did not.' But despite the denial he saw the guilty realization dawn in her eyes. Her face contorted with terror.

'Yes, you did. You told him where to find me,' he laughed at her.

'Please. You don't understand.' He ignored her protests, and his voice dropped to a kindly and reassuring tone.

'Don't worry; just do as I tell you and everything will be all right. Take your left ear and pull it out to one side as far as it will go.' She stared at him in dumb incomprehension.

'Do it, Victoria. Do it, if you really love me,' he urged her, and still staring at him she lifted her hand and took the lobe of her ear between her two fingers and stretched it out.

'That's perfect,' he said, and with a single quick stroke of the silver blade he sliced the ear off cleanly at the level of her scalp.

She shrieked once and then stared with fixed horror at the severed ear that she held between her fingers.

'Now eat it. Put it in your mouth and swallow it,' he told her softly.

The blood from her wound dripped onto her chest and ran down between her breasts. She ignored it and kept staring at her severed ear. He pricked her neck and she started and looked up at him.

'Open your mouth,' he told her and pricked her again. She opened her mouth.

'Now put it in your mouth and swallow it.'

'No!' she said. 'I am sorry. I didn't mean to do it. Let me explain . . .'

He touched her eyebrow with the point of the knife. 'Eat it or I will cut out your eyeballs, one at a time.'

She put her own ear into her mouth.

'There you see. That's not so bad. It probably tastes pretty good, doesn't it?' Her shoulders heaved again. 'No. Don't do that. Swallow it.'

She made a determined effort to obey. Her face and her throat contorted. At last she gulped it down. She was panting but she blurted out hoarsely, 'It's gone. I swallowed it.'

'That's really cool. I am proud of you.'

'Please, please stop now. Please don't hurt me any more.' She was weeping bitterly and still rolling her head from side to side.

'Stop?' he asked with mock surprise. 'But we have only just gotten started. There is still something you want to tell me about, isn't there, Vicky? You want to tell me who you have been talking to about me, don't you?'

'I never told anybody about you, I swear it on my mother's grave.' Tears were streaming down her face, and she was breathing in great shuddering gasps.

'You are lying, Vicky. I have to make you eat your other ear.' He forced her to her knees and he seized her remaining ear and stretched it out like a piece of rubber. He laid the blade against it, and Vicky screamed.

Nastiya heard that scream.

N astiya picked up the cab at the front door of the Portals of Paradise. It was dropping off four giggling and squealing Polish girls.

She pushed one of the girls aside, jumped into the back seat and told the driver, 'Forty-seven Gardens Lane and the postcode is TW9 5LA. It's on the corner with Kew Gardens Road. It's about three hundred yards down the road from the Kew Gardens tube station.'

'I know where it is, love,' the cabby said.

'An extra fifty pounds if you can get me there in under a quarter of an hour, cabby.'

'Buckle your seat belt, and have your fifty-pound note ready, lady,' he told her. 'Here we go.'

The streets were almost deserted and he drove very fast. He pulled into Gardens Lane with minutes to spare. Nastiya pushed two fifty-pound notes through the pay window and told him, 'Keep the change, you earned it.' She jumped from the taxi and ran across the road to No. 47. As she went through the gate into the tiny garden she heard Victoria scream. She kicked off her stiletto heels and dropped her sequin-covered bag. She pulled her pencil skirt up around her waist and ran at the door, building up momentum. She remembered from her last visit that the lock was old and flimsy. However, she also remembered the two substantial security chains, so she launched herself with both feet together and at the last moment kicked out like a mule.

To her astonishment the lock gave way readily and the door crashed back against the inner wall. Nastiya flew through it, feet first, into the passageway beyond. She rolled back onto her feet and was running again with barely any check in her charge.

She remembered the exact layout of the shabby little apartment. The living room and the kitchen were to the right. But she could see the light under the door of the single bedroom. She kicked it open and then dodged aside and flattened her body against the side wall. She glanced around the door jamb into the bedroom.

It was a charnel house. Blood splattered the pink linen of the single bed. It had been dashed across the walls and was pooling on the fluffy white rugs in the centre of the floor.

Vicky was on her feet facing her, but Nastiya could hardly recognize the girl. She was naked. Her ears had been hacked away. Blood cascaded from the fresh raw wounds. It ran down into her mouth and dyed her teeth crimson. Blood poured off her chin and ran down her body in sheets. The room stank of blood and vomit.

Nastiya recognized Aleutian at once from the video. He was standing behind Vicky. He had her in a headlock, pinning her helplessly. In his other fist he held the bloody knife with which he had committed the carnage. He was reaching around Vicky's body and holding the point of the long blood-caked blade against her belly button. Using Vicky's body as a shield, he was glaring at Nastiya over her shoulder.

'Listen to me, Aleutian. Let Vicky go and you can walk away from this,' Nastiya told him in a calm and reasonable tone of voice.

'I don't know who the hell you are, blondie, but I like what I see of you. I think I have got a better plan than yours. First I am going to finish what I started with this cow I have here. Then I am going to come after you, and when I catch you I'm going to give you the best fuck you have ever had in your life. Then I am going to kill you also, but very slowly. Now I am only going to do this once, so watch closely please.'

He drew the knife swiftly from side to side across Victoria's naked belly, cutting down deeply through her skin and muscle and her stomach wall. Her intestines bulged from the wound. The knife had sliced through them and the contents spilled from them. Then he changed the angle of the blade and stabbed it up through her sternum.

Vicky's eyes flew wide open, staring into eternity, as the blade pierced her heart. The breath rushed from her open mouth and then she sagged in Aleutian's grip as she died. Even Nastiya was for an instant frozen by the brutality of it.

However, her dominating concern had switched from saving Vicky's life to the knife in Aleutian's hand. The knife gave Aleutian control.

She'd seen from the way he handled the weapon that he was a skilled knife fighter, probably the most dangerous she had ever faced. He knew how good he was, and he was supremely confident. He was enjoying himself. Obviously he thrived on the smell of blood and the stink of ripped bowels that filled the room. She knew she underestimated him at her peril.

She, on the other hand, was unarmed, barefooted and dressed in restricted clothing. The tiny bedroom was made even smaller by the bed in the centre. For her particular fighting style she needed space in which to manoeuvre, to retreat and feint. Most of all, she must have space in which to keep clear of that blade.

Clearly, Aleutian had reached the same conclusions, and he moved swiftly to restrict her movements even further. Still holding Vicky's corpse in front of him as a shield, he tried to crowd Nastiya into a corner of the room. But she broke away, slipping around his left side, away from the knife.

Before he could swing his human shield around to block her, she had regained her position in the doorway. The door jambs on each side of her covered her flanks. She faced him again and fell into a fighting crouch with her hands held high and stiff as axe blades, crossed at the wrists.

'Cool! You've been watching the Jackie Chan Kung Fu movies, blondie,' he mocked her, and he lifted Vicky with her legs dangling and ran straight at Nastiya. He was attempting to force her into the passageway where he could get at her more readily.

Nastiya saw the opening; his feet were visible below Vicky's dangling legs. Instead of retreating she ran to meet him. Just before they collided she launched herself feet first under Vicky's legs and shot out her favourite mule kick. Both her feet landed solidly on Aleutian's left ankle, exactly where she had aimed.

Clearly, she heard the bone and cartilage in his leg give with a snap. She felt a surge of triumph, she knew for certain he would go down and she would get her chance to take the knife from him.

Aleutian grunted with pain, but to her dismay he stayed upright. She back-flipped onto her feet and faced him again. However, before she could fully recover her balance he used Vicky like a battering ram and slammed her limp body into Nastiya with such force that she was hurled backwards through the doorway. She came up hard against the far wall of the passage.

Aleutian came after her. He was limping on his injured ankle, but nevertheless moved surprisingly fast. He was still holding Vicky's mutilated body in front of him. He drove Nastiya back against the passage wall, and he stabbed at her face over Vicky's shoulder. Nastiya grabbed his wrist, but it was slippery with blood and he twisted free, still holding the knife. She was against the wall and he was shoving Vicky into her, keeping her hedged in and off balance. Vicky's head rolled about loosely on her shoulders. Her eyes were glazed and unseeing.

Aleutian stabbed at her face again and she ducked under the blade, losing sight of him for an instant. He let Vicky's corpse drop, and Nastiya's lower body was no longer shielded by it. With the speed of an adder he struck at her belly. Nastiya twisted violently aside to avoid the thrust, but the corpse was lying across her feet, inhibiting her movements. She felt the sting of the steel as it opened a long shallow cut across her hip. She tried to jump over the corpse and get into the open before he could strike again, but the rope of Vicky's intestines wrapped around her ankle and she tripped. She went down on one knee and threw up her hand to counter the knife thrust that she knew must surely come, but instead Aleutian grabbed her wrist and dragged her face down on the floorboards. He put one knee in the small of her back to pin her while he swiftly readjusted his grip. Then he forced her to her knees and knelt behind her, holding her in a single-handed head lock. He put enough pressure on her larynx to prevent her calling out.

'You are quite good, blondie,' he commended her. 'You know how to use yourself in a fight.' He was breathing heavily and chuckling. 'Now you get your chance to show me how good you are at the famous old doggy style.'

At that moment the front door of the apartment crashed back on its hinges, and Hector and Paddy burst through it into the passageway together. They paused for a moment to take in the scene.

Aleutian rose to his feet without losing his choke-hold on Nastiya. Using her body as a shield, he faced them.

'Stay where you are,' he warned them. 'Come any closer and this slut gets it.'

He held the knife to Nastiya's neck with the blade pressed up under her ear. He saw the pistol. Hector was holding it in a double-handed Weaver grip. He had taken up the classical gunfighter's crouch; balanced on the balls of his feet with the pistol pointed at Aleutian's forehead.

Aleutian ducked his head and tucked himself in closely behind Nastiya, offering a minimal target. He began to sway his head from side to side like a standing cobra to frustrate Hector's aim.

'Welcome, Mr Cross. It's such a pleasure to see you again. Please accept my condolences on the recent loss of your lovely wife,' he said.

It was as though a shutter flickered across Hector's eyes and his vision seemed to glow red with the heat of his fury. He just managed to control it.

Once again his mind was working like a computer, calculating range and aiming point. The pistol sights were set to shoot one and a half inches high at twenty-five yards. This range was eight, maybe nine yards to target. He would have to compensate for the rising bullet. Aleutian was moving all the time, giving him only intermittent glimpses of his head.

'You can take him, Heck,' Paddy breathed as he crouched behind Hector's shoulder. His words were only just audible.

Hector's lips tightened into a hard straight line; he knew that the chances of pulling off the shot without touching Nastiya were about even money.

'We can do a deal, Mr Cross,' Aleutian said. 'I know you have a car outside. You could not have gotten here so quickly without one.

You give me the keys and I give you this piece of blonde pussy. Fair exchange?'

The weapon in Hector's hand was unwavering. 'Who gave you the contract on my wife?' he asked.

'That's not the deal, Mr Cross.'

'That's the only deal, Aleutian.'

'Look what I did to your friend Victoria. No ears and no guts. Please don't annoy me.'

Hector's eyes never even flickered towards Vicky's mutilated corpse.

'I want the name,' he insisted.

'And I want to go on living. No names.'

'I can wait,' Hector said.

'I don't think you can,' Aleutian said. 'Watch this.' He brought his knife down behind Nastiya's back and placed the point on her naked tricep, and then slowly he pushed the long blade cleanly through her arm. Nastiya's face contorted with the pain as the point emerged from the front of her biceps.

'It's okay, Hector,' she said but her voice was hoarse and her eyes were filled with agony.

'Tough cookie!' Aleutian acknowledged her stoicism, and jerked the blade out of her flesh. 'Next one goes through her leg.' He stabbed the blade through her thigh. When he pulled it out dark blood spilled from the wound and pattered onto the floor.

'Take him, Heck,' Paddy demanded.

'Hazel!' With a single word, Hector explained his reluctance to fire.

'You can't save Hazel, but you can save Nazzy. Take him, please.' Now Paddy was pleading, and Hector had never heard him plead before. But never before had Paddy been forced to watch helplessly as the woman he adored was cut to ribbons.

Hector knew he had to take the shot. He also knew that it would be the most crucial shot he ever fired, and the consequences should he miss.

However, the pistol in his hands was a very special weapon. Dave Imbiss had persuaded a military master-armourer to work on it for him. First the armourer had obliterated the serial numbers, so there could be no paper trail linking the pistol to Hector. He had hand-polished the chamber to accept the rounds so cleanly that there was no possibility of a jam. He had put the barrel through a classified machine in the US Defense Sniper Division that rendered the rifling and lands mirror perfect. The cartridges were also part of a specially prepared batch. The ballistics were perfect; every bullet would rotate through the barrel and fly to the target on an identical trajectory, with no wobble or roll and almost zero deflection. Finally, the crude iron sights had been replaced with state-of-the-art optics. The end result was that its accuracy was fined down to thousandths of an inch. Hector had spent so many hours on the practice range with it that the pistol was now almost an extension of his own body.

Moreover, Aleutian was a wild animal at bay and he was on the cusp of panic. He was no longer thinking like the cold-blooded killer he really was. He was making a little mistake. He was beginning to sway his head to a rhythm, moving it from side to side with the regularity of a metronome. Aleutian was showing Hector one eye and an inch and a half of the right-hand side of his head at intervals of two seconds. Hector would have to let his bullet pass a millimetre clear of Nastiya's cheek.

He drew a long slow breath and then let it out just as slowly. He lined up on the space into which he anticipated he would fire. His pressure on the trigger was a mere feather off the point of release. His concentration was so intense that for him everything seemed to slow down and go very still and quiet. The pistol went off of its own accord. It seemed to Hector that a force beyond his own volition had made the shot.

He saw a lock of Nastiya's golden hair snipped off cleanly by the bullet, and her ear flicked as the turbulence of the passing shot caught it, and then he saw Aleutian's right eye explode in a burst of pale jelly as the bullet passed through. The back of his skull blew out. The pale matter of his brains splashed across the wall of the passage, and he went down hard and lay on his back. His heels drummed spasmodically on the wooden floor.

'We must get tourniquets on those wounds right away, but don't touch anything in the room which will leave fingerprints!' Hector shouted at Paddy as he rushed forward. Nastiya took a pace towards him and then fell forward as her damaged leg collapsed under her weight. Paddy caught her and lowered her gently to the floor.

Hector moved swiftly to the spot were Aleutian had been standing. He did not have to concern himself too much with fingerprints on the expended cartridge cases. The only fingerprints of his were on the external parts of the weapon. He pulled a cotton bandanna from his pocket and wiped the pistol meticulously, then used the cloth as a glove. He went to where Aleutian's corpse lay on its back. Hector had noted his grip on the handle of the knife so he knew that he had been right-handed. He knelt beside his corpse, picked up his limp right hand and folded his fingers around the hand grip and pressed them onto the blued steel. Then he did the same with Aleutian's left hand on the slide. He paused for a few seconds to examine the Maalik tattoo on the dead man's wrist, and grimaced with anger. Kneeling behind Aleutian with an arm under his armpits he stood up slowly, lifting the corpse into a standing position.

'Keep your head down, Paddy,' he warned. 'I'm going to let another one off.' He forced Aleutian's dead finger onto the trigger. The pistol fired and the bullet smacked into the passage wall beside the front door.

Then he released his grip on Aleutian's dead body and let it fall to the floor under its own weight.

He stood for a few seconds reviewing the scene. The angles were right. Aleutian's right hand was now covered with burnt gunpowder. When the police forensic team applied the paraffin test they would get a positive. His body had fallen in a natural attitude, with the knife that he had used on Vicky under him. It was all convincing.

He turned away from the body and squatted beside Paddy as he worked on Nastiya's leg. Paddy had taken down a length of sash cord from the window in the end wall of the passage. He tied the cord high up around Nastiya's thigh above the wound. Now he was twisting it tight. The cord gradually cut into her flesh and the bleeding from the wound was pinching off. Hector knelt beside him and used his bandanna as a tourniquet on her arm.

'You saved her life. I don't know how to thank you, Heck.' Paddy spoke without looking up.

'Then don't!' Hector said.

'I can do better than my stupid husband,' Nastiya told Hector.

'Soon as I can stand up I am going to give you a big fat kiss.' She was very pale, her voice hoarse, but she smiled.

'I'll hold you to that,' he warned her.

'How come you made Aleutian fire a second shot even after he was dead?' Paddy asked.

'To put burnt powder on his hands and his fingerprints on the pistol,' Hector told him.

'What are the police going to think when they find this big mess that we have made?' Nastiya asked.

'We hope they are going to think that Aleutian killed Vicky with the knife after a lover's tiff, then in remorse and fear of the consequences he shot himself.'

'It took him two shots?' Paddy asked incredulously. 'His aim must have been a bit wild!'

'Suicides often fire a clearing shot first, to check the gun and bolster their courage before they make the killing shot,' Hector explained. 'I think we have cleared our tracks. We have left nothing here that the boys in blue can trace back to us. Let's get the hell out of here.'

Nastiya made no sound as Paddy picked her up and carried her out through the front door. Hector stood up and walked back to where Vicky Vusamazulu lay. Even to one accustomed to death in all its most hideous aspects, this mutilation was sickening. He gave her a few seconds of silent respect.

'Silly little thing. But she didn't deserve to go out like this.'

Then he went to Aleutian and stood over him. With his hands thrust into his pockets, he stared down at the ruined head. The single remaining eye stared back at him. Anger and dismay washed over him in alternating waves. Anger for what this man had done to Hazel; dismay for the fact that his death had wiped out the trail that might have led Hector to the lair of the ultimate Beast.

Now he knew he was staring at the veritable mother of all dead ends. He turned away and followed Paddy out to where the Q-car was parked. The street was deserted.

Hector opened the driver's door and slipped behind the wheel of the Q-car. Paddy was in the back seat holding Nastiya. She was silent and pale. Hector drove away without revving the engine. As they passed the gates to the Botanical Gardens, Hector spoke again.

'Well, it looks like another lucky one. We've got away clean except for Nazzy. How are you bearing up, tsarina?'

'I've been worse, but I have also been a lot better,' she said. 'Where are we going?'

'We are going to see a man that Paddy and I both know rather well,' Hector told her, as he passed his iPhone back over his shoulder. 'Grab my phone, Paddy. You will find Doc Hogan in my contacts list. Tell him we are on our way. We will be with him in about an hour and a half.'

Doc Hogan had been the Royal Medical Corps doctor attached to the SAS regiment in which Hector had served. When he retired he had settled down on the family farm in Hampshire. However, behind the country gentry façade he was still in the practice of medicine, albeit unofficially and on the quiet. His speciality was trauma management. His small and select list of patients were all ex-army friends and comrades who had suffered minor misadventures such as impregnating a lady who was not their wife, or getting themselves stabbed, or carelessly standing in the way of a flying bullet.

Paddy and Nastiya stayed with Doc Hogan as his guests for ten days, before he allowed her to fly down to Abu Zara in the Bannock Oil jet to complete her recuperation.

The demise of Aleutian and Vicky Vusamazulu hardly raised a ripple of interest. It was reported as a domestic violence on the back pages of a local news-sheet, but it never made it to the TV news channels or the national radio broadcasts.

Agatha had accepted Hector's offer of permanent employment and was now his chief personal assistant, but it had tested his powers of persuasion to talk her into accepting an increase in her salary.

'I don't know what I would do with all that money, Mr Cross.'

'You are a clever girl, Agatha. You'll think of something,' he assured her. 'However, I'm going to need you in Abu Zara, where you will be close at hand to help me, with business and Catherine Cayla. We may return to London once the Trust has sold Number Eleven and we can set up alternative lodgings.'

Apart from the fact that she was such a dedicated and experienced secretary, she was the world's living expert on that period of Hazel's life prior to Hector's appearance on her horizon. Every day Hector was involving her more intimately in the research that he was carrying out on her accumulated records to try to identify the hidden enemy in Hazel's past. In this, Agatha's experienced advice was invaluable.

During one of their long and probing discussions of the killer's identity, it was Agatha who reminded him of the existence of Henry Bannock's stepson, the son of the wife who had preceded Hazel in the role. His name was Carl and at first Henry had welcomed him into his family with open arms. He had provided him with the finest education and when he left college had given him a highly paid job at Bannock Oil. However, their relationship had exploded in a terrible family scandal which had affected Henry Bannock deeply.

'What was it all about, Agatha?' Hector asked her. 'I heard the rumours when I came to work for Bannock Oil. But I never learned any of the details.'

'Very few people did. It was long before my time. But I only know that Mr Bannock was deeply ashamed of the whole business. He never allowed anybody ever to talk about it in the Bannock household. There was no reference to it in any of his personal records; he must have expunged them all. It was as though it had never happened. I heard that Carl Bannock was released from prison after serving a long sentence. But then he simply disappeared, until after Mr Bannock died and Hazel took over his job as CEO. Then Carl popped up again out of nowhere, and started hounding Hazel. I don't know what he was on about, but I think he was trying to blackmail her. I think he forced her to pay him out a large sum of money, because he suddenly disappeared again and I haven't heard anything of him since then. Did Hazel ever speak of him to you?'

'Never. I didn't ask and she didn't tell. I knew there was a deep and dark family secret and I didn't want to rake up old and hurtful things connected to Henry Bannock, who she revered,' Hector admitted. 'It was as if this Carl fellow never existed.'

'In any event I cannot see how Carl could be implicated in Hazel's murder. What would he stand to gain by killing her, or by having her killed? He had already gotten all the money out of her that he could.'

'I can't see any motive either, apart from sheer vindictiveness. But if Hazel had paid him off, as you suggest, why would he come back all these years later to murder her? I agree it doesn't make sense. I think we must look for her killer elsewhere. But we will bear Master Carl Bannock in mind, although I think he is pretty far down the line of possible suspects.'

As soon as they were settled back in Seascape Mansions, Hector and Agatha started drawing up a list of possible villains, but there had been so many hostile people in Hazel's life that the list expanded until it threatened to stretch out to unwieldy proportions. It was impossible for Hector to travel back and forth across the globe to follow up every lead and run down every possible culprit. So Agatha had to find a reputable private detective in each country where Hazel's erstwhile enemies were now scattered. Hector employed them to carry out the local search. Only when the report from the hired detective was hot and promising would Hector fly out to follow up the blood spoor in person.

One such journey was to Colombia to investigate a notorious local cocaine and oil baron who had once had dealings with Bannock Oil, dealings which had ended in mutual recriminations and anger. Agatha recalled that Señor Bartolo Julio Alvarez had sent death threats and referred in public to Hazel Bannock as a *Yanqui putain de bordel de merde.*

To Hector the meaning of this was obscure but Agatha explained with relish that it meant something along the lines of, 'An American lady of easy virtue who plies her trade from a house of ill repute built from excrement.'

'That's very unflattering,' Hector agreed. 'Best I go down there to reason with him.'

When Hector arrived in Bogotá he found that he had just missed by a week the opportunity to attend Señor Alvarez's funeral. He had been sent to his celestial reward by six rounds from a Scorpion SA vz. 61 submachine gun fired at a range of two feet into the back of his skull by a trusted bodyguard who, it seemed, had recently transferred his allegiance to the head of a rival cocaine syndicate.

When Hector flew back to Abu Zara he was more fortunate. Nastiya was now sufficiently recovered from her injuries to be with Paddy to meet Hector at the airport.

'You'll never guess what has happened,' Nastiya told him as they embraced.

'Whatever it is, it's got to be good,' Hector replied. 'You are grinning like an idiot.'

'Catherine Cayla is crawling!'

'She's what?'

'Crawling! You know, hands and knees. We are talking about the next Olympics already,' Nastiya told him with pride.

'Congratulations, Heck!' Paddy laughed.

'Thank you, Padraig. Clearly, my daughter is an infant prodigy.' He spoke in tones of awe. 'I have to see this.'

'Your reception committee is anxiously awaiting your arrival at Seascape Mansions. I warn you that the preparations have been quite extensive,' Paddy told him.

They rode up in the private elevator and when the doors opened the entire household was drawn up in the entrance lobby, under an elaborate banner that had been strung from one wall to the other. The slogan in gold glitter paint read WELCOME HOME, DADDY!

At the rear of the lobby were the ranks of house servants. The chefs were wearing spotless whites with their traditional tall hats. The uniforms of the lesser members of staff were clean and freshly ironed, and maids wore frilled white aprons over their navy blues. In front of them were the security operatives in their number-one dress uniforms, shining belt buckles and highly polished boots. In the forefront were the three nursemaids. Bonnie was front stage centre, and in her arms she held Catherine Cayla Bannock-Cross.

Catherine was dressed in an embroidered pink romper suit, and enough of her fluffy blonde hair had been scraped together to support an enormous pink bow.

The assembly burst into applause as Hector stepped out of the elevator. Catherine swivelled her head, looking around at them in astonishment, and then her eyes came back to Hector as he approached. Hector saw that her eyes had changed colour. They were a deeper and brighter shade of blue. They were Hazel's eyes. Their gaze was steady and focussed. Hector realized that she was actually seeing him, possibly for the first time.

Hector stopped in front of her and she thrust her thumb into her mouth and regarded him solemnly.

'You are very beautiful,' he told her. 'You are as beautiful as your mother.'

He held out his arms towards her and he smiled.

'May I hold you, please?'

He knew she was still too young to remember or recognize him. They had told him that it would only happen when she was one year old. But he kept smiling and looking into her eyes.

He saw her thoughts coming to the surface like pretty little fish in a deep blue pond. Suddenly she echoed his smile and held both her arms towards him, leaning forward in Bonnie's arms and bouncing so violently that the nurse almost lost her grip.

Stone the experts! Hector thought joyfully. *She does so recognize me!*

He took her up, and she sat erect in the curve of his arm, balancing herself easily. She was light and soft and she smelled like fresh warm milk.

He kissed the top of her head and she said clearly, 'Ba! Ba!'

'We mean Dada.' Bonnie supplied the translation. 'We have been working on it, but it's a rather difficult word for us.'

He carried Catherine to her nursery and her three nurses trooped after them. He placed her in the centre of the floor, and backed away to the door.

'Okay, you little beauty,' he said to her. 'Let's see you crawl.' He clapped his hands. 'Come, Cathy. Come to Baba, my baby!'

She rolled over onto her belly and then came up on her hands and knees and shot towards him at a flying crawl. When she reached him she grabbed a double handful of his trouser leg and tried to haul herself to her feet. She flopped back on her nappy-cushioned bottom, and all three nurses burst into excited cries of, 'Did you see that?'

'She tried to stand on her two feet!'

'She's never done that before!'

It was lunchtime and Hector played his part by spooning a mush of minced chicken and pumpkin into her mouth. Most of this was returned. It dribbled down her chin and splattered her bib and Hector's shirt front. As she swallowed the last spoonful her eyes closed, her chin fell on her chest and she was asleep where she sat.

Hector worked out in the gymnasium for two hours while Catherine took her nap, then he changed into his running shoes and retrieved Catherine's papoose and went to find her. When she saw the papoose she kicked her legs and uttered sounds of strongest approval.

They ran along the almost deserted beachfront, followed at a discreet distance by two of Dave Imbiss's best men. Hector sang to her and pulled faces that made her laugh. She explored his face. She stuck her chubby pink fingers into his mouth to see where the strange sounds were coming from, and she tried to emulate them. She blew spit bubbles and chortled.

She soothed the loneliness. It no longer hurt so badly when he thought of Hazel.

Too soon he had to return to London.

Against all the odds, the estate agent had found a buyer for No. 11. Ronnie Bunter on behalf of the trustees asked Hector to oversee the takeover. So he had to be there when the removals company packed up the contents of the huge house. The purchaser was an Indian steel magnate. He was giving it to one of his sons as a wedding present. Hector was able to unload most of the furniture from the great house onto them. He sent the antiques and artwork that Hazel had accumulated to Sotheby's to be sold at auction, and felt a sense of almost physical relief as the last heavily laden removal van pulled away down the driveway.

The astute estate agent had a list of a dozen replacements for

No. 11 at hand. He took Hector on a viewing tour. Third on the list was a lovely mews house in Mayfair. It had been completely renovated, and the paint had hardly dried on the walls. It comprised all the usual offices together with four large bedroom suites, under-ground garaging for three cars and accommodation for five servants in the basement. It took Hector forty-five minutes to make the deci-sion to buy it.

As he signed the documentation for No. 4 Lowndes Mews, Mayfair, he had already chosen a name for his and Catherine's new home: 'The Cross Roads'. And it occupied a little more than twenty per cent of the floor area of the Belgravia mansion.

He called in his usual firm of interior designers and gave them a deadline of six weeks to have the property completely furnished and ready for occupation. He began to feel that at last he had succeeded in putting the past behind him and he was ready to start living his own life afresh.

The trial at the Old Bailey of the two thugs who had fire-bombed Brandon Hall was set down for a few weeks later. It lasted six days.

Between them, Nastiya, Paddy and Hector spent two of those days on the witness stand, and their combined testimony combined with that of Paul Stowe, the gamekeeper, was overwhelming.

The jury returned from their deliberations in only two and a half hours with a 'guilty on all counts' verdict.

When the list of previous convictions was read out to the judge, he brought the full might of the law to bear on the accused.

He sentenced them each to twenty-two years' detention, and ordered that they must serve a minimum of nineteen years of their sentences.

They had attempted to burn Catherine Cayla and Hector felt only partially mollified by the severity of the sentence. He consoled himself with the thought that, lacking the death sentence, it was about as steep as the feeble current laws allowed.

When the three of them flew back to Abu Zara, Paul Stowe went with them at Hector's invitation. He no longer needed a head keeper at Brandon Hall, but Paul was too good a man to lose so Hector had found a new job for him at Cross Bow Security.

Hector was able to devote himself to Catherine and to following up the paper trail that he hoped might eventually lead him and Agatha to the shadowy assassin.

However, doubts were rising in the recesses of his mind. The list of suspects was dwindling rapidly as the negative reports came in from his field operatives. He began to experience bouts of helplessness and inadequacy. Those were sensations to which he was unaccustomed.

He tried to fight off these swings in mood by heavy physical exercise and hours spent on the firing range. He also had the distraction of having to fly to the US for the annual general meeting of Bannock Oil, Inc., of which he was still a director.

Then news came from his interior decorators in London that they had completed the refurbishment of The Cross Roads in Lowndes Mews only five days past the deadline he had set for them.

With relief he returned to the bustle and excitement of London.

The interior decorator and two of his assistants showed Hector over The Cross Roads. It was complete in every detail. The dominant colour scheme Hector had chosen was light blues and yellows, with shades of brown as counterpoints. It was welcoming, functional and masculine.

His carefully selected team of domestic servants from No. 11 and Brandon Hall were already in occupation of the servants' quarters. Cynthia, the chef, was in the kitchen, busy with her pots and pans.

A new Bentley Continental and a brand-new Range Rover were parked in the underground garage, with their pristine bodywork gleaming.

The bar and the wine cellar were stocked with his favourite wines and liquors.

In his study the lighting was easy on the eyes and his computer was online.

The master bedroom was a work of art, with an emperor-size bed. The bed was made up with his favourite silk duvets. There was a gleaming white-tiled boy's en suite bathroom, and a soft-pink girl's bathroom with, naturally enough, a bidet. His suits and shirts were ironed and hanging in the master dressing room. His shoes were on the racks and polished to a high gloss.

Across the passage was Catherine's nursery suite.

Before Hector moved in he had Dave Imbiss fly out from Abu Zara with his box of electronic tricks. Dave swept the house from the basement to the roof loft and declared that it was free of bugging devices or any other nastiness.

He had decided that in future he would live between The Cross Roads in London and Seascape Mansions in Abu Zara, spending ten alternate days in each. That way he could indulge in both the excitement of the metropolis and the tranquillity of the desert kingdom.

The first evening Hector was in residence in The Cross Roads he invited three of his old comrades-in-arms from his SAS days and their spouses to dine with him. It was a convivial evening and he only fell into bed well after midnight.

The next morning as he stepped out of the shower his mobile phone rang. He dried his right hand on the towel, flicked the water from his sodden hair and picked up his phone from the top of the washstand.

'Cross!' he barked into it. His head was still paining him a little from the previous evening's jollifications.

'Oh, I do hope I am not disturbing you, Mr Cross?' a woman's voice said.

'Jo?' he asked cautiously. 'It is Jo Stanley, is it not? Or should I have said Miss Stanley?' He knew it was her, of course. For almost a year now he had been aware of the musical strains of her voice echoing softly in the backwaters of his memory.

'Jo sounds better to me than your second choice, Hector.'

'This is a surprise. Where are you? You're not in England by any strange chance, are you?'

'Yes, I'm in London. I got in fairly late last night.'

'Are you staying at the Ritz, as before?'

'Goodness gracious, no!' He smiled when she said that. It was so old-fashioned. 'I can't afford that kind of extravagance.'

'You can if you send the bill to Ronnie Bunter,' he suggested.

'I don't work for Mr Bunter any longer,' she replied, and it caught him off balance.

'Then, who are you working for?'

'To use the well-travelled euphemism, I am currently between jobs.' Again she had him stumped.

'So what are you doing in London Town?'

'I came to see you, Hector.'

'I cannot bring myself to believe that. Why me?'

'It's complicated. Besides, there are better and safer ways to discuss it than over the telephone.'

'Your place or mine?' he asked, and she laughed again. It was a sound that pleased him.

'Would it sound forward if I said yours?'

'We'll never get anywhere if we don't move forward. Where can I find you? Where are you staying?'

'In a rather cute little hotel with a cute name, just at the top end of Chelsea Green.'

'What's the name?'

'It's called My Hotel.'

'Okay, I know it. I'll pick you up at the front entrance in forty-five minutes. I'll be driving a—'

'You'll be driving a silver Bentley with licence plates CRO 55, am I correct?'

'An inspired guess, Miss Stanley,' he chuckled. 'But that was my old jalopy. The new banger is black. However, the number plates are the same.'

'Goodness gracious! Only the angels can understand men and their motors.'

Jo was standing outside the hotel entrance, wearing denim jeans and a navy windcheater over a roll-neck white cable-stitch jersey, and she was carrying a leather briefcase. She had changed her hairstyle; now it was bobbed and fringed. It suited her even better. It made her neck seem longer and more swanlike. He had forgotten how tall and elegant she really was, even in denim pants.

When he reached across and opened the passenger door for her, she slipped into the seat and fastened her seat belt before she turned to face him.

'I don't have to ask how you are. You are looking very well, Hector.'

'Thank you, and you are looking pretty good yourself, Jo. Welcome back to London.'

'How is Catherine Cayla?'

'Now you have pressed the right button. I could go on about her all day. Catherine Cayla is fifty leagues beyond gorgeous.'

'Never mind the small print; just give me the headlines.'

'She has blue eyes and already she can crawl. She can even say Dada, however she pronounces it Baba, which proves to me beyond any shadow of a doubt that she is a prodigy.'

'Do you think I will ever get to meet her?'

'Now that is a rare and beautiful thought.'

After they'd parked in the cobbled mews outside The Cross Roads he carried her briefcase to the house and then ushered her into the entrance lobby. She looked around at the sweeping circular staircase and the open doors into the sitting room.

'Nice,' she approved. 'Very nice. Beautiful taste, Hector. Is that a real Paul Gauguin?' She indicated the large oil on the facing wall of the sitting room.

'I wish! Hazel had her entire art collection copied, so she could keep the originals in safe storage without paying iniquitous amounts of insurance on it. I am sure you will recall that the originals all belonged to the Trust. I kept this copy in memory of Hazel.' He surprised himself with how easily he could now speak of Hazel, with pleasure rather than pain.

He set down her briefcase and helped her to divest herself of her jacket. Standing close to her, he remembered her perfume from their first meeting. It was Chanel No. 22 and it suited her perfectly.

'If you are agreeable, we can work in my study. I presume we came here to work rather than to admire my fake masterpieces?'

She laughed softly. 'You presume correctly.' She liked the way he readily admitted that some of his paintings were copies. It was proof of what she had suspected when she first met him. He was straight down the middle, without side or pretence. A man that a woman could trust, and that bad men should walk wide of.

He took her elbow to assist her up the stairs. His study was very masculine. But she had never expected such a large collection of books. The floor was covered with Persian carpets in pleasing colours and patterns. His carved teak desk dominated the large room. On the facing wall was an oil portrait of Hazel. She was standing in a golden wheat field, holding a wide-brimmed straw hat in one hand. With the other hand she was shading her eyes and laughing. Her hair was darker gold than the wheat, blowing in the wind. Jo dropped her eyes; she felt a strange emotion that she could not define. She was not sure whether it was envy or admiration or pity.

Hector placed her briefcase on the long antique library table, and then patted the buttoned-leather chair. 'This is the most comfortable seat in the room.'

'Thank you,' she said, but instead of sitting immediately she wandered along his bookcase looking at his collection.

'Can I get you something to eat or drink?' he asked.

'I would die for a cup of coffee.'

'Dying is not called for,' he told her, and went to the Nespresso coffee machine that was concealed behind an antique Chinese screen in the corner.

'I don't like to let anybody else brew for me,' he explained. 'Not even Cynthia, my chef.'

At last she took the seat he had offered her, and he placed the porcelain on the table beside her. He went to his own chair behind the desk.

'How secure are we here? We have some highly sensitive issues to discuss,' she asked quietly.

'You don't have to worry, Jo. I had a thorough check run on the entire building by somebody I trust implicitly.'

'Sorry I had to ask. I know you are a pro, Hector.' He inclined his head to acknowledge the apology, and she went on. 'The whole way across the Atlantic I have been pondering how best to explain this all to you. I decided the only way was to start at the beginning.'

'That sounds logical to me,' he agreed.

'That's why I am going to start at the end.'

'When I think about it, that also sounds very logical, but only if you are a woman, of course.' She ignored the sarcasm. Her expression began to change. The animation and flippancy faded away. Her lovely eyes filled with shadows.

He wanted desperately to help her, but he realized that the best way to do that was to remain silent and listen. She spoke at last.

'Ronald Bunter is a fine lawyer and an honest and noble man but, as the head trustee of the Henry Bannock Family Trust, he has been faced with a soul-destroying decision. He has had to decide which he must betray: his professional honour or the lives of innocents that have been given into his keeping.'

She broke off and he knew with an intuitive flash that she had been faced with the same dreadful choice.

Then she sighed and it was a harrowing sound. She laid her hand on her briefcase and said, 'In here I have a digital copy of the Henry Bannock Family Trust Deed. I stole it from the law firm to which I had sworn my fealty. Ronald Bunter gave me the duplicate keys and the codes so that I was able to enter the strongroom while the building was deserted and he shielded me from discovery. He was my accomplice. We did not commit this act without long and deep discussion and soul searching. But in the end we decided that justice must take precedence over the strict letter of the law. That is something almost impossible for a lawyer to accept. Nevertheless, when I had finished what I had set out to do I felt it was my duty to my God and my own self-esteem to resign from the firm whose trust I had so woefully betrayed.'

Hector realized that he had been holding his breath as he listened to her. Now he let it out in a long soft sigh, and then he said, 'If you did this for me, I cannot let you do it. The sacrifice is too great.'

'I have done it,' she said. 'I cannot go back on it now. It's too late. Besides which it is the right decision. I know that it's the right thing. Please don't argue. This is my gift to you and Catherine Cayla.'

'When you explain it that way I have no choice. I must accept it. Thank you, Jo. You will not find us ungrateful.'

'I know that.' She dropped her eyes and looked at her hands, which she was holding in her lap. When she looked up at him again she had regained complete control of her emotions.

'The Trust Deed that Henry Bannock put together is a three-hundred-page monstrosity. It would take you an age to wade through it, because you would drop off to sleep every two or three pages.'

She opened her briefcase and took out two small USB flash drives. She balanced them in the palm of her hand, as though she was reluctant to hand them over.

'So, what I have done for you is to prepare a digital copy of the actual Trust Deed.' She placed one of the flash drives on his desk in front of him. 'Then on this second drive I have set out the background and history that led up to the formation of the trust that Henry Bannock created; then to the chain reaction that this set in motion. With Ronnie Bunter's full cooperation I think that I have been able to put the facts into some sort of logical and cohesive order, which is also readable. I suppose I must have always had a deep-rooted ambition to be an author, because I found myself deeply involved in the writing of it.' She smiled self-deprecatingly. 'For what it's worth, I offer to you my first attempt at narrative literature. It is not a novel or even a novelette, because everything it contains is factual.'

She stood up and placed the second flash drive beside the first on the desk in front of him. Hector picked it up and examined it curiously. Jo returned to her seat and watched him. He leaned across his desk and plugged the USB drive into his desktop computer.

'It's formatted in Microsoft Word,' she said.

'It's opening without any hassle,' he told her. 'But now it's asking for a password.'

'It's poisonseed7805,' she told him. 'All lower case. All one word.'

'That's done it. Here we go. It's opening. "Karl Pieter Kurtmeyer:

The Poisoned Seed".' He read aloud the title from the heading of the document.

'I hope you find the contents of more interest than the title suggests,' Jo said.

'I am going to start reading it immediately, but it looks as though it will take me a good few hours, maybe even days. Is there something you can do for your own entertainment? Would you like to read a book or watch TV, or go out sightseeing or shopping? London is a fun town.'

'I am shattered by jetlag.' She hid her yawn behind her fingers. 'It was a horrendous red-eye flight in tourist class. What with the turbulence and my obese neighbour snoring like a rampaging lioness and overflowing from her seat into mine, I slept hardly a wink.'

'You poor girl!' He stood up. 'Never mind. Your problem is easily solved. Follow me.' He led her up to the guest suite. When she saw the bed she smiled. 'I have seen polo fields smaller than this.'

She was equally impressed with the bathroom. He led her back into the main bedroom and told her, 'The dressing gowns are in the wardrobe. Take your pick, then lock the door and say farewell to this cruel world for as long as it takes.'

He left her to it and returned to his study. He settled down in front of his computer, and started on the first page of 'The Poisoned Seed'.

Karl Pieter Kurtmeyer was born in Düsseldorf in the Rhine-Ruhr region of western Germany.

His father was Heinrich Eberhard Kurtmeyer. During World War II Heinrich had been a junior officer in the Nazi Gestapo. In the final days of hostilities he was captured by the British forces liberating the concentration camp of Bergen-Belsen. Heinrich was sentenced by a war crimes court to four years imprisonment for his part in the atrocities committed in the death camp.

On his release from prison he returned to his home town of Düsseldorf and found work in a nightclub called Die Lustige Witwe or The Merry Widow. He was a good-looking young man with cultivated manners. He was also a shrewd businessman and hard worker. He bought the nightclub on the death of the original owner from the widow. From these meagre beginnings he had built up a chain of clubs across Germany, and he was soon a wealthy man.

He employed a young dancer in the original Düsseldorf club. Her name was Marlene Imelda Kleinschmidt. She was bright, vivacious and beautiful. She was nineteen years of age when Heinrich Kurtmeyer married her. The following year she gave birth to a boy who they named Karl Pieter. Eighteen months after the birth of his son, Heinrich Eberhard Kurtmeyer succumbed to cancer of the colon. It was a demise almost as unpleasant as the ones he had meted out to the Jewish men, women and children in the death camp.

Marlene Imelda found herself widowed at the ripe old age of twenty-one years.

When the assessors came in to evaluate Heinrich's estate for tax purposes they discovered that he had another secret vice, quite apart from that of slaughtering defenceless Jews: he had been a compulsive gambler. Contrary to what most people in Düsseldorf believed, Heinrich was not a wealthy man. He had frittered away his substance. Marlene Imelda and her infant son were left almost destitute.

However she was young, beautiful and resourceful. She knew where the money was. She emigrated to the United States of America and within months of her arrival she had found employment as a secretarial assistant with a fledgling oil exploration company based in Houston.

The founder and owner of the company was a man named Henry Bannock. He was a handsome, rumbustious and larger-than-life character. In appearance he resembled John Wayne with a touch of Burt Lancaster. In his youth he had flown F-86 Sabre Jets in Korea and was officially credited with six kills. Later in Alaska he had run his own charter company which he named Bannock Air. He had flown a great deal for the big oil exploration companies and in the course of business he met many of the top executives. They taught him the ropes and gave him entrée to the oil world. Soon he had acquired several drilling concessions of his own. Shortly before Marlene Imelda came to work for Bannock Oil he had brought in his first field on the Alaskan North Slope, so he was already a multimillionaire.

Marlene was in her twenties and even more beautiful than she had been at age nineteen when she met Heinrich. She knew how to please a man both in bed and out. She pleased Henry Bannock inordinately. The fact that she had a young son made her even more desirable to him.

Karl Pieter Kurtmeyer took after his mother. If anything he was even better-looking than she was. He had thick blond hair, a strong jawline and a slight epicanthic fold to his eyelids, which gave him a mysterious and thoughtful air. This minor imperfection seemed to emphasize the perfection of his other features.

Karl was intelligent and articulate. Even at this tender age he already spoke Spanish, French, German and English. His school grades were consistently A level. Henry was impressed by good-looking people who were also clever and compliant. Like his own mother, Karl was all those things.

When Henry Bannock married Marlene Imelda he formally adopted Karl and changed his name to Carl Peter Bannock, dropping the Teutonic spelling of his given names. Henry called in several markers to get Carl a place in St Michael's Elementary, one of the most prestigious prep schools in the state of Texas. There Carl flourished. He was always one of the top three scholars in his class, and he played football and basketball for the school teams.

At home, Marlene Imelda proved that Henry was not infertile, as was rumoured by his many enemies. Within a short time of the wedding she gave birth to a seven-pound daughter. Like her mother, Sacha Jean was an exceptional beauty. She was also a gentle and sensitive child, and musically gifted. She started learning the piano at the age of three and by the age of seven she could play even the most technically challenging compositions in the standard classical repertoire, including Rachmaninov's Third Piano Concerto.

She doted on her big brother, Carl.

Sacha was almost nine years of age when Carl forced fully penetrative sex on her. He had been grooming her for this over the previous six months by inducing her to fondle his genitals when they were alone. Carl was thirteen years old and precociously sexually developed. He taught Sacha how to manipulate his penis, holding her hand onto his organ and moving it back and forth until he ejaculated. He was patient and kind to her, telling her how much he loved her and what a clever and pretty girl his sister was and how much she pleased him. In her innocence Sacha looked upon these games as a delightful secret between the two of them, and she dearly loved secrets.

Carl's favourite place to be intimate with her was in the changing rooms of the swimming pool in the ten-acre gardens of the family home. The best time was when their father was away on business in Alaska and their mother was resting after lunch. Marlene had fallen into the habit of taking three or more gin-and-lime cocktails at lunchtime, and her gait was unsteady when she stood up from the table and headed for the bedroom. That was when Carl took Sacha for a swim.

The first time that Carl ejaculated into her mouth Sacha was taken fully aback. She was disgusted by the taste of it and she cried and told him she was not going to play any more. He kissed her and said that if she didn't love him it was all right, but he still loved her. However, he didn't act as if he still loved her. For weeks thereafter he was very distant and he said spiteful and hateful things to her. In the end she was the one who suggested they should have a swim together after lunch. Soon enough she became accustomed to the taste. But then sometimes he pushed it too far down her throat and she cried herself to sleep at night. The only thing that mattered was that her brother loved her again.

Then one afternoon he made her take off her panties. He sat on the bench in front of her and he touched her down there. She closed her eyes and tried not to wince and pull away when he put his finger inside her. In the end he stood up and squirted onto her tummy. Afterwards he told her she was disgusting and she must wipe herself clean and not tell anyone. Then he left her without another word.

She refused her dinner that evening and her mother gave her two tablespoons of castor oil and kept her back from school the next day.

Three weeks before her ninth birthday party Carl came to Sacha's bedroom when the house was quiet. He took off his pyjamas pants and climbed into bed with her. When he pushed his thing inside her it was so painful that she screamed, but nobody heard her.

After he had gone back to his own room she found that she was bleeding. She sat on the toilet and listened to her blood dripping into the pan. She was too ashamed of herself to call her mother. In any event she knew that her mother was locked in her bedroom and would never answer her knocking or pleading.

After a while the bleeding stopped and she wadded her nightdress up between her legs. She hobbled down to the end of the passage and found a clean sheet in the linen cupboard to replace the bloody one. Then she crept down to the deserted kitchen and stuffed her soiled pyjamas and the bloody sheet into a garbage bag and put it into the dustbin.

The next day in school she knew everybody was staring at her. She was usually one of the stars of the mathematics class but now she could not work out the answers to any of the questions. Her teacher called her after the class ended and berated her for her poor attempt.

'What is wrong with you, Sacha?' She threw the paper down on the desk in front of her. 'This isn't like you at all.'

Sacha could not reply. She went home and stole a razor blade from her father's bathroom. Then she went to her own bathroom and slit both her wrists. One of the housemaids saw the blood coming from under the door and she ran screaming to the kitchen.

The servants broke open the door and found her. They called an ambulance. The cuts she had inflicted on her wrists were not deep enough to be life threatening.

Marlene kept her out of school for three weeks. When she returned Sacha told her music teacher that she was not going to play the piano ever again. She refused to attend the musical evening that was scheduled for the following Friday. A few days later she hacked off all her hair with a pair of scissors and clawed her face until it bled, convinced she was breaking out in acne pustules. Her features grew haggard and her manner furtive and nervous. Her eyes were haunted. She was no longer beautiful. Carl told her she was ugly and he didn't want to play with her any more.

A month later she ran away from home. The police picked her up eight days later in Albuquerque, New Mexico, and took her home. A few months later she ran away again. This time she made it as far as California before the police caught up with her.

When she was sent back to school she set fire to the music rooms. The fire destroyed the entire music wing, with damage amounting to several millions of dollars.

After a prolonged and thorough medical examination Sacha was sent to the Nine Elms Psychiatric Hospital in Pasadena, where she began a long and difficult treatment and rehabilitation programme. Never once did anyone suspect that she had suffered abuse of any kind. It seemed that Sacha herself had completely expunged the memory of it from her mind.

She put on weight rapidly. Within six months her body was grossly swollen and she was clinically obese. She kept her hair clipped close to the skull. Her eyes grew dull and moronic and she chewed her nails so deeply into the quick that her fingertips were stubby and deformed. She sucked her thumb almost continually. She became increasingly nervous and extremely aggressive. She attacked the nursing staff and other patients at the least provocation. In particular she was intensely antagonistic towards any of the staff who attempted to question her about her relationship with her family. She suffered from insomnia and began walking in her sleep.

When the family were allowed to visit her for the first time Sacha was sullen and withdrawn. She replied to questions from her parents with animal-like grunts and mumbled monosyllables. She did not recognize her once-beloved brother.

'Aren't you going to say hello to Carl Peter, darling?' her mother chided her gently. Sacha averted her eyes.

'But he is your own brother, darling Sacha,' Marlene insisted. Sacha showed a small spark of animation.

'I don't have a brother,' she said, using full sentences for the first time but still without raising her eyes from the floor. 'I don't want a brother.'

Henry Bannock stood up at this, and he said to his wife, 'I think that Carl and I are doing more harm than good by being here. We will wait for you in the car park.' He jerked his head at Carl. 'Come on, my boy. Let's get out of here.'

Henry abhorred being presented with misery and suffering in any form, particularly if it was related to him personally. He simply closed his mind to it, disassociated himself from it and walked away. Neither he nor Carl Peter ever returned to Nine Elms.

On the other hand, Marlene never missed a visit to her daughter. Every Sunday morning the chauffeur drove her a hundred miles to Pasadena and she spent the rest of the day chattering to her silent and withdrawn child. On one visit she took along a cassette of Rachmaninov's piano concertos to play to Sacha on her portable tape recorder, hoping that it might reawaken Sacha's musical talents.

As the first bars of the opening movement of the third concerto in D minor sounded, Sacha sprang to her feet, seized the machine and hurled it against the wall with maniacal strength. The recorder shattered. Sacha threw herself to the floor, drew her knees to her chest in the foetal position, thrust her thumb into her mouth and bumped her head rhythmically on the floor. It was the last time that Marlene attempted to intervene in her treatment.

From then onwards she confined herself to reading poetry to Sacha or reciting a detailed account of the past week's trivial events. Sacha remained silent and totally withdrawn. She stared at the wall, swaying backwards and forwards in the chair as though it was a rocking horse.

Months later, Marlene Imelda discovered she was pregnant once again. She waited until the sex of the foetus was confirmed by her gynaecologist; then on her next visit to Nine Elms she confided in Sacha, 'Sacha, darling, I have the most wonderful news. I am pregnant and you are going to have a baby sister.'

Sacha turned her head towards her and looked Marlene in the face for the first time during the visit.

'A sister? My own sister? Not a brother?' she asked in a clear and lucid voice.

'Yes, darling. Your very own little sister. Isn't it exciting?'

'Yes! I want a sister very much. But I don't want a brother.'

'What do you think we should call her? What name do you really, really like?'

'Bryoni Lee! I love that name.'

'Do you know anybody with the same name?'

'There was a girl at school who was my best friend.' She smiled. 'But her father found a new job and they moved to Chicago.' She was animated and talking like a normal child of her age.

Week after week they discussed the new baby, and week after week Sacha asked the same questions in the same order. She laughed at her mother's replies.

After Marlene's eighth month of gestation Sacha sat next to her throughout the entire visiting period and Marlene held her daughter's hand against her stomach. When the baby moved under her hand for the first time Sacha shrieked with excitement so loudly that the duty sister rushed into the visitors' room.

'What on earth is the matter, Sacha?' she demanded.

'It's my little sister! Come and feel her.'

Marlene brought Bryoni Lee to visit Sacha for the first time when she was three months old. Sacha was allowed to hold her new sister and she sat with her on her lap for the entire visit, cooing and laughing at her and asking her mother questions about her.

After that first visit with Bryoni, Marlene never missed a week and Sacha was able to watch Bryoni Lee growing up. Her therapists recognized the beneficial effect that the infant was exerting on Sacha and they actively encouraged the relationship.

And so the years passed.

Bryoni Lee grew into another beautiful child. She was petite and dainty with pixie features and striking dark eyes. Her heart-shaped face was mobile and expressive. People were naturally attracted to her and they smiled whenever she entered the room. She had an enchanting singing voice. Her feet seemed to have been designed to dance. Yet she was strong willed and assertive.

Bryoni Lee's natural place was at the head of the pack. Like her father Henry Bannock she was a born leader and organizer. In any group of children she effortlessly assumed control and even the elder boys bent readily to her will.

It took Henry some time to become accustomed to having a child in his household who he was unable to dominate entirely, especially in as much as this was a female offspring who was willing to stand up to him. Henry had strong views on the divides between the genders and the roles of and relationships of parents to children and men to women. Equality did not figure on his list.

Bryoni Lee delighted him in that she was clever and good to look upon, but she alarmed him in that she answered back and argued with him. Henry would fly into rages at her. He shouted at her and threatened her with corporal punishment. Once he actually carried out the threat. He pulled his belt out of its trouser loops and whacked her across the back of her bare legs. It raised a red weal but she stood her ground and refused to cry.

'Daddy, you shouldn't do that,' she told him solemnly. 'You were the one who told me that a gentleman never hits a lady.'

Henry had shot the Commie jets out of the sky over Korea and beaten the living daylights out of any number of the big tough rough-necks and roustabouts who worked his oil rigs, but now he backed down from an eight-year-old girl.

'I'm sorry,' he told her as he threaded the belt back through his trouser loops. 'You're right. I shouldn't have done that. I won't do it again. I promise you. But you must learn to listen to me, Bryoni Lee!'

In turn he began to listen to what she had to say, a courtesy that he had seldom extended to any other female. He discovered to his surprise that more often than not Bryoni Lee made good sense.

The year Bryoni Lee turned ten years of age was a memorable one in the Bannock household. In May Henry brought in his first off-shore deep water oil well. The market capitalization of Bannock Oil reached ten billion US dollars. And he purchased his personal Gulfstream V private jet, which he generally flew himself.

In the same month the Bannock family moved into their new home in Forest Drive. Designed by Andrew Moorcroft, of Moorcroft and Haye Architects, it was set in fifteen acres of gardens and contained eight bedroom suites. It won the Best House of the Year Award from the American Institute of Architects.

Carl Peter Bannock had graduated cum laude from Princeton and in June he went to work for Bannock Oil at its head office in Houston.

In July Henry Bannock asked his old friend and lawyer Ronnie Bunter to set up the Henry Bannock Family Trust to protect his close family from all harm and evil for the duration of all their lifetimes. The two of them laboured and agonized over the wording and the provisions of the trust deed until August when Henry finally signed it.

Ronald Bunter kept the original deed in his firm's strongroom and Henry placed the only copy in his own strongroom at Forest Drive.

In August of that same year the doctors at Nine Elms told Henry and Marlene that Sacha Jean would never be able to live outside an institution and would be in care for the rest of her life. Henry made no comment and Marlene locked herself in her sumptuous new bedroom suite with a bottle of Bombay Sapphire gin.

In September Marlene Imelda Bannock began a spell of three months in the Houston drug clinic on a rehabilitation programme for alcoholics.

In October Henry Bannock divorced Marlene Imelda Bannock and was given full custody of both their daughters; Sacha and Bryoni. Carl was already an adult so his name never figured in the divorce documents. When she was released from the drug programme Marlene went to live alone in the Cayman Islands in a magnificent beachside property where she was tended by a large domestic staff. All this was a part of the divorce settlement.

In late October the Directorate of Civil Aviation refused to renew Henry Bannock's commercial pilot's licence. He had failed his medical check.

'What the hell are you talking about?' Henry demanded furiously of the physician who was conducting the examination. 'I have just bought myself a Gulfstream for twelve million dollars. You cannot pull my licence now. I am as fit as I was when I was flying Sabre Jets in Korea.'

'If I may respectfully remind you, Mr Bannock, that was some two decades ago. Since then you have worked yourself as if you were a one-man prison chain-gang. When did you last take a vacation?'

'What the hell has that got to do with it? I haven't got time for vacations.'

'That's my point exactly, sir. Then tell me how many Havana

cigars you have smoked since Korea? How many bottles of Jack Daniel's have you demolished? How much exercise do you take?'

'You are being insolent, sonny boy.' Henry's face turned puce. 'That's my private business.'

'I apologize for that. However, I have to tell you that you have a classic case of atrial fibrillation.'

'Cut out the technical gobbledegook. What the hell are you fibrilling and drivelling about?'

'I am trying to tell you that your heart is dancing around like Gene Kelly on steroids. But that's only the half of it. Your blood pressure is up there in outer space with Neil Armstrong. If I were your physician I would immediately place you on Coumadin, Mr Bannock.'

'Thank God you are not my doctor. I know about this Coumadin stuff. I know it was used as rat poison and that it doesn't taste like Jack Daniel's; so you can take it, roll it into a small ball and stuff it up your rear end, Doctor Menzies.' Henry stood up and marched out of the office.

Even without his pilot's licence Henry continued to fly his beloved Gulfstream. He had two highly paid commercial pilots who covered for him.

However, sometimes in the still midnight hours he woke up with his heart stuttering and fluttering in his chest. He refused to see another doctor. He did not want to hear his death sentence being read to him.

With this warning that his days were numbered, he worked himself even harder. The idea of giving up his Havanas and his Jack Daniel's was intolerable, so he put it out of his mind.

In November Bryoni Lee won a state-wide mathematics competition against other students three and four years senior to her and was voted by her classmates the most likely to succeed and the most likely to become the president of the United States of America. She took over from her absent mother the visiting duties for her older sister.

Every Sunday Bonzo Barnes, Henry's chauffeur and bodyguard, drove her up to Nine Elms to spend the day with Sacha. Bonzo was a former heavyweight boxing contender. Like most others he loved young Bryoni. Bryoni sat up in front with him and they chatted happily all the way to Pasadena and back.

In December of that same year while his father was in Abu Zara reviewing the Bannock Oil concessions in that country, Carl Peter Bannock finally worked out the passwords and codes to Henry Bannock's strongroom. Carl had found a spot on the swimming pool terrace from which he was able surreptitiously to overlook his father's study. One Saturday morning he watched through the lens of a pair of 10x Zeiss binoculars as Henry sat at his desk and prised back the silk lining of his black leather desktop diary. Then he drew from beneath the lining one of his own business cards which he had concealed there.

On the back of the card in Henry's large bold hand was written a long string of letters and numbers. He crossed the room to the steel door of his personal vault. Consulting the writing on the card, Henry rotated the dial of the lock back and forth to register the password and then he spun the locking wheel in a counterclockwise direction and swung open the massive door.

Carl had to wait several weeks until Henry left on his next business trip, but then he had ten days and nights to work with.

The first night, after many frustrated attempts, he was able to master the complicated sequences to deactivate the locking mechanism and to open the steel door to the vault.

The next night he photographed the interior of the vault and the arrangement of the contents. Before he dared move anything he knew he must be able to replace all of it in exactly its original position. He knew that his father would immediately notice any changes. He wore surgical gloves at all times so as to avoid leaving his fingerprints on any of the contents of the vault and he worked with painstaking attention to all the details.

On the third night he could start exploring the contents of the vault. The bars of gold bullion were stacked on the floor where their weight was borne by the steel and concrete foundations. He estimated that there must be about fifty or sixty million dollars' worth of gold in the hoard.

Henry's behaviour had always been dictated by a peculiar mixture of reckless daring and prudent caution. This hoard was his little emergency fund.

On the next line of shelves were Henry's decorations and citations from his US Air Force days, and photographs and memorabilia of particular significance to him. On the steel shelves above were files of documents and share certificates, bonds and deeds of title to the numerous properties and concessions that Henry owned in his personal capacity. The other significant assets were held in the name of Bannock Oil Corporation.

On the fourth shelf from the top Carl found what he was really looking for.

He already knew of the existence of the Henry Bannock Family Trust. While he was still at Princeton he had begun hacking into his father's telephones in his bedroom and in his study. He had even attempted to access Henry's private phone lines at Bannock Oil headquarters, but the security cordon protecting the Bannock Building was impregnable.

Carl had been restricted to listening in on the line to the main bedroom suite to numerous conversations between Henry and his ex-wife and mistresses. But Carl had also made transcripts of conversations that Henry had conducted from his downstairs study, which included numerous conversations between Henry and his business associates and, more importantly, his lawyers.

Carl had been able to follow some of the discussions between Henry and Ronald Bunter, his principal lawyer, while they put together the Deed of Foundation of the Family Trust. But he had only a vague picture in his mind of the exact content and provisions of the final Trust Deed.

Now he found Henry's copy of this large tome sitting in the middle of the fourth shelf.

Still he did not rush at it. He examined the deed minutely with a magnifying glass before opening it. He marked the pages that Henry had stuck together with tiny droplets of glue. He separated these carefully and re-glued them as he passed on.

Between page 30 and page 31 he found the hair that Henry had placed there to trap interlopers. He recognized it as one of Henry's own hairs, wiry and springing, that he had plucked from his sideburns. Carl kept it in a clean white envelope and replaced it between the pages when he had finished with the document.

All these preliminaries left Carl with three uninterrupted nights before his father's return from the Middle East to peruse the deed of the new Henry Bannock Family Trust.

What he read filled him with a soaring sense of his own supremacy. The Trust Deed had endowed him with almost god-like powers. He was armed against the world and shielded by billions of dollars. He was invincible.

Sacha Jean had gradually regressed over the years until she had reached the equivalent mental age of a five- or six-year-old. Her world had shrunk as her brain was stifled and shut down. She no longer recognized anybody except one of the middle-aged nurses, who had been especially kind to her, and her baby sister Bryoni.

When her nurse reached retirement age, Sacha's already limited world was halved again and she became pathetically dependent on Bryoni. When the weather permitted it, the two of them spent all of every Sunday in the gardens of Nine Elms. Over time the physicians had learned just how reliable and responsible Bryoni was. They had no hesitation in giving her full care of Sacha for the day.

Sacha was now in her early twenties and obese. She towered over her little sister. Bryoni mothered her and led her by the hand to her favourite spot beside the lake, where they picnicked and fed the ducks. Sacha could no longer concentrate long enough to read for herself but she loved nursery rhymes. Bryoni read them to her. They played hopscotch, follow the leader and hide and go seek. Bryoni's patience was endless. She fed Sacha the picnic lunch that she had brought with her from home, and wiped her face and hands when she had finished eating. She took her to the toilet and helped her wipe herself and readjust her clothes when she had finished.

Sacha particularly loved having her back tickled. She liked to take off her blouse and lie face down on the picnic rug and make Bryoni tickle her back. Whenever she stopped Sacha would cry, 'More. More.'

One Sunday Bryoni was tickling her when Sacha said quite distinctly, 'If he ever wants to touch your nunu, don't let him do it.'

Bryoni paused in mid stroke and thought about what her sister had just said. Nunu was their baby name for the vagina.

'What did you say, Sash?' she asked carefully.

'When?'

'Right now.'

'I never said nothing.' Sacha denied it.

'Yes, you did.'

'I never did. I never said nothing.' Sacha was already becoming agitated and nervous. Bryoni knew the symptoms. Next she would curl up in a ball and start sucking her thumb or bumping her head on the ground.

'My mistake, Sash. Of course, you didn't say anything.' Slowly Sacha relaxed and starting talking about her puppy. She wanted her puppy back. For her last birthday Mummy had brought her a puppy, but Sacha was very strong and she loved and squeezed the puppy to death. They had to tell her it was sleeping to get the carcass away from her. She always asked Bryoni to bring it back to her, but the doctors would not let Sacha have another pet.

The next Sunday was bright and sunny and they picnicked at the same spot on the lake shore. Sacha didn't like anything to change. Change made her feel nervous and insecure. When they had eaten their lunch, Sacha demanded, 'Scratch my back.'

'What is the magic word?' Bryoni asked her. Sacha thought about it, scowling with concentration, but at last she gave up.

'I forgot the word. Tell me what it is.'

'Is the word please, do you think?'

'Yes. Yes. It's please.' Sacha clapped her hands with joy. 'Please, Bryoni. Pretty please scratch my back.' She pulled off her blouse and stretched out on the rug. After a while Bryoni thought she had fallen asleep, but suddenly Sacha said, 'If you let him touch your nunu he will stick his hard thing into you and make you bleed.'

Bryoni froze. The words shocked her deeply, to the extent that they made her feel physically sick. However, she pretended not to have heard and went on stroking Sacha's back. After a while Bryoni began to sing: 'Humpty Dumpty sat on the wall.' Sacha tried to join in but she got the words all muddled up and they both laughed.

Then Sacha said, 'If he sticks his thing in your nunu it will be very sore and you will bleed.' It was a trick of her damaged mind to repeat things over and over again.

'It's time for me to go now, Sash,' Bryoni said at last.

'Oh, no! Please stay a little longer. I get very frightened and sad when you go and leave me.'

'I will come back next Sunday.'

'Promise?'

'Yes, I promise.'

The next Sunday Bryoni brought with her a Dictaphone she had 'borrowed' from Henry's study.

She and Sacha walked hand in hand down to the lake. Bryoni carried the rug and the picnic basket. When they reached their special spot Sacha spread the rug and made certain there were neither folds nor tucks in it. Arranging the rug was her responsibility and she was very conscientious and proud of her ability to spread it to perfection. While her sister was concentrating all her attention on the rug, Bryoni slipped the Dictaphone out of the pocket of her jeans, switched it on and then returned it to her pocket without Sacha having noticed.

The day followed its familiar pattern; they fed the ducks and spoke about Sacha's puppy that was staying with its mummy dog in heaven. They ate their lunch and Bryoni took Sacha to the toilet. They returned to the lakeside and lay on the rug. Sacha asked her to scratch her back and Bryoni made her say please. Then, while she was tickling Sacha's back, she started humming 'Humpty Dumpty'. It set off a train of ideas in Sacha's crippled mind, as Bryoni had hoped it might.

Suddenly Sacha said, 'I didn't like it when he made his thing squirt into my mouth. It tasted awful.'

Bryoni shuddered but kept on humming quietly. For once Sacha was at ease and she rambled on.

'I have been trying to remember his name. He said he was my brother, but I don't have a brother. He showed me how to hold his thing and go up and down with it until it squirted. I liked it when he told me how clever I was and how much he loved me.'

She fell silent again and Bryoni went on humming softly and soothingly. Suddenly Sacha sat up and exclaimed, 'I remember now! His name was Carl Peter and he really was my brother. But then he went away. They have all gone away. My mummy and daddy; all of them have gone away and left me; all except you, Bryoni.'

'I'll never leave you, Sash. We will always be together like sisters should be.' Sacha was placated and she subsided back onto her stomach. Bryoni stroked her back and hummed softly.

Suddenly Sacha spoke out in a tone of voice more resembling the woman she was, rather than the five-year-old she had become.

'Yes, I do remember now that it was my brother Carl who came to my bedroom that night and climbed into my bed. It was Carl who pulled my legs open and put his big hard thing deep into me and made it squirt. I screamed but nobody heard me. I was bleeding and it was so sore, but I never told anybody because Carl had told me not to. Do you think I did the right thing, Bryoni?'

'Of course you did, my darling sister. You are such a good girl, and you always do the right thing.'

'Promise you will never leave me, Bryoni.'

'I promise you I will never leave you, my dearest Sash.'

When Bryoni arrived back home from Nine Elms that Sunday evening Carl's brand-new Ford Mustang was parked in the driveway. As she entered the front doors Carl was coming down the main staircase at a run. He was dressed in a suit and tie. His shoes were polished and his hair was slicked and glossy with oil.

'Hi, Bree!' he called down to her. 'How's our coo-coo sister? Is she still playing with the fairies?'

'Sacha is just fine. She's a very sweet and lovely girl.' Bryoni couldn't look up at his face; that smug arrogant face.

Carl swiftly lost interest in Sacha. He had only mentioned her name to rile Bryoni. He stopped in front of the full-length mirror at the foot of the stairs and adjusted the knot in his necktie. Then he took out his comb and carefully rearranged a few hairs that were out of place.

'Big date tonight. She's been panting after me for a month or more. Tonight is her lucky night. How do I look, Bree?' He turned to face her and spread his arms. 'Ta-ra! Ta-ra! Every woman's dream, yes?'

Bryoni stopped in front of him and forced herself to study his face. Many of her girlfriends said that he was the most handsome man they had ever laid eyes on. She realized that she hated him. He was a sick twisted sadistic swine.

'You know, Carl, this is the first time I've noticed that your right eye is bigger than the left one,' she said, and he turned back to the mirror in consternation. She brushed past him as she ran up the stairs to her own room. She knew that for weeks he would agonize about the relative size of his eyes, and she was pleased.

Her dad was out of town. He had gone off in his new jet plane to some funny little country in the Middle East called Abu Zara, and would not be home for two days more. She was alone in the big house. She phoned down to the kitchen and asked Cookie if she could eat dinner in the staff dining room with the other household servants, instead of alone in the big old dining room. Cookie was delighted. They all loved Bryoni.

'I baked an apple pie especially for you, Miss Bree.'

'You are a darling, Cookie. You know that's my absolute favourite.'

After dinner Bryoni locked herself in her study adjoining her bedroom and she copied the recording she had made at Nine Elms onto a spare tape. As she listened to Sacha's sweet baby voice reciting such disgusting perversions she grew very angry all over again.

She caught herself thinking of the twelve-gauge shotgun in her dad's den downstairs. Henry had taught her to shoot clay pigeons, and she had become a good little shot. Now she realized that she was in danger of losing her good sense and reason. She forced herself to return to her original plan.

When she had completed the copy of Sacha's rambling recollections she locked the recorder in her bedside drawer and went back to her desk to complete her homework assignment for the next day. She switched off her light at a little before ten o'clock but she could not get to sleep until almost midnight. Then she was awakened again by the roar of Carl's Mustang coming up the long driveway. He always drove very fast when he had been drinking. She checked the time and it was ten minutes past three.

The next morning she ate her breakfast in the kitchen with Cookie, and Bonzo drove her to school before Carl had emerged from his bedroom.

At mid-morning break she gave the back-up recording of Sacha's confessions into the safe keeping of her best friend, Alison Demper. She knew that if she kept the recording at Forest Drive Carl would find it.

'You have to swear a "Cross your Heart and Hope to Die Double Dixie Oath" that you'll not tell anybody I gave it to you,' she told Alison, who was intrigued. She dutifully spat on her finger, crossed her heart and swore her life away.

After school Bryoni pleaded a headache and was released from her art class. She went directly home and was waiting for her brother Carl when he returned from his job at Bannock Oil headquarters. He usually stopped for a beer with his chums at the Troubadour Inn, but this evening he came thundering up the drive in the Mustang a little before seven.

Bryoni was sitting in the window seat of her bedroom. She leaned out of the window and called down to him as he climbed out of the car and slammed the door. 'Hi, Carl! If you have a few minutes I would like to talk to you. Please can you come up to my bedroom?'

'Right on, sis.'

She heard him pounding up the stairs and then he knocked on her bedroom door.

'Door is open,' she called and he opened it, and paused in the doorway.

'What's up, sis?'

She was sitting on her bed but she had moved the armchair to the centre of the room for him.

'Come in, Carl. Take a seat. I want to talk to you about Sacha.'

215

He closed the door and sauntered across to the chair. He sprawled into it with one leg hanging over the arm.

'So, what is it about Sacha? Is she seeing little green men from Mars, or does she think she has turned into a pink polar bear at last?' He laughed at his own wit.

'Please listen to this.' She held up the Dictaphone.

'Is it your new all-time favourite rap recording, perhaps?'

Bryoni couldn't bring herself to reply to him, she hated him so much. She switched on the recorder and placed it on the bedside table.

There was silence as the recorder ran through its backing and then Sacha's voice spoke out. Carl knew it was her at once. He straightened up in the chair, unhooked his leg from the arm and placed both feet together on the floor in front of him.

'I didn't like it when he made his thing squirt into my mouth. It tasted awful,' Sacha said and Bryoni saw her brother wince, and his eyes shifted towards the window as though he was seeking an escape. But then they were drawn back to the recorder as Sacha went on.

'I have been trying to remember his name. He said he was my brother, but I don't have a brother. He showed me how to hold his thing and go up and down with it until it squirted. I liked it when he told me how clever I was and how much he loved me.'

Bryoni picked up the recorder and fast forwarded the tape for a few seconds. Then she hit the play button and replaced it on the bedside table. Sacha's voice was firmer and more mature as she began speaking again.

'. . . it was my brother Carl who came to my bedroom that night and climbed into my bed. It was Carl who pulled my legs open and put his big hard thing deep into me and made it squirt. I screamed but nobody heard me. I was bleeding and it was so sore, but I never told anybody because Carl had told me not to. Do you think I did the right thing, Bryoni?'

'Of course you did, my darling sister. You are such a good girl, and you always do the right thing.'

Bryoni reached out and switched off the recorder, and then in the silence that followed she asked quietly, 'Do you think that you did the right thing, Carl?'

His mouth was working but was forming no words. He wiped his face on the sleeve of his jacket and then stared at the sweat traces left on the fine cloth.

Then abruptly he sprang to his feet and snatched the Dictaphone off the bedside table and in the same continuous movement hurled it against the door to Bryoni's bathroom. It shattered into its component parts. He crossed the room with quick and decisive strides and stamped on the remains.

His hands were trembling and his entire body was shaking as he turned back to face Bryoni.

'The slut. The filthy little whore. You and your crazy whoring sister dreamed that all up. Admit it: you are as raving mad as she is. You are both jealous of me. You are trying to discredit me with my father. But my father loves me.'

'Your father was a Nazi war criminal,' Bryoni said quietly. 'Your father was somebody called Kurtmeyer who murdered people in gas chambers and ran a chain of brothels. You are your true father's rotten seed, Karl Kurtmeyer.'

'That's a lie,' he shouted at her. 'You made that up. You are a lying little bitch,' he screamed at her.

'I did not so make that up,' Bryoni replied without raising her voice. 'Our mother told me all about your father one afternoon when she was drinking gin.'

'It's a lie! My father is Henry Bannock. I am his only son. He loves me and I am his heir. You and your dirty little whoring sister are jealous of me. You want to poison his mind against me. That's why you are telling these filthy lies about me.'

'We aren't doing anything to you. You are the one who brutalized and debased your own little sister. You forced her to do terrible and disgusting things, and then you raped her and drove her out of her mind.'

'Lies!' he shouted at her. 'My father will never believe your lies.'

'He will when he listens to my recording.' Bryoni stood up from the bed and confronted him calmly. He spun round and ran to where the shattered pieces of the recorder lay and dropped on his knees. He swept them up and stuffed them into his pockets.

'There is no recorder,' he said. 'It's gone. It never was. It was only a mad girl's fantasy.'

'I made a copy,' Bryoni said. And he stood up and advanced on her menacingly.

'Where is it?'

'Where you will never find it.'

'Give it to me.'

'Never!' she hissed at him fiercely and he hit her. It was an open-handed, full swing across her face. It knocked her backwards onto the bed. She pushed herself up on her elbows and there was blood in her mouth and it ran down her chin. She snarled at him again through bloody lips, fierce as a wounded lioness, 'Never!'

The sight of her bright blood inflamed him. Blood always had that effect on him. It tipped him past the point of reason. He threw himself on top of her and forced her shoulders back on the bed. He was more than twice her age, and much more than twice her body weight. His strength was overpowering. He tore at her clothing and grunted, 'You are going to have to learn a lesson in respect. The same lesson I taught your crazy sister.'

She screamed but he locked the fingers of his left hand around her throat and squeezed hard, while with the other hand he pulled down her underclothes and forced one knee up between her thighs.

'Scream as much as you like. No one will hear you. No one will come to help you. No one will believe you.' His voice was thick with lust. 'I have to teach you respect.'

He sprang the buckle of his belt, and tore open the fly of his trousers so violently that one of the buttons flew off. Now he had her skin to skin.

Her lower body and loins were childlike and totally devoid of hair. She was unripe fruit; tiny, tight and dry. But he tore her open and forced his way into her.

In a paroxysm of agony she sank her teeth into his shoulder and he swore at her and released his strangling grip on her throat to prise her jaws open. Now they were both bleeding.

She threw back her head, and she screamed and screamed as he continued pounding into her.

Cookie in the kitchen below them heard her screams and she shouted for Bonzo Barnes, the chauffeur. The two of them raced up the stairs and burst into Bryoni's bedroom just as Carl's whole body contorted, and he bucked and groaned in orgasmic ecstasy over Bryoni's slim half-naked form.

Bonzo hauled Carl off his sister and threw him across the room.

'What you doing, man? She only a baby, man. She your little sister, man. What you think you doing to her, man?' Bonzo bellowed at him. He picked up Carl from the floor by his throat and shook him like a rat.

'Don't hurt him, Bonzo,' Cookie shouted at him. 'Police going to take care of him.' Bonzo dropped him in a heap, and Carl sat up.

'No, don't call the police,' he pleaded desperately. 'My father will be home tomorrow. He will take care of everything. He will pay you—'

'Shut your face, you pig-dog animal. I'm warning you, man,' Bonzo growled at him.

Bryoni was weeping bitterly with shock and pain. Cookie hugged her to her bosom and told her, 'Hush up, my baby. He not going to hurt you no more. You safe now.'

She reached out and lifted the bedside telephone handset from its cradle and dialled 911. The call was answered almost immediately.

'Young girl just been raped here. She's bleeding pretty bad. We caught the pervert done it to her. Send the police.'

The blue-uniformed police arrived in two squad cars within twenty minutes. They listened to what Cookie and Bonzo had to tell them and then turned to Bryoni.

Bryoni stood up from the bed where Cookie had laid her down. She faced the officers. Her clothes were torn and bloodstained. Her face was swollen and one eye was blue and half closed. She was still shaking.

She took one step towards the police sergeant, but a thin ribbon of blood snaked from under her skirt and ran down her thigh. She moaned and clutched at her lower belly. She doubled over slowly and sagged to her knees. Cookie picked her up and held her to her bosom.

'Holy Moses!' said the sergeant. 'Get the cuffs on that sad bastard and take him down to the station.'

His men grabbed Carl and twisted his arms up behind his back.

'Take it easy, damn you,' Carl protested. 'You don't have to act so tough.'

'Like you didn't have to act so tough with that little girl?' one of them asked as he locked the cuffs on Carl's wrists. Then he looked across at his sergeant. 'Prisoner is resisting arrest, Sarge. Better we slap the leg irons on him just in case.'

The sergeant nodded approval, then turned back to Cookie. 'We have to get this child to the hospital. She needs a doctor.'

Cookie wrapped the blanket around Bryoni's shoulders. Bonzo picked her up and ran with her to the waiting squad car.

Ronald Bunter phoned Henry Bannock at the Bannock Oil installation in Abu Zara, and Henry's voice was thick with sleep.

'This had better be good, Ronnie. It's three in the morning here.'

'Sorry, Henry, but I have news for you. It isn't good,' Ronald told him. 'In fact it's about as bad as it gets. Is there somebody there with you?'

'Of course there is. Do you think I am a monk?'

'She doesn't have to listen to this.'

'Hold on. I'll move to another room.' There was a short exchange between Henry and his mysterious companion, a pause and then Henry said, 'Okay, Ronnie. I am sitting on the john and the door is locked. Give it to me.'

'Carl Peter has been arrested.'

'Oh no! The little monster,' Henry groaned. 'What is it this time? Speeding? Drunken driving?'

'I wish it were, my old friend. It's far, far worse, I'm afraid.'

'Come on, Ronnie! Stop being coy! Out with it!'

'They have charged him with a number of different offences. The most serious are common rape, statutory rape, aggravated sexual assault, common assault and grievous bodily harm, battery, incest and corrupting a minor. They are still investigating and questioning witnesses, but they have warned us that they expect to bring other charges of repeated aggravated sexual assault on a person or persons under the age of fourteen years. A couple of those felonies are capital offences in the state of Texas.'

There followed a long silence broken only by the crackle of static. 'Hello! Hello! Are you still there, Henry?'

'Yeah, I'm still here. I'm thinking.' Henry's voice was bleak. 'Give me a second or two, Ronnie.' Then he asked, 'Who do they accuse him of raping?'

'Sorry, Henry! This is the worst part of it. He is accused of raping both Sacha and Bryoni.'

'No!' Henry said softly. 'It's a mistake. It can't be true. I don't believe it. Bryoni is my baby.'

Ronald wanted to say, 'Sacha is also your baby,' but he bit back the words. He didn't want to add to his old friend's suffering.

'We are going to fight this, Ronnie. We are going to fight this with all we've got, do you hear me?'

'I hear you, Henry. But just consider this for a moment. They have the testimony of both your daughters, they have the testimony of two reliable eye witnesses, they have samples of Carl Peter's sperm taken from Bryoni's vagina and mingled with her blood. They have photographs of the bruises he inflicted on her.'

'Christ!' said Henry Bannock. 'Jesus Christ and Mary!'

Ronald could almost hear the pillars and rooftops of Henry's universe crashing down upon him. He thought he heard him sob, but that was not possible. Not sobbing. Not Henry.

'Do you think he did it, Ronald?'

'I am a lawyer, I don't sit in judgement.'

'But you think he's guilty, don't you? Don't talk to me like my lawyer. Talk to me like my best friend.'

'As your lawyer I don't know and I don't care. As your friend I care very much, and I think your son is guilty as hell.'

'He's not my son!' Henry said. 'He never was my son. I have been fooling myself all these years. He is the get and spawn of some rotten Nazi bastard I picked up along the way.'

'You better come home, Henry. We need you here. Your two little girls need you here very much.'

'I am on my way!' Henry said.

'Look here, Ronnie.' Henry leaned over the desk and pointed his finger at Ronald Bunter. 'I want that dirty Nazi rapist struck off the list of the beneficiaries of my Family Trust, and I don't want my Trust to have to pay for the legal fees of defending him from the crime of raping both my daughters. I have spoken to Bryoni and he's as guilty as all sin and I want to see him swing on the gallows.'

Ronald swivelled back in his chair, placed his fingertips together and looked at the ceiling, as though he was seeking higher help and guidance.

'You know we have been over this numerous times, Henry. However, I will address your three separate wishes in the order you expressed them.' He sat straight upright in his chair, placed his elbows on the desk and looked Henry directly in the eye.

'Firstly, you placed Carl Bannock on the list of beneficiaries and you made damned sure that nobody can ever remove him; not me, or you, or the Supreme Court in Washington. My hands are tied and you tied them. Secondly, you do not want the Trust to pay for his legal defence. The trustees, me among them, have no option in the matter. You made it abundantly clear in the deed of trust that you signed that we are duty bound to pay for all the expenses of protecting him from any legal action brought against him by any person or any government, be it the Department of Justice or the Department of Internal Revenue. It is out of our hands. Carl chooses his own defence team and the Trust must pay for it.'

'But he raped my daughters,' Henry protested.

'You never made an exception for that eventuality,' Ronald pointed out, and then he continued, 'Lastly you have just expressed a wish to see Carl swing from the gallows. This can never happen. The State of Texas abolished execution by hanging in 1924. The best I can offer you is a lethal injection.'

'I realize now that setting up that trust was the biggest mistake of my sweet life.'

'Again I have to disagree, Henry. Your trust is a fine instrument. The sentiment behind it is a noble one. It ensures that Marlene,

Sacha and little Bryoni, together with all their own children and your future wives and their offspring, will never want or lack anything that money can buy. You are a good and great man, Henry Bannock.'

'I bet you say that to all your clients.'

The trial of Carl Peter Bannock lasted twenty-six court days. The preliminary deliberations of the Grand Jury covered four of those days before they returned a 'True Bill', which was the equivalent of a felony indictment. The case was assigned to a court and the process of law was set in motion.

The judge was Joshua Chamberlain. He was a man in his sixties. He was a committed Democrat. He had the reputation of being pedantic and meticulous. During almost twenty years on the bench none of his judgements had ever been overturned on appeal; which was in itself a remarkable achievement.

In line with his liberal beliefs, he had meted out the death sentence in less than three per cent of the capital cases that had come before him.

The prosecutor was a woman. Her name was Melody Strauss. Although she was a little under forty years of age, she had handled many extremely difficult cases, and had built up a solid reputation for herself. She was assigned two legal assistants.

The defence team comprised five of the most expensive lawyers in the state of Texas. They had been carefully selected by counsel for the defendant. Their combined fees cost the Henry Bannock Family Trust a figure somewhat north of two hundred thousand dollars a day.

The first order of business was choosing and swearing in the twelve members of the jury from the fifty possibilities that had been put forward. This took more than a week, as the defence strove to exclude as many women as was possible. They used up all their ten peremptory challenges to strike out prospective female jurors, and then they grilled the remaining women on their attitude to the death sentence and their stance on female enticement and instigation to rape.

Melody Strauss met the defence head on and slogged it out with them. She strove to retain as many women as possible on the final list of jurors. Melody was quick-witted and persuasive. She questioned all the male candidates rigorously to detect any tendency towards male chauvinism. She reserved all her peremptory challenges to dismiss only male candidates who revealed traces of this defect. In the final count she managed to square the odds with an equal number of men and women on the jury.

On the tenth day of the trial Melody Strauss rose to present the case for the prosecution and was met by a barrage of objections from the defence. From the outset they challenged the competence of Sacha Jean Bannock to give evidence, on the grounds of her mental condition.

Both sides called expert witnesses. Melody Strauss called two members of the staff of the Nine Elms psychiatric clinic who had dealt with Sacha over many years. They both testified that Sacha had recently shown marked and sustained improvement in her memory and recall. They attributed this to the influence of her younger sister, Bryoni Lee, and to the catharsis she had experienced after she had recalled a traumatic event or series of events from her early childhood.

Under questioning they gave further evidence that Sacha's symptoms and mental condition were a textbook example of the effects of repeated and aggravated sexual abuse in early childhood.

The expert called by the defence was a professor emeritus of UCLA Department of Psychology who testified that he had examined Sacha and he gave his opinion that Sacha was not capable of giving evidence under oath because she did not understand the significance of doing so. He further gave his opinion that any evidence she was able to impart would be completely unreliable and that the process would be so traumatic to Sacha that there was a high probability that she would suffer significant and permanent mental damage from the experience.

Melody asked the judge to give special permission to allow Sacha to give evidence in his chambers with the defence and the jury in the next room watching and listening over CCTV without Sacha being aware of their presence. After learned debate Judge Chamberlain denied the request.

Melody then petitioned the judge for leave to play Bryoni's tape recording of Sacha speaking about her relationship with her brother Carl to the jury.

Again this raised a storm of objection from the defence, and again Judge Chamberlain denied the request of the prosecution.

Melody was left with a fateful choice. She could defy the odds and call Sacha Jean to the stand, or she could drop the charge of 'repeated aggravated sexual assault on a person or persons under the age of fourteen years'. And go to trial with only testimony from Bryoni Lee as to her rape.

Melody Strauss turned to Bryoni Lee Bannock for final advice. The two of them had developed a special relationship in the short time since they had first met. Bryoni had swiftly come to like and trust Melody, and Melody had been impressed by Bryoni's maturity, courage and good sense. More especially she had been deeply moved by her loyalty and devotion to Sacha and her intuitive understanding of the troubled girl's condition.

'What will Sacha do if I question her in front of all those people about what Carl did to her?' she asked Bryoni, who answered without hesitation, 'She will fall down and curl up like an anchovy; then she will suck her thumb and bump her head on the ground and go away into her own special dreamland.'

The next day, to protect and shield Sacha, Melody Strauss formally withdrew the capital charge of repeated aggravated sexual assault on a minor.

Spurred on by this partial failure, Melody threw herself with freshly rekindled vigour into pressing the other charges against Carl Bannock to their utmost.

She called Bryoni Bannock to the stand. The defence raised another storm of protest. Bryoni was an immature child. She did not understand the questions put to her. She was incapable of giving plausible and meaningful evidence.

Judge Chamberlain called a two-hour recess to consider the objection. He spoke to Bryoni alone in his chambers and returned to tell the jury, 'This young lady has demonstrated to me more intelligence and maturity than many of the thirty- and forty-year-old persons who have stood before me in this court. The objection of the defence is denied. Miss Bryoni Lee Bannock may take her place in the witness box.'

In the witness box was where John Martius, the leading defence counsel, strove to destroy her credibility.

Melody Strauss had groomed Bryoni for the ordeal and instructed her as to how she should comport herself while she was on the stand, and the kind of questions she might be asked.

'Keep your answers short and to the point,' she said. 'Don't allow yourself to be side-tracked.'

In the event Bryoni conducted herself like a veteran. She answered every question firmly and politely.

'When did you first suspect that your sister had been sexually molested?' Melody asked her.

'When she warned me not to let anybody touch my private parts or else they would hurt me. I was sure that somebody had done that to her.'

'Objection! Supposition!' John Martius was on his feet in a flash.

'Objection denied,' said Judge Chamberlain.

'Did she say who it was that had done it to her?'

'Not at first, but the longer she spoke the more she remembered. I think she had tried to forget the ugly things that had happened to her.'

'In the end did she remember the name?'

'Yes, ma'am. I can remember her exact words. She said, "Now I remember it was my brother Carl who came to my room that night and climbed into my bed. It was Carl who pulled my legs open and put his big hard thing deep into me and made it squirt. I screamed but nobody heard me. I was bleeding and it was so sore, but I never told anybody because Carl had told me not to."'

'Objection!' howled John Martius. 'Hearsay!'

'Objection denied,' said the judge. 'The witness is describing a conversation to which she was a party. The jury will take cognizance of that reply.'

Melody Strauss moved on to cover the events after Bryoni had confronted Carl Bannock with the tape recordings she had made of Sacha describing the series of assaults upon her.

'Objection! The alleged tape recordings have no provenance and have been excluded from evidence,' cried John Martius.

'Miss Strauss?' The judge invited her to refute.

'Your Honour, I am not seeking to introduce the recordings as evidence, I am using them merely as a time reference to the events of that evening.'

'Objection is denied. You may continue, Miss Bannock.'

Bryoni described Carl's assault upon her.

'He demanded to know what I had done with my copy of the recording of what Sacha had told me. I refused to tell him. Then he struck me in the face and knocked me onto my bed.'

'Did he cause you any injury?'

'My left eye was swollen and bruised. My nose was bleeding and my lip was cut so that my mouth was filled with blood.'

The female members of the jury gasped and murmured and exchanged horrified glances.

In the front row of the visitor's gallery Henry Bannock scowled and glared at his stepson in the dock. He had been there every hour of every day of the trial, hoping with his presence to bolster and encourage Bryoni in her ordeal.

'After he had struck you and knocked you down on the bed, what happened next, Bryoni?' Melody Strauss asked her.

'Carl told me he was going to teach me respect, just as he had done to my sister, Sacha.'

'When you say Carl, do you refer to your brother, Carl Bannock, the accused?'

'That is correct, ma'am.'

John Martius intervened swiftly. 'Objection! Carl Bannock is not the brother of the witness.'

'I stand corrected.' Melody Strauss was just as quick. 'I should have said, half-brother. That relationship is also covered in the definition of incest in the felony code of the State of Texas.'

'Objection!'

'I withdraw that remark, and reserve it for my summation.' She turned back to Bryoni. 'Then what did the accused do?'

'He climbed on top of me and opened my clothing.'

'Did you try to resist him?'

'I tried my best, but he is much bigger and stronger than I am, ma'am, and I was dizzy from the blow he had given me.'

'After he had opened your clothing what happened?'

'He took out his penis . . .'

Seated at the defence table Carl Bannock covered his face with both hands and started to sob loudly. John Martius sprang to his feet.

'Your Honour, my client is overcome by these accusations. I ask for your indulgence, and request a recess for him to recover.'

'Mr Martius, by all the evidence your client is a powerful and determined individual. I am sure that he can endure a little longer. The witness may reply to the question.'

'He took out his penis and forced it inside me, into my vagina.' Bryoni gulped, and wiped at her eyes. 'It was so sore. The worst pain ever I had. I screamed and struggled but he wouldn't stop pushing it into me. Then Bonzo came and pulled him away, but the pain did not stop and I saw I was bleeding down there. Cookie came and held me close and told me that it was over and Carl would never be able to hurt me again. She said she wouldn't let anybody hurt me again.' Bryoni folded up in her chair and buried her face in her arms, sobbing brokenly.

'No more questions, Your Honour,' Melody Strauss said softly.

John Martius jumped to his feet.

'Cross, Your Honour.'

'The court will recess until ten o'clock tomorrow morning. You must reserve your cross-examination until then, Mr Martius.'

Henry Bannock, Ronnie Bunter and Bonzo Barnes were waiting outside the courtroom to meet Bryoni when she was released and they shepherded her through the mob of reporters and journalists that crowded the sidewalk and shouted questions at her. Bryoni held her head up high and looked straight ahead but her face was ashen and her lips trembled. She clung to her father's arm. Bonzo Barnes broke trail for them, and his bulk and his scowl cleared a lane for them to the waiting limousine.

That evening Cookie brought Bryoni's dinner to her bedroom on a tray and Henry sat beside her bed and talked to her while she ate. He told her how much he loved her, and how he wished he had been able to protect her and Sacha from the terrible things that Carl had done to them. He promised her that he would never let harm come to either of his daughters again.

Then he stayed with her and stroked her hair until she fell asleep.

At ten o'clock the next morning Bryoni was on the witness stand again. The courtroom was packed and in the press section there was standing room only. Bryoni had been briefed by both Melody Strauss and Ronnie Bunter so she ignored them completely and looked at her father in the front row of the public gallery, and at Bonzo and Cookie sitting three rows further back.

John Martius stood up from his seat at the defence table and came to stand in front of her.

'You understand that I am going to ask you some questions, Bryoni?'

'Yes, sir.'

'You don't mind if I call you Bryoni?'

'No, sir.'

'Do you love your brother, Carl?'

'Objection! The accused is not the witness's brother.' Melody paid him in his own coin.

'I will rephrase,' Martius conceded. 'Do you love your half-brother, Carl?'

'Perhaps I did once, but not since he raped me and Sacha, I don't, sir.' A buzz of approbation swept the courtroom at this and Judge Chamberlain rapped his gavel and said sternly, 'Silence in court, if you please.'

'Did you ever ask him to kiss you?'

'No, sir.'

'Are you saying you never kissed Carl?'

'I said I never asked him to kiss me, sir.'

'Did you ever kiss him?'

'Carl and I just naturally kissed cheeks to say hello or goodbye, like everybody does, sir.'

'Did you ever ask Carl to kiss you on the mouth, Bryoni?'

'No, sir. Why would I do that?'

'Just answer my questions, please, Bryoni. Did you ever put your tongue in Carl's mouth when he kissed you?'

'Objection! Witness has already testified that she never kissed the defendant on the mouth,' Melody pointed out.

'Objection sustained,' Judge Chamberlain said. 'Counsel will withdraw that question.'

'Question withdrawn.' Martius bowed slightly to the judge, and then turned back to Bryoni. 'Did you ever enter the bathroom when Carl was showering, Bryoni?'

'No, sir. I have my own bathroom. I never went to Carl's bathroom.'

'Did you ever walk into Carl's bedroom when you knew he was changing?'

'No, sir. I have my own bedroom. I have never been to his bedroom.'

'Never?'

'Never, sir.'

'What would you reply if I told you that Carl says that you wanted to watch him shower, and that you once went to his room at night and climbed into bed with him?'

'Objection! Asked and answered! Witness has testified that she has never been in the accused's bedroom.'

'Objection sustained. Counsel will withdraw the question.'

'I withdraw the question, Your Honour.' But he was well pleased; he had placed a seed in the minds of the jury. He consulted his own notes for a moment, and then looked up at Bryoni.

'Did you ever ask your half-brother Carl if he would like to see your breasts?'

Melody Strauss seemed on the point of objecting, but then she remained silent, and she let Bryoni reply spontaneously and tellingly.

'I don't have any breasts, sir. Not yet, anyway.' She looked genuinely puzzled when two of the jurymen laughed out loud, but it was kindly laughter, without any trace of mockery. Two or three of the female jury members frowned in disapproval of their male counterparts' levity.

Henry Bannock saw that Melody had withheld her objection deliberately. It was a shrewd decision. He hoped the jury would punish Martius for harassing a child, especially a pretty one.

.Martius had taken a gamble when he introduced the element of female enticement. Now he knew it was a losing bet, and he changed tack at once.

'Do you know that your father had such a high opinion of your half-brother Carl that he formally adopted him as his own son, and after Carl achieved singular distinction at Princeton he gave him a highly paid and responsible job at Bannock Oil Corporation?'

'Yes, sir, of course I knew. Everybody knew.'

'Did this make you think that your father loved Carl more than he loved you? Did it make you very jealous? Did it make you and your sister Sacha decide to make up hurtful stories about Carl?'

'My daddy loves me, sir.' She looked at Henry Bannock and she smiled. 'One of the reasons that my daddy loves me is because I always tell him the truth. He wouldn't love me so much if I lied to him.'

Henry Bannock smiled back at his daughter and nodded affirmation of her declaration. His craggy and obdurate features softened.

'No further questions for this witness, Your Honour.' John Martius realized he had been bested by a child and he decided to retreat in some sort of order.

'Thank you, Bryoni,' Judge Chamberlain told her. 'You have been very brave. You may go to your father now.'

Henry Bannock came to meet his daughter and placed one arm protectively around her shoulders. He shot a last vitriolic look at his adoptive son and then led Bryoni from the courtroom. Bryoni clung to him and began to weep quietly but bitterly.

Melody Strauss called her next witness. She was the police physician who had examined Bryoni on the fateful evening. Her name was Doctor Ruth MacMurray. She was mature and grey-haired, composed and quietly spoken.

'Doctor MacMurray, did you examine Bryoni Lee Bannock on the evening of August fifteenth last in the emergency room at Houston University Hospital?'

'I did.'

'Can you please relate to this court your findings at the time, Doctor?'

'The subject was a prepubescent female. She presented with superficial facial injuries consistent with having been struck with the hand. There was contusion and swelling of the left eye. There was also laceration of the soft tissue of the mouth. In addition the left incisor and first premolar teeth had been loosened by trauma.'

'Were there any other bodily injuries?'

'Yes, indeed. There was extensive bruising of both upper arms and throat.'

'What would that bruising indicate to you, Doctor?'

'It would indicate that the subject had probably been forcibly restrained by being held by the upper arms, and that she had in addition been held by the throat either in an attempt to strangle her or to prevent her crying out.'

'Thank you, Doctor MacMurray. Did you find any other injuries?'

'The subject showed all the symptoms of her genitalia being penetrated by a large rigid object.'

'Were these injuries consistent with the immature subject having been forcibly penetrated by a mature and erect human penis?'

'They were entirely consistent with that possibility. The hymen had very recently been ruptured and was still bleeding. The perineum between the vagina and the anus had been torn and had to be surgically repaired. In addition there was internal tearing and rupturing of the lower vaginal wall which also required repair.'

'In your opinion were these injuries consistent with the subject having been raped?'

'In my opinion these injuries were entirely consistent with aggravated rape and forcible penetration of the genitalia.'

'Did you manage to collect samples of the bodily fluid that you found in the subject's vagina, Doctor?'

'I collected thirteen swabs from the damaged vagina. And blood samples from the subject's clothing.'

'What were the findings from the pathologic examinations of these samples, Doctor?'

'In the case of the clothing samples two types of blood were found to be present. One was AB-negative and the other O-positive.'

'Do these match with the blood of the accused and the victim, Doctor?'

'Carl Bannock is blood type AB-negative, and Bryoni Bannock is type O-positive.'

232

'Is type O a rare or is it a common blood type, Doctor?'

'It is the most common type. About forty per cent of human beings are type O.'

'And type AB-negative; is it rare or common, Doctor?'

'It is the rarest blood type; possessed by only one per cent of humans.'

'So does that mean that there is a forty to one chance of the AB-negative blood samples belonging to Carl Bannock, the accused?'

'I am not a bookmaker, madam. I would not be able to quote you exact odds. I will say, however, that there is a much higher chance that the AB-negative blood samples belong to Carl Bannock than to anybody else on earth.'

'Thank you, Doctor. My next question is regarding the swab samples you took from Bryoni Bannock's vagina, Doctor. What were the pathological results of these swabs?'

'In each case without exception both blood and seminal fluid were present.'

'What was the blood type or types, Doctor?'

'Only type O-positive.'

'That is Bryoni Bannock's blood type, is it not?'

'Yes, it is.'

'Now, Doctor, was there any other bodily fluid on the swabs that you took from Bryoni Bannock's vagina?'

'Yes, there was also male seminal fluid present.'

'Male seminal fluid? Was the pathologist able to establish a match to the samples collected from Carl Bannock, the accused?'

'The seminal fluid taken from Bryoni Bannock's vagina was an eighty to ninety per cent match to those samples provided by Carl Bannock for the police surgeon.'

'How were these samples tested against each other, Doctor?'

'Three techniques were applied: the RSID strip test, the PSA test and the acid phosphatase test.'

'Thank you, Doctor. I have no more questions,' Melody told her, and looked across at John Martius.

'Your witness, sir.'

'No questions,' Martius said without looking up from his trial brief.

Judge Chamberlain glanced at the courtroom clock before he

instructed Melody. 'Please call your next witness, Miss Strauss.'

'The prosecution calls Mrs Martha Honeycomb.' Cookie stood up from her bench in the public gallery and made her way down the aisle towards the witness box. Despite the advice from Melody Strauss that she should wear subdued clothing, Cookie had not been able to resist the temptation to wear her finery for the occasion. On her head she had a tiny straw hat set at a jaunty angle and a small black veil over one eye. Her dress was patterned in large sunflowers which had the effect of emphasizing the size of her posterior. Her white shoes were very high heeled, which made walking a little awkward.

Once she was seated in the witness box Melody Strauss led her through a brief account of her relationship to the Bannock family.

'How long have you worked for Mr Henry Bannock?'

'Since I left school, ma'am.'

'How long have you known Bryoni Bannock, Mrs Honeycomb?'

'You can call me Cookie, ma'am. Everybody else does.'

'Thank you, Cookie. How long have you known Bryoni, Cookie?'

'Since the day she were born. Cutest little thing she were, too.'

'And her brother, Carl. How long have you known him?'

Cookie swivelled her large frame around and glared at Carl sitting at the defence table. 'Since the day he come to live by our house, and a sad and sorry day that were too, though none of us knowed that at the time. We all thought he were a good little fella.'

'Counsel, please ask your witness to confine herself to answering the questions.'

'Did you hear the judge, Cookie?'

'Sorry, ma'am. Mr Bannock also say I talk too much.'

Judge Chamberlain coughed and covered his mouth with one hand to smother both the cough and his grin. Melody Strauss led Cookie through the events leading up to her and Bonzo's rescue of Bryoni from Carl's attack, and to his arrest by the State Police.

'How did you know that the accused had gone upstairs to his sister's room?'

'Bonzo and I hear him coming up the driveway in that fancy machine his daddy give him for his birthday. Then we hear Bryoni calling to him from her room to come up 'cos she wanna talk to him.'

'Then what happened, Cookie?'

'We hear Master Carl running up the stairs and the door to Bryoni's bedroom slam. Then there silence for a long while. Then Bonzo and me hear Carl shouting like he going out of his head. I say, "Bonzo we better go see what they up to." But Bonzo he say, "Man, they just arguing like always. You and me, better we leave them to get on with it. I am going to polish the Cadillac for when Mr Bannock come home," and off he go down the stairs.'

'So he left you alone in the kitchen and then what happened, Cookie?'

'Then there was a bit of quiet, and suddenly Miss Bryoni start screaming like she having her throat cut. Even Bonzo hear it down there in the garage. But I shout, "Bonzo, you better come quick. Sounds like there big trouble." We runs up the stairs and Bonzo runs straight through that big ol' door like there nothing there. I runs in just behind him and I see Master Carl on top of Miss Bryoni on the bed and she fighting him like a crazy girl and screaming her head off and he on top of her having sex with her.'

'How did you know he was having sex with her, Cookie?'

'Nuff good ol' boys have done it to me for me to know for sure when one of them doing it to someone else, Miss Strauss.'

'Please continue telling us what took place next, Cookie.'

'Well, Bonzo go out of his head. Like all of us he just love little Miss Bryoni. He shouting at Carl, "What you doing to her, man? She your little baby sister, man. What you doing to her?" and stuff like that. Then he grab Carl and throw him clean across the room. Then I see Carl got his pants all open in front and his big ol' hard-on sticking out a yard in front of him, all wet with my baby's blood and stuff and then I want to kill him also, but I tell Bonzo leave him 'cos the police going to take care of him and we gotta take care of Bryoni. Then I call the police and they come pretty damn fast and they arrest Carl and Bonzo carry Bryoni to the police car 'cos she hurt so bad she can't walk and they take her off to hospital.'

'Thank you, Cookie. I have no further questions for you.'

Judge Chamberlain looked towards the defence table. 'Counsel for the defence, do you wish to cross-examine the witness?'

John Martius seemed about to refuse, then he stood up slowly.

'Mrs Honeycomb, you say you heard Bryoni inviting the accused up to her bedroom?'

'Yes, sir, I heard her tell him to come up, but I don't think she want him to play hide the ol' pork sausage with her. I think she gonna play him the tape of Sacha telling what Carl did—'

'Your Honour! Witness has answered my question that Bryoni Bannock invited her brother into her bedroom. The rest of her testimony is supposition.'

'Please don't speculate, Mrs Honeycomb. The jury will pay no heed to the rest of witness's reply.'

'Thank you, Your Honour. I have no further questions for this witness.' Martius sat down again.

Next, Melody Strauss called Bonzo Barnes to the witness box. Bonzo corroborated every detail of Cookie's evidence, but not as articulately nor as colourfully as she had delivered the original.

John Martius asked a single question in cross-examination. 'Mr Barnes, did you hear Bryoni Bannock invite her brother Carl into her bedroom?'

'Yes, sir. I heard her.'

'Did Bryoni often entertain her brother Carl in her bedroom with the door closed?'

'If she did then I never seen or heard her do it, mister.'

'But you are not certain that she never had him alone in her bedroom?'

Bonzo thought about the question deeply and darkly. 'It ain't my job to stand guard at Miss Bryoni's door every minute of the day.'

'So you don't know if Bryoni Bannock made a habit of entertaining her boyfriends in her bedroom behind closed doors?'

'I am sure of one thing, mister. If I catch any boy in her room trying to do what Carl done to her I gonna break his neck.'

'Thank you, Mr Barnes. No further questions for this witness, Your Honour.'

Bonzo rose to his full height and stature and glowered at John Martius. 'I know what you trying to make me say, but what you hear me say is our little Bryoni is a good girl. I gonna break the neck of anybody who say she not!'

'Thank you, Mr Barnes.' John Martius backed away hurriedly

236

out of the reach of Bonzo's long arm. 'You may leave the witness box.'

Melody called her next witnesses. He was Sergeant Roger Tarantus of the Houston Police Department. He gave evidence that he and his team had responded to an emergency call and gone to No. 61 Forest Drive, the residence of Henry Bannock and his family, on the evening in question. Melody led him through a detailed description of what he had found on the premises on arrival, and the actions he had taken. Sergeant Tarantus's evidence tended to confirm the evidence of all the other prosecution witnesses, including Bryoni Bannock and both Bonzo Barnes and Martha Honeycomb.

'So, Sergeant Tarantus, on the strength of what you had seen and heard at Number Sixty-one Forest Drive you arrested Carl Bannock for rape and sundry other offences and took him into the Houston police headquarters, where you booked him?'

'That is correct, ma'am.'

The defence team declined to cross-examine the sergeant, and the other witnesses called by the prosecution were all character witnesses for Bryoni Bannock. These were Bryoni's school teachers and the psychiatrists from Nine Elms who had come to know Bryoni well over the time she had been a regular visitor to her sister Sacha. One after another they described Bryoni as an exemplary student and an intelligent, well-balanced and normal child.

In cross-examination the defence attempted to lead the witnesses into agreeing that Bryoni had an abnormal interest in the opposite sex for a child of her age. In every case this was strongly resisted by all of them.

At last Melody was able to tell Judge Chamberlain, 'No further questions. The prosecution rests. We are ready to make our summation to the jury, if it pleases Your Honour.'

'Thank you, Miss Strauss.' The judged turned to the defence table and asked, 'Does counsel for the defence wish to call any witnesses in rebuttal, Mr Martius?'

A hush of anticipation held the courtroom. Everybody knew the defence had to call the accused, Carl Peter Bannock, to the witness box to give testimony in his own defence. Not to do so would be an admission of his guilt. To do so would be a calculated risk.

John Martius rose slowly, almost reluctantly, to his feet.

'The defence calls the defendant, Carl Peter Bannock, Your Honour,' he said. There was an audible sigh of released tension and Melody Strauss smiled thinly in anticipation, like a lioness with the scent of the gazelle in her nostrils.

Carl rose from his seat at the defence table and made his way in the palpable silence of the courtroom to the witness stand. His demeanour was that of profound contrition. He stood in the box with his hands clasped in front of him and his head bowed. His expression was tragic.

'You may take a seat, Carl,' John Martius advised him.

'Thank you, sir, but I prefer to stand,' Carl mumbled like a broken man.

'Please tell us how you feel about these legal proceedings.'

'I am completely devastated. I feel that I have lost the will to go on living. If this court places me under sentence of death I will welcome the executioner with open arms.' Carl lifted his head and looked across the floor to his adoptive father, Henry Bannock, seated in the front row facing him. 'I feel I have let down and disappointed my father. He had such high hopes for me and I tried to live up to his expectations but I failed.' He sobbed and wiped his eyes on his sleeve. 'I am deeply sorry for any hurt or damage that I might have inflicted on my two darling sisters. I am just as guilty as they are in leading me into sin. I forgive them, and I beg them to forgive me. I am overcome with remorse.'

Henry Bannock snorted with disgust and deliberately turned his face away from the sorry spectacle.

'Are you guilty of the charges that have been brought against you, Carl Bannock?' John Martius demanded.

'I am guilty only of succumbing to temptation and to female enticements, to the sin of Adam and the wiles of Eve.' The phrase was so theatrical and contrived that some of those that listened to it winced.

'No further questions of this witness, Your Honour.' John Martius sat down.

Melody Strauss came at the accused, the lioness now charging from ambush. 'Are you suggesting, Mr Bannock, that you were deliberately lured into committing rape by your two underage sisters?'

'I am confused and deeply distressed. This has all come as a terrible shock to me. My memory fails me. I hear the accusations levelled against me and I think that there must be some truth in them, but I remember only very little of any of it, madam.'

'How do you suggest your sperm found its way into your twelve-year-old sister's vagina? Did she place it there herself, Mr Bannock, do you suppose?'

'As God is my witness, I don't know. I don't remember any of this, but I am profoundly sorry for anything I might have done.' He was blubbering again.

'Do you suggest that your twelve-year-old sister inflicted the bruises and contusions on her own body? Perhaps she ripped open her private parts to shame you, do you think that possible?'

'Maybe that is what happened, and if so I forgive her as I hope she will forgive me.'

'Do you believe that those twelve law-abiding and upstanding citizens of the jury are naïve and gullible to the point of lunacy to fall for this claptrap? Is that what you believe, sir?'

'No! I certainly do not believe that. It is only my own memory that I doubt.'

'When did this strange bout of amnesia first strike you, sir? Was it when you realized that you were going to be made to pay for the hurt and shame you so readily inflicted on your young sisters?'

'I don't remember. I truly don't remember.'

Melody threw up her hands in disgust. She was too shrewd to labour a point that she had taken so convincingly. She knew that the defence had paid a high price to allow their client to express his repentance in open court, and she was well pleased.

'No further questions for the accused, Your Honour.'

'Very well, ladies and gentlemen.' Judge Chamberlain glanced up at the clock on the wall. 'The time is a few minutes short of four o'clock. So I am going to adjourn this court for today and we will resume at ten o'clock tomorrow morning, to hear the prosecution's summation.'

Melody Strauss's summation lasted almost three hours. She laid the established facts before the jury in a cogent and logical fashion which demonstrated how she had earned her reputation. The jury and everybody else in the courtroom listened with total fascination. The manner in which she presented her case was flawless.

In contrast, John Martius made no attempt to address the evidence. He worked on the theory that his client had been the victim of enticement and entrapment by his two sisters. He put forward the theory that the motive of the girls was to bring Carl into disfavour with Henry Bannock and to replace him in their father's affections. His rebuttal took only forty-eight minutes.

Judge Chamberlain summed up for the jury. He told them to consider carefully if Carl Bannock's remorse for the crimes he was accused of was genuine or if it was merely rather poor acting, and if Bryoni Bannock's horrendous injuries were self-inflicted.

'Were those real tears of remorse that we saw in the eyes of the accused yesterday, or were they perhaps more saurian in nature?' he asked them.

He sent the jury out directly after lunch to commence their deliberations.

Henry took Melody Strauss, Ronnie Bunter and Bryoni down the road to lunch at the local Burger King. Bryoni and Melody shared a double cheeseburger. Now that her ordeal was almost over Bryoni was once again chirpy as a songbird, but she held her father's hand for reassurance, and once she whispered to him, 'If Carl goes to prison, he is going to be real mad at me. Do you think he will come to get me when they let him out again?'

'Carl is going away for a very long time. And we are going to make sure that he can never bother you again, my darling.'

By the time Henry called for the check it was after three o'clock. He was still paying it when a clerk of the court hurried into the restaurant.

'The jury is back, Mr Bannock. They have reached a verdict. You had best hurry, sir.'

'Good Lord! Well under three hours, that's either very good or very bad.' Ronnie Bunter gave his opinion.

'Let's get out of here.' Henry grabbed Bryoni's hand and hustled her down the street to the courthouse. The courtroom was full and the press section included reporters from as far afield as New York City and Anchorage, Alaska.

Hector Cross had left orders that he was not to be disturbed. He had diverted any incoming telephone calls to Agatha's office in Abu Zara. He was so deeply engrossed in the typescript of 'The Poisoned Seed' that he had not been conscious of the passage of time until there was a discreet little double tap on the door of his study.

Hector jerked back from another time and a faraway place to the present. He had been so engrossed in Jo Stanley's writing that for another few seconds he was slightly disorientated. He glanced at the window and saw by the outside light that it was already dusk. The day had sped away. He had not eaten since breakfast and had subsisted on cups of coffee that he brewed himself. He had barely taken the time to visit the toilet that adjoined his study.

He jumped up from the desk and crossed quickly to the door. He opened it, and she stood there smiling at him. She wore one of the white terry towel bathrobes and her legs and feet were bare. Her hair was damp and she had twisted it up on top of her head. She had bathed away the last traces of her make-up and her skin glowed. She looked young as a schoolgirl. She had obviously slept well for her eyes sparkled and the whites were clear. The irises were green, like tropic sunlight through seawater, sea green and serene.

'Are we going to stand here staring at each other all night, or are you going to invite me into your lair?'

'Forgive me. I had almost forgotten how good you look.'

'You saw me just six or seven hours ago.'

'Has it been that long?' He was genuinely surprised and he checked his wristwatch. 'You are right. I must learn not to argue with you.' He took her hand and drew her into the room. 'I do apologize for neglecting you. But it's your own fault, I am sorry. You had me mesmerized with your literary genius. You had me hooked and hog-tied.'

'You old flatterer, you!' she said, but she smiled with genuine pleasure.

'Sit down, please.' He led her to the leather easy chair. She sat down and curled her legs under her. Then she tucked the skirts of the bathrobe around them when she saw him looking. They were lovely legs, he noted. 'What have you been doing during the time I was so busy neglecting you?'

'I had three or four hours of heavenly sleep. Then I availed myself of your gymnasium. I found a tracksuit in the gym cupboard that fitted me when I rolled up the sleeves and trouser legs. I changed all the settings on your machines, for which I apologize.'

He shook his head and laughed. 'You are more than welcome.'

'Then I had a sauna, and I shampooed my hair. I helped myself to all the Hermès and Chanel girlie goodies in your guest bathroom, and was pleased to note that none of them had been opened by previous visitors.'

'You are the first.'

'I am naïve enough to believe you. Perhaps that is because I want to.'

'Cross my heart! But have you eaten?'

'I wasn't hungry. I was too busy exploring.'

'Oh my God! You will die of starvation and I will never forgive myself. You have two options. Cynthia, my chef, is the finest cook in London, and possibly the universe. The Ivy Club runs her a close second.'

'We both have been in this house, albeit this lovely house of yours all day. Perhaps it would be better if we went out to dine,' she said, but at the same time she dropped her eyes demurely from his. Already he knew her well enough to divine what she was actually hinting: that it was still too soon for her to spend the evening in intimate seclusion with him.

'The Ivy it shall be. It's pretty relaxed with its dress code, but if you would like to change I can run you past your hotel.'

'Thank you, Hector. I would prefer that.'

'I will throw on something suitable while you change back in your togs, and then I will wait for you in the car outside the hotel while you put on something fresh.'

He was impressed by the fact that she kept him waiting only twenty minutes, and that when she returned she was wearing something understated but elegant.

'Perfect!' he said as he opened the door of the Bentley for her. 'You look smashing.'

'That's an adjective that sounds odd to an ear from west of the Atlantic, but I shall take it as a compliment.'

He took her on his arm through the entrance that pretended to be a flower shop and they rode up in the grand glass elevator. The girls at the reception fussed over Hector when they took the coats and one of them led them up in another elevator to the dining room.

'Do you own the place?' Jo whispered to him.

'Wherever one goes in this naughty world, a decent tip performs miracles,' he assured her.

'I suppose it doesn't hurt either if you look the way you do.'

'I hope you are not allergic to champagne,' he said as they settled at the table.

'Try me!' Jo invited.

When they had tasted and approved both the wine and the first course she asked the question which had been on the tip of her tongue since they had left The Cross Roads.

'So tell me, where did you get to in my story?' she asked.

'I reached the part where Henry and Bryoni are waiting to hear the jury's verdict on that horrible little shit, Carl Peter Bannock. Forgive my language but you have made me hate him.'

'You are totally justified in that. I think that Carl Bannock is one of those people who is truly evil from the core and without any redeeming sides to his character.'

'So where is he now, this monstrous creature?'

'Read what I have written, Hector. Don't try and jump ahead of the story. If you do it my way you will understand much more of the characters involved here, and there are many of them. However, I assure you that you haven't come to the best part yet, or should I rather say the worst part.'

'Okay, but indulge me with one more question that is eating holes

243

in me. Did Hazel know any of this? If she did, she never told me about it.'

'Hazel had not appeared on the scene yet. She was still learning to play tennis is South Africa.'

'But she must have known about it when she married Henry?'

'I doubt Henry ever told Hazel the details. Ronnie Bunter says Henry was deeply ashamed of the dreadful scandal of it all. Henry felt terrible guilt that he had not been able to protect his daughters. On the other hand, perhaps it is possible that Hazel did know but she never told you. It is such a tragic and sordid tangle that perhaps, like Henry, Hazel just wanted to pretend it had never happened.'

'What has become of Bryoni Lee? That little one was a heroine. I would love to meet her, if that is at all possible.'

'Contain yourself. I am not going to tell you. You will just have to read to the end of the story.'

'I warn you, madam. Patience is not one of my numerous virtues. When I want something I want it now.'

'There are some situations in which the ultimate pleasure is multiplied many times over by the anticipation,' she told him. 'And storytelling is only one of those.' Her expression was enigmatic, and only remotely touched with prurience.

'I am certain that advice is the best available.' He scarcely could forbear to smile, but he managed to match her restraint. 'How did you meet Ronnie Bunter?' He changed the subject.

'He was at law school with my father. I come from a long line of lawyers.'

She took his lead and they talked at large throughout the excellent meal, getting to know each other. Afterwards he took her on to a private nightclub named Annabel's. She had never been there before but Hector was joyously received by the staff. When they danced they discovered that they moved very well together. Then the music changed and became soft and sentimental. It seemed perfectly natural that he held her closer and that she laid her head against his chest. He drove her back to her hotel and he escorted her as far as the entrance, where she told him, 'Goodnight, Hector. I enjoyed the evening immensely. Will you call me in the morning,

please? We still have so much to talk about.' Then she offered him
her cheek to kiss, and was gone in a swirl of skirts.

H e woke at sunrise the next morning feeling rested and cheerful,
with an expectation of something good about to happen to
him. He lay for a few moments wondering at the source of
this ebullient mood. Then it all came back to him with a rush. He
chuckled gleefully and swung his legs out of the bed.

While he hurried through his ablutions he phoned down to the
kitchen and told Stephen to lay out his breakfast on the desk in his
study, rather than in the dining room. When he ran down the stairs
showered and fully dressed, he met Stephen just leaving the study.

'Morning, Stephen,' he greeted him. 'There is one other favour
you can do for me.' Stephen followed him back into the room and
listened with an expression of disbelief as Hector gave him his instructions.

'Are you certain that is what you want, Mr Cross?' he asked when
Hector had finished.

'Tell me, Stephen, when last did I ask you to do something that
I did not want you to do?'

'I don't think that has ever happened, sir.'

'And it's not happening now,' Hector assured him.

'I shall see to it at once, Mr Cross.'

'I can always rely on you, Stephen.'

Hector settled himself at the desk and woke up his computer.
When the screen was aglow, he picked up the telephone and dialled
the number of Jo's mobile, which she had given him the previous
evening. While he waited for her to answer he speared a slice of
ripe mango and slipped it into his mouth.

Jo answered on the fourth ring. 'Good morning, Hector. How did
you sleep?'

'I fell into a deep dark hole and woke up half an hour ago, ready
to slay dragons.'

'There are enough of those out there,' she agreed. 'Slay one for
me. I am still in bed with a cup of coffee.'

'Lazy girl!' he chided her. 'Life is for living.'

'All your fault, keeping me up into the small hours. But it was fun, wasn't it? We should try that again sometime.'

'Soon!' he agreed. 'Like this very evening, if not earlier.'

'I have to see some people in the city this morning. I promised Ronnie Bunter. It's nothing to do with "The Poisoned Seed". It's a totally different matter. However, I shall be free after lunch.'

'Come. I shall be waiting for you.'

'You get on with your reading. I warn you, there will be questions.'

'And I'll have a few for you.'

He hung up the receiver, and turned his full attention to the computer screen.

Henry Bannock, with Ronnie Bunter on one side of him and Bryoni on the other, had only just taken their seats in the courtroom when Judge Chamberlain came through the door from his chambers and the bailiff called the court to order.

The twelve members of the jury, led by the foreman, filed from their room and took their places in the jury box. None of them looked to where Carl Bannock was seated at the defence table.

'Good sign!' Ronnie whispered to Henry. 'They seldom look at a man they have condemned.'

'Have the members of the jury considered their verdict?' asked Judge Chamberlain.

'We have, Your Honour,' replied the foreman of the jury.

'What is your verdict?'

'On the charge of common rape we find the accused guilty as charged.

'On the charge of statutory rape of a minor we find the accused guilty as charged.

'On the charge of aggravated sexual assault we find the accused guilty as charged.

'On the charge of common assault and grievous bodily harm we find the accused guilty as charged.

'On the charge of a commission of incest we find the accused guilty as charged.

'On the charge of corrupting the morals of a minor we find the accused guilty as charged.'

'Six out of six,' breathed Ronnie Bunter. 'Full marks to Melody Strauss.'

Judge Chamberlain thanked and dismissed the members of the jury and then conferred with the counsels for the defence and the prosecution. Finally, he addressed the court. 'We will adjourn until tomorrow at ten o'clock, when I will pass sentence on the prisoner.'

That evening Henry hosted a celebratory dinner party at Forest Drive for twenty close friends and relatives. Cookie served a baron of prime Texan beef, comprising two full tenderloins left uncut and joined at the backbone, rare and oozing juices.

Henry opened a dozen bottles of Château Lafite Rothschild 1955, to complement the beef.

Ronnie leaned across the table to bet Melody Strauss that Carl would only get ten years in the state pen. Joshua Chamberlain was a notorious liberal, Ronnie claimed. Melody put ten dollars on a sentence of at least fifteen years. However, they both agreed that the Château Lafite was the best wine they had ever tasted.

Bryoni could not make it through to the dessert course before her eyes closed and she slumped head down onto the table. Henry carried her up to her room and tucked her into bed. He sat on the edge of her bed and stroked her hair until she had fallen asleep for the second time before he went back to rejoin his dinner guests. As soon as he was gone Cookie smuggled a large bowl of chocolate ice cream up to Bryoni's bedroom by the back stairs. Bryoni found sufficient reserves of strength to wake up and polish off the bowl.

The following morning at eight o'clock Bonzo Barnes drove Bryoni to school. Henry wanted her to return to her normal routine as soon as possible. He had arranged long-term counselling for her and he had spoken at length to the school principal and Bryoni's class teacher. Henry was satisfied that he had done everything in his power to help her weather the hurricane and get her life back on an even keel. He had been warned that it might be a long process, but Henry had faith in his daughter's strength of character and her maturity.

Henry left for the courthouse in an angry and vengeful mood. At ten o'clock precisely the bailiff called the court to order.

Henry Bannock sat with Ronnie Bunter in his usual place in the front row of the visitors' gallery.

Carl Peter Bannock was led up the staircase from the holding section by two uniformed guards. He was manacled and restrained by leg irons. He was pale, unshaven and unkempt. There were dark shadows under his bloodshot eyes. He looked pleadingly across the courtroom at Henry.

Henry's expression was cold and angry. He held Carl's eyes for a long moment. Carl smiled uncertainly and his lips quivered. Deliberately, Henry turned his face away from him in total and final rejection.

Carl's shoulders slumped and he shuffled across the floor to stand in the dock facing Judge Chamberlain.

'Prisoner at the bar, you have heard the verdict of the jury. Do you have anything to say in mitigation of the sentence which will be passed upon you?'

Carl looked down at the irons locked to his ankles. 'I am truly sorry for the anguish I have caused to my father and the other members of my family. I will try to make it up to them all in any way I can.'

'Is that all you have to say?'

'Yes, Judge, I am very sorry.'

'This court takes cognizance of your contrition in mitigation of sentence,' Judge Chamberlain said, and looked down to rearrange the papers on the desk in front of him. He looked up again.

'The sentence of this court is as follows:

'On the charge of corrupting the morals of a minor I sentence you to five years' detention in a federal penitentiary.

'On the charge of incest I sentence you to six years' detention in a federal penitentiary.

'On the charge of common assault and grievous bodily harm I sentence you to six years' detention in a federal penitentiary.

'On the charge of aggravated sexual assault on a minor I sentence you to twenty years' detention in a federal penitentiary.

'On the charge of common rape I sentence you to fifteen years' detention in a federal penitentiary.

'On the charge of statutory rape of a minor I sentence you to fifteen years' detention in a federal penitentiary.

'I direct that the sentences shall run concurrently, and that you shall be incarcerated for a minimum period of fifteen years.'

Judge Chamberlain looked across at John Martius expectantly. Martius rose to his feet.

'Your Honour, I beg your permission to lodge an appeal to the Supreme Court against the sentence.'

'Permission is granted,' Joshua Chamberlain said. 'However, the prisoner will be taken directly from this court to the Holliday Induction Unit in Huntsville and from thence to the penitentiary assigned to him to commence serving the sentence of this court immediately.'

He looked back at the two guards. 'Gentlemen, please do your duty.'

Each of the guards seized one of Carl Bannock's arms and they guided him to the head of the staircase. His leg irons clanked as he descended the stairs to the holding area.

'The court will rise,' called out the bailiff.

Henry and Ronnie were the last two remaining in the courtroom.

'It could have been better,' Ronnie gave his opinion. 'I was very much hoping for twenty-five years minimum. But fifteen years will have to do. At least it's all over at last, and you have gotten rid of the rotten seed that has poisoned your family.'

'I wonder,' Henry said darkly. 'Is it really over, and have my girls and I truly seen the last of that perverted animal?'

The truck was parked hard up against the rear door of the court building, in the gated secure compound. The rear doors were open to receive Carl Bannock. The sides of the truck were signwritten with the letters TDCJ–CID, for Texas Department of Criminal Justice – Correctional Institutions Division. Carl was bundled in through the rear doors and his leg irons were locked into the ring-bolts on the floor between his legs. The doors were slammed

shut and locked and the truck pulled away on its seventy-mile journey
to the Huntsville induction centre.

The Holloway Induction Unit was a square concrete block four
levels high, with heavily barred windows. It was protected by guard
towers and a triple row of ring-fencing. At each of the three gates
the truck passed through heavy security checks. When it reached
the main building Carl's leg irons were unlocked, and he was shepherded by his guards through a series of electronic gates to the primary
reception area.

His papers were checked once again and Carl's name and details
were entered in the register. Then the sergeant behind the desk signed
the receipt for his delivery. Two new guards took over from those who
had brought him down from Houston. He was led through another
remotely controlled gate into the main reception area. All his personal
possessions, including his gold signet ring, his wallet and his gold Rolex
wristwatch, and his civilian clothing were taken from him. They were
inventoried and bagged. When the guard gave him the receipt book
to sign he handed him back a ten-dollar bill from his wallet.

'What's this for?' Carl asked.

'You are a sex offender. It's for essential toiletries.'

'What has my conviction got to do with it?'

'You'll find out.' The guard gave him a sly grin.

He led Carl to the barber shop, where his hair was cropped down
to the skull. The barber stood back to admire his handiwork.

'Stunning!' He gave his opinion. 'Them good ol' boys in Holloway
are going to love you, baby.'

The guards took him on to the showers to scrub up. Then, naked
and wet, he went on to the tailor, where he was handed his uniform
through a hatch. His new uniform was made up of a white tee shirt
and underpants, baggy white canvas jacket and trousers with a draw-
string waist, and white canvas slip-on shoes.

Through another electronic gate he was taken to a single cell in
a long row of cells and locked down. The furnishing consisted of a
squat-pan toilet and a wooden bunk that was fixed firmly to the floor
and side wall. There was a single blanket but no mattress. Later, his
dinner was handed to him through the hatch. It was a bowl of watery
stew with a thick slice of bread dunked in it.

Early the next morning he was taken from his cell to the interview room, where three members of the induction board were waiting for him, seated at a steel table. All three of them were uniformed members of the Correctional Institutions Division staff.

'Carl Peter Bannock. Is that correct?' the man seated in the middle of the trio asked without looking up.

'Yes,' Carl replied.

'Sir!' the inquisitor corrected him.

'Sir,' Carl agreed dutifully.

'Fifteen years' sentence, minimum. Is that correct?'

'Yes, sir.'

'Sex offender and paedophile. Is that correct?'

'Yes, sir,' Carl said through gritted teeth.

'Better send him to Holloway Long Term Correctional Unit,' said one of the other members of the panel.

The senior member of the panel suggested, 'Send him to the sixth level, where the other long-termers can't get at him?'

'The only place those good ol' boys won't get at him is in heaven, and this pretty boy ain't never going that high.' The third member of the panel sniggered and the others chuckled.

That afternoon another TDCJ–CID truck carried Carl a further twenty miles south into the historic cotton slavery belt where the Holloway penitentiary stood in a bleak and featureless landscape like a massive grey concrete monument to the infamy of mankind.

Here the security was even more forbidding than it had been at the induction centre. It took twenty minutes for the vehicle to pass through the three ring-fences and to park at the prisoner reception entrance. Then it was a further twenty-five minutes before Carl had his manacles and leg irons removed and he was transferred from the ground level to his final destination on the sixth and top level of the building.

From the elevator he was marched down a short passageway to a green-painted door which was signed OFFICE OF THE LEVEL SUPERVISOR. One of the guards knocked on the door and was rewarded with a muffled bellow from within. He opened the door and jerked his head at Carl to enter. The level supervisor was sitting behind his desk. The plastic name tag pinned to his shirt proclaimed him to be LUCAS HELLER.

His chair was teetering on its two back legs and Lucas's booted feet were planted on the desktop. With a crash he let the chair fall forward onto all four legs and he stood up. He was tall, round shouldered and lean. His sandy hair was thinning, but what was left of it flopped onto his forehead. His ears were disproportionally large for his long pale face. His eyes were also pale and watery, but the tip of his nose was pink and the nostrils moist with rhinitis. His two upper front teeth protruded to give him the air of an anaemic rabbit.

He carried a riding crop in his right hand. He came around from behind his desk and circled Carl slowly on his long stork-like legs. He sniffed wetly as he reached out with the riding crop and stroked Carl's buttocks with the leather flap on the end of the crop. Carl started with surprise and Lucas sniffed again and giggled like a girl.

'Nice,' he said. 'Very nice. You should fit in very nicely here.' He winked at one of the guards. 'A nice tight fit. Get it?'

'Yeah! I got it, Super.' The guard guffawed.

Lucas came around in front of Carl and sat on the edge of his desk.

'Have you got your ten dollars for the essential toiletries, Beauty Bannock?'

'Yes, Super.'

'Let's have it.' Lucas held out his hand and snapped his fingers. Carl groped in the pocket of his white canvas pants and brought out the crumpled bill. Lucas plucked it from his hand. Then he went back behind his desk and opened one of the drawers. He took out a large plastic bottle and slid it across the desktop towards Carl.

'There you have it.'

Carl picked up the bottle and examined the label. 'Best Quality Macassar essential oil. Great for the hair,' he read aloud and looked puzzled.

'What should I do with this, Super?'

'You will know when the time comes,' Lucas assured him. 'Just keep it handy.' Then he glanced at the guard. 'Have you got the check for this piece of goods?'

'Right here, Super.' The guard laid the check-in book in front of him, and Lucas dashed off his signature.

'Okay, boys. Bring him along.' They marched Carl back along the passageway, through another massive door and into a long gallery of grey steel and darker grey concrete. The vaulted ceiling high overhead was covered with armoured glass. Sharp rectangular shafts of brilliant sunlight burned down, filled with dancing silver dust motes. On each side of the gallery stood a long row of barred steel cages. Shadowy figures clung to the bars or crouched behind them, peering through as Carl was led past. Some of them called out sardonic greetings and blew wolf whistles, giggled and hooted and reached through the bars to make obscene gestures at him.

Lucas stopped at the last cell in the row and opened the door with his electronic master key.

'Welcome to cell number 601. The Honeymoon Suite.' Lucas grinned and waved him through. As Carl stepped over the threshold the door slid closed behind him. Lucas and his escort left him and returned the way they had come, without looking back.

Carl went to sit on the single bunk, and surveyed cell 601. It was no larger than his cell at the induction centre had been. The only improvement was the tiny stainless-steel washbasin beside the squat pan of the toilet and a stool set at a bare writing desk. Every piece of furniture was bolted to the walls so it could not be used as a weapon.

This was to be his home for at least the next fifteen years, and his spirits quailed.

At six o'clock that evening a bell rang and Carl, taking his cue from the other inmates, went to stand at the door of his cell. All the cell doors on the level opened simultaneously, and the prisoners stepped out into the gallery.

On shouted commands from the armed guards on the steel catwalk high above, they turned and filed down to the canteen at the other end of the gallery. As each prisoner passed the kitchen hatch a small plastic tray was shoved at him by one of the kitchen staff. Dinner was a bowl of soup, another bowl of mutton stew and a round of white bread. Carl took his place at one of the bare steel tables, but none of the other inmates came to join him. They formed cliques with others of the same ethnic backgrounds. Some of them were obviously discussing Carl, but he could not hear what they were saying, so he ignored them. He told himself bitterly that he would have many more years to find his place in this warped society.

They were given twenty minutes to eat, and then the guards on the walkways up above chivvied them back to their cells.

Lock-down was at precisely seven thirty. Carl lay on his back on the bunk with his ankles crossed and his hands behind his head. He was exhausted. It had been a day of worry and uncertainty. At least the dinner had been edible and he longed for the arc lights that burned down into his cell to be switched off for the night. But he had been warned by the guards that was never going to happen.

Gradually he became aware that the voices of the prisoners in the cells around him had sunk to expectant whispers and muffled sniggers. Carl sat up and looked out through his bars into the long gallery, but his view was limited and he could see no reason for the charged mood that seemed to grip the other inmates on Level Six.

Then he sat up again and swung his legs off the bunk as he became aware of the tramp of many feet approaching down the gallery. Lucas Heller, the level supervisor, came into his line of sight. He was carrying his riding crop. He wore a regulation hat and a crisply ironed uniform.

'Prisoner, on your feet!' he ordered.

Carl stood up from the bed.

'How are you enjoying your first night in Holloway, Bannock?'

'Fine, Super.'

'Dinner okay?'

'No complaints, Super.'

'Bored, are you?'

'Not really, Super.'

'That's bad luck, Bannock. Because I brought some good ol' boys to keep you company. A number of them been here twenty years and more, and they bored as all hell. None of them had a woman in all that time, and they hot as all hell, too, I can tell you!'

Carl stood to attention, and he felt his skin crawl. He had heard the jokes and rumours, but he had wanted to believe they were not true and that it would never happen to him. But there were strange men crowding forward behind Lucas.

'May I introduce to you Mr Johnny Congo?' Lucas put his hand on the shoulder of the man nearest to him. Lucas was tall but he had to reach up to his own head level to do so. The man seemed to be a massive mountain of anthracite. His head was round and smooth as a cannon ball. He wore only a tee shirt and shorts, so Carl could see that his limbs were like baulks of ebony hardwood, solid muscle and bone almost devoid of any trace of fat.

'Mr Congo lives on death row downstairs while the Supreme Court considers his appeal. He has been with us eight years and is highly respected here in Holloway, so he's got special visiting rights.' Lucas held his hand out, palm upwards, and Johnny Congo placed a twenty-dollar bill in it. Lucas smiled his thanks and pressed the door release. The bars slid aside.

'Go ahead, Mr Congo. Take all the time you want; just enjoy yourself.' Congo stepped into the cell, and the other men crowded up to the barred cell door behind him, jostling each other for position, grinning in anticipation.

'You got your Macassar oil, white boy?' Congo asked Carl. 'You got about thirty seconds to get yourself lubed up, and down on your knees, otherwise I'm coming in dry.'

Carl backed away from him. He was speechless with terror, and he was beginning to blubber. 'No. No, please leave me alone.'

The cell was small and with three giant strides Congo had him trapped in the corner. He reached out and grabbed Carl's upper arm. With a casual flick of the wrist he hurled him face down on his bunk.

'Get your pants down, white boy. Give me the oil.' Then Congo saw for himself the Macassar oil bottle on the shelf above the wash-basin where Carl had placed it. He took it down and screwed off the cap. He went back to the bunk. Carl had rolled himself into a ball, with his knees under his chin. Congo flipped Carl over onto his face, then placed his knee between Carl's shoulder blades and ripped down the elastic top of his pants. He held the bottle up high and poured half the contents over Carl's buttocks.

'Ready or not, here I come!' Congo said as he got into position behind Carl.

'No . . .' Carl blubbered, and then he screamed. It was a sound of utmost anguish. Each of the waiting men handed their entrance fee to Lucas, like the spectators at a ball game, and then they crowded into the cell behind the pair on the bunk. Their voices were thick with lust and excitement. One of them sang out, 'Go, Congo! Go, go, go!'

The others laughed and took up the refrain.

'Go, Congo, go!'

Suddenly Congo arched his back, threw back his head and gave a cry like a bull moose in rut. The man behind him helped him off, and then immediately took his place. Carl screamed again.

'My Lordy, but he do sing sweet,' said the third man in the line.

By the time the fifth man came over him Carl was no longer screaming. When the last man was finished, he shook his head sorrowfully as he pulled away.

'Seems to me like he gone and died on us, man.'

Congo had been resting on the bunk beside Carl. Now he stood up and said, 'Naw, he still breathing. If he breathing, he still ripe for love.' He stepped up behind Carl once more.

The trusty orderly from the sick bay had been invited to the party in both his personal and professional capacity. At last he came forward in his professional role and felt for Carl's pulse under his chin at the carotid artery.

'This old boy had enough for tonight. Help me get him downstairs and he will be ready for some more fun come two, three weeks.'

By dawn Carl was in a critical condition from shock and blood loss. The doctor from headquarters was called in. He ordered Carl to be moved to the main medical facility at Huntsville State Penitentiary.

In the operating theatre Carl's lower abdominal cavity was aspirated by suction pump and almost two litres of blood and human semen were removed from inside him. Then the physician sutured the torn and leaking blood vessels and surgically repaired the injuries to his lower colon and finally administered three whole litres of blood by transfusion.

During the time he was in the Huntsville sanatorium Carl was allowed to make telephone calls and receive visitors. He phoned the Carson National Bank in Houston and asked his account manager to visit him. Carl was an important client, so the account manager responded promptly.

Carl had worked for his adoptive father and the Bannock Oil company for two years and two months before his arrest. At the beginning his salary had been set by Henry at a handsome one hundred and ten thousand dollars a month. Henry was a firm believer in both the carrot and the stick. He also believed that his only son deserved to be treated like royalty.

To Henry's amazement and deep gratification Carl almost immediately displayed extraordinary business acumen far beyond that which Henry had expected from one of his age and experience. By the end of the first year Henry realized with immense pride that Carl was a financial genius whose natural endowments matched and in some cases exceeded his own. Carl soon demonstrated an uncanny ability to smell profits from as far down wind as a hungry hyena can smell a rotting carcass. Carl's salary climbed steeply as his talents unfolded and blossomed. By the end of his second year he had earned his place on the board of Bannock Oil, and his salary and his director's fees totalled in excess of two hundred and fifty thousand dollars a month. The Henry Bannock Family Trust in terms of its trust deed had been obligated to pay him out an additional sum three times greater than the amount of his personal earnings. The consequences of his father's largesse were that even after meticulously paying his taxes Carl had amassed a credit balance of well over five million dollars, so the account manager responded promptly.

On the sixth day Carl was sufficiently recovered from his rectal injuries to be transferred from Huntsville back to the sick bay in the Holloway unit. He took with him the new cheque book which his account manager had provided. From the sick bay Carl was able to get a message to Lucas Heller via the medical orderly. The message was that Lucas should visit him if he wished to learn something to his benefit.

Lucas condescended to come downstairs to see Carl, mainly for the opportunity to mock him as he lay in bed.

To get the conversation rolling, and as a token of his good faith, Carl handed Lucas a cash cheque for $5,000 drawn on the Carson National Bank. Lucas read the figures with awe. He had seldom had that much money in his hands at one time, but experience had taught him not to place his trust in fairy godmothers. He refused to believe this stroke of fortune until he had an opportunity to hurry into town and present the cheque at the local branch of the bank.

The cashier honoured it without a quibble. The scales fell from the eyes of Lucas Heller and he became a believer. He rushed back to the Holloway unit and visited Carl again. On this occasion his manners were deeply deferential and obsequious.

Carl ordered him next to carry a message to Johnny Congo on death row. Carl had by now fully appraised all the underlying political structures of the Holloway unit. He had learned that Johnny Congo wielded enormous influence throughout the prison. Like some grotesque man-eating spider he sat at the centre of his web and manipulated the strands that reached as far as the warden's office.

The warden had come to rely heavily on Congo to keep order among the prison inmates. If Johnny passed the word for 'Peace and cooperation' then the administration of the unit was able to maintain some semblance of order in the midst of a system which seemed specifically designed to produce chaos.

However, if Johnny Congo said 'Riot!' then fires broke out throughout the unit; guards were knifed in the workshops, or in the galleries or on the catwalks; the inmates seized control of the dining halls and the prison yard. They broke up the furniture and fittings. They murdered a few of their companions to work off old grudges or in obedience to Johnny Congo's orders. They hurled missiles and chanted abuse at the guards, until the National Guard was called out in full riot gear, and the warden's performance ratings plummeted.

Johnny Congo had won special privileges from the administration for his cooperation. He had his pick of the prettiest new prisoners as soon as they arrived in the unit, as Carl had experienced at first hand. His cell was never searched, so his stash of drugs and other luxuries was inviolate. He was even allowed to have a telephone in his cell so he was able to communicate with his contacts and criminal associates in the outside world. His death sentence was blocked somewhere in the system; rumour was that the state governor had seen to that. The smart money was betting that Johnny would die of old age without any help from the man with the lethal needle in the white-tiled execution chamber.

If any person incurred Johnny Congo's displeasure it was only a matter of days before the issue was terminally settled with the blade of a knife in the prison yard, or in the small hours of the morning in the privacy of the offender's own cell, which would have been conveniently left unlocked by the Level Supervisor.

It was bruited abroad that Johnny Congo's influence reached out far beyond the prison walls. It was believed that he had maintained strong ties with criminal syndicates and gangs in all of Texas and the surrounding states. For a very reasonable price he could fix things in cities as far off as San Diego and Frisco.

It took Lucas Heller almost a week to set up the meeting between Carl and Johnny Congo, but finally the office of the supervisor of death row was put at their disposal, and the two of them came together at three o'clock on a Sunday morning when the rest of the unit had been locked down for the night. The Level Supervisor and four of his guards waited outside the door, but did not interfere.

Once Carl and Congo were alone they assessed each other warily, like two black-maned lions from rival prides meeting in disputed territory on the African veld. By this time Congo had learned that Carl was not just a pretty face. He knew that Carl was Henry Bannock's son, and he knew the power and wealth of the Bannock Oil Corporation.

'You wanna talk with me, white boy?'

'I need your protection, Mr Congo.' Carl wasted no time.

'You can bet your sweet ass you do, else sure enough it ain't gonna be sweet or pretty much longer. But why should I want to protect you?'

'I can pay you.'

'Yeah, man, that might make me wanna do it. But how much money we talking about here, boy?'

'You tell me, sir.'

Congo picked his nose while he pondered the question. Finally he examined the crust of dried mucus he had retrieved from his left nostril and flicked it off his finger, before he stated his price. 'Five thousand dollars each and every month, in ones and fives delivered here in Holloway. Ain't much good to me on the outside.' He had set the figure outrageously high, expecting Carl to bargain.

'That figure is ridiculous, Mr Congo,' Carl said, and Johnny Congo bridled. His fists clenched into mighty black hams. 'For a man of your stature and exalted position I would expect to pay ten or even fifteen thousand dollars a month.'

Johnny Congo blinked and his fists unfolded. He began to smile in a fatherly manner. 'I hear you, white boy, and I like what I hear. Fifteen thou' sounds just about right to me.'

'I am sure I will be able to arrange the delivery route from my bank to wherever you want it. Just tell me what I must do and I will do it. My hand on it, sir.'

Congo took the proffered hand and as he shook it he rumbled, 'There is more than your hand on it, boy. Your sweet life is on it.'

'I understand that, Mr Congo. However, if you really want to make a great deal of money we should go into business together.'

'What kind of business?' Congo stopped just short of scoffing. 'Lay it on me, white boy.'

Carl spoke for the next forty minutes and Congo leaned forward and listened almost without interruption. By the end of that time he was grinning and his eyes were shining.

'How do I know you going to deliver, boy?' he asked at last.

'If I don't, then you can withdraw your protection, Mr Congo.'

It was a momentous meeting out of which would emerge an unholy alliance; a crooked young genius combining his talents with those of a ruthless monster who wielded the powers of life and death. Both men were psychopaths; totally lacking compassion, scruples or remorse.

Over the following years the profits of their various enterprises, initially conceived by Carl and then fostered by Johnny Congo, were first laundered and sanitized. Johnny's friends on the outside were eager to assist in this process. After the money was clean it was distributed to Carl personally in the form of dividends and director's fees through a company in the British Virgin Islands that Carl had set up while he was still at Princeton.

The value of the end receipts was quadrupled by the Henry Bannock Family Trust. Finally, the grand total was shared by Carl and Johnny Congo and secreted in numbered bank accounts in Hong Kong, Moscow, Singapore and other cities around the globe where even the muscled arm of the US Internal Revenue Service could not reach.

To facilitate the operation of their enterprises both in and outside of the prison it soon became necessary for Carl and Johnny to take in Marco Merkowski, the warden of the Holloway Correctional Unit, as a sleeping partner. Once they had involved him in his first illegal scheme Marco found himself completely in the thrall of Carl Bannock and Johnny Congo.

Carl was moved from the sixth level of the unit to the first level, where jail trusties and other inmates with unblemished records of good behaviour were accommodated. The cell that Carl was allocated was three times the size of his old one on the sixth level. Carl was provided with a television set and his own private telephone.

The telephone was an essential element in the management of the business interests of the alliance. Fortuitously, Carl was working into a raging bull market. All his former contacts were still in place and his instincts for profit were unimpaired.

There was still a great deal of time in his unhurried prison days for Carl to turn his fecund mind to planning for the future. By this time he had passed over five years in detention. His prison record was spotless; Warden Merkowski had taken care of that. The original minimum sentence of fifteen years handed down by Judge Chamberlain had been reduced on appeal to a minimum of twelve years. Carl had nearly reached the halfway mark. He was still only thirty-one years old, a cunning street-smart multimillionaire, eager to take on the world on his own terms as soon as he stepped out of the gates of the Holloway Correctional Unit.

Through his own and Johnny Congo's multitudinous outside contacts Carl was kept fully informed of his father's movements, and the movements of all the other beneficiaries of the Henry Bannock Family Trust.

Most unfortunately for Carl's ultimate financial aspirations, his father had met a professional women's tennis champion thirty years his junior, considerably younger than Carl Bannock himself. Carl had seen photographs of this woman. Her name was Hazel Nelson and she was blonde, athletic and lovely. Only a few months after meeting, his father and Hazel were married in a splendid wedding ceremony at the Forest Drive residence in Houston. Less than a year later Hazel gave birth to a girl they named Cayla. Henry's record of fathering only female offspring remained intact. From Carl's point of view, this awkward new adventure of his father's had added two more names to the role of beneficiaries of the Henry Bannock Family Trust.

The full list including Carl himself now amounted to a total of seven persons: Henry Bannock and Hazel Bannock and her infant daughter Cayla; Carl's mother Marlene Imelda Bannock, who had retained his name after Henry had divorced her; and Carl's two half-sisters, Sacha Jean and Bryoni Lee. Using the market value of the Bannock Oil Corporation stock as quoted on the NY Stock Exchange as a guide, Carl estimated the present total value of the assets of the Henry Bannock Family Trust to be in the region of $111 billion. Carl fiercely resented having to share even that vast sum with five or six other persons.

From his prison cell Carl followed with intense and partisan interest his father's long-running petition to the Supreme Court in Washington DC to have Carl Peter Bannock removed from the list of beneficiaries to the Family Trust on the grounds that he was not blood related to the donor and that his conviction on a series of major felony charges had disqualified him. When the learned justices of the Supreme Court eventually rejected Henry Bannock's motion unanimously, Carl knew that death alone could deny him his share of the Trust funds.

Carl and Johnny Congo hosted a discreet little celebratory party in death row, attended by Warden Merkowski and a number of young female escorts brought down from Huntsville for the occasion. Although Carl and Johnny Congo had years ago become lovers, they were quite happy to share their conjugal bed with one or two pretty girls or even young boys if these were available.

The Supreme Court judgement in his favour set Carl applying his mind seriously to the many remarkable conditions that his father had laid down in the Trust Deed of the Henry Bannock Family Trust.

Carl had developed an excellent memory during his years of study, and though he had not held a copy of the actual Trust Deed in his hands since the day he worked his way into his father's strong-room, he had made detailed notes of its contents. All this time one particular provision that his father had written into the deed had tantalized Carl. The provision was that when there remained only a single living beneficiary, then the trustees of the Henry Bannock Family Trust must wind up the Trust and the entire remaining assets must be divided equally between a charity that Henry favoured and the sole surviving beneficiary, be it man or woman.

Carl decided that the time had come for him to take full advantage of this clause while he was still hidden from public view in the depths of the Holloway Correctional Unit, and while the concrete walls that imprisoned him would also act as a shield to deflect suspicion from him, and provide him with an unshakeable alibi.

Henry himself was invulnerable, but he was by now aging rapidly. At the rate that he lived his life he could not last very much longer. The word from Carl's informants was that Henry was already beginning to falter. Carl knew that he had the Grim Reaper as his ally and he was prepared to wait.

Hazel and her young daughter Cayla were protected by the heavy mantle of majesty that Henry Bannock cast over all who surrounded him closely. Hazel and Cayla were not yet vulnerable. Their time would come once Henry was out of the way.

The same did not apply to his drunken mother, Marlene Imelda, whom he despised, nor did it apply to his half-sisters, whom he hated deeply and bitterly. They were directly responsible for his incarceration and the many wasted years of his life that he was being forced to spend behind concrete and steel barriers in the company of creatures more vile than any jungle beast.

Carl learned that the mental condition of his eldest sister Sacha had improved so dramatically after he had been imprisoned that her doctors had been able to discharge her from the Nine Elms clinic into the care of her mother. Sacha had gone to live with Marlene in the Cayman Islands. Mother and daughter had flourished in this new intimate relationship. Marlene was not cured of her dipsomania; however, charge of her firstborn daughter had given her the incentive she needed to become teetotal. She now devoted all her love and attention to Sacha, and Sacha responded gratifyingly.

When Henry Bannock married Hazel Nelson and Cayla was born, Bryoni decided to leave Forest Drive and move to the Caymans to be with her mother and her own sister. At this time Bryoni was not much younger than Hazel, her step-mother. Both girls had very strong and competitive personalities and they were both fiercely possessive of Henry Bannock. In different circumstances they would have probably become friends, but when baby Cayla was born the advantage swung heavily in Hazel's favour. Now she was not only the new mistress of Forest Drive, but was also the mother of Henry's youngest daughter. Henry was besotted with Hazel, and when she began to take an intense interest in the affairs of the Bannock Oil Corporation he encouraged her. Soon Henry elevated Hazel to the role of company director that Carl had vacated when he was convicted.

Hazel took her seat at the boardroom table at Henry's right hand.

She became all things to Henry Bannock: lover, wife, mother of his child, business partner and boon companion.

On the other hand, Bryoni had no particular interest in the Bannock Oil Corporation. She had all the money she needed from the Family Trust, and she was not avaricious. She had few of the other talents that Hazel possessed in abundance and which made her so valuable and desirable to Bryoni's father. Bryoni could not compete with her at any level. So she flew down to Grand Cayman in the Caribbean where Marlene and Sacha welcomed her with pathetic eagerness, and where she was able to serve a purpose that was both highly valued by the two people she loved dearly and totally fulfilling to Bryoni herself.

From Carl's standpoint the move was also highly favourable. He now had three of the beneficiaries of the Family Trust removed from under the shield of his father and from the jurisdiction and protection of the government of the United States of America to an isolated island where they were a great deal more vulnerable and accessible to the attentions of the friends of Johnny Congo.

Carl laid his plans with great care and attention to detail. Congo was an enthusiastic participant in the enterprise. He had cocaine syndicate connections in Honduras and Colombia who were always interested in making a few extra dollars in more mundane side projects.

Johnny's contact in Honduras was Señor Alonso Almanza. He based himself in the port of La Ceiba, where he kept two very fast forty-foot ocean-going speedboats. These were usually employed in nocturnally running white goods north to Mexico, Texas or Louisiana. However the US Coast Guard had recently become a trifle bothersome and so his fine boats were underutilized.

The distance from La Ceiba to the Cayman Islands was less than five-hundred nautical miles; an easy run for one of those big fast Chris-Craft.

'Alonso is a good man, very trustworthy. He doesn't mind a little wet work if the price is attractive. I think we could do a lot worse,' Johnny Congo told Carl.

'I like the sound of him, and his price is good. But, what about the initial survey? Do you have somebody on Grand Cayman who can do that for us?'

'No problem, white boy.' The nickname which had started out as deliberately pejorative had now become a term of endearment between them. 'There is a realtor in George Town who once did a bit of work for me. He isn't fussy. We just tell him we want to make an anonymous bid for a property on the island and that we need a full description of everything in it including the servants and occupants.'

'Get on to him, Blackbird.' Anybody else who called Johnny Congo that to his face would die prematurely and painfully. 'Most of all we need to know about the security on the estate. If I know my daddy, and that I do, it will be tight. Obviously we must know which bedroom my mother sleeps in and where to find my two sisters. It's a good bet their bedrooms will be close alongside their darling mama's.'

Johnny's contact on Grand Cayman was a retired Englishman named Trevor Jones who had decided to spend his autumnal years in a tropical island paradise. He had discovered to his chagrin that paradise comes at a price and his pension was not stretching as far as he had hoped. He took this lucrative assignment from Carl Bannock to heart. He uplifted from the government surveyor's office a copy of the blueprint plans of The Moorings, the Bannocks' beachfront home. Then he ran to earth a former chambermaid of Mrs Marlene Bannock who had been fired from her employment for stealing a pair of pearl earrings from Miss Sacha Bannock's jewellery box. Her name was Gladys, and she had left The Moorings with a chip on her shoulder large enough to qualify as a log.

Together Gladys and Trevor Jones pored over the house plan. She showed him in which bedrooms the three members of the family slept and where the security guardroom was located. She knew the patrol routines of the guards. There were punch-clocks set up at various points on the property that kept the guards working to a strict timetable. The shifts changed precisely on the hour. So the movements of the security guards were predictable. Gladys was also able to provide a roster of the domestic staff. Most of these were not required to work on Sunday. They only returned to their duties after the weekend.

Gladys knew the exact location of every one of the numerous alarm sensors on the property. Naturally, the passwords had been changed after she was fired, but her common-law husband was still employed at The Moorings as a sous-chef. He willingly supplied her with the new passwords.

The gap through the coral reef was marked with light buoys and the channel to the anchorage in front of The Moorings was also buoyed. Jones went out in his little fishing skiff and took surreptitious soundings and made one or two other arrangements. At high spring tides the channel was a goodly three metres deep at the shallowest point, more than sufficient water for even one of the big Chris-Craft.

This entire package of information was sent to Johnny Congo. Its total cost to Carl was well under $4,000, which he considered excellent value.

The information was forwarded to Señor Alonso Almanza in La Ceiba with further detailed instructions and a bank transfer payment of $75,000 against a contract completion price of $250,000.

'I'm going to tell you a little secret, Blackbird.' Carl grinned at

Johnny Congo. 'If you have enough money, you can do anything you want, and have anything you want. Nobody is going to stop you.'

'Right on, white boy!' Johnny lifted his right hand and gave him a high five.

Twenty-eight days later Señor Almanza's Chris-Craft *Pluma de Mar* used the light of the full moon to creep quietly through the gap in the reef into Old Man Bay on the north side of Grand Cayman. Her hull was painted matt black, so even by the light of the moon she was almost invisible. She had cleared La Ceiba at noon the previous day, and had timed her arrival precisely for a quarter to three on a Sunday morning; the witching hour when only highwaymen, werewolves and pirates should be abroad.

The *Pluma de Mar* carried a crew of eleven. They were dressed in black tracksuits and wore black head-hoods with cut-outs for their eyes and mouths. They tied up to one of the channel markers seventy metres off the beachfront of The Moorings. Trevor Jones had placed a tiny radio beacon on the marker to guide them in. Leaving one crewman on board to take care of the vessel, they launched an inflatable dingy and the battery-powered outboard engine carried them silently ashore.

They hit the beach at exactly three o'clock, when they knew that the security patrols would be gathered in the guard room changing shifts and drinking coffee. Two of the masked men ran ahead to bypass and disable the alarm sensors and clear the way for those who followed. When the assault team burst into the guard room they took the four men gathered there completely off-guard. Within minutes they had gagged and bound all of them with duct tape, and shut down the alarm system at the main control board.

Then they raced around the swimming pool and jemmied open the door into the main house. They knew exactly where they were headed, through the living rooms and up the main staircase to the bedroom suites. At the head of the stairs they split into three groups. Each group went quickly to the suite that they had been allocated.

They rushed in while the occupants were still sleeping soundly. They hauled them out of their beds and bound their hands at the wrists with duct tape. Then they were dragged down the staircase and out onto the pool deck. The pool deck was discreetly screened by high walls and tropical vegetation to allow the Bannock women to indulge their penchant for nude sunbathing.

One of the gang produced a movie camera from his rucksack. He was a professional maker of hardcore pornographic films from Guadalajara in Mexico. In passable English he told the three terrified and weeping captives, 'My name is Amaranthus. It is my pleasure to make a documentary film of you. Please take no notice of me and try not to look into the lens of my camera unless I ask you to.' He stepped back and aimed his camera at them.

The gang leader took his place in front of them. 'I am Miguel. You will do as I tell you, or I hurt you bad. Name? *Nombre?*' he yelled at them, forcing each of the women in turn to announce her name for the benefit of Amaranthus and his camera. Sacha Jean was struck dumb with terror. Bryoni spoke up for her and gave her name.

'She is my sister Sacha Jean Bannock. She is sick. Please don't hurt her.'

Sacha fell to her knees and explosively soiled her pyjama bottoms. Miguel laughed and kicked her. 'Filthy cow! Stand up!' He kicked her again. Bryoni reached down with her trussed hands and helped Sacha back onto her feet.

The gang leader turned to Marlene and he produced a slip of paper from his zip pocket. 'These are my orders.' He read from it in his thick Hispanic accent. 'Marlene Imelda Bannock. You are to be executed. Your death is to be witnessed by your daughters, Sacha Jean and Bryoni Lee. Your execution will be filmed for the benefit of all interested parties. Thereafter your daughters are to be imprisoned for life in a foreign country.'

Sacha's legs collapsed under her again. Bryoni could not hold her and she fell to the marble coping that edged the pool. She rolled herself into a ball and wailed shrilly. She started banging her forehead on the marble with such force that one of her eyebrows split open and blood trickled down into her eyes. Bryoni knelt beside Sacha and tried to prevent her injuring herself further.

As three of the men dragged Marlene away she called back desperately. 'Be brave, Sacha! Don't cry, baby. Take care of her, Bryoni.'

They took Marlene down the pool steps and into the water. It was waist deep. Bright underwater floodlights lit the stage for Amaranthus, who knelt on the edge of the pool and filmed it all.

One of the crew members stood on each side of Marlene, holding her arms. They looked up at Miguel on the edge of the pool above them.

Miguel told them, '*Bueno!* Hold her under.'

Two of them forced Marlene's head below the surface of the water. The third man grasped her ankles, and lifted them up high. The top half of Marlene's body was completely immersed. She kicked her legs wildly and her entire body bucked and convulsed so violently that the men had difficulty holding her.

'Enough!' Miguel shouted. 'Bring her up for a minute.' They lifted Marlene's head from the water and she gasped and struggled for breath. Then suddenly a mixture of pool water and vomit shot from her gaping mouth, and she choked on her next breath.

'*Bueno*, that's good. Put her under again.' They ducked her head under just as she drew breath and Marlene took down a mouthful of water rather than air. They repeated the duckings at progressively longer intervals as Marlene's struggles weakened. Amaranthus behind the camera wanted to make the most of this scene. This was one of the stipulations that his sponsors had set, and Amaranthus understood how fascinating this would be to them.

Torn by her love for her sister and her mother, Bryoni left Sacha and crawled to Miguel and tried to hold his legs.

'She is my mother. Please don't do this to her.'

He kicked her away, and called to the three men in the pool, 'Now we will finish it. Keep the old bitch under.'

There was a violent burst of bubbles on the surface as Marlene's lungs emptied completely. Her struggles grew weaker and at last stopped.

'*Ha muerto?*' one of them asked. 'Is she dead?'

'*No, esperar un poco más,*' Miguel ordered. 'No, wait a little longer.'

Bryoni understood enough Spanish. She crawled back to Miguel and clutched at his legs again, 'Please, señor. Have mercy, I beg of you.' This time he kicked her in the mouth and she fell over backwards, holding her bleeding lips.

'Your turn will come soon enough,' he jeered at her. 'But first we must sample your meat; both you and your loco sister.' He pulled back his sleeve and looked at his watch. Then he spoke to the men in the water. '*Bueno!* That should do it. Bring her up. Let's take a look at her.'

One of the men grabbed a handful of her hair and lifted Marlene's face out of the water. Her skin was waxy pale. Her eyes were wide open and staring. Her hair had come down in streamers over her face like seaweed exposed on a rock at low tide. Water drooled from her open mouth.

'Leave her there,' Miguel ordered and they released her and waded to the steps, leaving Marlene's corpse floating face-down in the pool.

'We have been here too long already. It's time to go,' Miguel told them. 'Get that dirty *puta* cleaned up.' He pointed at Sacha. 'The *jefe* will kill us if we get shit all over his beautiful boat.'

They stripped Sacha's soiled pyjamas off her and threw her naked into the pool beside her mother's corpse. One of them stooped over Bryoni and cut the duct tape from her wrists.

'Get in there with your pig sister and wash the shit off her,' he ordered her in Spanish.

Bryoni waded out to Sacha and washed her body and cleaned the blood from the wound above her eye, then led her back to the pool steps with one arm around her shoulders. Sacha kept whimpering and looking back at Marlene's floating corpse. 'What is wrong with Mummy? Why doesn't she want to talk to me, Bryoni?' Sacha had regressed to her five-year-old state.

The dawn was a riot of majestic cumulus clouds set alight by the rays of the rising sun. The *Pluma de Mar* was running hard for the south over an easy and unctuous swell. She was two hundred nautical miles south of Grand Cayman, but she was not on a direct return course for La Ceiba in Honduras.

She was headed instead for the port of Cartagena in Colombia.

This was a deliberate ploy ordered by Carl and Johnny Congo. The *Pluma de Mar* had left La Ceiba with only eleven crew members on board. She must return with the same complement; otherwise the suspicions of the port officials would be roused.

As soon as the sun cleared the horizon Miguel ordered the captives to be brought up from the forecastle to the cockpit. Sacha was completely confused and disorientated. She did not understand what was happening to them. She was even unaware of her own nudity. She stood blinking in the bright sunlight, and she kept asking Bryoni where their mother was. 'Who are all these strange men, Bree? Why are they staring at me? Why did we leave Mummy behind, Bree?' She had retreated into the profound depths of her dementia.

The crew had brought up some of the gaily coloured cushions from the benches in the main cabin and strewn them on the deck of the cockpit to serve as a mattress. All of them had removed their black tracksuits and hoods, and had stripped down to tee shirts and shorts. Now that the raid was successfully completed, they were in a jovial and celebratory mood. They were joking and laughing, drinking Mexican Corona beer from the can as they crowded around the two girls. Miguel came down the companionway ladder from the flying bridge. He pointed at Bryoni. 'Get the clothes off that one. No secrets on board this boat. Let's see what she has got there for us.'

While Amaranthus filmed them, they pulled Bryoni away from her sister and tore her flimsy nightdress from her back. One of them balled it in his fist and threw it over the side of the boat. The crew crowded around her, reaching out to grope her buttocks and fondle her breasts. Bryoni tried to fend them off by twisting her body around and striking out at their hands. Miguel intervened and pushed them back. 'No fighting!' he warned them. 'Everybody gets a go. By the time we reach Cartagena you will all have had so much of this pussy that you'll be sick of the sight of it.' He held up a fan of playing cards. 'Draw your card, *caballeros*. The numbers are Ace to Jack. Ace gets first turn, and Jack comes last.' They pushed forward to take a card out of his hand. One of them let out a triumphant whoop and held up the ace of spades.

'Beat that you whore-sons!' he challenged them.

'Stand back!' Miguel chuckled. 'Feliciano gets first shot. Which one do you want, amigo?'

'I'll take the fat one.' Feliciano elbowed his way towards Sacha. She smiled at him as he took her hand. She still didn't understand what was happening. She followed him compliantly as he led her to the pile of bench cushions on the deck and pushed her down on them.

'No, Sacha! Don't let him touch you.' Bryoni was struggling with the men who were restraining her. 'He is going to hurt you, baby.'

Sacha was smiling happily now. Her mood swings were quick and unpredictable. 'It's all right, Bree. I like him. He is such a nice man.'

Then Feliciano knelt in front of her and pulled down his shorts. Sacha's damaged brain made another instantaneous connection to her brother Carl Peter in a similar pose and she recoiled in fear. It took four of the crew to hold her down before Feliciano was able to enter her. Sacha was still shrieking as Feliciano rolled off, and grunted, '*Fantástica! Mejores de la historia!* Fantastic! The best ever! I love to feel them buck and hear them squeal.'

Bryoni was dragged over and thrown down on the floral patterned cushions as the next man in line came forward eagerly. She also began to scream and struggle, but the same four men pinioned her limbs, and spread her legs wide apart. Amaranthus kept on filming.

By the middle of the afternoon as the *Pluma de Mar* roared on into the south both the sisters were in a stupor. Neither of them had the strength nor the will to continue resisting. One of the gang stood up after covering Bryoni for the third time, and complained to Miguel, 'She is like meat in the butcher shop; dead and cold.'

'*Bueno*, I can fix that. Bring them down to the main cabin,' Miguel told him.

They carried Bryoni down the companionway and laid her on the mess table. Miguel wound a length of surgical rubber tubing around her upper arm and tightened it until the veins in the crook of her elbow stood out blue and proud. He poured a heaped teaspoonful of white heroin powder into a small bottle of distilled water and shook it until the powder dissolved. Then he drew it up in a disposable syringe and shot it into Bryoni's distended vein. Within a few minutes Bryoni was resuscitating as the rush of the drug hit her. She started screaming and struggling again. They dragged her up to the cockpit where the man whose turn it was came forward, lowering his shorts and working up his penis with his hand.

In the cabin below Miguel turned his attention to Sacha and prepared a second shot of heroin for her. Amaranthus recorded the entire process.

That evening, twenty nautical miles off the Colombian port of Cartagena, in the short tropical twilight, the *Pluma de Mar* made a rendezvous with a working barge from the port. Once again the two sisters were trussed and gagged with duct tape. Then they were transferred across to the barge, and concealed under an old stained tarpaulin in the stern. Amaranthus with his ubiquitous camera followed the girls across to the barge. His brief was to stay with them and continue filming to the very end.

The *Pluma de Mar* reversed her course and headed at thirty knots for La Ceiba. The barge trundled on into the port of Cartagena.

There was an old Ford three-ton truck waiting to meet the barge on one of the wharves in a remote section of Cartagena harbour. A fresh team of men was waiting to receive them: a driver, his mate and two thugs. The girls were quickly transferred ashore and bundled into the back of the truck. Another tarpaulin was thrown over them. Amaranthus and the thugs climbed into the rear of the truck. The driver and his mate scrambled into the cab. The driver started the engine and drove to the harbour gates. A customs official came out of his hut. There was a muttered conversation with the driver and a wad of banknotes changed hands. The customs man stood back and waved them through and they drove into Colombia.

They headed southwards for the next six days, over progressively rougher unmade roads, through jungle and mountains. At some point they left the state of Colombia and crossed another river by ferry into Venezuela. At each stop along the way the driver climbed into the back of the truck and gave the girls a shot of intravenous heroin. By this stage, as soon as they saw the needle, the sisters were holding out their right arms willingly, eager for the solace that the drug provided them.

As soon as they were revived the driver's mate flagged down any other passing vehicles on the road and opened the canvas flap on the back of the Ford to display the girls to these prospective customers. If the girls tried to resist they were beaten, and denied their next fix of heroin. By the time they reached Minas de Ye each of the sisters had been used so often that they had lost count of all the men who had climbed into the back of the old Ford to be with them.

Minas de Ye was deep in the jungles of the Amazon basin. It was an area along both banks of the Rio de Oro, a tributary of the Amazon, which cut through the mountains. An army of illegal gold miners laboured in the diggings, risking their lives for a few grains of the alluvial yellow metal.

The truck stopped for the last time at a large ramshackle building on the river bank, where one of the many gold buyers from the city of Calabozo had set up business. The buyer was a fat and shaggy rogue named Goyo who sat behind his gold scales on the veranda and haggled with the miners who brought down the meagre yellow flakes and beads from their sluice boxes in the hills.

Goyo's woman was a shrewish creature, as thin as her husband was fat. Her name was Dolorita. She sold marijuana, heroin and home-brewed tequila to her husband's customers. She also operated a brothel in the back rooms of the rambling building. Sacha and Bryoni were unloaded from the truck and handed over to Dolorita, who seemed to be anticipating their arrival. She at once forced the girls to strip off the rags that covered them and she examined them quickly.

'They have already been used up. This was not what I saw in the photographs,' she complained when she saw their bruises. 'But it is too late now. I can't send them back. I have already paid over a hundred dollars each for them. Anyway, we always need new girls.' She turned to her overseer. His name was Silvestre and he was a villainous-looking brute with a marked squint. When he smiled, which was seldom, he exposed one gold tooth and another jet black one sitting side by side in the front of his lower jaw.

'You better try to get some of my money back, Silvestre. Do you hear me? Make them work hard,' Dolorita ordered him.

Silvestre led the two sisters around to the back of the building and shoved them into a dingy little room in which they would live and work on the two filthy mattresses that were laid side by side in the centre of the mud floor. There was no plumbing, and the girls had no alternative but to bathe in and drink from a bucket of river water in one corner of the room. There was an identical bucket standing beside the first one. This was the latrine which served not only Sacha and Bryoni but any of their clients who felt the need. The contaminated river water gave both the girls intermittent low-grade dysentery.

Dolorita set her prices so low that at all times there was a line of three or four men waiting their turn at the door. They were all miners and their bodies reeked with the sweat of their labour, while their mouths stank of rotting teeth and cheap tequila. Their bodies and ragged clothing were plastered with red mud from the gold diggings.

Bryoni never knew how many other girls were working in the adjacent rooms. All she knew was that there were many of them. Dolorita fed her working girls on a diet of minimal amounts of plain boiled cassava and much larger doses of low-grade heroin. Her turnover of girls from disease, malnutrition and drug overdose was brisk.

The roof of the shack was thatched with palm fronds. The tropical rain dripped through and the girls were seldom completely dry. Within the first week Sacha developed a persistent cough. She refused to eat more than a few mouthfuls of the foul food, and she lost weight at an alarming rate.

The walls of their room were made from unpainted cardboard packing cases, so flimsy that they were able to hear almost everything happening in the other rooms around them. Two or three times a week Bryoni would hear Dolorita call Silvestre and tell him, 'This bitch is finished. Take her down to the farm.'

Bryoni had no idea what she meant by the farm. She had long ago descended into a fog of pain, exhaustion and heroin. Like Sacha, she was slowly losing her grasp on reality.

Every few days Amaranthus would come to drink tequila with Silvestre and to take more film footage of Bryoni and Sacha in their squalor. Bryoni was hardly aware of his presence. The only thing that she agonized over was the swift deterioration of Sacha's health. Bryoni realized at last that Sacha was dying.

She pleaded with Dolorita and Silvestre in her elementary Spanish to fetch a doctor, but they laughed at her.

'Who is going to pay for this doctor, *querido*?' Dolorita mocked her. 'If your sister worked harder, I might buy a little medicine for her cough, but she is a lazy cow. Why should I spend good money on her?'

Three days later Sacha developed a burning fever, and again Bryoni begged Dolorita to get help for her. 'My sister is very sick. Just feel how hot her body is.'

'*Bueno!* The men they like it that way. They like putting their bread into a nice hot oven.' Dolorita cackled with laughter.

In the early hours of the following morning Sacha died. Bryoni was holding her in her arms as she felt the life go out of her. Her body began to cool and Bryoni hardly had the strength to weep for her one last time.

In the dawn Dolorita and Silvestre came to the little room and stood over Sacha's skeletal naked body.

'*Si*,' Dolorita said briskly. 'She is finished. Take her down to the farm, Silvestre.'

Bryoni still did not know where or what the farm was and she did not care. She had lost Sacha, and after that nothing else mattered. At last she had given up the struggle. She just wanted to die and be with Sacha, wherever she had gone.

Amaranthus the cameraman came the next afternoon and he was furious to learn that Sacha was dead. Bryoni heard him shouting at Silvestre on the veranda. 'Why didn't you send for me? They are going to be angry with me now. This is going to cost me money. It is my job to film everything; especially if one of the bitches dies. They will cut my pay. You should have sent a message to me.'

One of the gold miners was with Bryoni while this conversation was going on outside her window. He was rutting noisily on top of

her, grunting like an animal in her ear, so she had difficulty understanding what Amaranthus had said, but she heard clearly Silvestre's
reply. 'Don't worry, Amaranthus my friend. The other *puta* won't be
too far behind her. I will call you when it happens. Now, come and
I will let you buy me a glass of tequila.' He took Amaranthus by the
arm and led him up to the barroom. They sat at one of the small
and grubby tables and drank the first tequila. Amaranthus's mood
improved and he brought Silvestre a second drink.

'I would like to see this farm that you and Dolorita are always
talking about. I would like to take some film. Will you show it to
me, Silvestre?'

'Buy me one more drink first.'

Silvestre drained his glass and then stood up. '*Bueno, amigo*. Come
with me and I will show you our famous farm.'

He led Amaranthus down through the banana plantation towards
the bank of the river and then turned into a grove of cashew trees.
Suddenly Amaranthus sniffed the air and exclaimed with disgust,
'Poof! What it is that revolting smell?'

'What you smell is our butchery and hog pens.'

'It's a pig farm, is it?'

'Yes, our pork sausages are the finest in South America. We send
all we can make to the big towns.'

They came out of the trees into a large clearing in the jungle.
Silvestre led him down a path between two rows of hog pens. The
animals in them were black Iberian pigs.

Silvestre stopped beside one pen in which there were eight enormous boars. Each of them stood as high as a man's hip. Short sharp
tusks protruded from their jaws. The coarse bristles on their humped
backs formed a dense mane. They snuffled the air hungrily and
champed their jaws, grunting with excitement, watching Silvestre
with glistening and greedy eyes.

'They recognize you. They are very happy to see you,' Amaranthus
remarked.

'They are my pets,' Silvestre agreed. 'I am the one who feeds
them.' He pointed at the largest animal. 'That one is called Hannibal.
By the time he goes to the butcher shop to be made into sausages,
he will weigh three hundred kilos.'

'He is a monster,' Amaranthus agreed. 'What do you feed them on? Cassava?'

'Yes, cassava.' Silvestre tapped his nose with one finger and his expression became cunning and conspiratorial. He dropped his voice. 'But meat also. We feed them plenty of meat.'

'Where do you get meat from to feed pigs?' Amaranthus wondered. 'Few men in Minas de Ye can afford to eat even a little of it more than once a month. Meat is very expensive.'

'Not if you run a bordello in Minas de Ye.' Silvestre was still grinning.

Amaranthus stared at him. 'No!' he exclaimed as he caught on to Silvestre's meaning. 'No. I don't believe it.' Then he began to grin also. 'The girls? Is that it?'

'*Si!*' Silvestre was snuffling and grunting with mirth, very much like one of his own pigs. '*Si!* When they finish work at the bordello for ever, Dolorita sends them down here to the farm.'

'Is that what you did to the first *Yanqui* cow when she died?' Amaranthus demanded. 'You fed her to the pigs?'

Silvestre was laughing so much he could not reply. Amaranthus turned away and leaned over the low wall of the hog pen. His mind was racing. As he rolled a joint of marijuana, his hands were trembling with excitement. He lit the joint and turned back to Silvestre. 'How would you like me to pay you one hundred dollars *americano*?'

Silvestre stopped laughing abruptly. He thought about what he could do with a hundred dollars. He decided he could do a great deal with that sum of money. It was almost twice as much as Dolorita paid him for a week of hard work.

'What do you want me to do?'

'I want you to let me film when you bring the other *Yanqui puta* to the farm, to visit your pet Hannibal.'

Silvestre grunted with relief. 'That is no problem, *amigo*. I will send word to you as soon as she dies. I don't think she will last much longer. She is pining for her sister. Soon she will give up. For a hundred *americanos* you can shoot all the film in your bag.'

'No!' Amaranthus contradicted him. 'No, you don't understand. I want you to bring her to the farm before she dies. I want you to bring her to see Hannibal while she can still struggle and kick. I want to film her while she is still able to squeal.'

Even Silvestre was stunned by the enormity of the proposition. His face paled and he stared at Amaranthus.

'You mean alive?' he stammered. 'You want me to let my pigs eat her while she still lives?' He could hardly believe what he was hearing.

'*Si, amigo.* Alive!'

'Beloved Maria! Now I have heard everything. Give me a suck on your *porro*.' Silvestre needed time to regain his wits. Amaranthus handed him the cigarette. Silvestre inhaled deeply and held the smoke as he spoke.

'One hundred dollars is not enough!' he wheezed. 'I want five hundred.'

'Three hundred and fifty,' Amaranthus countered.

'Four hundred.'

'Okay! Four hundred,' Amaranthus agreed happily. He had heard of someone who had made a hundred thousand dollars with a six-minute tape by selling it on the black market. He had seen that tape. It was as nothing compared to what his tape would be.

A million! he dreamed. *It could make me a million; perhaps even more.*

It was Monday morning so Silvestre knew that Dolorita and Goyo would be locked in their office behind the bar. They were counting the takings of the week before Goyo carried them down to the bank in the town. Silvestre knocked on the door.

'Who is it?' Dolorita screeched. 'What do you want? We are busy!'

'It is me, Silvestre. The second *Yanqui puta*, the cheeky one, she died during the night.'

'So what do want me to do about it? Take her down to the farm, and leave us alone. You know that we are busy.'

'*Perdóname, señora.* I will not bother you again.'

Silvestre went around to the back of the house. Even this early in the morning there were two miners waiting at the door of Bryoni's room. The door was open and the men were smoking and watching with interest what was happening inside. Silvestre shoved them away from the door, and pointed down the veranda.

'Go to one of the other girls,' he told them. 'This one is finished for the day.'

'I want this one,' one of the miners started to argue. 'I know her well. She is lively. She fights. She does not just lie there like a dead catfish . . .'

Silvestre turned on him with a scowl. The man backed down hurriedly. Silvestre's reputation as a knifeman was almost as ugly as his face.

Silvestre kicked the naked buttocks of the miner who was on top of Bryoni. He jumped to his feet, hoisted the trousers of his overalls and scurried from the room. Silvestre went to kneel beside Bryoni.

'Are you ready for a little of the good stuff?' he asked her and took the box containing his heroin kit from his pocket. Bryoni sat up eagerly and offered him her left arm. He examined it briefly. The crook of her elbow was inflamed and ulcerated. One of the big veins had collapsed and the ulcers were festering and oozing pus. Her other arm was in a similar condition.

'I will use your foot,' he decided. He put the rubber tube around her leg just above the ankle and twisted it until the veins puffed up. He shot the drug into her leg. Bryoni closed her eyes in anticipation. Then she opened them again and smiled at Silvestre. She had lost two of her front teeth a few weeks previously in an argument with Silvestre, but that no longer mattered. All that mattered was the glorious surge of the heroin through her body.

'Thank you, Silvestre,' she whispered dreamily.

'I am taking you out for a while,' he told her.

'Okay,' she agreed. She had given up caring what happened to her next.

'I am going to cover you with a blanket, so people won't see you without your clothes.'

'Thank you,' she murmured again.

He wound the mud-and-semen-stained blanket around her naked body, and draped a fold of it over her head to cover her face. He picked her up in his arms and carried her out through the back door of the building and headed into the trees. When he came out into the hog farm he saw that Amaranthus was there before them. Amaranthus had climbed onto the wall of Hannibal's sty and he had set his camera on its tripod. The animals were milling around below him, grunting and squealing. They had seen Silvestre coming down the hill, carrying a familiar burden.

'Are you ready?' Silvestre called to him. 'We mustn't waste too much time.'

'Camera is already rolling!' Amaranthus laughed with excitement. Beneath where he stood Hannibal reared up on his back legs and placed his front hooves on top of the wall of the sty. He peered over it as Silvestre approached.

'How do you want to do this?' Silvestre asked as he placed Bryoni on her feet. He removed the blanket that covered her. With a puzzled expression on her face Bryoni stared at Hannibal's massive black head that was looking at her over the wall of the sty. She cowered back against Silvestre's chest. Hannibal was snuffling through his flat pink-blotched snout and champing his jaws.

'I am ready if you are,' Amaranthus assured him.

'I think we need a little blood to get Hannibal worked up,' Silvestre said. He stepped back from Bryoni. She was so fascinated by the huge animal in front of her that she did not notice what Silvestre was doing. Earlier that morning he had left a flat-bladed spade propped against the wall of the sty. He picked it up in one hand and said softly, 'Hey, Bryoni, look at me.'

She turned to face him and he swung the spade at the level of her knees. The steel cut through to the bone and shattered her kneecap. Blood spurted from the wound. Her leg collapsed under her and Bryoni shrieked with pain and shock as she started to fall.

Silvestre dropped the spade and caught her up in his arms. He glanced over her head at Amaranthus on the wall above them.

'Yes?' he asked.

'Yes. Do it!' Amaranthus shouted.

With a heave of his shoulders Silvestre tossed Bryoni over the wall. She fell amongst the hogs on the far side.

Bryoni was stunned by the fall, but she recovered swiftly. She pushed herself up on her elbows and started to drag her body through the black filth of the sty, back towards the illusory safety of the wall.

Hannibal led the charge of great black bodies that descended upon her. He locked his tusks into her wounded leg. He worried the mutilated limb, trying to tear off a mouthful of flesh, dragging Bryoni on her back through the mud. Bryoni lifted her face towards the camera.

'Please!' she cried. 'Please somebody help me.'

Then another animal bit into her shoulder and heaved back, until he and Hannibal had Bryoni's body racked between them. A third boar surged forward and bit into her stomach and then pulled back, tearing out a tangled mass of her entrails.

Bryoni opened her mouth for the last time.

'Daddy!' she cried out in a piercing but slowly descending pitch. And the pigs tore bloody chunks from her body and gulped them down.

Carl Bannock and Johnny Congo sat side by side in Johnny's prison cell and watched the video on the TV screen. This was the third night that they had watched it, but both of them were just as excited and animated by it as they had been the first time.

From hundreds of hours of tape Amaranthus had, with professional expertise, edited out forty minutes. The final result was both sickening and harrowing to any but the most sadistic and warped mind. Carl and Johnny rejoiced in it. They bellowed with laughter at the highlights as though they were moments of sheer comic genius.

'Run it back!' Johnny pleaded. 'That's so funny. I love it when they drown the old mother bitch. I love the way the water and shit shoots out of her nose when they pull her head out.'

'Yeah, that's good. But I like it even better when Bryoni kneels in front of the head honcho and begs for her mother's life, and then he kicks her in the mouth and she sits there spitting out blood and broken teeth. That's really cool, man.'

However, both of them were agreed that the final scene was by far the best part of the show. They leaned forward in anticipation of the moment when Bryoni, broken and disembowelled, lifted her head out of the mud and called out to her father. In chorus they mimicked her, imitating her falling and sobbing inflection: 'Daddy!'

Then both of them burst into delighted laughter as Bryoni's eyes swivelled up towards the sky in agony and the pigs swarmed over her.

'That scene just freaks me out.' Carl almost choked on his own laughter. 'This Amaranthus guy you found for us should get an Oscar for this.'

'Yeah, man, he is a genius. When I watch that Daddy bit, it gives me a full hard-on every time,' Johnny confessed.

'That doesn't mean too much. Anything at all can give you a bone, Blackbird, even a passing bus,' Carl teased him.

'Passing bus will do it,' Johnny agreed. 'As long as it's full of school-girls. But don't you want to take a look at what I got down there this time?'

'Okay,' Carl said with aroused interest. 'Show it to me.' Then as Johnny leaned back in the chair and exposed himself fully, Carl laughed out loud.

'You could sink a Russian battleship with that big black torpedo.'

'What you going to do about it, white boy?'

'You know damn well what I'm going to do, Blackbird,' said Carl, and knelt in front of him.

Later, when they had both recovered their breath, Johnny asked, 'So tell me, when you going to send the video to your daddy?' He used the same inflection on the last word as the dying girl had done in the video, and they laughed again together.

Then Carl said seriously, 'Soon as we can work out a way that Henry Bannock won't be able to trace it back to us.'

'Your daddy didn't get rich by being stupid,' Johnny pointed out. 'As soon as he gets it he's going to know where the tape came from.'

'Yeah, man, that's what I want. This is his punishment for what he did to me. I want him to know that, but he will never be able to pin it on me.'

Ronnie Bunter and his wife Jennie were opera fanatics. They seldom missed a premiere at the Grand Houston 1894 Opera House. *La Bohème* was one of their absolute favourites and the travelling La Scala production was visiting Texas. The two of them were there on the opening night. After the performance they walked back to the underground car park discussing the show with animation. Ronnie opened the passenger door of his Porsche 911 and helped his wife into her seat, and then he went around to the driver's side. As he slid into his own seat he suddenly exclaimed, 'Now what on earth have you left here, darling?'

'I haven't left a single thing, Ronald.'

Ronnie groped around the back of his seat and pulled out a small oblong cardboard box. 'Then how did this get here?'

'Careful! It could be a bomb, Ronald,' Jennie said with alarm.

'If it was we would both be dead by now.' He examined the package, and then read the handwritten label on the front of the box. *To Mr Ronald Bunter. To be viewed in private.* 'It seems to be a video tape.'

'Not something nasty, I hope,' Jennie said primly.

'I doubt it.'

'Then why does it say "in private"?'

'I'll take it with me to the office tomorrow and have a look at it on the projector in the conference room.'

'Better not let your new assistant watch it. She seems to be a nice girl.'

'Don't worry about Jo Stanley. She has just finished three years in law school. You can bet your bottom dollar she could teach two old fogeys like us a thing or two.'

As soon as he had viewed the video the next morning Ronnie phoned the Bannock Oil Corporation offices in Anchorage, Alaska. When Henry Bannock came on the line he asked, 'Henry, when will you be back in Houston?'

'I'm flying back Friday.' Henry detected the gravity in his old friend's voice. 'What is it, Ronnie? Is something up? Have you received any news from the police about my daughters yet?'

'Listen, Henry, you must get back here right away. No, I can't tell you why until you get here. Just come, Henry. Come to my office just as soon as you can. Do not bring Hazel with you, do you understand? Come alone.'

'Hold on, Ronnie.' Ronald heard him speak to somebody with him and then he came back on the line, 'Okay. We will be airborne in an hour. But the flying time is more than seven hours. We will get in to Houston pretty late.'

'No matter how late you get in, come straight to my office, Henry. I will be waiting for you. Someone will be downstairs to let you into the building.'

'I'll phone you soon as we land,' Henry assured him.

Bonzo Barnes in his chauffeur uniform was waiting at the VIP fast-track gate of Houston airport when Henry Bannock and Hazel came through.

'Welcome home, sir and madam. We missed you.'

'How you been, Bonzo?'

Henry shook his hand. Mr Bannock was a real gentleman. He treated even his employees with respect; but his grip was no longer firm. Bonzo turned to Hazel and during their brief handshake he asked a silent question; cocking his great black head slightly on one side and lifting an eyebrow. He was fearful of mentioning the missing girls in front of their father.

Sacha and Bryoni had been gone for almost a year. They had left only sorrow and despair behind them. Perhaps the worst part of their loss was the uncertainty; month after month of agonizing suspense.

Henry Bannock was suffering far worse than any of them. His powerful and rugged features seemed to be crumbling. His eyes no longer sought new horizons to conquer; they had become dull and introspective. His shoulders were slumped and his back bowed. He walked like an old man, shuffling along and clinging to Hazel's arm for comfort and support. But now he rallied and gave Bonzo a weary smile.

'Subtlety has never been one of your many outstanding gifts, Bonzo Barnes. The answer is no. We have heard nothing about the girls.'

Bonzo winced. He had worked for Mr Bannock for nigh on thirty years. He should have remembered that he had eyes in the back of his head.

'Sorry, Mr Bannock, sir.'

Henry clapped his shoulder with some of his old vigour. 'We must all bear up, man. Now you can drop me off at Mr Bunter's office. After that you can take Mrs Bannock home. Then come back to town and wait for me. I don't know how long I am going to be.'

On the back seat of the Cadillac Hazel sat close to Henry and hugged his arm. 'If you have changed your mind, Henry, I'll come with you to hear what Ronnie has to tell us.'

'Cayla hasn't seen her mama for four days. You go on home.'

'In my life you come first, Henry Bannock; Cayla comes second.'

Henry turned in his seat and looked into her eyes. 'You're a good woman. The best I ever knew. I'm going to miss you.'

'Why did you say that?' She looked at him with alarm.

'I don't know why. It just came out.'

'You aren't planning to do something stupid, are you?'

'No, I promise you.'

'You think Ronnie has bad news, don't you?'

'Yes, I know Ronnie Bunter has bad news for me.'

Hazel walked with him from the car to the front door of the tall building that housed the law firm of Bunter and Theobald, Inc.

Beyond the double glass doors Jo Stanley, Ronnie's new legal assistant, was sitting on one of the white leather sofas in the spacious lobby, reading a glossy woman's magazine. She looked up and saw them crossing the sidewalk. She dropped the magazine and came to meet them. As she stooped to unlock the door Hazel turned and hugged Henry.

'Take note of what I tell you, husband!' she said softly. 'I shall never miss you, because I will always be walking close beside you.' She reached up on tiptoe and kissed him on the mouth and then she turned away and hurried back to where Bonzo held open the back door of the Cadillac for her.

Henry watched them drive away and then he went into the lobby through the door that Jo Stanley held open for him.

'Sorry to keep you at work so late, Jo.'

'It's no trouble, sir. I don't have much reason to hurry home.'

'Is Ronnie still here?'

'He's waiting for you on the tenth floor in the main conference room. I'll show you up, Mr Bannock.'

'I know the way better than you do, Jo Stanley. I have been coming here from before you were born. Off you go home like a good girl.' He smiled at her but she saw the smile was forced and his eyes were tired.

When the elevator doors opened on the tenth floor Henry found Ronnie waiting for him on the landing. 'Sorry to put you through all this palaver—' he started, but Henry cut him short.

'Cut the bullshit, Ronnie. Give it to me straight, have they found Bryoni?'

'It's not quite as simple as that, Henry.' He took Henry's arm.

Henry shrugged his hand away. 'Come on, Ronnie. I can still walk.' He straightened his shoulders, stood to his full height and marched to the conference room. He took his usual seat at the long table and glowered at Ronnie. 'I am listening,' he said.

Ronnie sat across the table from him. 'I received a video cassette,' he said.

'From whom?'

'I don't know. While Jennie and I were at the opera Saturday evening somebody left it on the driver's seat of my Porsche.'

'Have you played it?' Ronnie nodded. 'What's in it?'

'I cannot describe it. It's the most harrowing and disgusting filth imaginable. Only a very sick and vicious mind could have conceived of this. That is why I asked you not to bring Hazel with you.'

'Does it involve my girls?'

'Yes. But now I have warned you, do you still want me to screen it for you?'

'If it affects my girls, do I have any other choice? Run the thing, Ronnie. Cut the crap and have done.'

Ronnie reached for the control panel on the desk in front of him and the lights dimmed as the silver screen unrolled from the ceiling to cover the far wall. Henry swivelled his chair to face it.

'Steel yourself, Henry, my old friend.' Ronnie's tone was compassionate as he pressed the 'Play' button on the console panel.

The lilting strains of violins playing a Strauss waltz filled the room as the screen lit with the image of a tall athletic man playing with a pretty little girl on the wide lawn of a magnificent mansion. In the background a lovely young woman was watching them fondly.

Henry straightened up in the chair. 'What the hell! That's a cut from one of my own home movies. That's me and Marlene with Sacha when she was a kid.'

The scene faded and then was replaced by a magnificent vista of a high summer sky and billowing cumulus nimbus clouds. Over this a line of prose appeared in golden script:

The extremity of joy is separated by merely the trembling of a leaf from the depths of despair . . .

The vista of sky jump-cut to a night scene of a swimming bath surrounded by the shadowy shapes of palm trees. Three masked men held Marlene in the water. The underwater lighting showed everything in stark and remorseless detail. Marlene was naked, and as Henry watched they drowned her, drawing out the process with exquisite sadism.

Then the camera cut away to Bryoni, naked on the edge of the pool, pleading and weeping for her mother's life. She was at the feet of another black-clad assailant. Sacha was curled up on the coping beside her. She was hitting her head on the marble slabs with such force that her blood flowed.

'In the holy name of Jesus Christ, don't let this be happening,' Henry whispered, and his voice was hoarse with agony.

Then he went silent and still as a statue cast in bronze as the horrors multiplied. He was unable to tear his eyes from the screen as rapes followed beatings, as his girls were forcibly injected with narcotics and then were held down by lewd sub-human creatures, and mounted by others even more obscene.

The recorded sounds: the thud of the lash impacting on flesh, the lascivious clamour of the tormentors and the agonized whimpering and sobbing of the tormented girls were almost as terrible as the images.

At the very end when his beloved Bryoni was down in the mud and filth of the sty, being ripped into bloody tatters by the slavering pack of pigs, Henry heaved himself painfully to his feet and stood swaying at the head of the long table.

On the screen Bryoni lifted her head and seemed to look directly at him.

'Daddy!' she cried.

Henry lifted his right hand in a gesture of supplication, as if he were begging her forgiveness for failing her in her hour of direst need.

'Bryoni!' Henry answered her with his own cry; one ringing with the utmost spiritual anguish.

Then he began to fall like a giant Sequoia redwood, slowly at first but swiftly gathering momentum, until he crashed face-down onto the long table and lay deathly still.

The time was already past midnight, but Hazel had asked Cookie to keep dinner for Henry. It was a warm evening and the sky was full of stars. She waited on the terrace for her husband.

She had chosen a sleeveless blue evening dress, a shade that matched her eyes. It left her back bare, and showed off her bosom and the fine musculature of her arms. She knew it would please Henry. She had been very strict with herself since the birth of Cayla and she was as lean and beautiful as she had been when she first met him.

She could not remain still. Impatiently she paced the terrace with panther-like grace, sipping the single glass of Pouilly-Fuissé that she allowed herself each evening, and humming softly in tune to the music from the concealed speakers. She thought about phoning Henry to make certain he was all right, but then she shook her head. Henry did not welcome interruption when he was in a business meeting.

She paused beside the dinner table and realigned the silver cutlery laid at Henry's place. The wine was in the crystal decanter. She had opened and poured one of Henry's favourite Burgundies to let it breathe and unfold. She decided to light the candles as soon as she heard the Cadillac coming up the hill, and she checked that the vintage Ronson lighter for that purpose was ready to hand.

'I know that something has happened to the girls. No matter what Ronnie has told Henry tonight I am going to be strong,' she promised herself. 'I am not going to break down and weep. I am going to be strong for him.'

She resumed her restless pacing. Suddenly the phone that she had placed beside her own seat rang and she ran back to the table and snatched it up with a great surge of relief.

'Henry!' she said. 'Darling! Where are you?' And her voice sang joyously.

'No, Hazel, it's me. Ronnie.'

'Oh God!' The music went out of her voice. 'Is Henry all right? Where is he?'

'There is only one way to tell you this, Hazel. With any other woman I would try to soften it, but you are different. You are as strong as any man I know.'

Hazel could hear her own heart beating in her ears. She did not speak for five slow heartbeats, and then she said quietly, 'He had a premonition. He's dead, isn't he, Ronnie?'

'I am so dreadfully sorry, my dear.'

'How?'

'A stroke. A massive stroke. It was almost instantaneous. He felt nothing.'

'Where is he?' She felt the cold, a searing arctic cold that struck down into the inner regions of her soul.

'Hospital,' he said. 'St Luke's Episcopal.'

'Send Bonzo to fetch me, please, Ronnie.'

'He's on his way already,' Ronnie assured her.

Hazel stood beside the high hospital bed and looked down on the human shape under the white sheet. The cold was still in her heart and in her bones.

Ronnie stood beside her. He took her hand.

'Thank you, Ronnie. I mean no offence, but I have to do this on my own.' Carefully she withdrew her hand from his.

'I understand, Hazel.' Ronnie took a pace backwards and then looked across the bed to the nurse who was standing ready. 'Thank you, Sister.' The nurse took the top edge of the sheet and drew it down gently.

In death Henry Bannock had recaptured the imperial mantle which grief had stripped from him.

'He was a beautiful man,' Ronnie said softly. 'He was the finest man I ever knew.'

'He still is,' Hazel said. She leaned forward and kissed Henry. His lips were as cold as her heart.

'*Au revoir*, Henry,' she whispered. 'God speed, my love. You should have died hereafter. Cayla and I are bereft. You have left us only dust and darkness.'

'No, Hazel,' Ronnie contradicted her softly. 'Henry has left you an empire and the shining beacon of his example to light the way ahead for both you and Cayla.'

'Astroke!' said Carl Peter Bannock joyfully. 'A massive stroke. The only thing bad about it is that they say he never suffered. His doctors are on TV saying that it was so quick that there would have been almost no pain. I would have enjoyed it even more if they told me that he went out screaming and blubbering in agony.'

Johnny grinned. 'I never knew him but I hate the old shit as much as you do. They should feed him to the pigs the way you did to his brats.'

'Unfortunately, my father built himself a big marble temple on top of a hill where he will lie for ever like Napoleon, stuffed and embalmed.'

'That's great, white boy. As soon as they turn you loose you should go up there and piss on him.'

Carl whooped with mirth. 'Great idea! While I am about it I might go all the way and curl out a turd on his head.'

'Did you know that this would happen when you sent him the video? Did you know that it would kill the old bastard?' Johnny Congo asked.

'Of course I did!' Carl gloated. 'Didn't you know, man? I have some weird powers. My father kept the ashes of all the filthy Jews he burned in the gas ovens in Bergen-Belsen, and on the day I was born he rubbed a pinch of those ashes on my head.'

Johnny stopped grinning and looked uneasy. 'Don't talk that sort of crap to me, man. It gives me the shits.'

'I am telling you, Johnny. Voodoo stuff, man! The evil eye! I got the evil eye.' Carl opened his eyes wide and stared at Johnny Congo. 'I can change you into a toad. Do you want to change into a toad, Johnny? Just look into my eyes.' Carl's face contorted into a horrible rictus and he rolled his eyes.

'Cut that out, man, I'm warning you. Stop fooling around with that sort of stuff.' Johnny jumped off his bunk and went to the barred window. He deliberately turned his back on Johnny and stared out at the tiny wedge of sky that passed for a view in Holloway. 'I'm warning you! Don't make me mad.'

'Your mother made you mad, Johnny. She made you mad when she dropped you on your head when you were a baby.' Johnny spun around from the window and glared at him.

'You leave my mother out of this, white boy.' Carl knew that this time it was not an endearment. Carl also knew just how far he could press his luck with him, and he knew that he had reached the absolute limit.

'Come on, Johnny.' Carl held up both hands in surrender. 'I'm your friend, remember? You told me I give you the best blow jobs you ever had. I don't have any voodoo powers. I love you, man. I was just kidding around, man.'

'Well, don't kid around about my mother.' Johnny had lost the main theme of the discussion. 'She was a saint, man. I'm telling you.' He was only marginally mollified.

'And I believe you, Johnny. You showed me her picture, remember? She looked pretty damn saintly to me.' He changed the subject quickly. 'Just think of this. You and me, we set out to get those three bitch relatives of mine and we got more than that. We got the main man as well. I brought down my own daddy. How cool is that?'

'That's cool. That's cool as a pound of shit in a deep freeze.' Johnny turned back from the window. He was smiling again.

'We got more than half of them with one punch. There are only two left now; my old man's bride and her bastard brat. Only two more to go down and the money is all mine.'

'How much is it, Carl baby?' Johnny had forgotten and forgiven the affront to his sainted mother's memory. 'Tell me how much money you going to get, man.'

'One day soon I am going to get me fifty billion green frogskins out of that old trust, Johnny baby.'

Johnny rolled his eyes theatrically. 'Man, that's so much money I still can't get my head around it. Tell me how much it is in a way that I can understand it. Tell me the stuff about the motor cars.'

Carl thought for a moment. 'Well, let me put it this way, Johnny. I will have enough money to buy every single motor car in the whole of the US of A.'

Johnny rolled his eyes as though he was hearing it for the first time. 'Awesome, man, Carl baby. That's just plain awesome!' Johnny Congo waggled his head and giggled like a teenage girl. It always took Carl by surprise when he did that.

'And I tell you something else. If one of my good friends is standing beside me when that all goes down he is going to get himself one – or ten – truckloads of those green goodies.'

'I'll be right there beside you, Carl baby, all the way.' Then Johnny's face puckered up into a bulldog frown. 'That is unless the man don't give me the hot needle first.'

The buoyant mood between them changed swiftly. Earlier that week Johnny Congo's lawyer had informed him that his appeal against the death sentence had finally reached the Supreme Court, and that in all probability the judgement would be handed down within the next eighteen months. Up to this stage the appeal seemed to have become totally bogged down in the legal system. As the years passed Johnny Congo had settled into a state of complacency. He had come to believe that his comfortable existence within the walls of the Holloway Correctional Unit would continue for the tenure of his natural life.

But now abruptly the spectral figure of the executioner with his dreaded needle had reappeared on Johnny's horizon and was closing in on him, slowly but inexorably.

He had long ago been found guilty in the High Court of Texas of multiple murders with aggravating circumstances. To date the exact number of his capital convictions was twelve. The state prosecutor had decided that this was sufficient to his purpose. However, in the event that this was not the case and that Johnny somehow managed to wriggle off his hook, he had dockets for a further twenty-eight cases of murder that he could bring against Johnny at any time in the future.

Texas law recognized nine capital felonies. As he had boasted to Carl Bannock on more than one occasion, Johnny had qualified for five out of the nine. They had convicted him of straight murder; for sexually aggravated murder because sometimes Johnny liked to spice up the job; and of murder for remuneration which had been Johnny's main profession after he had completed his two tours of duty with the US Marine Corps. They had also got him for multiple killings, which were inevitable in his line of business, and murder in the course of a prison escape. In his case the jail break had not been a success.

As Johnny very reasonably complained to Carl, 'How they expect anyone to break out of here without blowin' somebody away? It's just downright illogical, man.'

All these birds of his were coming home to roost, and Johnny's birds were all vultures. He was a worried man.

'Calm down, Blackbird. Don't worry,' Carl counselled him.

'Soon as anybody tells me "Don't worry", that's when I really start worrying myself to death, man.'

'We have gotten Marco and half the guards eating out of our hands. When the time comes to spring you they will lay down the red carpet for you to waltz out through the gates without getting your shoes dirty.'

'When is that going to happen, man?' Johnny insisted.

'They are not going to hit you with the needle for another two years, like your lawyer says. So we have got that long at least,' Carl explained. 'In ten months' time my own jail time ends, and I am out of here. We already have everything set up. As soon as I am released I will get everything else set up on the outside. We will make it all infallible.'

'So then we will go into business with each other on the outside, just like we done in here.'

'You can bet your sweet ass.'

'I don't know, Carl.' Johnny looked dubious. 'I have been thinking about this. When I get out I'll be a marked man. With twelve murder raps on my score card the man will put a million dollars on my head, and they will have wanted posters stuck up on every wall in Texas and across the whole US of A. With a face like mine people are going to recognize me pretty damn easily. I'll have every bounty hunter in the northern hemisphere after me.' Gloomily Johnny reeled off the list of his woes. 'Where am I going to hide?' They were both silenced by the question.

'Where're you from, Johnny?' Carl demanded suddenly, and Johnny stared at him blankly.

'That's a stupid question. I told you I'm from Nacogdoches, the toughest town in the entire Lone Star State, didn't I?'

'I mean where were you born? You don't speak like you were born in Texas.'

'I was born in Africa, man.'

'Whereabouts in Africa?'

'What you think my name is, white boy?' Johnny cheered up and grinned.

'Johnny.'

'Johnny who?'

'Johnny Congo.'

'Right on, man! Johnny Congo. That's me. My grandpappy owned half the entire country. He were the paranormal chief of the whole damn place.'

'Do you mean the paramount chief?'

'Whatever, man. He was the king. He had five hundred wives, man. That's as much a king as anybody can get!'

'Do you speak the language?' Carl asked.

'My mammy taught me well. There are two languages. Inhutu is the language of where I come from. And Swahili is the lingo of all of East Africa. I speak them both.'

'Why did your father decide to leave Africa, Johnny?'

'When my grandpappy died my father was his son number twenty-six. He got himself the hell out of there before his big brother, who was son number one, could put him in a pot and cook him for dinner. Where I come from we don't piss around. We are real mean bastards, I tell you, man. The Congo is a big country. It has been split up into three or four separate countries.'

'Which one do you come from, Johnny? Where were you born, man?'

'My country is called Kazundu.'

'How do you spell that?'

'Shit, I don't know. I was only born there, white boy. I didn't discover the place.'

Suddenly there was a rattle of keys on the steel bars of the cell, and Carl stood up.

'It's time for me to go,' he said with resignation. With the influence that the two of them wielded in the institution, they had been able to meet every night from midnight to three a.m. Every visit cost them a few thousand dollars in bribes. Neither of them grudged the money. Over the long period of their association Johnny had become a multimillionaire, carried to those heights on the back of Carl's financial smarts.

Apart from Carl, Johnny had been deprived of many other forms of convivial, intimate and sympathetic human contact. The cells on death row were arranged so that the inmates were unable to see each other. Their only contact was verbal, shouting to each other down the echoing gallery.

Johnny Congo had been a certifiably crazy psychopath even before he was jailed. Without the benefit of Carl's company over the past nine years he would most likely have become a suicide or a raving lunatic.

On the other hand, Carl's prison routine as a trusty was relatively easy. He was allowed four hours a day in the exercise yard where his contact with other sub-humans was, if anything, overly unrestricted.

He was allowed visitors twice a week, though nobody from the outside came to visit him, unless it was his bank manager. Once Carl had numbered his friends in their hundreds, but now he had none, other than Johnny Congo. The notoriety of his crimes had placed the mark of the Beast on his forehead for all the world to see. He had been shunned and abandoned by everybody outside of Holloway.

However, Carl had a deep-seated need of human contact, of syco-phants to flock around him and tell him what a marvellous person he really was. He knew that when he left prison he would have to buy his friends, or seek them in the ranks of the outcasts from society wherein he now found himself numbered.

Suddenly the idea of Africa was very attractive. His father had taken him on a hunting safari to that land when he was sixteen. He had killed over fifty wild animals, and had sex with a number of Maasai and Samburu girls. He had enjoyed it all immensely.

The two guards who picked Carl up from Johnny Congo's cell led him back through the security gates and scanners to his own cell on the ground floor. Carl palmed a roll of hundred dollar bills to the senior officer who winked at him and then locked him down for the rest of the night.

Even at this late hour Carl could not sleep. Restlessly he roamed around his cell. He was excited and his imagination was sparking. He did not know why he had fired the question at Johnny Congo regarding his place of birth. The idea had sprung into his mind as though it had always been there, lying concealed until the right moment. He accepted it unquestioningly as further proof of his own natural genius.

He and Johnny needed a refuge, a fortress in which they would be safe from the enemies that surrounded them. For both of them America was now an exceedingly hostile place. They needed to find another more congenial country as a haven from which they could operate.

Carl stopped in front of his desk, which was concealed behind a curtain in the back corner of his cell. He sat down and switched on his computer. As soon as the screen came alive he typed in the name 'Kazundu' and he hit the Google search key.

Within seconds the page filled with rows of data and the legend at the head of the page read, 'About 32,000,000 results'. Carl's eyes raced down the screen as the facts sprang out at him. The descriptions of the country were overwhelmingly inauspicious.

Kazundu was the smallest sovereign country on the African continent. In extent it covered about 3,500 square miles; roughly half the size of Wales or the American state of New Jersey. Its total population was estimated at a quarter of a million. There had never been an official census.

It was also the poorest country on the African continent with a gross domestic product per capita of $100 per annum. Carl whistled softly. 'Each of those poor suckers is pulling down less than $10 per month! What would ten million dollars buy out there?' he asked himself in an awed whisper. 'The answer, my dear friends, is it would probably buy the whole damned country.'

Carl went on scanning the information on his screen, and he learned that Kazundu was situated on the north-western shore of Lake Tanganyika, like a tiny bush-tick clinging to the belly of the great elephantine mass of the Democratic Republic of Congo.

Lake Tanganyika is a vast inland sea. It is one of the longest and deepest lakes in the world, with a north to south length of over four hundred miles. On average it is thirty miles wide. Kazundu had a lake frontage of a mere twenty-two miles. Fishing and primitive agriculture were its only sources of income and sustenance.

Back in the dark days of the Arab slave traders it had been an important link in the chain of trading posts that led down to the shores of the Indian Ocean to the east. Slaves captured in the interior of the Congo were held there in barracoons before being shipped in Arab dhows across the lake to Ujiji, and thence down to the coast.

In AD 1680, at the height of the traffic in human beings, the Sultan of Oman constructed a castle on a high promontory of a rocky cliff overlooking the lake. The slave-trading harbour nestled in the small inlet below the cliff.

When the Arabs were driven out of the Great African Lake districts by the European colonists and the anti-slavery forces of France and Great Britain, the paramount chief of the local Inhutu tribe moved with his entire court and harem into the abandoned castle of Kazundu. His heirs had been ensconced there ever since.

The present ruler of Kazundu was the hereditary King Justin Kikuu Tembo XII. The Swahili name translated as Great Elephant. His portrait revealed him to be an impressively large man with a sombre expression, a scraggly grey beard and an enormous paunch that sagged over his kilt of leopard tails. On his head he wore a turban of leopard skin, and he sat on a throne of elephant tusks. He was surrounded by his multitudinous wives and his bodyguard of five uniformed Askari armed with automatic rifles.

According to the numerous derogatory comments on the internet, he ruled the tiny state with a high hand, unencumbered by such modern eccentricities as parliaments and elections. He was treated by the rulers of the surrounding countries with benign indifference. None of them had ever shown much interest in wresting the insalubrious little country out of King Justin's hands. His father had been a close associate of General Idi Amin in Uganda, and he was an ardent admirer of President Robert Mugabe of Zimbabwe.

Carl clicked on a collection of pictures and photographs of the kingdom. There were many views of the lake shore and the mountainous and densely forested land that rose beyond it. The settings were splendid and the panoramas across the lake were magnificent, wild and barbaric. White-headed fish eagles circled high above the creamy beaches, and lines of pink flamingos undulated low across the lustrous lake waters.

There were shots of the airport that had been built by South African Airways to attract the tourists who never came. The buildings were now abandoned and derelict, but the runway which ran parallel to the lake shore looked as though it was still serviceable.

The castle was built in the Indo-Islamic style. Elegant minarets rose above the formidable walls. The gateways were curlicue shaped, and the windows were covered with fretwork panels. Photographs of the interior depicted spacious and lofty public rooms. The walls were covered with glazed ceramic tiles in shades of blue ranging from azure to indigo and ultramarine. These were overlaid with verses from the Koran in black serpentine Arabic script.

These state rooms contrasted sharply with the dingy cellars and dungeons where the slaves had once been chained.

Carl Bannock had difficulty restraining himself and his ambitions until he could resume his interrupted discussion with Johnny Congo. As soon as the two of them were alone again he picked up their discussion at the point it had been interrupted.

'You remember what we were talking about last time, Johnny my man?'

'I sure do, Carl baby.' Johnny grinned. 'I was telling you how my daddy and all the family had to get the hell out of Kazundu before my mother-loving uncle ate us.'

'What was your uncle's name?'

'Justin Kikuu Tembo.'

'So your name isn't really Congo, is it?'

'My daddy changed it to Congo when we reached Texas, but before that it was also Kikuu Tembo. People here in the US can't get their stupid tongues around my real name, man.'

'How would you like to change back to King John Kikuu Tembo?' Johnny blinked and then began to chortle.

'You not kidding me, are you? You are real serious, aren't you, white boy?'

'You remember how we talked about if you have enough money you can take anything and you can do anything, and nobody is going to stop you?'

'I remember.'

'Well, Johnny, you and I have got enough money. Just give me a little time and Kazundu is going to be ours, Your Majesty.' And he gave Johnny Congo a high five.

Three nights before his release from the Holloway unit Carl Bannock came to visit Johnny Congo on death row for the last time.

First they had sex. They had been lovers now for twelve years and each of them knew exactly what the other liked best. As it was a farewell occasion Carl acted the role of the queen and let Johnny have it his way.

Afterwards they shared the flat bottle of Dimple Haig whisky that Carl had smuggled into the cell with him. Sitting on the bunk with their heads close together, drinking the whisky from plastic tooth mugs and speaking in guarded whispers, they discussed Johnny's escape.

The previous week Johnny's lawyer had come to visit him. He was the only person from the outside who had that right. He told Johnny bluntly that they had reached the end of the line after many years of legal manoeuvring.

The Supreme Court had finally considered Johnny's appeal against the death sentence and had turned it down flat. The governor of the State of Texas had set Johnny's execution date for 12 August.

'That's much sooner than we were banking on,' Carl reminded him. 'It leaves us only a couple of months to spring you out of this joint. It was lucky that we started working on the planning so much earlier. Now we have only a few minor details to work out.'

By the time that the unit controller came to let Carl out of Johnny's cell and escort him back to the trusties' level on the ground floor, they had settled every one of those minor details.

The unit controller was Lucas Heller who had been the first to welcome Carl into Holloway twelve years previously. Since then he had been promoted to his present elevated rank in the prison hierarchy. When they reached the ground level Lucas took Carl into his own office and locked the door while the two of them discussed the final details of the plan that Carl had just agreed with Johnny Congo. When they had finished, Lucas tactfully brought up the matter of payment of the bribes. Lucas referred to these euphemistically as the motivational considerations.

Carl had agreed to make the payments in tranches; half the agreed fee immediately, and the balance on the day previous to the actual escape.

The prison warden, Marco Merkowski, would receive a total of $250,000 paid into a numbered account in the Bank of Shanghai in Singapore. The $100,000 for the two level supervisors would be transferred to an account in the British Virgin Islands. Lucas Heller was the main mover and shaker. He would be paid $200,000 in the Cayman Islands and an additional $200,000 once Johnny was outside the walls of Holloway and running free. Carl would personally hand over this final tranche to Lucas Heller in used $100 bills, and then they would shake hands and part as friends, never more to meet.

The traditional manner in which a prisoner was released from Holloway was firstly to take him down to the induction area and make him hand over his prison uniform. Then he would sign for, and be handed, a bag containing the same clothing in which he had entered the establishment all those years ago. Finally two armed guards escorted him as far as the main gate. There he was pushed firmly out into the sweet air of freedom and the gate slammed just as firmly behind him. If one of the guards was in a beneficent mood he might point the way to the Greyhound Bus terminal, only a three-mile hike down the road.

On Carl Bannock's release day Warden Marco Merkowski came to his cell to shake his hand and bid him Godspeed. Then Lucas Heller escorted him to the induction centre, where he handed over his prison-issue uniform and received and signed for the large parcels that his tailors in Houston had consigned to him. These contained a custom tailored suit in pale grey flannel, a Sun Island cotton shirt, gold monogrammed cufflinks; a black string necktie with a lapis lazuli pendant; a wide-brimmed cream-coloured Stetson hat and a pair of high-heeled Western boots.

Lucas rode with Carl in the prison bus to the main gates, where a black hire limo with a uniformed chauffeur that he had ordered online was waiting. The limo carried Carl in air-conditioned silence to the Four Seasons Hotel on Lamar Street in Houston.

The receptionist escorted him up to his suite. After he had tipped her a $50 bill, he ordered a bottle of chilled Dom Pérignon from room service. He sipped a flute of the champagne as he phoned down to the concierge. His name was Hank and he well-remembered Carl and his generosity from the old days.

'I want a couple of lady friends for the evening, Hank.'

'Certainly, Mr Bannock,' Hank agreed. 'One blonde and one black, as usual; is that right, sir?'

'You have a good memory. Make sure they are as young as possible, just short of jail-bait. Tell them I'll want to see a piece of photo ID to prove their age.'

The following week was extremely busy as Carl picked up the severed threads of his previous existence, re-established old contacts and made new ones from the list that Johnny Congo had provided for him.

He spent a morning with his private account manager at the Carson National Bank in Houston, rearranging and fine-tuning his accounts and portfolios. Then he passed a glacial hour at the law firm of Bunter and Theobald, Inc., with the head trustee of the Henry Bannock Family Trust.

Ronald Bunter treated him as though he was a species of poisonous reptile and answered his questions only as far as a strict interpretation of the Trust Deed would allow.

Ronald had his legal assistant at his side. She was a young woman named Jo Stanley. She was attractive and seemed extremely efficient, but she was a little too old for Carl's particular tastes. Although he did consider that she might be able to obtain for him a more comprehensive and up-to-date overview of the affairs of the Trust than Bunter was prepared to divulge.

The following morning Carl phoned Jo Stanley from his suite to invite her to dine with him. He had decided to explore the extent of her libido and the effect of his irresistible charms upon it. If this proved to be negative then she would certainly be amenable to a bribe. Carl had never yet met anybody who was not responsive to both of these two stimuli.

However, Jo Stanley declined to accept his call and, to Carl's mild embarrassment, had it transferred directly to Ronald Bunter's desk.

Carl broke the connection as soon as he recognized Ronnie's voice.

He decided to postpone his assault on the Family Trust until he had freed Johnny Congo. Johnny was running out of time.

One of the names on Johnny's list of reliable contacts was a certain Aleutian Brown.

'Aleutian is young but he is bright and mean. He is well connected. He has never let me down yet. He is just about the best man on the entire west coast.' Johnny had recommended him and provided Carl with his contact number.

In response to his phone call, Aleutian Brown flew in from Los Angeles and Carl picked him up from the airport. During the short drive from the airport to the hotel where he had made reservations Carl learned enough to accept Johnny Congo's assessment of the man.

Aleutian was one of the top honchos in a black gang known as the Angels or the Maaliks. The gang was international. Its tentacles reached out from the USA across the oceans to all the major cities world-wide, wherever there was a significant Muslim segment of the population. Within a few days Aleutian had taken care of all the planning and logistics of the operation, and Carl was able to set a final date for Johnny's rescue. He decided on 29 July, two weeks before the date appointed for Johnny's execution.

On 23 July there was an explosion in the laundry of Holloway prison. Two inmates were killed and all the washing and drying machinery was destroyed or severely damaged. This was critical to the smooth functioning of the entire unit. Emergency measures had to be taken by the prison administration. One of the commercial laundries that serviced some of the major hotels in the city was located only fifteen miles from the Holloway prison.

Polar White Laundry was chosen from a shortlist, and the selection was endorsed by the prison warden, Marco Merkowski, on the suggestion of Johnny Congo and a motivational consideration from Carl. Thirty per cent of the employees of Polar White were members of the Maalik Angels.

On the early morning of 29 July a five-ton white International truck pulled up at the main service gate of Holloway. On each side of the truck body was emblazoned the name of the laundry, and images of a smiling female polar bear with her three frolicking cubs wearing spotless white napkins. Over the past week, since the destruction of the prison laundry, the guards at the main prison gates had become accustomed to the daily traffic of these vehicles.

Today there were five men on board. All of them were dressed in white overalls with the company's name and logo embroidered on their backs.

Carl Bannock was the driver of the truck, and Aleutian Brown was his mate. The other three riding in the body of the truck were all Maaliks. Carl was a cautious person and much concerned by his personal safety. He had evaluated the risk factor of being one of the rescue party, and decided it was minimal. Nevertheless he was nervous and jumpy as he drove up to the main gates of Holloway.

He sweated lightly across his forehead as his forged ID was carefully checked by the prison guards on the gate. As last they waved the truck through.

After his long residence in Holloway Carl knew the layout of the unit intimately. He drove to the service entrance of the prison's utility block. There he reversed the truck up to the loading bank of the laundry. Once the double doors at the rear were opened, the trolleys were trundled out of the truck. In the laundry they were loaded with canvas sacks of dirty washing which were then pushed back to the waiting Polar White truck.

The three switches and substitutions that ensued were as neat and smooth as a magician's illusions.

In one of the last laundry sacks to be loaded into the truck Johnny Congo was concealed. The sack had been marked and was manhandled with great care into the cargo body. Aleutian, who was overseeing the loading, made certain that it was placed in a position where it was screened by the other laundry bags, but where Johnny Congo would not be in any danger of suffocation.

The last trolley that was pushed from the truck into the laundry already had a single sack on board. It also contained a human body, but this one was very much deceased.

The previous week Aleutian had visited the suburb of Gulfton, one of the poorest areas of Houston populated mostly by Hispanics and immigrants. In a cheap bar he had picked out somebody with a passing resemblance to Johnny in that he was big, black and formidable-looking. Aleutian had bought him a drink and offered him a well-paid job. The man had accepted enthusiastically. Aleutian had given him $200 as an earnest of good faith, and arranged to meet in the same bar on the evening of 28 July.

They had met again as arranged. Johnny had plied him with liquor until he was jovial and unsteady on his feet, then he had strangled him in the parking lot behind the bar and had packed his body into the laundry sack in the trunk of his rental car. This sack was the last to be unloaded from the Polar White truck.

The corpse in the sack was taken down to Death Row. It was swiftly placed in Johnny Congo's bunk with its face to the wall and covered with a blanket, leaving only the back of its head exposed. To a casual observer it would seem that Johnny Congo was still securely tucked up in his bunk.

Lucas Heller climbed into the empty sack and was trolleyed back to the Polar White truck, and placed alongside Johnny Congo.

Now that the Polar White truck was fully loaded the rear doors were slammed shut. Carl Bannock climbed into the cab and started the engine. Aleutian was already in the passenger seat, and Carl drove sedately back through the inner checkpoints and finally out onto the Interstate.

Ten miles down the highway they pulled off into a service area and Carl parked among the other large vehicles in the truck stop. He and Aleutian opened the rear doors. The three laundry employees jumped down and immediately set off to where they had left a small Toyota sedan the previous evening. They drove away without looking back. None of them ever showed up again at the Polar White Laundry.

Carl and Aleutian climbed into the back of the laundry truck and closed the doors behind them. They released Johnny Congo and Lucas from their canvas bags.

Johnny and Carl embraced ardently while Aleutian and Lucas Heller looked on with amusement. Then Johnny turned to Aleutian and lifted him off his feet in a bear hug.

'Aleutian Brown, you are one hectic dude. I told Carl we could rely on you, man.'

Lucas Heller went to Carl and held out his hand. Carl took it and squeezed. Lucas squirmed at the pressure.

306

'Okay, Carl,' he said uncomfortably. 'If you'll just give me what you owe me now I will leave you and your pals to celebrate and I'll be on my way.'

Still holding his hand Carl told him seriously, 'Thank you, Lucas. It's been a real pleasure knowing you, it really has.' Then, still holding Lucas's hand firmly, he nodded at Aleutian. 'Okay, Aleutian. Give him what we owe him.'

From the inside pocket of his overalls Aleutian slipped out a small-calibre pistol fitted with a silencer. He fired a single bullet into the back of Lucas Heller's skull.

Carl released his hand and Lucas's body dropped to the floor. His legs kicked and his body juddered. Aleutian stooped over the corpse and fired two more spaced shots into Lucas's right temple. His legs stopped kicking.

'What the hell?' said Johnny Congo. 'What the hell did you do that for?'

'I never liked the bastard,' Carl explained reasonably. 'And I just saved us two hundred grand.'

'I love you, Carl Bannock.' Johnny clutched his belly and guffawed.

Aleutian had brought a change of clothing for each of them packed into one of the laundry bags. They discarded their uniforms and dressed quickly in street clothes. Then they jumped down from the back of the truck. Carl locked all the doors and they left the International and walked unhurriedly to the far side of the car park where the previous afternoon Aleutian had left a Ford rental car.

They climbed into it and drove north on Route 45 for forty miles and then they turned onto a secondary road and headed west towards Waco. In the late afternoon they reached a crop-spraying airstrip in the centre of a wide area of cultivated sorghum. There was a twin-engine Baron G58 prop-driven aircraft waiting for them on the strip. The aircraft was owned by one of Aleutian's drug contacts and its short take-off and landing capabilities were ideal for their needs.

The pilot already had the engines ticking over, and the nose lined up with the runway. Carl and Aleutian shook hands with Johnny Congo. Then Johnny scrambled up on the wing root and stooped to cram his bulk through the open cabin door.

The co-pilot locked the door behind him, and the pilot gunned the engines and roared away down the strip, outward bound for La Ceiba in Honduras where Señor Alonso Almanza was looking forward to the pleasure of Johnny's company.

Johnny and Carl met again fourteen days later in a suite on the top floor of the Hotel La Lasjitas in the Argentine capital, Buenos Aires. Carl had a Gold Rewards Card issued by Four Seasons. He always enjoyed the ambiance and the service that the company provided.

After they had sex, they showered together, and then took a cab down to the Puerto Madero and ate huge juicy steaks at Cabaña las Lilas. They washed them down with a bottle of Catena Alta Malbec. Afterwards they returned to the hotel suite.

The concierge had been forewarned and as soon as they arrived he sent two young people up to their room.

Carl checked the ID of the two visitors carefully. The girl looked to be about twelve years old, but her papers proved that she was sixteen years and two months. Carl kissed her and squeezed her skinny little buttocks. 'You are very beautiful, my angel,' he told her.

The boy was four months older than the girl. He was also very comely, if overly effeminate. When Johnny smiled at him from the sofa, he minced across the room and sat down on Johnny's lap.

The following evening Carl and Johnny settled into the first-class cabin of the Air Malaysia flight to Cape Town on the southern tip of Africa. From the Presidential Suite of the One and Only Hotel at the Cape Town waterfront Carl phoned an unlisted number and spoke with General Horatio Mukambera in Harare, the capital city of Zimbabwe.

The general informed Carl that President Mugabe had been fully briefed on their proposal and had ordered the cooperation of the military. He confirmed that the funds had been received in the bank in Singapore, and that he would meet them in person when they arrived at Harare airport on board South African Airways.

Carl then passed the call on to Johnny Congo. Johnny had served two full tours of duty with the US Marine Corps in Vietnam, so his combat experience was extensive. He had reached the rank of sergeant major, and had been in the thick of the action on numerous occasions.

Within minutes he had established his credentials, and General Mukambera was aware that he was speaking to a man who knew the business. Their conversation became more relaxed and cordial as they discussed the logistics of the operation.

'I am able to put at your disposal up to two companies of first-line assault paratroopers,' the general told him.

'How many men in one of your companies, General?'

'One hundred and twenty.'

'We do not want to be under-gunned. We will need both your companies,' Johnny told him. 'You have a secure location where I will be able to meet the men and work with them before we head north?' Johnny switched into Swahili, leaving Carl unable to follow the conversation. But the general warmed to him even further as he replied in the same language.

'Yes, we have an operations area that I can put at your disposal. But tell me how you speak one of our languages so well? I thought you were an American.'

'I was born in East Africa. I am a member of the Inhutu tribe.'

'Ah, I see! That explains a great deal. Welcome back to your homeland, Mr Kikuu Tembo.'

'Thank you, General Mukambera.' Johnny reverted to English. 'I understand you have been informed that we also need air transport.'

'I am able to put at your disposal a Douglas Dakota C-47 Skytrain.'

'That type is a veteran of World War II,' Johnny protested.

'I assure you that it has been meticulously maintained, Mr Kikuu Tembo.' Johnny glanced at Carl for guidance.

'What is its range, General?' Carl asked.

'Its range is fifteen hundred nautical miles, fully loaded, but this machine has long-range fuel tanks that give it an additional five-hundred miles. I personally have flown from Harare to Nairobi in this same plane on a number of occasions.'

'What is the load capacity?'

'The Skytrain will carry seventy fully battle-equipped men.'

309

'So we will need to make four flights,' Johnny mused. 'What do you estimate the turnaround time, General?'

'We can operate from Kariba on our northern border. Turnaround Kariba to Kazundu will be under seven hours.'

'The transport doesn't have to land at Kazundu. The men will jump. This means that on Day One we will be able to put a hundred and forty men on the ground. The second wave can come in early on Day Two.'

'I have had a report on the present strength of Kazundian forces. They will not be able to put up much of a fight against those numbers. I think that after your first strike the survivors will almost certainly be very happy to change sides.'

Four days later Carl and Johnny parted company at Harare airport. Johnny was picked up by a Zimbabwean army transport truck and driven two hundred miles down into the Zambezi valley to a military training camp in the remote bush.

Lieutenant Samuel Ngewenyama was waiting there to greet him and escort him to his quarters in one of the camp's prefabricated huts. There Johnny changed into the camouflage fatigues and para-trooper boots that had been laid out on his bunk. Then Sam Ngewenyama paraded the men for his inspection.

Johnny Congo was satisfied with the turn-out. He had expected something much worse. These were certainly not US Marines, but he judged they were spirited fighting men. With a little brushing up they would be good enough for the job ahead.

He was especially pleased with Sam Ngewenyama. He was a veteran of the dirty little bush war against the Rhodesian forces of Ian Smith. He was a hard man with the cold eyes of a man-eater. Sam soon recognized the same qualities in Johnny Congo.

Over the following days Sam and his men struggled to keep pace with Johnny's powers of endurance. They were unable to match his skill with knife, pistol and rifle, nor his expertise in unarmed combat and bush-craft. It did not take long for Sam Ngewenyama to give Johnny his unconditional respect and loyalty.

Johnny drove the men hard and at the end of three weeks he had transformed them, almost but not entirely, into marines.

In the meantime Carl flew north to Kinshasa, the capital of the Democratic Republic of Congo. Joseph Conrad's Heart of Darkness was one of the largest countries in Africa, ravaged by decades of internecine warfare in which an estimated 5.4 million people perished. It also had the world's highest incidence of HIV.

Congolese governments rose and fell. Corruption was routine. Warfare, mass rape and pillage were the way of life. Marauding gangs of thugs without affiliations to any recognized authority roamed the back-country.

Back in the mists of time when the Great Rift Valley split the crust of the earth it exposed a vast treasury of natural resources. These included columbite-tantalite, locally known as coltan. This mineral is the ore of tantalum, a metal essential to the manufacture of capacitors, cellular phones, pacemakers, GPS, laptop computers, ignition systems, anti-lock braking systems, video and digital cameras and the whole array of modern super-gadgetry. Pound for pound, tantalum is worth half as much again as pure gold.

Eighty per cent of the world's known reserves of coltan are found in the eastern regions of the Congo, abutting Kazundu.

The other minerals mined in the eastern Congo were diamonds of industrial and gem quality, gold, cassiterite and wolframite. These were the notorious conflict minerals and blood diamonds, the production of which Europe and the West sought to suppress and control. Paradoxically the industrial nations themselves had developed an insatiable hunger for them. In the process of attempting to embargo them the altruists had driven their market value up to astronomical heights.

The tiny kingdom of Kazundu was situated on the border of the remote and dangerous eastern areas where the local population, including women and small children, was coerced by armed soldiers of rogue factions into labouring forty-eight-hour shifts in the mudslides and collapsing tunnels of the primitive mines.

For a man like Carl Peter Bannock this situation could be summed up with one sweet and melodious word . . . *Profit*.

In Kinshasa Carl met clandestinely with three men who were blood-related to the newly declared state president. French is the official language of the Congo, a language in which Carl Bannock was fluent, so there was no impediment to their negotiations. At first the Congolese gentlemen were cautious and guarded, even though Carl had come highly recommended by senior members of the Zimbabwean government. However, they slowly warmed to Carl as he laid out for them a detailed and convincing plan in which the neighbouring state of Kazundu could be transformed from a forgotten appendage without utility or real value into a vital export channel through which the conflict mineral could be safely and lucratively exported.

Carl emphasized the fact that it would not cost them anything in hard cash. All that was required was for the government of the Democratic Republic of Congo to look the other way while King Justin, that brutal and hated tyrant, was deposed in favour of his benevolent and enlightened nephew King John Kikuu Tembo, who was the legitimate heir to the throne. Naturally, once the change of monarchs had been effected, the Congo would place its tiny neighbour under its protection, coming to its defence in the conclaves of the United Nations and the African Union if the change in the monarchy were ever placed under scrutiny.

In this manner it could be ensured that the supply of blood minerals across the borders would not be hampered by the prudish sensibilities of the American and Western European governments.

Finally, it was agreed that the Congo government would pass a diplomatic message to King Justin to inform him that Carl Bannock and his associates wished to meet with him to discuss a scheme to build a luxury holiday resort and spa on the Kazundu lake shore. They would inform him these visitors had tens of millions of dollars to invest in the project.

The meetings ended with smiles, handshakes and the utmost bonhomie.

Carl and Johnny were reunited in the imperial suite of Meikles Hotel in Harare. They reviewed and discussed their progress, and put the final touches on the master plan.

The following day Johnny introduced Carl to Lieutenant Sam Ngewenyama. Carl was delighted with him. Carl was not much given to acts of derring-do, but he recognized and valued the killer instinct in others. He did not need Johnny's endorsement to see that Sam was a hard man. He gave Johnny a nod of approval and listened as Johnny gave Sam his orders. He was to go into Kazundu in the guise of an itinerant work seeker, and carry out a preliminary reconnaissance.

The only feasible way into Kazundu was by lake steamer. Sam flew on Air Zambia from Harare into the port of Kigoma on the eastern shore of Lake Tanganyika. In the airport toilet he changed into distressed and tattered clothing and assumed his role of work seeker. From there he boarded the MV *Liemba*, which had originally been commissioned as a German gunboat in World War I.

There were two hundred other passengers on board. All of them camped on the open deck. There were no toilets. This in no way discommoded any of them; both sexes merely backed up to the ships rail when necessity called.

It took four days and eight ports of call before the MV *Liemba* sailed into the beautiful little port of Kazundu. Sam was one of only six passengers to disembark. They were met on the dockside by two armed militiamen who ordered the new arrivals to open their luggage. Then they picked over the contents of the various bundles and cardboard cartons to select anything that took their fancy. One of the passengers was a teenage mother with an infant slung on her back. Laughing and joking, one of the militiamen handed his rifle to Sam to hold for him and took the girl into the public toilet at the end of the wharf. As short while later she returned giggling, with her infant still on her back, seemingly more cheerful and sanguine for the brief interlude.

Sam handed back the rifle to the militiaman. However, he had taken the opportunity to check the weapon in his absence. It was a

VZ-58 copy of the Russian AK-47 of 1950s vintage. There was no blueing remaining on the metal of the barrel and no ammunition in the magazine. Sam grinned as he considered the kind of resistance they might expect when they returned to Kazundu with more serious intentions.

Sam left the harbour and walked into the town, stopping to talk to every person he met about the chances of finding a job. All of them were dressed in rags. They had gaunt faces and either fearful or apathetic expressions. Many of them seemed to be in the advanced stages of starvation. Most of them hurried away without replying to his questions.

Sam walked across Kazundu's deserted landing strip on his way to King Justin's castle. He judged that the Dakota Skytrain would have no difficulty landing once some of the more bulky rubbish, which had rendered the strip unserviceable, was dragged off the runway. There were a handful of militiamen and their women camped in the ruins of the terminal building. In contrast to the other Kazundians he had met they were well nourished.

He climbed the pathway to the castle on the summit and squatted with the other work seekers and beggars in the courtyard while he studied the layout of the building. There was only one entrance, facing towards the lake. The gate sagged on its hinges. It was clear that it had not been closed for many years.

Despite the magnificent vistas of the lake and the forested hills of the interior there was an air of despondency hanging over it all like a poisonous miasma.

Finally, one of the inner doors of the castle was flung open and four armed men emerged and ordered them to disperse. They reinforced the order with the butts of their rifles. One of them struck Sam in the face. When Sam made an instinctive move to retaliate he stepped back and pointed the barrel at Sam's face, at the same time pumping a round into the breech of the weapon.

'Yes!' he encouraged Sam, grinning. 'Come!'

Sam checked his anger and returned the man's gaze for a few seconds, and then he touched his bleeding lip and said softly, 'I will come back, and I will remember your face.' He turned away and the guard jeered at him as he went out through the open gate.

Three days later Sam reboarded the MV *Liemba* and returned to Kigoma on the eastern shore of the lake. As the *Liemba* made fast to the passenger pier, Sam noticed there was a large motor launch lying at moorings in the bay. One of the assignments that Johnny Congo had given him was to look out for this vessel and to gather as much information about it as he could. It had not been in the bay when he passed through on his way to Kazundu, but now it had returned.

Dressed once more in his new and stylish clothing, Sam went down to the harbour master's office at the head of the pier and spoke to the clerk he found sitting on the veranda. The clerk told him that the launch belonged to the government administration of the district of Kigoma. It was used mainly by the provincial governor on his official business, however on occasion it was chartered out to other parties. The clerk assured Sam that it was a very seaworthy vessel and capable of crossing to the far shore of the lake in even the heaviest kinds of wind and water conditions.

Johnny Congo had given him one other task to perform. Kigoma was an important centre of food distribution for the entire western side of the lake. Sam caught the full attention of the local area manager by giving him a fifty-dollar bill to cover his 'personal expenses', then they discussed the supply of large quantities of maize meal, the staple diet of Africa. The manager assured him that any amounts of this foodstuff could be placed at his disposal at short notice.

Sam caught the late-afternoon flight back to Harare and reported to Johnny Congo and Carl. The conversation was in Swahili, which Carl was unable to follow. Johnny listened intently and asked a few questions, and then he leaned back in his armchair and crossed his arms.

'Well, Carl baby,' he said. 'Everything is arranged. We have received a cordial invitation from my Uncle Justin to visit him and bring our ten million dollars with us and we have chartered the governor's launch to get us there. So we are off to our new home.' Carl stroked his chin and looked thoughtful.

'I think I'll let you go on ahead,' he said tentatively. 'I'll follow you as soon as you call for me.' Knowing Johnny as he did, Carl had no doubt at all that the air would be blue with flying bullets when Johnny Congo arrived in Kazundu.

'I'm calling for you now, baby. I don't want you to miss any of the fun,' said Johnny expansively and Carl's shoulders slumped with resignation.

On the passenger jetty of Kigoma port Carl made his last attempt to sidle out of the path of looming danger. He shaded his eyes and gazed out across the lake. The banks of early morning mist had not yet been dispersed by the rising sun.

'It looks very rough out there,' he said. 'I think there is a storm brewing. I'm not a good sailor. I think it would be best if—'

'Yeah, man. I agree with you,' Johnny said. 'It is fifty clicks to the far side. It would be best if we move our hairy asses and get cracking right now.' He picked up Carl's kit bag and hurled it over the rail of the motor launch onto the open deck. Then he grabbed Carl's arm and marched him across the gangplank.

When they had the castle and the port of Kazundu in sight, Johnny made a call on his satellite phone. While he waited for the pilot of the incoming Dakota Skytrain to respond he searched the southern sky, although he knew it was still too soon for him to pick out the aircraft amongst the towering cumulus nimbus clouds.

'This is crunch time, white boy,' he warned Carl. 'If there has been a fuck-up, if somebody has blown the whistle on us, those bastards there . . .' he pointed with his chin at the small reception committee on the wharf of Kazundu harbour '. . . are going to shoot the shit out of us before we can get one foot on the dock.'

Carl said nothing but his handsome face turned a pale shade of green.

At that moment the pilot of the incoming Zimbabwean Dakota answered Johnny's satellite call.

'This is Chicken Soup,' he said.

'This is Mother Hen. What is your status?' Johnny asked him.

'Forty-two minutes to drop.'

'Roger that. Keep coming,' Johnny told him. 'Over and out.'

Suddenly the men waiting on the Kazundu wharf began to wave and their shouted greetings reached them across the closing gap of lake water. Carl leaned over the rail and in relief threw up into the lake, copiously and noisily.

His Majesty had sent his ancient Land Rover down from the castle to fetch them. It was the only functioning motor vehicle in the kingdom. When Johnny, Sam and Carl were on board, four of the militiamen push-started the Landy and as soon as the engine fired they clung onto the sides.

Nearing the top of the hill the Landy began to falter. Clouds of blue smoke blew out of her exhaust. The militiamen jumped off and shoved her the last fifty yards through the gates of the castle and into the courtyard.

The riff-raff had been cleared out, and the courtyard was deserted. However, as soon as the engine of the vehicle, with a final backfire, subsided into silence the court chamberlain emerged from the main gates with a small retinue to welcome them. He was a plump personage with a pair of pendulous dugs dressed in only a kilt of white colobus monkey tails.

He beckoned them from the gateway. The three of them dismounted from the Land Rover and climbed the stairs. Johnny and Sam were carrying their leather briefcases. Carl hung back behind them. They went in through the gate with the chamberlain dancing ahead of them, leading them through a series of state rooms that were devoid of any furnishing or decorations. They had to pick their way around groups of women squatting at the cooking fires which had been laid on the beautifully patterned ceramic floor tiles. The walls and high ceilings were blackened by soot from the wood fires. Rubbish and animal droppings littered the floor. Naked black toddlers with dried mucus encrusting their noses squalled and wailed, tumbling over each other like puppies on the filthy tiles. They fell silent and with enormous dark eyes watched the three strangers pass. The sleeping dogs woke and rushed forward barking furiously, until Johnny Congo kicked the leader of the pack in the guts with such force that it skidded on its back across the tiles, howling in shock and agony. The rest of them scattered in panic.

The air reeked of unwashed humanity, wood smoke and raw sewage.

As they approached the doorway at the end of the hall the chamberlain began to chant in a high falsetto and cavort in a grotesque rheumatic dance.

'What's he saying?' Carl demanded anxiously.

'He is the praise singer to the king,' Johnny translated. 'He is telling us how King Justin, the mighty elephant, devours the trees of the forest and shits them on the heads of his enemies.'

They entered the throne room. On a raised dais against the far wall King Justin sat on his throne of elephant tusks. As his official portrait had depicted him, he was a large man clad in leopard-skin kilt and turban. His beard was thick, grey and curling. His eyes were bloodshot and he smelled richly of millet beer. He held a large clay pot of this home brew balanced on his lap.

At the king's feet sat two young girls, bare-breasted and nubile. On each side of the throne were arrayed his bodyguards. There were six of them. Their uniforms ranged from faded denim jeans to goat-skin kilts. They were all barefooted. One of them was a boy no older than thirteen years of age. The Russian automatic rifle that he was leaning on reached as high as his shoulder.

'Good God!' said Carl softly. 'That one is still a baby.'

'He has probably killed more people than you have swatted flies,' Johnny Congo warned him. Then, still in English, he told Sam Ngewenyama at his side. 'Give the old bastard the usual greeting and tell him that his fame is known as far away as America. Men whisper his name in fear and deep respect.'

Sam repeated the greeting in Swahili and King Justin nodded and his sombre expression lightened perceptibly as he spoke to his chamberlain in Inhutu.

'Say that I am pleased to welcome these people to Kazundu. I am told that he is a rich man who has many thousands of cows. These two girls . . .' he prodded them with his bare toes '. . . are his wives for as long as he stays here as my guest.'

The chamberlain genuflected deeply to the king and then turned to the visitors and repeated it all in Swahili. Sam Ngewenyama then translated it into English.

Carl smiled at Johnny. 'The chick on the left has a raging dose of syphilis, and the one on the right is riddled with AIDS. Take your pick, my old darling.'

The tedious and meaningless conversation with His Majesty continued at length while Johnny glanced at his watch from time to time.

'The Dakota is four minutes overdue,' he grumbled softly to Carl. 'I hope the pilot hasn't lost his way.' Then suddenly he brightened. 'Here he comes!'

Carl cocked his head, and caught the soft throbbing of a multiple-engined aircraft. It was still merely a tremble of sound in the air, but it increased rapidly in volume. Johnny left the group gathered in front of the throne and with a few long strides reached the open doors which led onto the ramparts and battlements of the castle. He stepped out into the open and looked up at the southern sky.

The big lumbering aircraft was banking steeply onto its drop run down the length of the derelict runway of the airstrip. It was at an altitude of only five or six hundred feet when the first human shape dropped out of the hatch and fell free for a few seconds before his parachute flared and his swift descent was checked abruptly. He was followed at close intervals by the other men in his stick jumping out of the doors on each side of the fuselage. Suddenly the sky was filled with white puffs of silk, like a field of daisies in early spring.

Johnny spun around and rushed back towards the throne shouting hysterically in Inhutu, 'Run! Run! The enemy is here. He will kill us all.' Neither the king nor any of his subjects questioned Johnny's sudden fluency in their language.

The girls leapt to their feet and raced for the door to the harem, screaming in terror.

King Justin heaved his bulk upright and harangued his bodyguard, pointing to the door onto the battlements, with his own flying spittle settling like dew drops on his snowy beard. His men ran towards the door, hefting their rifles and loading them with a clatter of breech-blocks. All of them had their backs turned to Johnny and Sam.

Johnny spoke quietly to Sam out of the corner of his mouth. 'Okay, Sam, let's rock and roll.'

Carl Bannock dropped flat with his hands locked protectively over his head, and one cheek pressed to the filthy tiles. He was already whimpering with fear.

Johnny and Sam drew their weapons. They were both toting CV-75 9mm machine pistols. These had been concealed in the brief-cases that each of them carried. The long, extended thirty-round magazines were already attached to the weapons. The stubby barrels were only accurate up to twenty-five yards, but the range was only half of that. They had the rate of fire selectors set at single rather than automatic. They started shooting.

Johnny took his uncle first, deliberately hitting him twice in the spine low down his back. The old man dropped to his knees and swayed, trying to keep his balance, until he crumpled forward onto his face. Then Johnny turned smoothly on the boy soldier. He was as dangerous as any of the older men. He head-shot him and saw the boy drop, his rifle clattering on the tiles beside his prostrate body.

By this time Sam also had two of his targets down, and the remaining militiamen were turning back to face them with astonished expressions. Johnny and Sam fired again simultaneously and two more went down. One of the surviving militiamen got off a short burst that hit the royal chamberlain and bowled him over backwards.

Johnny and Sam turned on him together. Sam tagged his right shoulder, but Johnny's bullet smashed into his open mouth as he yelled a challenge. The two incisor teeth in the bottom of his jaw snapped off at the gums and the bullet went on to exit from the back of his skull. He went over backwards. Behind him the last man standing had dropped his piece and was racing for the door out onto the ramparts. Sam missed him, but Johnny hit him just above the left knee, shattering the bone of his femur. He went down sprawling and crawled through the open door, dragging the leg behind him and leaving a glistening blood-trail across the stone slabs. Johnny lifted his weapon to finish him off, but Sam stopped him.

'He is mine. I know him. I owe him one.' Johnny lowered his weapon and pointed it towards the floor.

'Okay, Sam. He is all yours,' he agreed affably.

Sam walked out onto the ramparts, changing the magazine on his CV-75 for one with a full load. He stood in front of the crippled man and said quietly but ominously in Swahili, 'Look at me, comrade. Do you recognize me?'

The man looked up at his face with tears of shock and terror making his eyes swim, and Sam went on, 'I am the one who you hit in the mouth with your rifle. I promised you that I would come back and now here I am.'

Recognition dawned in his eyes as he looked up at Sam's face and read the promise of his death there.

'Good!' said Sam. 'I see that you do remember me.' Sam walked around him in a slow circle. He fired a shot into the back of his unwounded knee, breaking the bones, then he shot him twice more, low down in the small of his back, ensuring that his spinal column was completely severed. Both these were mortal wounds, but it would be a lingering death.

In the throne room Johnny went to where Carl had crawled into a corner and was covering his face with his folded arms. He was still whimpering. Johnny nudged him with his foot.

'Everything is okay, Carl baby. Daddy has made the bogeyman go away. You can come out from under the blankets now and watch me say goodbye to my Uncle Justin.'

Carl lowered his arms and looked around timidly. He saw that all the opposition were down. He grinned with relief and scrambled to his feet. 'I did not want to get in your way. I wasn't afraid; really I wasn't,' he protested.

'Of course you weren't. I know you really are a brave little hero. You just don't like loud noises.' Johnny explained his behaviour for him. Carl followed him as he went to where King Justin lay. Standing over his uncle's sprawling body, Johnny reloaded the machine pistol with a fresh magazine of ammunition.

'He is still breathing,' he exclaimed cheerily. He clapped Carl on the shoulder. 'Have you ever killed a man, Carl baby?'

Carl shook his head wistfully. 'I never had the chance. There is always somebody else to do it for me.'

'Well, you've got the chance now. You can finish off Uncle Justin. Would you like that, white boy?'

Carl's face lit up. 'Hell, yes!' he exclaimed. 'Thank you, Blackbird, I always wanted to try it.'

Johnny handed him the machine pistol and Carl took it and held it awkwardly.

'Now, what do I do with it?'

'You point it at the old bastard and pull the trigger.'

Carl lined up on the king's body, turned his head away and closed his eyes. He pulled the trigger until his forefinger turned white with the pressure. Then he opened his eyes and turned back to Johnny. 'It won't shoot,' he said plaintively.

'Don't point that piece at me.' Gently Johnny pushed the barrel of the pistol to one side. 'First, you have to let off the safety catch. Now try again. But this time try keeping your eyes open.'

Carl lined up again, braced himself and held the trigger down. The magazine emptied with the sound of tearing silk and the bullets ripped into the old man's back like a chainsaw. Then the weapon fell silent.

'It's stopped shooting again, Johnny,' Carl complained.

'That's because you have used up all the rounds.'

'Is he dead yet?'

'He should be. You nearly cut the old bastard in half. But did you enjoy that, Carl baby?'

'Shit, yes! That was really cool. Thank you, Johnny.'

'Any time, Carl baby. Any time at all.'

They sauntered out onto the ramparts to watch the last of the Zimbabwean paratroopers landing on the airstrip below the hill, and immediately begin securing the area. There was the sound of desultory gunfire. The Dakota circled the hill at low level and Johnny called the pilot on the satellite phone.

'Good job, Chicken Soup! By the time you return we will have the strip serviceable. We will mark the runway for you with parachute silk.'

The Dakota banked away towards the south. Johnny turned to Sam.

'Get down there and take command of your men. Round up as many of the locals as you can before they disappear into the bush. Get them cracking on cleaning up the airstrip. There is no call for celebrations until we have landed the remainder of the troops and seized total control of the country.'

Sam and his Zimbabweans had a section of the runway cleared by that evening when the Dakota returned. The aircraft landed and disembarked another sixty men and rations for the next ten days. There was just sufficient daylight remaining for the Dakota to take off and head back to Harare for its next load.

Over the next four days they shuttled in the rest of the Zimbabwean troops from Kariba and rations to keep them fed for the next few months. Then the motor launch delivered a full cargo of maize meal sacks from the depot in Kigoma across the lake.

At the first sound of gunfire King Justin's little army, along with the entire civilian population of Kazundu, had vanished like smoke on a windy day.

This did not cause Carl and Johnny any real concern. With the lake in front of them and the jungle behind there was very little choice for these unfortunates. They knew what awaited them on the far side of the Congo border. They would be captured and put to work in the treacherous tunnels of the mines until they starved to death or were drowned or smothered in one of the inevitable mud rushes or cave-ins.

When the initial preparations had been completed Johnny was flown in the Dakota at low altitude over the lake shore and the jungle behind the port. The aircraft had a 700-watt Sky Shout loud-speaker system fitted under the fuselage. Through this King John Kikuu Tembo addressed his subjects in Inhutu. His voice boomed and echoed off the hills.

'King Justin is dead! I am your new king. I am King Johnny. You will give me your total loyalty and obedience. In return I will care for you and feed you. Come to the old airport below the castle. Do not be afraid. I will not harm you. The boat from the south has brought a mountain of maize meal to feed you, so that you will not know hunger again. Your new King Johnny loves you. He will not harm you. He will feed you. He will give you work and pay you many silver shillings.'

Within hours the first of Johnny's new subjects to test the veracity of the royal assurances issued timidly from cover. Only a fool would volunteer for such a hazardous assignment. These had been dragooned into the task. They were three skinny little black girls, all under the age of ten, dressed only in ragged loincloths. They were holding each other's hands and weeping with terror.

When they saw Johnny Congo waiting for them on the airstrip they turned and fled squealing, back into the jungle. A short while later they were driven out again by their parents, still clinging to each other and sobbing. His Majesty patted them on the head and gave each of them a handful of cheap boiled sweets, a short length of brightly patterned cotton cloth and a large scoop of maize meal wrapped in a banana leaf. The trio raced back bearing their treasures, to be swiftly relieved of them by their waiting elders.

After another short interval the three little heroines came back again, leading their mothers and most of their other female relatives. The warriors of the tribe were still testing the waters. The ladies received their rations and rushed back to their menfolk ululating with joy. Then the boys were sent out. When they also survived their first encounter with the new King John, finally the men appeared.

Soon the airfield was filled with a noisy throng celebrating the death of the old king and the ascension of the munificent new monarch to the ivory throne of Kazundu.

Sam Ngewenyama and his men moved among them sorting the men and women into work battalions. The first task awaiting them was the repair of the airstrip and the lengthening of the runway to accept heavy modern freight-carrying aircraft. After that they could concentrate on the enlargement of the tiny harbour to prepare for the arrival of the shipments of building material and the heavy equipment.

The first aircraft to touch down on the renovated airstrip was an Antonov An-124 Condor of 1985 vintage which had seen many thousands of hours of service in the Russian military, before being sold on. It was a four-jet cargo carrier, one of the largest in service, with an enormous load-carrying capacity. Carl Bannock was the sixth registered owner. He had purchased it from an army-surplus dealer in Bulgaria. It was flown by two pilots who had been retired from the Russian air force on account of their age. They were both desperate for a job and Carl got them and the aircraft at a very favourable price.

With the reconditioned engines that Carl had ordered installed in Dubai, the Condor had sufficient range for a non-stop flight from Kazundu to Hong Kong or to Tehran. China was one of the world's largest buyers of conflict coltan ore, while Iran desperately needed tantalite to pursue its quest for nuclear capability. Carl and Johnny were now able to provide their largest customers with a direct delivery service to their front doors.

The first cargo that the Condor flew into Kazundu comprised the massive diesel generator to power the castle and the satellite antenna and the full array of electronic communications apparatus that Carl needed to keep in instantaneous contact with the financial markets around the world. On the same flight came a team of seven highly paid experts who installed and operated all this equipment.

There was also a doctor on board the Antonov. He was taking up full-time employment with the new government of Kazundu to be instantly on hand to deal with the low-grade hypochondria with which Carl was afflicted.

From the same Bulgarian dealer who supplied the Condor, Carl had also procured a fleet of two Russian ex-naval landing craft. He had them fitted with new engines and delivered by freighter from the Bulgarian port of Varna on the Black Sea to Dar es Salaam, the chief port of Tanzania. The Condor flew down to the coast and flew them back to Kazundu, one at a time. They were capable of crossing the lake to Kigoma in a little over two hours and delivering fifty tons of cement or other building material on site with each crossing.

While this heavy labour was in progress Johnny Congo picked out all his deceased uncle's former militiamen from amongst his subjects. The chosen men were amazed by his ability to identify them so readily. Johnny earned the reputation of possessing supernatural powers, which contributed largely to the awe in which he was regarded by his subjects. None of them tumbled to the simple fact that they were the best nourished segment of the entire Kazundian population and stood out belly and buttocks from the herd.

Johnny handed these conscripts over to Sam Ngewenyama to be fully trained as soldiers and enforcers to keep the rest of their tribal brothers and sisters hard at work. Breaking heads and kicking back-sides was their employment of choice. They went to work with gusto in the service of King John and his white prime minister, His Excellency Carl Peter Bannock.

O nce the infrastructure of the new Kazundian government was in place and running smoothly, Johnny assembled a band of his new bodyguard, thirty men strong and heavily armed. He sent envoys ahead of him to announce to the local Congolese warlords his imminent arrival in the Democratic Republic of the Congo and then, accompanied by Sam Ngewenyama and his bodyguard, he marched across the border. Carl decided against joining the expedition on the grounds of being unsuited to the job by his inability to speak any of the native languages and the importance of him staying in close contact with the movements of the global financial markets. For once Johnny did not brush his excuses aside and he left him with a lingering kiss on the mouth.

Johnny's tour of the eastern Congolese provinces was a triumph. Every province was run by a local warlord and his own private army. They listened in barely suppressed glee as Johnny explained that he would pay in good American dollars for every ounce of coltan concentrates, every gram of gold, every carat of diamonds and every hundred-weight of cassiterite or wolframite delivered to him at the Kazundian border, where Johnny had his own accredited assayer waiting to test the purity of the ore and minerals.

As Johnny pointed out to the warlords, there was no risk to them. They would not lose sight of their goods until the money was safely in their hands.

It was only a few weeks after Johnny returned from this visit that long columns of porters began to arrive at the border crossing. They were shepherded and urged along by the shouts, kicks and whips of the armed men who accompanied them. These porters were mainly women, reeling along under sacks of raw minerals which they balanced on their heads. The men and the children were more usefully employed back in the underground workings of the primitive mines.

The weight of each porter's burden was carefully matched to her individual strength and endurance. When one of them fell she was whipped to her feet and urged onwards. When she was finally unable to rise, her burden was shared out amongst the others in the column, who were already nearing their breaking points.

Then she was shot and her body left beside the track as an example and a warning to those who followed. The road to Kazundu through the forested hills soon became clearly defined not only by the passage of thousands of feet but also by the stench of the decaying corpses that lined the verges.

Very soon the first full load of coltan ore was ready for the Antonov Condor to carry to Hong Kong. On the return journey the Condor was ordered to stop over in Thailand to refuel and take on board a number of young Thai prostitutes, both male and female. Both Johnny and Carl found the Thai faces and petite bodies particularly pleasing. Johnny and Carl were particularly enamoured of the Thai ladyboys who pandered so perfectly to Johnny and Carl's penchant for either or both sexes.

Johnny and Carl had assiduously shunned physical contact with the local Kazundians, who were, in contrast to the carefully screened Thai prostitutes, walking skeletons riddled with venereal disease.

After the first two years of King John's rule, when the profits of the trade in the conflict minerals and Carl's financial genius were reluctantly quadrupled by the trustees of the Henry Bannock Family Trust, Carl and Johnny turned their combined energies and vast fortune to transforming the castle on the hilltop from a pestilential ruin into a bright jewel mounted in the stupendous setting of lake, mountains and verdant jungle.

Over the next four years they flew in architects, landscape designers, hydro-engineers, master builders and others with specialized skills to help them to realize this vision. They shipped in high-quality building materials across the lake. They collected rare and beautiful artefacts, various types of exotic timber, paintings, silks and ceramics and other works of art and decorations from around the globe. They pumped up the lake waters to irrigate their hanging gardens on the hilltop, and to flow through subterranean caverns and pools, and then to tumble down artfully contrived cascades and waterfalls back into the mighty lake from which they had arisen.

To assist them in the realization of this masterpiece Carl Bannock selected the celebrated award-winning American architect Andrew Moorcroft of Moorcroft and Haye, who had designed the mansion on Forest Drive that Henry Bannock built for his family.

It gave Carl malignant pleasure to employ the man originally selected by his adoptive father and benefactor who he had destroyed, and whose family he had decimated.

Carl had carefully transferred to DVD several copies of the documentary movie that he had commissioned Amaranthus, the Mexican pornographic film maker, to shoot for him. Carl and Johnny never tired of watching it. Every few weeks they would sit entranced for a whole evening running and re-running the video. They always laughed delightedly at Bryoni's final struggles in the mud and filth of the hog pen with the great black boar Hannibal.

Then at the end they joined in unison to mimic her death cry to her father; the cry that had killed Henry Bannock.

'Daddy!'

It was Johnny who made the momentous suggestion. 'Why don't we build our own death pen?'

Carl seized upon the idea with glee. 'Blackbird, you are a genius. It's a brilliant idea. We could have our own live show whenever we wanted it.'

'It would also be great for the discipline around here. Anybody who pisses us off, we just feed him to the pigs and make the others watch it.' Johnny expanded the proposal, and Carl giggled like a teenage girl and hugged himself at the thought.

'We could build an amphitheatre like the Colosseum in Rome; you know, where the ancient Roman emperors made the gladiators fight each other to the death and where they fed beautiful women to the lions and good stuff like that.'

'I never heard about these guys before, but I like what you tell me about them. They must be real hectic dudes. We should go and see them sometime.'

'We're about two thousand years too late for that,' Carl told him. 'But we are just as cool as any spic with a bunch of leaves on his head. Like the man said, we can have anything we want because we are mega rich and super cool.'

'You think pigs are that super cool, white boy?' Johnny scoffed. 'Surely we can do better than a bunch of pigs. How about a few lions, man? This is Africa, for Chrissake! Lions are cooler than pigs any day of the week.'

Carl thought about the suggestion for a moment and his expression sobered. 'I don't like lions.' He shook his head. 'They are dangerous, man.'

'What's so dangerous about a bunch of lions in a cage?' Johnny demanded.

'They run faster than pigs, if they escape from their cage. What if one got out of the cage? What about that, man? I don't want to be there when that happens.'

'Okay, what runs slow but eats people,' Johnny pondered his own question.

'How fast does a crocodile run, Johnny? Do you have any idea?'

'I seen pictures of them crocodiles, man. They got short legs. I guess they don't run so fast as no lions.'

'Where would we get a couple of big man-eating crocodiles, Johnny?'

'If you turn your head real slow and look behind you, man, you'll see the biggest goddam lake in the world.'

Carl did as he suggested and swivelled around in his chair. They were sitting out on the castle battlements and the view across the water was stupendous. Nevertheless Carl corrected him primly. 'That is not the biggest; it's only the second biggest lake in the world.'

'Looks like the biggest to me.' Johnny brushed aside his protest. 'I bet there are some monster crocodiles in there, white boy.'

'I'll go online and find out.' Carl stood up and went into the throne room, which he had converted into his communications centre. He came back onto the battlements a few minutes later with a smug expression. 'Pour me another Tusker beer, Blackbird,' he said as he sat down opposite Johnny. 'Give yourself one as well. You deserve it. You were right on both counts. Crocodiles can't run as fast as a man, and anyway they would never run after you. They are stealth killers, not chasers. You just never see them coming, especially if you are near water. That's score one to you.' Carl took a pull at the beer can and belched. 'Score two to you is that Lake Tanganyika and its tributary rivers . . .' he indicated the inland sea with a sweep of his arm '. . . is the absolute homeland of *Crocodylus niloticus.*'

'What the shit is that?'

'That is the Nile crocodile, Johnny boy. There is one in that lake there that they say is twenty-five feet long. They call him Gustave. They say he could swallow even a big sucker like you without chewing.'

'Just let one of those scaly bastards try that on me,' said Johnny belligerently, then he threw back his head and let out a bellow. 'Sam! Samuel! Get your lazy black ass out here!'

Sam came sauntering out onto the terrace, totally unperturbed by the wording of King Johnny's summons. Johnny had only started referring to him in truly pejorative language after they had become true and trusted comrades in arms. Sam had signed on as Johnny's second in command after the capture of Kazundu, when all the other Zimbabwean troops had been repatriated. Johnny had promoted him immediately to the rank of colonel. His scale of pay was several times greater than he had received in the Zimbabwean army. Among his other side benefits and perks he was granted third shot at any of the visiting oriental ladies or ladyboys after Carl and Johnny moved on down the line. Samuel Ngewenyama was a happy man.

'Hello, Mr King. Did you call me?'

'You know I did, you black bastard.' Johnny handed him a can of Tusker beer. 'We need some crocodiles, Sam.'

'How many, boss?'

'I don't know, for sure. Let's say two for a start, but make sure they are really big suckers, and make sure they are alive and hungry.'

'I'll put the word around, but it might take some time. Not a lot of people around here are happy to mess with crocodiles.'

'That's okay, Sam. We have still got to build a croc pen.'

Over the next few months they spent a great deal of time and energy planning and building the crocodile arena. The forced-labour gangs laboriously excavated the circular pit halfway down the front slope of the newly named Castle Hill. It did not have to be spacious, but Carl insisted that it was deep enough to prevent any of the inmates escaping and engaging him in a speed trial.

The walls of the arena were lined with stone blocks and flared inwards to make them unscalable. One of the artificial waterfalls was diverted so that the stream fell into the large pond that took up almost half the total area of the arena. The dry ground was strewn thickly with the golden brown beach sands of the lake. This would provide a basking ground on which the cold-blooded reptiles could sun themselves, and a wallowing basin in which to cool down again. On the stone coping that surrounded the top of the pit was seating for a hundred spectators and a special royal box for King John and his prime minister, which gave them an unimpeded overview of everything that happened on the floor of the amphitheatre. There was also a camera platform from which the action could be filmed.

There was a subterranean tunnel through which the floor of the pit could be reached via a sturdy croc-proof iron gate. In the stone lintel above this gate was chiselled the stern admonition: ABANDON ALL HOPE, YE WHO ENTER HERE.

When Johnny read it for the first time he demanded, 'Who the hell is Ye?'

'Ye is anybody who goes through the gate,' Carl explained patiently.

'Did you think up that shit yourself?'

'What a silly question, Blackbird. Of course I did,' Carl assured him, and Johnny shook his head in admiration.

'You pretty smart for a white boy; you know that, Carl baby?'

They heard the drums and the ululation in the harbour area, even from high up on the castle battlements.

'We better go down and see what the hell is going on down there!' Johnny suggested. The climbed into the brand-new white Range Rover that Carl had recently imported as Johnny's birthday gift. Johnny took the wheel and they hurtled down the hill to the port, and parked on the wharf. The crowd had been driven back by the rifle butts of the Royal Bodyguards to leave them space.

Carl and Johnny stood on the edge of the stone wharf and shaded their eyes to stare out across the lake. A flotilla of native dugout canoes was coming down from the north. It was impossible to count them at this distance, but Carl estimated that there were at least twenty smaller craft, surrounding and escorting two much larger war canoes.

The drummers were seated amidships in the smaller canoes. They were pounding out a triumphant and primordial rhythm. The rowers were standing upright in bows and sterns, the long paddles dipping and swinging to the beat of the drums, tall lean men whose naked bodies gleamed in the sunlight like freshly washed anthracite. They chanted as they rowed.

The two great war canoes in the centre of the formation were deeply laden; each had only a few inches of freeboard. There were a dozen or more paddlers aside. As they came abeam the harbour they turned and headed in towards the beach. The crowds on the shore ran down the wharf and jumped onto the beach to meet them. Johnny and Carl followed them with Sam and his men running interference for them, whacking woolly heads and bare black shoulders with the heavy bamboo rods they always carried to clear the way.

They arrived at the water's edge just as the largest war canoe ran its bows ashore. The spectators plunged waist deep into the lake to help run both the long canoes high and dry. Then they crowded around them laughing and jabbering with excitement and amazement as they saw the cargo that they carried. The bodyguards cleared them away to allow Carl and Johnny to come forward and stare down on the massive beasts that lay in the bottom of the canoes. Their jaws had been roped closed with plaited papyrus reeds, and they had been blindfolded with old maize sacks to keep them quiescent.

Johnny paced out the length of the largest crocodile, and then he whistled with awe. 'This sucker is five paces long, that makes him over sixteen feet. How the hell did they catch him?'

'They built a long trap of poles and put a goat into it for bait,'

Sam Ngewenyama explained. 'Once they cover his eyes the crocodile goes to sleep.'

It took a gang of twenty men to drag the quiescent monster up
the loading ramp of one of the Russian landing craft, and only then
could they motor him up to the crocodile arena. Another gang of
fifty men lowered him into the pit on the ropes.

The second crocodile was a mere twelve feet long. She was a
presumed female, although in the absence of external genitalia it was
not possible to be certain. They laid them side by side on the basking
sands of the arena beside the pool while Carl and Johnny leaned over
the railing around the top of the arena, shouting instructions.

'Take the blindfolds off their eyes now!' Johnny gave the order in
Swahili. Two of the bolder spirits obeyed and the rest of them scattered and fled, jamming in the exit tunnel in their haste to return
to safety.

The two monstrous saurians sluggishly roused themselves from
their stupor. Then they waddled on their stubby legs to the algae-
green pool and slid down the bank into the lukewarm water. There
they lay submerged with only their eyes and nostrils showing above
the surface.

Johnny shouted at Sam to pay the croc hunters their bounty. Sam
counted out the thick wads of Tanzanian shillings into the hands of
the tribal headman who had commanded the capture operation. It
was sufficient cash to buy a large herd of cattle. The headman marched
away down the hill, followed by his men singing and drumming with
exultation.

Johnny and Carl were left alone on the stone seats of the royal
box to gloat over their new pets.

'We have to give them names,' Carl mused. 'What do you suggest?'

Johnny frowned with concentration and then said, 'How about
we call them Big Sucker and Little Sucker?'

'Not a bad idea! Very poetic!' Carl nodded thoughtfully. 'But I
like the name Hannibal the same as in the Daddy video.'

They both laughed at the memory, and Johnny punched his arm
fondly. 'That's cool, Carl baby. I am glad you thought of that one.
We call the big sucker Hannibal and the little sucker Aline.'

'Who?' Carl looked puzzled.

'Aline, man, Hannibal Gaddafi's wife. She was a super cool chick. She liked to pour boiling water on the heads of her servants if they pissed her off.'

'I thought we were speaking about Hannibal the son of Hamilcar Barca the scourge of Rome, not Hannibal the son of Muammar Gaddafi,' Carl chuckled. 'But never mind me, anybody can make a silly mistake. Aline, the lady crocodile shall be.'

'I love her already,' Johnny confessed.

'Let's prove your love. Have you got anybody in mind for dinner with our Aline? Has anybody pissed you off recently?' Carl asked. 'People are always pissing you off, aren't they, Johnny baby?'

'You are right on, white boy. I don't know why they always take advantage of me. I guess I am just too kind to all these assholes.'

'Pick one of them, any one of them.'

'Sam caught one of them in the grain store last night stealing a bucket of maize meal. Stupid cow claims her snivelling kids were starving.'

'That's unforgivable,' Carl agreed. 'Anyone in their right mind gotta be pissed off at that kind of behaviour. Tell Sam to bring her up here.'

The woman was so paralysed with fear that she could not walk. Two of Sam's men dragged her up the hill to confront King John.

'Do you know what is in that hole?' Johnny pointed at the pit. The woman shook her head.

'Well I am going to put you in there to find out for me.' The woman stared at him in dumb incomprehension.

'Her expression is so beautifully comical. Does she know what's going to happen, do you think?' Carl asked.

'No,' Johnny replied. 'Sam has had her chained in one of the castle dungeons since her arrest. She hasn't seen the crocs yet. It will be a nice surprise for her.' Johnny turned to the men that held her and told them, 'Get her clothes off. Take her down the steps and put her into the hole.'

They stripped the woman's limbo cloth off her body and dragged her down the stairway to the barred gate. While Carl and Johnny hung over the rail to watch they opened the gate and thrust her through it, then slammed it shut behind her.

She beat on the iron bars of the gate with her bare fists until her knuckles bled. Then she looked up at the men above her, wailing and pleading for mercy.

'Come here,' Johnny called to her in Swahili. 'Come and I will lift you up.' She left the gate and went hesitantly towards where he was leaning over the coping of the stone wall and beckoning to her. She skirted the edge of the pool without looking down at the water.

Suddenly the algae-green surface of the pool exploded with such violence that the two men leaning over the rail high above were dashed with spray. Hannibal launched himself from the pond like a great grey torpedo.

He did not open his jaws to seize his victim; instead he kept them tightly closed so that the protruding fangs in his top jaw overlapped his lower lip in a fixed sardonic grin. He swung his whole head at her. The scales that covered his skull were tough as chain mail. He hit the woman in her rib cage as she lifted her arm towards Johnny Congo. She was hurled by the blow into the stone cladding of the pit wall. Her ribs crackled like fire kindling as they snapped. She fell in a heap at the foot of the wall.

Hannibal opened his jaws to their full gape as he reared over her, and then he locked his long yellow fangs into her body. His jaws clashed together like the slamming of the iron-barred gate. Hannibal lifted the body high, holding it crosswise in his jaws, so that just the woman's toes and fingertips dragged in the sand as he carried her back towards the pool.

Then the green water erupted a second time.

'Here comes the gorgeous Aline to join the fun,' Carl shouted with excitement. The female rushed out of the pond at Hannibal, but he made no move to avoid her. Instead he checked and turned his head towards her, almost as though he was offering her the naked body he held in his jaws.

Then with a toss of his monstrous head he threw the woman high and caught her again as she dropped; but now he was gripping only one of the woman's arms.

The woman was screaming shrilly as Aline gaped and then snapped her jaws shut on her legs. When both of the great reptiles had a grip on her they performed an extraordinarily well-rehearsed manoeuvre. Both of them went into the death roll. Hannibal spun his huge body to the right. His butter-yellow belly flashed in the sunlight for a moment before he came back onto his clawed feet. At the same time Aline rotated herself to the left. Neither of them released their grip on the woman as they spun in opposite directions.

'Will you look at that?' Johnny shouted. 'What the hell are they doing?'

'They can't bite off lumps of meat with their spiky teeth. They have to twist it off.' Carl had read up online about crocodile behaviour, and he was eager to show off his knowledge.

Between the two great beasts the woman's limbs were plucked from her trunk like the wings from a well-roasted chicken.

'Look at that! Those suckers are doing just like you said.' Johnny was properly impressed by Carl's erudition.

As her body was torn apart and the blood spurted from the ruptured arteries, some of it splashed Carl. He was so engrossed with the spectacle that he did not seem to notice it.

Both crocodiles backed away, crunching flesh and bone in their jaws and gulping it down.

Then Hannibal came back to the remains of the corpse and lifted it in his jaws, and waddled with it into the pool. Aline followed him into the water and they resumed their cooperative feeding. In the water they were able to spin themselves with less effort. It was an unhurried and orderly dismemberment and feasting.

Aline spun the entrails out of the woman's remains. Then Hannibal took his turn and twisted the woman's head off her shoulders. He crushed her skull in his jaws, popping it like an overripe melon, and swallowed it with one convulsive gulp.

The two men on the top of the wall watched with total fascination. As Aline tore off the woman's remaining arm and chewed the bones to splinters the pink palmed hand flapped out of the corner of her mouth.

'Look at that.' Johnny roared with laughter. 'She's waving us goodbye!'

'Just like my little sister Bryoni, she's saying goodbye to Daddy.' Carl put the cadence on the final word, and they hugged each other with glee. At last Johnny pulled back, still panting with laughter.

'I'll say it again, only a living and breathing genius could have thought up a crocodile live-show. That was one of the coolest things I have ever watched. We have to do this more often.'

'Don't have any sleepless nights about that, Blackbird. I will see to it that Hannibal and Aline will always have as much as they can eat.'

A week after the opening and stocking of the crocodile pen, and the first human offering, there was the usual convivial pre-dinner gathering in the throne room of the castle.

Samuel Ngewenyama was dancing with the Thai ladyboy who had ultimately been passed down to him by Carl and Johnny. King Johnny was playing strip mah-jong with another ladyboy and a female who was fully equipped by nature rather than by surgery. Johnny set the rules of the mah-jong game, which differed widely from the original Chinese version. Johnny's two opponents had picked up his linguistic foibles and there was much chatter and giggling over 'fluckin klongs' and 'flucking flowers'.

Carl and one of the other Thai visitors, who was appropriately named Am-Porn, were watching the CNN channel on satellite television. Carl in particular was waiting for the closing prices on the NY Stock Exchange. Am-Porn was seated on his lap, modestly dressed in a high-neck silk cheongsam, but the tight skirt was rucked up as high as her belly button. Below that it was abundantly apparent that she was not a ladyboy. Carl was passing the time before the news reports by idly exploring this exposed area.

On the TV screen the CNN anchorman began reading the news. Suddenly Carl leapt to his feet, depositing Am-Porn on the Persian carpet as he snatched up the remote control and pointed it at the TV set and boosted the volume. The voice of the anchorman boomed through the throne room.

'The gruesome murder of Cayla Bannock is reminiscent of the 1974 horror movie *The Texas Chainsaw Massacre*. The head of the decapitated girl was sent to her mother by the killer.' A series of photographs of the lovely blonde Cayla flashed on the screen. In one she was riding a thoroughbred Arab stallion and in another she was dressed in an evening gown for her high school prom.

'The girl's mother is Mrs Hazel Bannock, the widow of the oil magnate Henry Bannock. She has succeeded her husband as the CEO of the Bannock Oil Corporation. Mrs Hazel Bannock is reputed to be one of the ten richest women in the world.'

Johnny jumped up from the mah-jong table and came to join Carl in front of the TV. They switched from channel to channel and found the story was being carried right across the American continent, but hard facts were limited and all the TV stations were relying heavily on their archives for fillers.

'There is only one thing that is certain,' Carl said as he switched off the TV. 'And there is only one thing that is important.'

'What is that, white boy?'

'That the bitch is dead.'

'They've got her head to prove it.' Johnny guffawed and flung one massive arm around Carl's shoulders. 'Congratulations, Carl baby. Only one more bitch to go down and all that sweet green lettuce is going to be yours.'

'You are talking about Hazel Bannock here,' Carl agreed. 'I think it's time for you to call in your boyfriend Aleutian Brown again.'

'I wonder what it's going to feel like screwing a billionaire?' Johnny pondered the question.

Hector read to the bottom of the last page of 'The Poisoned Seed' on the screen of his computer. Then he rocked back in his chair and shook his head, as if to clear it. It was a long way back from the riotous and bizarre halls of Kazundu Castle to his civilized and urbane study in The Cross Roads.

He glanced at his wristwatch and grimaced with disbelief. Then he checked the time on the screen of his computer.

'Good God! Where did the day go?' It was after four o'clock in the afternoon. He reached for the phone and dialled Jo's number.

She answered on the second ring. 'So, you finally remembered that I exist. How very nice of you, Hector Cross,' she said. 'I have been waiting on the edge of my seat for you to call.'

'Forgive me, Jo. I am an utter bastard.'

'I defer to your superior knowledge on that subject.' But there were undercurrents of laughter in her tone. 'Has anything interesting happened since we met so long ago?'

'I read a book,' he said.

'Your first, no doubt?'

'Who is being wicked now? Shall we call a truce?'

'Okay,' she agreed. 'How was the book?'

'Stunning! Absolutely riveting. I have to see you immediately, if not sooner, to discuss it with you. Where are you, Jo?'

'Sitting all forsaken and forlorn in the lobby of the Dorchester Hotel. My business lunch broke up earlier than I expected.'

'Why on earth didn't you just grab a cab and come here?'

'I don't know the address. I was thinking about other things when you took me there yesterday.'

'Don't go anywhere. I am coming to fetch you. I'll be there in ten minutes.'

She came dancing down the hotel entrance steps as he drew up in the Bentley at the kerb. She was dressed in a dark business suit, and mink bunny jacket. He jumped out to open the passenger door for her, but she came directly to him and offered her cheek for him to kiss. Her cheek was silky and warm. She ducked into the front seat of the Bentley and her skirts pulled up well above the knee. She saw the direction of his gaze and she smoothed them down. Her expression was inscrutable.

He took the wheel and as he pulled out into Park Lane he said, 'If I told you that I missed you, it would be a lie, because you have been with me since early this morning.'

'I have got your attention then, have I?'

'My sweet Lord, Jo, you have written some tough stuff in there. A lot of it's enough to turn the strongest stomach.'

'That is why I could not bring myself to tell you. It was enough to write down the words, let alone to speak them to your face.'

'Still and all, I have a few questions,' he said, and she turned in her seat towards him.

'I would be very worried if you didn't.'

'When I say a few questions, I mean plenty of questions.'

'I'm not planning on going anywhere soon. I'm yours for as long as you need me.'

'That may be longer than you anticipate.'

Her eyes softened, and she smiled. 'Must you read a double meaning into everything I say? Ask your questions, mister, and try to be serious.'

'First question: is what you wrote the truth?'

'Yes. It's absolutely true.'

'But how did you gather so much detail?'

'Both Henry Bannock and his daughter Bryoni were avid diarists. I suppose Bryoni learned from her daddy. I have access to all their diaries. These are detailed descriptions of their lives. I know everything and I have written it all down for you.'

'But, how did you get hold of the diaries?'

'When both Henry and Bryoni died your wife, Hazel, went through all their belongings. She picked out all the valuable and very sensitive material, including their diaries, and asked Ronnie Bunter to seal it all in the Bunter and Theobald archives. Ronnie and I unsealed it. Reading it was like speaking directly to the dead. I found it a terribly moving experience.' Hector shook his head in wonder, and Jo went on speaking. 'Of course, that was not my only source of information. I had all the accumulated records of the trust open to me; all Henry's letters and emails, not to mention all correspondence with the beneficiaries.'

'Carl Bannock? Did you actually meet him just as you wrote in The Poisoned Seed?'

'Yes; I had that dubious pleasure.'

Hector laughed. 'So you were on the inside track when it came to describing him.'

'I also have a raft of his photographs from elementary school days right up to the present time. I know the exact amount of every payment he received from the trust. I have copies of all his correspondence and records of all his meetings with the trustees, and the records of his trial; all of it and more.'

'What about Johnny Congo?'

'That is him in real life, just as I described him. I have his military records and the court records of his trial and conviction for
multiple murders. Most of it is on those flash drives I gave you
yesterday.'

A scarlet Maserati with Saudi registration plates changed traffic
lanes abruptly in front of them, and forced Hector to brake sharply.

'I suggest that you should concentrate on the traffic until we get
back to your home, Hector.'

'Excellent advice,' Hector conceded.

Hector parked in his exclusive slot at the front door of The Cross
Roads, and let them in with his own key before Stephen could get
up from the basement.

'We are going to be in the study for a while,' he told the butler.
'Make sure we are not interrupted. Not even a phone call, please.'

As soon as Hector ushered her into his study Jo's eyes went to
the wall facing his desk. She came up short, staring at the wall. He
bumped into her from behind, but placed his hands on her hips to
steady her.

'What is it, Jo?'

'You have changed the painting,' she said in a small voice. The
summer portrait of Hazel in the wheat field was gone. In its place
there hung a colourful David Hockney landscape of the English
countryside.

'Don't you like it? Unlike the Gauguin you noticed downstairs,
this is an original.'

'Hazel has gone?'

'Yes, Hazel has gone. I had a lot of resistance from Stephen. He
didn't want to do it.'

'Why?' she asked. 'Why did you change it?'

'Let me take your jacket.' He slipped the mink off her shoulders
and led her to a chair. 'Make yourself comfortable while I get us
some coffee. Then I will explain to you why I did it.'

He placed the coffee cup in front of her, but she did not touch
it. He went to his seat and sat facing her. He lifted his own cup
halfway to his lips and then replaced it on the saucer without tasting

it. He interlocked his fingers and leaned back in his swivel chair, touching his chin with his thumbs.

'Hazel left me a posthumous letter,' he said and she nodded without taking her eyes off his. 'It was a long letter but the last paragraph was the one that was the most poignant.' His voice broke slightly and he coughed to clear his throat before he went on. 'I remember every word of it by heart. I want to tell it to you, because it affects us directly. May I recite it to you, Jo?'

She nodded slowly. 'If you feel you would like to,' she agreed.

'This is what Hazel wrote. "Do not pine too long over my departure. Remember me with joy, but find yourself another companion. A man like you was never designed to live like a monk. However, make sure she is a good woman, or else I will come back and haunt her."'

She said nothing, but she went on staring at him. Then her expression softened and she began to weep silently. 'My poor Hector,' she whispered. Still without lowering her gaze she opened the handbag in her lap and took out a Kleenex tissue; she dabbed at her eyes.

'Please don't pity me, Jo,' he said. 'I have done enough of that on my own account. I have passed through the valley of the shadow, and now I am coming out into the sunshine again; back into the happy land of laughter and love. I have Catherine Cayla and now I have found . . .'

She raised her hand to stop him. 'Please, Hector. I need a few minutes alone. I look a mess when I cry. Please let me go to the bathroom to fix my make-up.' He jumped to his feet solicitously and came to her, but she smiled at him through the tears.

'I know my way around here,' she said. 'Drink your coffee and I will be back presently.'

When she returned she had fully recovered her composure. 'I am so sorry for that performance, Hector,' she told him. 'Female histrionics is the very last thing you need now. I promise that it won't happen again.'

'Don't apologize, Jo. It is proof that you are the lovely caring person I judged you to be.'

'Stop,' she said. 'You'll start me off again, blubbering all over the place. We were talking about Johnny Congo. We can come back to this other subject later.'

'Very well. I agree both of us need to calm down a little before one of us says something they may regret. Johnny Congo it shall be. My last question was "How do you know so much detail about him?"'

'My reply was that I have a huge amount of documentation on him from his military records to his court and prison records.'

'I accept that, Jo. But here in "The Poisoned Seed" you have given us his direct speech. I am going to play the Devil's advocate now. The language you have put into Johnny's mouth seems very mild and proper for somebody like that.'

'That's very perceptive of you, Hector.' Jo dropped her eyes from his. 'I could not bring myself to write down his exact words. He has the filthiest mouth I have ever conceived of. Almost every sentence that he utters includes the four-letter copulatory expletive. Of course the overutilization of that sort of language is the hallmark of a limited vocabulary and a stunted intelligence. Ronnie and I have hours of tape recordings of Johnny and Carl in conversation with each other. That is how they speak to each other. After a very short time it loses its shock effect and becomes trivial and boring. But I could not bring myself to include it, not even to portray Johnny Congo's character more accurately,' Jo replied. 'I simply edited it out. I don't think it changed the sense and meaning in the least.'

'No, I don't accept that without further explanation. Where did you and Ronnie get all these tape recordings from?'

'This is why I wanted to write it all down in chronological order. It's such a complicated story that I don't want to chop and change backwards and forwards trying to explain and justify myself and my story. It will only make it all more confused and difficult to understand. I want to present it in a logical sequence.'

'Okay. I will try and restrain myself.'

'Before we deal with the provenance of the recordings, I want to tell you what else I have for you. I have all the floor plans and architectural drawings of the interior of the Kazundian castle on the hill. I think you might find them useful, for finding your way around if you ever get inside.'

He stared at her for a moment in astonishment. 'Good Lord; where did you get your hands on all this . . .' He broke off in mid-sentence. 'You already told me in your story; the architect from Houston, what's his name? Andrew Moorcroft, wasn't he? You must have had a reason for including his name so early in the story.'

'Full marks!' Jo applauded him. 'Go to the top of the class. Andrew is a friend of Ronnie Bunter. They were classmates at Harvard. They drifted apart but they met up again at the memorial service for your lovely wife Hazel in the Presbyterian Church in Houston. The two of them picked up their friendship again and were discussing events that had taken place in the interim. Andrew knew Ronnie was the trustee of the Bannock Trust and so he casually mentioned the work he had done for Carl Bannock in Africa. He took it for granted that Ronnie would know all about it, but of course Ronnie jumped on it, and asked for all the details. Andrew was able to give him copies of all his plans of the castle on the hill in Kazundu.'

'Now it all starts to make sense,' Hector conceded. 'That explains how you got your hands on the architect's drawings, but what about the voice recordings of Carl and Johnny Congo that you spoke of?'

'That was also with Andrew Moorcroft's assistance,' Jo explained. 'Apparently Carl had asked Andrew for a recommendation; somebody to install his electronics. Andrew told him about Emma Purdom and her team who are based in Texas. Emma is an electronics whizz-kid. Carl went along with Andrew's recommendation and employed Emma; and she took her team out to Kazundu. She installed all the communications and surveillance in the castle. However, Carl treated Emma badly. He swindled her out of several hundred thousand dollars. Like many acknowledged geniuses, Carl can sometimes be really stupid. Emma is not a good person to cheat. When Ronnie and I approached her she was delighted to help us out. It was a breeze for her, while sitting in her workshop in Houston, to hack into her own bugs in Kazundu. She downloaded Carl's tapes for us, all of them from the first to the last.'

344

'It all fits together. Except for one small detail: the crocodile arena. If I have followed the story correctly, Carl set that up very recently, long after Andrew and Emma Purdom had returned to Texas. How do you know about it?'

'Thanks to Emma Purdom again,' she told him. 'While Emma was in Kazundu she struck up a friendship with the local missionary priest who was in charge of the little church and school across the lake in Kigoma. Emma set up a computer program for the black schoolkids. Even after she left Africa she kept in regular touch with the priest and his kids. She chats with them online all the time. They kept her informed about everything that was going on around the lake shore. The capture of the giant crocs was big news for them. Then later there were ugly rumours about how Carl and Johnny fed their pets. They passed all this on to Emma. I knew about the fate they had meted out to Bryoni. It didn't take much imagination to put the two stories together.'

'Okay, I'll buy it all. I think you have a great future as a novelist. In fact I think you are a marvel; a living and breathing gift from the gods.'

'I think the same of you,' she replied. 'However, I suggest that you allow me to hurry along with my story.'

'No great hurry,' he told her. 'It's getting on towards dinner time and I know Cynthia has dreamed up one of her masterpieces. You will stay for dinner, won't you?'

'That sounds wonderful. I would love to dine here with you.'

Hector phoned through to the kitchen to warn Cynthia of the extra guest.

'That will be perfectly fine, sir. I have already made provision for Miss Stanley,' she answered.

'They are always well ahead of me,' Hector grumbled as he hung up. 'But at least we have the whole evening ahead of us. You don't have to rush.'

'Very well, then; I intend to make the most of it, I warn you,' she assured him. 'Next bit of breaking news is that the FBI is also interested in the affairs of Carl and Johnny.'

'Damn it! Are they going to beat me to it? This is my business entirely; they should keep their noses out of it.'

'This is how it stands now,' Jo replied. 'Congo is one of the most wanted men in the USA. In addition to the multiple murders for which he was convicted, there was also the killing of Lucas Heller during the prison break. Lucas was regarded as a law enforcement officer. It's not a good idea to kill one of those. When it was clear that Johnny had fled the US of A, the FBI was called in. The investigation was difficult and protracted. In the beginning nobody suspected that Carl Bannock was implicated. Congo had simply disappeared, and there were no clues to his whereabouts. The time passed, but the FBI never let up.'

Jo paused to gather her thoughts, and then she went on, 'Finally, in a seemingly unrelated matter the IRS began to investigate Marco Merkowski, warden of Holloway Prison, for tax evasion. He had been unable to account for being in possession of large sums of money in offshore banking accounts. Merkowski was brought to trial for tax evasion and sentenced to five years' detention. The FBI was able to link the timing of Johnny Congo's prison break with Marco's unexplained cash windfall. They offered Marco a deal if he would cooperate with their investigation of the Congo escape.'

'I bet Merkowski jumped at the chance to get out of jail free,' Hector suggested.

'He nearly tripped over his own feet in the rush,' Jo agreed. 'So the FBI was finally able to make the connection between Carl, Congo and the Henry Bannock Family Trust. They came to Ronnie Bunter as the head trustee. Even though over the years Ronnie had been in regular contact with Carl by email, Ronnie still had no idea where Carl was hiding. Living a double life and protecting Johnny Congo, Carl had become an expert at covering his tracks. Nevertheless Ronnie Bunter had to tell the FBI that his relationship with Carl was client and attorney, and he could not divulge any information about the Trust or its beneficiaries without committing breach of trust.'

The intercom rang and Jo broke off to let Hector reply. 'Thank you, Cynthia. Yes, we are ready for dinner right about now.' He glanced enquiringly at Jo and she nodded agreement. 'You can ask Stephen to be ready to serve it in about ten minutes.' Hector switched off the intercom and turned back to Jo. 'Would you like to wash your hands and then we can go down. Cynthia has the temperament of a great artist. When she says "Eat!" we eat.'

Once they were seated at the dining table Jo picked up the tale again. 'So the FBI petitioned the Supreme Court for a Disclosure of Information Order against the Henry Bannock Family Trust and its trustees. Ronnie, as was his duty as head trustee, defended the case and when it went against him he appealed. We lost again on appeal, so Ronnie had to admit defeat and do what his own moral principles had urged him to do all along. He gave everything we had on Carl and Johnny Congo to the FBI. This happened long before Ronnie and Andrew Moorcroft met again. Even with what we gave them at that time the mighty FBI were still unable to locate Carl and Johnny.'

'So are you and Ronnie now obliged to give the FBI the information that you gained recently from Andrew and Emma Purdom, pinpointing Carl's whereabouts?' he asked, and Jo sighed.

'That's a moot point, Hector. Ronnie and I have convinced ourselves that the Disclosure Order is only valid for information that we received up until the date of the order, and we are willing to take a chance on that assumption. Even if the FBI gets wind of the true situation and demands that we give them up-to-date information we are prepared to appeal their decision. So you have about a year without interference from Big Brother to do what you have to do.'

'What do you think I have to do, Jo Stanley?'

'My throat is sore from all this talking.' She smiled sweetly at him. 'I cannot say another word. As a lawyer, I certainly cannot incite you to commit a felony, such as killing or kidnapping anybody. You are a big boy, Hector Cross. You know what you must do. You don't need me to tell you.'

'I agree with you on the last bit, Jo. I do know what I must do right now. I must see to it that you enjoy your dinner, and pay full respect to the rather decent wine that I have chosen for us. I think that we have both had enough of Carl and Johnny for one day. Let's talk of more salubrious matters for the rest of the evening, and come back to them again tomorrow morning.'

For the rest of the dinner they spoke only about each other. Of course she knew almost everything about him, but he knew very little about her. He listened with his full attention and almost everything she had to tell him tended to confirm the high opinion he was forming of her. By the time they had finished the main meal there was a powerful and almost tangible undercurrent running between them. He realized that the removal of Hazel's portrait from his study wall had set their relationship on a new course. They could look into each other's eyes candidly and with trust. Each of them knew that they had reached an unspoken agreement. They were relaxed and trusting in each other.

When Stephen cleared away the plates, and Hector asked her, 'Dessert? Cheese? Cigars?' she laughed and shook her head.

'It was a great meal, but I think I will pass on the cigars, thank you.'

'We can go through to the sitting room for coffee, then,' he suggested. He stood up and went behind her seat and helped her draw back her chair, and then he gave her his arm and took her through to the sitting room.

'Oh, how lovely,' she said when she saw the fire in the grate. They stood in front of it with their backs to the warmth. She moved a little closer to him, and looked up to him. They held each other's gaze as he bowed his head over her, and her lips parted slightly, her breath came quicker.

It was their first real kiss, a statement and a promise. At the end of it they were clinging to each other. He spoke at last with their lips only inches apart, and they each had the taste of the other in their mouths. 'I mean this, Jo,' he said.

'So do I,' she whispered.

'Please stay with me tonight,' he said, and she hesitated for a long moment before she replied.

'Hector, I am not going to pull any punches. I knew a great deal about you even before we actually met, and I thought you must be a fascinating man. Then I met you for the first time and I discovered you were exactly what I had hoped you would be.' She looked up at him and there was green fire in her eyes. 'I have wanted you ever since that day, but I knew it was still far too soon for you. I was prepared to wait. But now I think that I have waited long enough. You have taken down the portrait in your study. For me that was an important statement. For me there is no turning back from here.'

He opened his mouth to reply to her, but she reached out quickly and placed her forefinger on his lips.

'Wait! Hear me out, please. I am not a simpering virgin, but neither am I a tramp. I was even married once, admittedly not for very long. However, I have never before jumped into bed with a man without a lot of careful thought and consideration.'

Gently he lifted her hand away from his mouth. 'We don't have to say anything more. From here onwards too many words may spoil what seems to me good and right. Being in love is fun, let's have fun, Jo, my darling.'

'That's the first time you ever called me darling, Hector darling.'

'May I show you the way upstairs?'

'Come along!' she said. 'Show me which stairs in particular we are talking about here.'

They stopped at the foot of the staircase. 'It's so far to the top,' she said. 'I swear I don't think I can make it without a little more encouragement.'

She turned towards him, took hold of the lapels of his jacket, lifted her face to his and stood on her tiptoes. He drew her closer and bowed his head to kiss her again. Her arms slipped around his neck. Their bodies melded. Her mouth was hot and he could smell the natural musk of her arousal blending with her perfume. He wanted her. His body was racked by the need for her. He picked her up in his arms and she kept her arms locked around his neck and her mouth glued to his.

He ran with her up the stairs and she laughed into his mouth. 'You crazy man! If you fall you'll kill us both.'

'I fell already, and we survived.'

'Only just,' she said.

Still with her in his arms he pushed open the bedroom door with his shoulder and carried her through. Then he kicked the door closed behind them and carried her across the room to place her on her feet, facing the floor-to-ceiling mirror.

He stood behind her with his arms clasped around her, looking over her shoulder and studying her image in the glass.

'I cannot get over how lovely you are,' he said.

She took his hands and placed them over her breasts. 'I think I look a lot better like this. It certainly feels better.' She was watching his eyes in the mirror.

He unbuttoned the front of her blouse and she dropped her arms to allow him to slip the blouse off her shoulders. He tossed it over the foot of the bed and then cupped her breasts again and squeezed them together softly.

'They are so big.' He kissed her ear from behind and she shivered.

'You are giving me goose bumps,' she said. 'Inside and out.'

He unhooked the clasp of her bra between her bosoms, and then he tossed the bra onto the bed on top of her blouse. He reached around again and took her nipples between finger and thumb of both his hands and milked them gently. Her nipples stiffened, thrust out their tips and turned the colour of ripening mulberries as the blood rushed into them. He pulled them out as far as they would go and then released them. They bounced back as though made of rubber.

'I hope you are having fun?' She tried to make her voice stern, but her breath was gusty.

'I cannot remember when I ever had more fun. As the man said, being in love is fun.' He kissed her shoulder. 'Your skin is so white and smooth.'

He ran his fingertips down from her breasts to her navel. Her belly was concave, white and warm as marble in the sunlight.

'Do you think I am fat?' she asked, the ubiquitous feminine question.

'I'll kill anyone who answers yes to that,' he warned her.

He unbuttoned the top of her skirt and worked it down over her hips. It dropped around her ankles and she kicked off her high heels.

Her bikini panties were of white satin with a little heart-shaped cut-out of lacework in the front. In the mirror he could see the shadowy haze of her pubes through the lace. He ran his fingertips lightly over the satin, and she whispered breathlessly, 'You are not teasing me; you are torturing me.'

'No more torture,' he promised and pulled open the elastic top of her panties, and ran his hand down under the satin. She moved her feet apart to allow him access.

'She is so wonderfully lubricious,' he murmured.

'That's just pussy's way of saying hello and it's so nice to meet you at last,' she explained.

'There is somebody else around here who also desperately wants to meet pussy,' he said.

'I know exactly who you mean,' she replied. 'He has been making his presence felt recently.'

'He has no manners. Please forgive his pushy and thrusting behaviour.'

'Pushy is good.' She laughed. 'Thrusting is even better. I think pussy would very much like to meet him. Do you mind if I make the introductions?'

'Please do,' he invited, and she turned in the circle of his arms to face him, and she kissed him. But at the same time she was drawing down the zipper of his trouser fly.

'Goodness gracious me!' she exclaimed suddenly.

'What's wrong?' he asked.

'That was an exclamation of delight, not dismay. I knew he had to be large but I never thought he would be that big. My immediate problem now is that you are over-dressed, but I intend to fix that.' With her one hand still deep into the opening of his fly and the other hand on his chest she forced him to reverse until he came up against the bed and he went over backwards onto the covers.

'Stay like that,' she ordered. 'Don't move!' She knelt and unlaced his shoes and pulled off his socks. Then she grabbed the bottoms of his trousers and told him, 'Lift your bum, chum!'

When he obeyed she whipped off his trousers with a flourish and then did the same with his underpants. She stood back brandishing his boxers over her head and giggling like a schoolgirl. 'Look at you, sticking up in the air and making the place all untidy. No, don't move! I'll have him tucked away neatly before you can say Jack Flash!'

She flipped the boxers over her shoulder and placed her fists on her hips and studied him with her head cocked on one side.

'Hey, there!' Hector said after a while. 'What are we waiting for?'

'Oh, I am sorry. I think I must have been hypnotized there for a moment, like the bird by the cobra. He is not only large but really rather handsome into the bargain, you know?' She hopped up onto the bed beside him, and swung one leg over him, straddling him. She busied herself for a moment and then she gasped, 'Oh my God, he fits in! I had serious doubts that it was possible.'

Their lovemaking was ebullient and joyful; mutually fulfilling after their long abstinence. Afterwards they clung together, their breath and their perspiration mingling. They talked, and then made love again. Long after midnight they fell asleep still conjoined.

In the dawn she woke first, but he felt her eyes on his face and he opened his.

'I was so afraid,' she said and hugged him fiercely. 'I dreamed you had gone away again.'

'That's not going to happen, I promise you.'

It was mid-morning when Cynthia sent up their breakfast and they ate in their bathrobes. They had shared a bath and their bodies still glowed from love and hot water. As Jo poured the coffee she asked, 'So what do we do now?' The plural pronoun came naturally to her lips.

'The time for talking is past, now we start moving.'

'Where to?'

'To Abu Zara for a start. I have to get the team assembled, briefed and focussed. You have to meet Catherine Cayla.'

'Great plan! When can we leave?'

'How soon can you be ready?'

'I am ready already. I travel light, remember?'

'You are a girl of infinite virtues.'

Agatha managed to book the last two available first-class seats on the Emirates flight out of Heathrow that same evening. Paddy and Nastiya met them at Abu Zara airport the next morning. They tried to conceal their fascinated curiosity when Jo walked out of the arrivals gate at Hector's side.

Hector shook hands with Paddy and kissed both of Nastiya's cheeks, and then he told them, 'I want you two to meet Jo Stanley.' Hector introduced her.

'Ah so!' said Nastiya as the ladies shook hands. 'I haven't seen that look on Hector's face for a long time. Be careful of this one, Jo Stanley. Hector has got a big handful.'

'I think my wife means rather that Hector *is* a big handful,' Paddy explained.

'So, a difference there is?' Nastiya demanded.

Paddy drove them to Seascape Mansions and when they rode up in the elevator to the penthouse Paddy was lugging Jo's heavy case. In the lobby the customary reception committee was gathered to greet Hector. Catherine Cayla recognized her father as he stepped out of the elevator and almost bounced herself out of Bonnie's arms with glad cries of 'Baba!'

'Put her down, Bonnie,' Hector ordered and then to Jo he said, 'Just watch this.' Catherine shot across the floor and tried to climb his leg. Hector picked her up and placed her on his hip, and turned to Jo. 'Pretty impressive, don't you think?'

'I think she is simply gorgeous. May I hold her?'

'She may wet you. If she does, take it as a sign of love. She pees on me all the time.'

'I'll take the risk.' Jo held out her arms. Catherine regarded her solemnly for a moment, then made up her mind.

'Man!' she said and went willingly into Jo's embrace.

'Man?' Hector asked incredulously. 'Did she ever get that one wrong!'

'It's her new word.' Bonnie rushed to the defence of her charge. 'She calls everybody that she likes Man.'

Dave Imbiss came forward to greet Hector and as they shook hands

Hector told him, 'Things are breaking, Dave. I want you with Paddy and Nazzy in the cinema right away.'

Hector led his main team to the cinema. Jo carried Catherine with her, and Catherine took the opportunity to explore the inside of Jo's nostrils with her finger.

When they were all settled Hector plugged the flash drive into the computer, and the first page of Jo's novella flashed up on the screen.

'"Karl Pieter Kurtmeyer: The Poisoned Seed". What the hell this is, Hector?' Nastiya demanded.

'Read it, Nazzy. All of you read it. Jo and I are taking Catherine to the beach for a swim. We will be back before dark to answer your questions, and to start the ball rolling.'

When Hector and Jo returned they went directly to the cinema and Hector opened the door quietly. The three of them in the seats were so engrossed that for a while they did not realize the two of them were standing watching them.

Nastiya said, 'Come on, Paddy. Read quicker. I want to find out the end.' Then suddenly she realized that she was being watched and she twisted round on the bench.

'Hector, is this the truth what is happening in the book, or just another bad joke of yours?'

'It's the truth, Nazzy. Even I would never joke about something like this.'

'Our baby! Our little Cathy! First we must stop them, both of these animals, before they can do this to our baby.'

'That is why we are all here,' Hector agreed. Both Paddy and Dave Imbiss were watching Hector. Their expressions were hard and cold.

'This Kazundu Castle . . .' Paddy cut in. 'Tell us about it. Are Carl and Johnny Congo still holed up there?'

'Have you finished reading Jo's story?' Hector avoided the question.

'Not yet,' Paddy admitted. 'Just a few pages to go.'

'Finish it. Jo and I are going to take a shower to get off the sea salt and sand. We will be back very shortly. In the meantime ring through to the kitchen, get Chef to rustle up a mess of food and a couple of gallons of coffee. We are going to be up late tonight.'

Half an hour later when they returned to the cinema they found an array of enormous silver platters heaped with sandwiches on the rostrum table. The room was redolent of the coffee in the silver urn.

'Have you finished reading the whole story?' Hector demanded of Paddy as they stood around the table wolfing sandwiches and swilling coffee.

'It's pretty fierce stuff,' Paddy said.

As soon as they had finished eating and the plates were cleared away, Paddy locked the door, and they settled back in the tiered seats. Jo fussed with the projector, connecting her laptop computer to it and focussing the beam on the screen on the back wall of the auditorium. Hector prowled back and forth across the stage.

'Okay, people. We all know now why we are going in.' There was a murmur of assent. 'This is a hunt-and-kill mission. No questions asked and no prisoners taken. We are going in to cancel Carl Bannock and Johnny Congo. We go in fast and come out just as fast. Are we all clear on that?' Again there was tacit agreement.

'Paddy has already asked the first question. Are the targets still in the castle on the hill? The answer is that as of forty minutes ago they were there.'

All three of them looked dubious, and Paddy spoke on their behalf. 'Forty minutes ago? That's pretty fast. The castle is almost three thousand miles from where we are now, so how can you be so sure so quickly? Come on, Hector, you don't expect us to believe in your new supernatural powers.'

'Jo is running a surveillance asset named Emma Purdom. She phoned in forty minutes ago while we were returning from the beach; she asked the question. The answer is that Carl and Johnny are still in the castle.'

They all turned and looked at Jo with dawning respect.

'Jo set up this asset?' Nastiya demanded.

'Jo found it and turned it on,' Hector confirmed.

'Just a pretty decoration your new lady isn't,' Nastiya said.

'Welcome to the team, Jo Stanley,' and Jo looked up from the projector and smiled her thanks.

'Hey, Jo! You have impressed Nazzy. That's not easy to do,' Hector told her. 'Are you ready to run your little show for us?'

'All set,' Jo replied. 'Give me the word.'

'Hold on a moment, please,' Hector said and then he turned to the others. 'First off, we need to make sure that you are able to identify the targets on sight and to recognize the sound of their voices. Jo is going to start with Carl Bannock. You know a great deal about Carl from Jo's story. So just to recap, then. Carl is an academic; a product of a good prep school and Princeton. He is smart and tricky. He is a financial genius. He is good-looking, polished and suave. He is bisexual and kinky. In particular he is a pathological sadist and a paedophile. He is a psychopath: no conscience; no pity and no remorse. He is a megalomaniac. Only one thing matters to Carl Bannock and that is Carl Bannock. Always bear in mind what he did to his own mother and sisters. You know what his plans are for Catherine Cayla.'

The room went suddenly tense at the reference to their child, and Nastiya's eyes were cold blue slits. Hector looked back at Jo. 'Thank you, Jo. You can start the show now.'

She dimmed the overhead lights and started the projector. The tape that she had prepared ran for a little under ten minutes. It began with footage from the Bannock family archives that Ronnie Bunter had taken from his files. It showed Carl as a Princeton undergraduate. This was followed by footage of Carl running, walking and playing golf and tennis so they could study his movements. Then there were short clips of Carl addressing the shareholders at the annual general meeting of the Bannock Oil Corporation, being interviewed on TV and in conversation with his friends. From there it cut to the courthouse scene of Carl's trial with him weeping and pleading for forgiveness. It ended with a few short clips from the concealed surveillance cameras in the castle on the hill. Emma Purdom had spliced these together for Jo. These were mostly clips of Carl and Johnny in conversation, but included brief and graphic scenes of Carl indulging in sexual congress with Johnny Congo and various other male, female and transvestite partners.

When the tape ended and Jo turned the lights up, Hector said, 'Well, now you should all be able to recognize Carl Bannock even from a distance or if he is wearing a disguise, or if he is without pants. Do you have any questions?'

'He is a snake, a poisonous snake,' Nastiya said. 'He is disgusting. He is the most repulsive thing I have ever seen.'

'That is not a question, Nazzy.'

'Okay, here is my question,' Nastiya agreed. 'Do we cancel him as soon as we can get a bead on him, or do we grab him so you can talk to him first?'

'Use your discretion, Nazzy. If there is the slightest chance that he is about to get clean away then take him down, and shoot to kill. However, if you can grab him, then I would be extremely grateful if you could bring him to me for a short farewell chat.'

'Hazel was a fine lady and her daughter is adorable. I want to be there when you are pointing out to Carl Bannock the error of his ways,' Paddy said without a smile.

'Are there any more questions or comments?' Hector looked around. 'If not we can go on to consider Johnny Congo. Here is another interesting and unusual subject.'

'I want to have a good look at this one,' Nastiya spoke up. 'I want to make up my mind which one of them I hate the most. I want they should no more think about messing with our baby.'

'Jo, you heard the lady. Please, can you show Johnny Congo to us?'

The opening sequence was of Johnny Congo as a US Marine sergeant being decorated with the Silver Star for valour in the Mekong River delta of Vietnam by his commanding general, while his company paraded behind them.

'No doubt about it that Congo is completely fearless,' Hector commented. 'He did two tours of duty in the US Marines. As you see he was decorated for courage and received an honourable discharge from the military with the rank of sergeant major. When he returned to civilian life he turned to the only role for which he was truly qualified and which gave him real pleasure; this was killing people. He became a hired gun; professional hit man. Like Carl, he is a psychopath and a sadist. Unlike Carl, he is a foul-mouthed brute, but do not for one moment underestimate him. He is possessed of innate animal cunning. You all know a great deal about him from Jo's descriptions. But I am going to remind you of some of the most important things to remember about him. Johnny has an omnivorous sexual appetite. Carl is his long-term sexual partner but the two of them copulate with all and sundry. Johnny Congo is immensely physically powerful and a fearsome adversary. Like a mad dog he should be shot at a distance, and not engaged at close quarters.'

The tape of Johnny ended with sequences put together by Emma Purdom from the hidden cameras in the castle on the hill. When the screen went blank and Jo turned up the lights Hector went on. 'Okay, you have all had a good look at our quarry. Now Jo will show you the hunting ground. We are expecting to find Johnny and Carl in or close to the castle and we might have to hunt them down within the walls. The castle is a large and rambling building. It is over three hundred years old and was built by Arabic stonemasons for the Sultan of Oman. It is a sprawling warren of hundreds of rooms. From the cellars and dungeons below to the towers and minarets on high it is a maze in which a stranger can very soon become completely lost. Jo will begin with photographs of the exterior.'

These photographs were all taken by professionals and were impressive. The backdrops of the lake and forest-covered mountains were magnificent. Jo ran through them quickly.

'Okay, that's the tourist commercial, but now we have something many times more valuable. Jo has managed to get her hands on up-to-date architects' drawings and blueprints of the castle interior.'

The first plan flashed up on the screen. It showed the layout of the dungeons beneath the castle walls.

Paddy became so excited that he pounded his knee with his fist. 'This is better than a winning lottery ticket. I am forced to admit that I was not very happy with the idea of following up blind through a labyrinth in which we could run into an ambush at every turn.'

'Where on earth did you get these from, Jo?' Dave Imbiss was as delighted as Paddy. 'You have probably saved our lives. I mean that literally.'

'Just remember what Maggie Thatcher said: when the going gets really tough send a woman in to do the job.' Nastiya joined in the chorus of approval. 'Luckily you men have now got another female on the team.'

Hector raised his voice to regain their attention. 'Jo has prepared a separate set of blueprints for each of you.' He glanced down at the notebook he was holding open in his left hand. 'Okay, so we now know our targets, and we know where we expect to find them. Now we must decide on how we are going to get into Kazundu. This is a tricky one. It's not an easy country to reach.' He nodded at Jo. She manipulated the projector to display a large-scale map of the area on the screen. Hector went on speaking.

'To the east of it lies Lake Tanganyika, like a gigantic moat. It's over thirty miles wide. Crossing it by some kind of vessel from the Tanzanian side is not really an inviting option. There's a saying: "Africa is an empty land with a pair of eyes watching from behind every bush". Johnny Congo is sure to have agents on the Tanzanian side. He would know we were coming before we pushed off from the eastern shore, and we would have to land on the Kazundian side of the lake under fire.'

'Can we go in from the west, through the Democratic Republic of the Congo?' Dave Imbiss asked, and Hector shook his head.

'That would mean an approach march of at least five hundred miles through dense jungle and across large rivers. There are virtually no roads. The tribal warlords who control that part of the country are all Johnny's staunch friends and business allies. He is the sales outlet for their conflict minerals. We wouldn't get very far.'

'So, it seems the only way in is by air. We will have to parachute in. That's no problem, then.' Paddy shrugged.

'Good Irish thinking,' Hector commended him. 'That's great for the entry. But how do we exit after we have done the job? We have already heard that it would be impossible to get out of Kazundu on foot.'

'The drop plane would land to pick us up,' said Paddy, defending his ideas. 'The same way Johnny did it originally.'

'Johnny wasn't on a hunt-and-kill raid, as we will be. He did not have to get control of the airport to have an escape route. He was there to waste Justin and take up permanent residence,' Hector pointed out. 'Anyway, this is a different situation. King Justin's army was a music-hall joke, a small bunch of palookas with no ammunition in rifles they didn't know how to shoot. Now Johnny's gang is made up of well-equipped men who he has hand-picked and trained with the help of Sam Ngewenyama. Both Johnny and Sam are military veterans. We can only land forty or fifty men at a time. Andrew Moorcroft, who was on the ground in Kazundu, estimates that Johnny has a couple of hundred trained men. We are up against pros; not a single palooka amongst them. What is more, we will be heavily outnumbered.'

'Shit!' Dave Imbiss said quietly but vehemently.

'Indeed,' Hector agreed. 'A big smelly lump of it. Andrew has also told us that Johnny Congo is fully aware that the airfield is his Achilles heel. He exploited it himself to get his men in. So what he has done is build a heavily sandbagged redoubt at each end of the runway. Set in embrasures in the walls are batteries of fifty-calibre heavy machine guns. No uninvited or unwelcome aircraft can land or take off without being raked by MG fire from both fore and aft, even before its wheels touch or leave the ground.'

They considered the proposition with expressions of cold distaste, until Jo Stanley broke the silence at last. 'Unless, of course, it is Carl's own Antonov Condor,' Jo said gently.

'Of course!' Hector agreed dismissively. 'But we are not going to be in his Condor, are we?'

'No, we are not,' Jo agreed demurely. 'Unless, of course, you hijack it for us.'

A solemn silence followed this statement. Nastiya broke it with a whoop of laughter. 'Look at their faces, Jo. They have run fresh out of smart-arse masculine replies. Come on, boys. What have you got to say to the lady?'

'Goodness gracious me, Jo Stanley!' Hector shook his head in mock disbelief. 'I knew you were bright, but I didn't realize that you are bright enough to light up the sky.'

'Hector Cross!' Jo tried to keep a straight face as she replied. 'Don't you dare hijack my terms of speech. Why don't you rather go and hijack an aircraft?'

I t took two more days of intensive planning before Hector was
satisfied with the logistics for the assault on Kazundu.

'The Condor will only be able to carry a safe limit of eighty-
four fully equipped men and sufficient fuel for a round flight from
Abu Zara to Kazundu and return,' Hector had decided. 'I estimate
we will need a force of around fifty. What is the present strength of
Cross Bow Security, Paddy? How many men can we field, right now?'

'We are short of about fifteen or so,' Paddy admitted, and glanced
across at Dave Imbiss. 'Am I right, Davie?'

'Here in Abu Zara we are shy of sixteen men. But I can fly re-
inforcements in from our other oilfields in South America and Asia.
Give me five or six days, and I can have the full complement assembled and ready to go on the airstrip of the Zara Number Thirteen
concession.'

'Get cracking right away, Dave,' Hector ordered him, and then
turned back to the others. 'Once we have landed at Kazundu airport
and overwhelmed the men in the two forts that guard it, we will
have control. We will leave the Condor under the protection of the
guns in the northern fort. That is the one closest to the castle on
the hill.'

'It's not a good idea to park it in the open,' Paddy advised. 'There
is going to be a lot of incendiary bullets and shrapnel flying about.
Just a single hit from one of those and the Condor goes up. Boom!'

'No!' Hector held up his hand. 'I don't have pictures of it, but
Emma Purdom has recorded conversation of Carl and Johnny
discussing the building of some type of laager to protect the Condor
when it is on the ground. It seems as though the floor of the bunker
is well below ground level with an entry ramp at each end. The sides
of the bunker are screened by walls of sandbags. Once the Condor
taxies down the ramp, it is immune from small arms and RPG fire.
Only problem is that this laager is situated well away from the main
buildings where we will be disembarking. Our pilot will only be able
to get the Condor under cover when we are clear.'

He looked around at their faces. 'Any more questions?' They
shook their heads, and Hector went on. 'I am assuming that we will

have to go after our targets in the castle. I am going to leave twelve men to hold each of the forts on the airfield. Their firepower will be enhanced by the captured heavy machine guns that Johnny Congo has mounted there. I am going to leave Dave in command of these contingents to cover and protect the airfield from counter-attack.'

At this stage Hector was presented with an unforeseen problem. It had never occurred to him that Jo Stanley would be any part of the strike team. She was not a trained warrior like the others. To his mind Jo's place would be in the safety of Abu Zara, possibly helping Bonnie to take care of Catherine Cayla. Now suddenly Jo spoke out in a stronger and more assertive tone than she usually used to express herself.

'The northern redoubt will also be the best place to site my comms post,' she said.

There was a sudden and complete silence in the cinema. Every eye turned to Jo, and then immediately went back to Hector.

Nastiya was at the water fountain drawing a mug of cool water. She was as surprised as any of them by Jo's outburst, but she recovered and went swiftly to stand at Jo's side, before Hector had decided on his reply. Hector was left in no doubt whose side Nastiya was on.

'I hadn't thought about you coming with the strike team to Kazundu, Jo.' Hector broke the pregnant silence carefully.

'Well, you should think about it now.' There was a tone in Jo's voice that he had never heard until that moment. 'I am arranging with Emma Purdom to set up special communications with her so that while the raid is in progress Emma will be able to keep us informed of everything that is happening in the castle. She will be shipping the equipment to me here in Abu Zara within the next few days. My specialized task will be to keep in constant contact with her in Houston. She is the only one of us who has eyes inside the castle. If either Johnny Congo or Carl Bannock goes to ground in there you will need Emma and me to provide you with live coverage of their movements.'

'Jo has a diploma in electronic communications, on top of her law degree,' Nastiya pointed out in the pause that followed Jo's announcement.

'How do you know that?' Hector snapped at Nastiya. He was under attack on two fronts.

'She told me when we were in the girls' room a short while ago. She knows the layout of the castle better than any of us sitting here,' Nastiya explained as if to a child. 'If you want to know how I know that, well, think about who gave us the drawings of the place.'

'Nazzy and Jo are making good sense,' Paddy chimed in. 'If one or both of those bastards gets away into the castle we will need all the edge we can muster. I for one will be happy to have Jo whispering in my ear to point out the way through the maze.'

'You are being heavily outgunned, Heck.' Dave Imbiss joined the discussion, 'A wise man would give up gracefully.'

'Who is talking about wise men here?' Nastiya asked ingenuously. 'I thought we are talking about Hector Cross.'

'Okay.' Hector carried on as though he was totally deaf to this fusillade of repartee. 'So, we are unanimously agreed on my suggestion that Jo goes along with us as field director of comms? Let's move along, then.'

He paused to pour himself another mug of coffee and to recover his equilibrium. Then he flashed Jo a conciliatory grin, before he resumed. 'We will use two kill teams, each comprising fifteen men. I will command the first and Paddy the second. Carl Bannock will be my prime target so my call sign will be "White". Paddy, your prime target will be Johnny Congo, so it follows naturally that your call sign will be "Black". Paddy, you can choose your number two.'

'I'll take Nastiya,' Paddy said.

'Why am I so surprised by your choice? I would have taken her if you had passed,' Hector mused aloud. 'I will have to settle for Paul Stowe as my number two.'

Hector's former head keeper at Brandon Hall had swiftly worked his way into the top echelon at Cross Bow after Hector had given him the job. He had proven himself to be a highly trained fighting man. He was quick-witted, intelligent and utterly reliable; a good man to have beside you in any scrape.

'By the way, where the hell is Paul?' Hector looked at Paddy.

'He is down on the old Number Twelve concession doing a routine inspection of the security there,' Paddy replied.

'Get him back here as soon as you can. He must be brought up to speed with our planning.'

Paddy grunted acquiescence and scribbled a note on his pad.

'We will go over the details again later, but that covers just about everything in broad outline, with one notable exception,' Hector summed up. 'How the hell do we get our hands on the Antonov Condor and who is going to fly it into Kazundu with fifty armed men on board without Johnny Congo and Carl Bannock knowing what we are up to?' He paused to let them consider the question and then he went on. 'I know who I want to fly it.'

There was a murmur of agreement from everybody except Jo, who looked puzzled. Hector addressed her directly.

'Sorry, Jo.' His expression softened. 'There is no way you could know that I am referring to Bernie and Nella Vosloo. They are a couple of commercial pilots, a husband and wife team, who own and run a small air charter company operating all across Africa. They can fly anything with wings, and they aren't too fussy about abiding strictly by aviation or any other laws. They did a tremendous job for us a while back.'

'I know about the Vosloos, Hector,' she corrected him mildly. 'They are the people who flew you and your team into Somalia to rescue Hazel's daughter from the pirate gang who had kidnapped her.'

'How did you know that?' Hector stared at her.

'Hazel told Ronnie and me about them. The Bannock Family Trust had to pay the Vosloos' bill, remember?'

'You get to the winning post before I even start running!' Hector conceded. 'Well then, perhaps you also know that the Vosloos operate only a single aircraft. It's an ancient Hercules C-130. But the type is about as close to the Antonov Condor as it is possible to get, except for the possibility that the user manual is printed in Cyrillic. But Bernie and Nella don't need a manual to fly a Russian copy of a Hercules.'

'Sure of that we are, Heck? Will they take the job?' Nastiya cut in.

'In both respects sure of that we are indeed, Nazzy, if you can follow that convoluted bit of grammar. I sent Nella an email last night. My question to her was, "Can you fly an Antonov Condor? Love Hector". I received her reply a few hours ago.' He held up his iPhone so they were able to read the text on the screen.

'This is the typical Nella Vosloo reply. "Can a peacock pee in the park? How far? How high? How much? Love Nella".' All of them chuckled. But Hector looked seriously at Jo.

'Can your friend Emma hack into the Condor's communications system, Jo?'

'I told you, Emma is the original IT whizz-kid. No worries.'

'Can she transmit a message to the pilots of the Condor as if it originated from Carl Bannock in Kazundu, and can she then intercept the reply from the Condor so that Carl Bannock is entirely unaware of the exchange?'

'Of course she can. She placed her own bug in the Condor and she can play it like Little Walter played his harmonica.'

'Who the hell is Little—' Hector began then changed tack. 'Scrub that question. Next question, I don't suppose our Emma would be able use her bug to track the Condor in flight, and give us a fix on it when we ask her?' Hector pressed Jo for more specifics.

'Absolutely. There are no secrets safe from our girl,' Jo responded without hesitation. 'She can read the Condor's instrument panel from three thousand miles away as though she was sitting in the pilot's seat.'

'Will you ask her for a breakdown of the Condor's recent flights and the destinations of each flight, covering the last six months?' He paused to consider and then went on. 'Also please ask her for the personal details of the two Russian pilots. If at all possible I would like her to give us ID photographs of the two of them, perhaps even copies of their licences?'

'I am sure she will be able to do all that for you.'

'How long will it take her, do you think? Please impress upon her that it's urgent.'

'It won't take long. Emma is totally switched on,' Jo replied. 'Even allowing for the different time zones it will only be a day or so. Emma sleeps with her computer on one pillow and her boyfriend's head on the other. Given a choice, I think she prefers the computer.'

'Okay.' Hector stood up and stretched, and then he checked his wristwatch. 'It's almost seven o'clock already. So we can take a break. Rumour has it that the chef has cooked up a feast for this evening, so you are all invited for eight p.m. That gives you an hour to primp and preen. See you all later.'

The dinner was heavy on the New Zealand green-lipped mussels, Maine lobster, bluefin tuna, gulf snapper and Chablis. Hector was the only one who stayed with the red burgundy.

Before they had finished eating they received proof that even Jo had underestimated Emma Purdom's efficiency. At the same time as the dessert was being served, Emma's response to Jo's queries was brought through to the dining room by one of the radio operators from the Cross Bow communications centre. Hector opened the envelope and scanned the page quickly, before he looked up again at his dinner guests.

'Ladies and gentlemen, hear the gospel according to St Emma. The Condor took off from Kazundu this morning at oh-eight-hundred hours GMT bound for Tehran in Iran with an unlisted cargo. Its ETA in Tehran is approximately one hour thirty minutes from now. On all its three previous visits to that city over the past six months the Condor remained in Tehran for twenty-four hours. Of course, that is in accord with DCA regulations to enable the pilots the stipulated rest period. After that it flew on to either Hong Kong or Russia. However, it always returns to Kazundu via Bangkok, where it takes on passengers. I am going to wager all my marbles on the Condor making the same homeward flight via Bangkok this time around. About now Carl and Johnny will be ready for some fresh Thai meat from the Bangkok flesh markets. According to St Emma, when in the Sin City the Russian pilots stay over at the Mandarin Oriental hotel for their requisite twenty-four-hour rest stop. So that gives Nastiya and Nella Vosloo a clear six days to get to Bangkok ahead of them and to be in the Oriental to meet the crew of the Condor when they arrive. Emma will send a message to the head pilot, purporting to emanate from Carl Bannock, to meet our two ladies and to ferry them down to Kazundu.'

Hector and Jo awoke early the next morning in each other's arms. It had been a busy night and they were both in buoyant mood.

'Do you mind if I invite Catherine Cayla to join us?' Hector asked.

'Oh, what fun! That's a brilliant idea,' Jo enthused and, very soon after his brief intercom call to Bonnie in the nursery, there was a discreet knock at the door.

'Who is it?' Hector demanded.

'It's just us,' Bonnie's voice sang back.

'Door is open. Put the smaller part of us through it, please, Bonnie.'

The door opened a crack and Catherine was deposited on the threshold. She was dressed in an immaculate pink romper suit and there was a matching ribbon in her hair. She sat four-square and looked about the room with an expression of mystification.

'This way, Cathy baby!' Hector called to her, and it took her a moment to focus on the two heads in the rumpled bed. Then it registered and she emitted a joyous cry of 'Baba' and came to her feet. She tottered halfway across the wide floor before she also recognized Jo. She chortled with glee. 'Man!' she greeted her distinctly. 'Good man!'

'Oh my God!' Jo exclaimed. 'Is good a new word?'

'And she used it for you, not me,' Hector grumbled. 'I am jealous.'

In her haste to reach the bed Catherine abandoned her upright gait and reverted to hands and knees. She completed the last few feet at a canter. Hector reached down and swept her up in his arms. She was warm and bouncy and she emitted a powerful aroma of baby talcum. They took turns to cuddle her as they talked.

'Can you two girls be serious for a moment, Jo?' Hector cut in at last.

'Of course we can, what do you want to be serious about?'

'Seeing as how I have made the decision that you are to be a member of the Kazundu strike team . . .' he began, but Jo blew him a raspberry. Cathy thought that was very funny. She laughed delightedly, and imitated Jo, splattering both of them with a fine cloud of baby spittle.

'Now that you two ladies have had your say, I shall continue,' Hector resumed. 'Jo, you and Emma Purdom will have to set up these communications you were boasting about pretty darn quickly. We may be in action in as soon as six or seven days' time.'

'You are absolutely right, my darling. I spoke to Emma as soon as I decided that I had to go with you. She knew exactly what we needed. She works on contract for the US Navy and she has developed for them a clever little gizmo that fits the bill exactly. It's classified, of course, but nevertheless yesterday evening she despatched one of these to me by courier. It should arrive here today, or tomorrow at the latest.'

The promised gadget was delivered by DHL to Seascape Mansions early that same afternoon. In size and appearance it resembled a Hermès Birkin handbag. This had given Emma the inspiration to name it the Birkin. It weighed a shade over eight pounds.

Hector and Jo drove out into the desert with the Birkin and parked the Range Rover off the main highway, well concealed behind a rugged ridge of black ironstone.

As Jo switched on the power she explained, 'The rechargeable battery has a life of seventy-two hours' continuous operation. The antenna is built in. Here we go, it is acquiring satellite contact.' She paused for a few seconds, and then she continued, 'Bingo! Now it will automatically contact Emma's station as its first option.'

Suddenly a young sweet girl's voice spoke out clearly. 'Echo Papa Seven Niner standing by.'

'Those are Emma's initials and her year of birth, but never tell her that I told you that. She will kill me,' Jo explained before she pressed the transmit button. 'This is Juliet Sierra. Hi there, Emma. This is just a radio check to let you know I have received your gift and I am online.'

'Good to hear your voice, Jo sweetie.'

'Are you still covering Little Boy and Big Boy?' Hector gathered that they were referring to Carl and Johnny Congo.

'Affirmative to that, Jo.'

'We will be going operational probably within the next six days. I will give you a heads-up as soon as it happens. In the meantime, keep it warm. Over and out.'

'I'll keep it warm, if you help him to keep it hard. Give him my love,' said Emma and she broke the contact.

'She knows about you,' Jo explained apologetically. 'And she can be very rude.'

'I gathered that.' Hector smiled. 'Now tell me what is so special about this Birkin. It looks very much run-of-the-mill stuff to me.'

'First of all there is its size and weight; and its incredible range and reception in the most adverse conditions.'

'Yes, you have just demonstrated those qualities, but still I am not sure what all the fuss is about.'

'It will support up to ten additional listening posts. That means as long as you are within ten miles you and your team leaders can follow simultaneously all Emma's transmissions to me on your in-ear headphones. This will leave your hands free to pick your noses or whatever else takes your fancy.'

'That's good,' Hector agreed. 'What else makes it unique?'

'It is completely secure. Nobody can possibly hack in on our transmissions,' she said, and Hector looked dubious.

'How is that again?'

'Did you notice the faint click every five seconds while Emma and I were transmitting?' she asked.

'Yes, now that you mention it. But I thought that was only static interference.'

'You'll hear no static on this set. It is modulated to be as clean as my mother's kitchen.' Hector smiled at the comparison, and she continued. 'What you heard was actually Emma's radio changing its frequency. Every five seconds it makes a random change, and my set follows suit and makes the change to exactly the same frequency at precisely the same instant. There are nearly five thousand AM frequencies for our sets to choose from. No other unlinked set can keep pace with us.'

'Now you have seriously impressed me, but what else, if anything, is so special about it?'

'At ranges up to ten miles there is virtually nothing that can interfere with transmissions from our Birkin to your headphones. Do you have any idea how thick the walls of Kazundu Castle are?'

'I don't know exactly, but I'm guessing they are plenty thick,' Hector said.

'In places, especially down in the dungeons, they are as much as fifteen or twenty feet thick; and that is solid rock!'

'Impressive,' Hector agreed. 'But go on and impress me a little more.'

'Okay, if you were down in the palace dungeons hunting for Carl and Johnny, Emma in Houston would be able to watch them on her planted cameras; however, she would not be able to report the information to you. Because of the thickness of the castle walls the two of you would not have comms.'

'That sucks,' Hector agreed. 'But I think I see where you are coming from.'

'Let's hear it from the lad. It's your turn to impress me with how smart you are.'

'I am in the Kazundu dungeon and I can't speak to Emma, but I can speak to you because you are on the airfield at the foot of the hill, or maybe you are even up on the battlements of the fort. Emma sees what our two beauties, Carl and Johnny, are up to, so she tells you and you relay it on to me.'

'You are just as smart as I hoped you were,' Jo admitted. 'So you see why this means that I have to come to Kazundu with you. You can't leave me behind to sit on my hands here in Abu Zara.'

'You are a scheming vixen, Jo Stanley!' Hector told her sternly, and then he went on, 'We will need in-ear headphones for each of our team leaders. We must be hands-free to use our weapons, if needs be.'

'Emma has sent me ten sets of headphones in the same package as the Birkin.' Jo opened the package and displayed them to him.

'She certainly is a switched-on young lady,' Hector conceded. 'And I like the sound of her voice. She sounds rather cute.'

'Just you forget it, buster,' Jo told him sternly. 'Emma is as ugly as an organ grinder's monkey. Besides, any time you feel the urge, this little Birkin right here beside you will be delighted to oblige.'

Nastiya and Nella Vosloo made the journey to Bangkok on separate airlines. Nastiya was the first to arrive and Nella followed eight hours later on a flight from Nairobi in Kenya. They met in Nastiya's suite in the Authors' Wing of the Mandarin Oriental hotel overlooking the Chao Phraya river. They had both changed into their best cocktail gowns, and after they had embraced they stepped apart still holding hands and examined each other with affectionate interest.

'You are looking so good, Nella. It seems like yesterday I last saw you,' Nastiya told her.

'And so are you! I love that dress. The colour suits you so well. Is it Prada?'

'Yes, it's Prada.' Nastiya hugged her again. 'Shall we have a nice-to-see-you drink? I found a bottle of good vodka in the minibar.' She poured two measures, filled them with ice cubes and they saluted each other with the frosted glasses, then Nastiya took Nella's arm and led her out onto the balcony.

'I have checked the room.' Nastiya dropped her voice. 'I think that it's clean. But it's best we take no chances, and we talk out here. Do you know what we have to do?'

'Yes, Hector has told me everything. He said you would have photographs of these other people we are taking over from.' Nella worded it diplomatically.

Nastiya left her for a moment to fetch her bag from the sitting room and she closed the door behind her as she returned. They studied the photographs together.

'This one is the captain,' Nastiya explained. 'His name is Yuri Volkov. In Russian Volkov means wolf. With a name like that his ancestors must have been aristocrats, before the revolution. When he was younger he flew MiG-29 Fulcrums for the USSR.'

'That's their top fighter. Only the hot-shot Russian pilots get to fly them.'

'*Da*,' Nastiya agreed. 'But now age and liquor have caught up with him, and he is no longer hot shot. His co-pilot is Roman Spartak. He also is old, but not as old as Yuri.'

Nella decided not to ask Nastiya for her definition of old. She had an uneasy suspicion that she might fall into that category. Instead she said, 'When are we going to meet them?'

'They checked into the hotel this morning. I spoke on the telephone to Yuri Volkov this afternoon just after you checked in. He has received the briefing that he believes was sent to him by Carl Bannock, and he is expecting our arrival. He and his second pilot are staying here in the hotel. I arranged with Yuri that we should meet them for a drink in the Bamboo Bar at seven thirty. That means we have an hour to go over our plans, to make certain we don't make any mistakes,' Nastiya told her.

At the arranged time the two women took the lift down to the Bamboo Bar.

'Remember that we mustn't recognize them,' Nastiya warned Nella as they walked into the room that throbbed with the rhythm of a Thai jazz band. The two Russians were sitting on the imitation tiger-skin high stools at the long bar and both of them were watching the door. They reacted immediately as the pair appeared in the entrance to the bar.

'They have spotted us.' Nastiya spoke without moving her lips. 'Emma Purdom sent them copies of our passports when she hacked into their comms. Here comes Yuri. He must have been a real hottie when he was younger.'

'I am Yuri Volkov.' The Russian bowed to the two women, then his eyes returned to Nastiya's face. 'You must be the one named Nastiya O'Brien,' he greeted her in English. 'That is a strange first name for an Irish girl.' He held out his hand and Nastiya took it.

'I was once Nastiya Voronova,' she replied in Russian. 'But I went and married an Irishman.'

'Ah so! It is good to meet such a lovely lady from home!' Yuri switched into their mother tongue.

'You can call me Nastiya,' she said, and then she reverted to English for the benefit of Nella. 'This is my friend Nella Vosloo. She is a South African business lady.'

Yuri turned to Nella and shook her hand. 'I hope you will forgive my English very bad.'

372

'Your English is very good,' Nella replied as she examined his once-handsome but now drink-raddled features.

'Thank you, but is not true.' Yuri turned back to Nastiya. 'I have instructions from my owner to fly you to Kazundu to meet him.'

'That is correct. We have special business with His Majesty King John,' Nastiya agreed.

'With your permission I present to you my colleague and co-pilot, Roman Spartak.'

Yuri introduced them and ordered vodka all round. They toasted each other and Yuri asked apologetically if he might be allowed to view the women's documents so that he could compare them to the copies he had been sent by his employer. After he had matched their passports to the scans Yuri relaxed further and ordered more vodka. An hour later Nastiya asked the men to excuse them and she took Nella to the ladies' room. As they repaired their make-up in the big mirror she asked tactfully, 'Do you have any personal interest in either of our new friends, Nella?'

'No thank you. Yuri is quite sweet. But I am happily married to a good man. I gave up playing those side games long ago.'

'The same goes with me. Besides which we have a busy day tomorrow.'

They said goodnight to the pilots and they agreed to meet them again in the hotel lobby after breakfast the following morning.

When they came down to the lobby, Yuri had two of the hotel courtesy cars waiting at the entrance and they drove out to the Don Muang private jet terminal in convoy. There were fourteen other passengers waiting in the private lounge to board the Condor. They were all startlingly good-looking Thai girls. They were in high spirits, chattering and giggling, excited to be embarking on this adventure to Africa.

'I don't think they are all girls.' Nastiya gave her opinion. 'Carl must be giving full run to his peculiar tastes. But keep your voice down, and try to wipe that frown off your face.'

Yuri gathered up all his passengers and shepherded them through immigration and airport security, after which they were allowed to board the minibus that took them all out to the gigantic four-engined

Antonov aircraft waiting on the hardstanding. They boarded her through the ramp at the rear of the fuselage.

A single African air hostess met them and led all the passengers forward through the empty cargo hold to the pressurized passenger compartment behind the galley and the flight deck. When all the passengers were seated in the cavernous compartment and strapped in, the hostess locked the airtight doors and demonstrated the emergency procedures. Meanwhile the pilots started the main engines and began to taxi to the head of the runway.

The Condor took off and climbed to cruising altitude and settled on course for Kazundu. Within a very short time the passengers lapsed into the torpor of long-distance flight as the Condor droned westwards at a little under five-hundred miles per hour.

An hour after take-off the hostess came back to where the two women were seated.

'The captain invites you up to the cockpit to see how the plane is flown.'

Nastiya glanced at Nella, who nodded acquiescence. They left their seats and followed the hostess back up the aisle. Without making it obvious, both of them took full advantage of this opportunity to study the layout of the forward area of the fuselage and the cockpit. They spent a pleasant enough half-hour with the two Russians. Yuri tried his best to impress them with the specifications of the Condor. He even allowed Nella to sit in the command seat and to hold the controls. She giggled with feigned excitement, and Yuri was so encouraged that he placed his hand on her knee. She removed it firmly, and the two women returned to their seats in the passenger compartment.

'You should be able to fly it now, after Yuri's instructions,' Nastiya teased her.

'I think he wanted to give me the full course.' Nella grinned, and reached into her bag for a paperback Stephen King novel.

Five hours later Nastiya surreptitiously switched on her hand-held GPS and confirmed that the position of the Condor was one hundred and fifty-two miles east of Male, the capital of the Maldives Republic in the Indian Ocean. She composed a single-code-word message and sent it to a one-off Hotmail address. This brief transmission was to alert Cross Bow Central that they were about to go operational.

Four minutes later she received the response and the order to proceed. This read simply 'KYBO'. She smiled at another example of Hector's boyish sense of humour. The acronym stood for 'Keep Your Bowels Open'.

Nastiya leaned across the aisle and touch Nella's arm. Nella opened her eyes, sat up straight and nodded at her. Nastiya unbuckled her safety belt, stood up and took her valise down from the overhead locker. Then she went up the aisle to the toilet between the galley and the flight deck. Behind the curtains that screened the forward area from the passenger cabin, the hostess was sitting in her jump seat in the galley reading a magazine. The door to the flight deck was hooked open, and through it Nastiya could see the backs of the pilots' heads as they sat at the controls of the Condor. Nastiya grimaced when for the first time she noticed that Yuri had a pronounced bald patch on the back of his scalp over which he had slicked down a few wispy grey locks.

All three members of the Condor crew were relaxed; bored and off-guard. They had obviously flown hundreds of hours together on this route, and their security precautions were minimal to non-existent.

The black hostess looked up and smiled at Nastiya. She returned the smile and went into the toilet. She locked the door and set her valise down on the floor. Then she unzipped and dropped her jeans and her panties around her ankles and lowered herself onto the seat. As Hector had reminded her with his coded text message, it was always a wise precaution to evacuate the bladder and bowels before going into action.

Still sitting, she leaned forward, placed her valise between her feet and opened it. From the bottom of the bag she took out a box of tampons. Carefully she removed four of the white cardboard applicator tubes from the box. In place of the advertised contents each tube contained one of the Hypnos knock-down hypodermic syringes that Dave Imbiss had provided for her. Nastiya had modified the inner pocket of her denim jacket by hand-sewing four slots into it. One of the Hypnos hypodermics fitted snugly into each slot, instantly ready to hand.

Nastiya packed away the tampon box and zipped her valise closed.

Then she completed her ablutions and readjusted her clothing. She checked her make-up and her appearance in the mirror above the basin. She frowned at herself, and made a mental note to make an appointment to see her dermatologist for another course of Botox injections, just as soon as she returned to London. She liked to look her best even when she was going into combat. She flushed the toilet and opened the door.

The hostess looked up and smiled at her again. 'There are some snacks, if you are hungry.' She indicated the array of plates on the galley table.

'Thank you so much.' Nastiya set down her valise to free both her hands. She selected a single ripe grape from the display, slipped it into her mouth and with her tongue popped it against the roof of her mouth. She savoured the sweetness as she waited for the hostess to switch her attention back to her magazine. Then she took one of the Hypnos tubes from her inner pocket, flipped back the cover to expose the needle and turned back to the seated girl.

The hostess wore a short-sleeved blue uniform shirt. Her back was turned half away from Nastiya.

'Please excuse me, miss.' Nastiya spoke in a soothing and placating tone, as she gripped the girl's shoulder lightly with her left hand. The hostess looked up in mild surprise as Nastiya slid the tip of the needle into her glossy black triceps. The needle was so sharp that its entry was painless. Nastiya squeezed the soft PVC tube and smiled into the girl's eyes. She returned Nastiya's smile, then her eyes glazed and her entire body melted into unconsciousness. Nastiya held her upright with one arm around her shoulders, and with the other hand she fastened the buckle of the girl's shoulder straps to keep her from falling out of her seat and injuring herself.

Nastiya took a pace forward until she was able to see through the doorway into the flight deck. Both pilots were still in their seats. They were wearing bulky radio headphones and tropical short-sleeved cotton shirts. Roman, the co-pilot, was speaking into the hand-held radio mike. Nastiya heard him reporting the present position of the Condor to Male control in the Maldives, which now lay only fifty miles off the port wing.

Nastiya leaned forward to peer over Yuri's head and to check the green light on the control panel which indicated that the Condor was flying on automatic pilot. The bulb was blinking reassuringly green. She waited for Roman to finish his radio transmission and cradle his hand-held mike.

Behind her back Nastiya held one of the Hypnos syringes in each hand. She flicked open the protective covers and exposed the needles. She stepped quietly through the door into the cockpit. The two Russians were oblivious to her presence. She came up behind them and simultaneously slapped a hand on each of their shoulders. The tiny needles slipped through cloth and skin without a check, and she shot the anaesthetic into them.

Both of the men had time to look around and recognize her. Yuri opened his mouth to speak, but before he could do so he sagged forward onto his shoulder straps. Roman followed him into oblivion a few seconds later. Quickly Nastiya checked to make certain that they were safely restrained, with no impediment to their breathing. Then she leaned over Roman's shoulder to reach the controls of the radio and she switched it off. Satisfied at last, she went back to the entrance of the passenger compartment and peered through the slit in the curtains. All the Thai passengers were asleep. However, Nella Vosloo was sitting forward in her seat, alert for her summons. Nastiya beckoned her with a jerk of the head, and Nella stood up and came up the aisle to join her.

In the cockpit Nella helped Nastiya to lift the two pilots out of their seats and lay them on the deck. From her valise Nastiya brought out a pack of heavy-duty PVC cable ties. With these they pinioned the pilots' arms and legs. Then they dragged them one at a time back into the galley.

'How long will the effects of the drug take to wear off?' Nella asked quietly.

'According to Dave Imbiss, they should be out for about three or four hours, depending on their individual resistance to the drug. But if we need them awake before then Dave has given me an antidote that will wake them up at once,' Nastiya told her and then went on briskly, 'We must separate the pilots. If we leave them together, when they wake up they will certainly try to plot some way to make trouble for us.'

377

They dragged Yuri into the small storage compartment between the toilet and the galley. They propped him in a sitting position on the deck, with his back against the storage racks. They used more cable ties to fasten him securely to the steel framework of the racks. Then they fixed a strip of duct tape over his mouth as a gag. They locked the door when they left him.

Next, they went back and dragged Roman into the toilet. They sat him on the floor and fastened his wrists to the grab-handles on the wall above his head. Then they gagged him as they had done with Yuri. Nella found the toilet key in the pocket of the hostess's apron. She locked the door and posted an 'Out of Order' sign on it.

They left the hostess still strapped to her jump seat, but they gagged her also, and used more cable ties to secure her hands behind her back so that she would be unable reach the release buckle of her safety belt. Then they drew the curtain over her alcove so that none of the Thai passengers might find her and raise a commotion.

Once all three crew members were immobilized Nastiya left Nella to take command of the aircraft while she returned to her seat in the passenger cabin from where she could cast a motherly eye over the other passengers to make certain that none of them wandered up the aisle into the forward area of the aircraft to use the toilet in which Roman was sleeping.

Nella went forward and locked herself into the flight deck. Then she took her place in Yuri's command seat. She punched into the satnav the coordinates of the airstrip at the Bannock Oil drilling installation on the Zara No. 13 concession. Then she disengaged the autopilot and assumed manual control of the Condor. She eased her onto a new heading of 325 degrees magnetic. The change of course was so gentle that it would not alarm any of the dozing passengers in the cabin.

Much later, with only an hour still to run before they reached their destination, Yuri Volkov regained consciousness. He began kicking the bulkhead with both feet still cabled together, and bellowing into his gag like a buffalo bull bogged down in a swamp. Nastiya hurried forward to the tiny luggage compartment and squatted in front of him.

'Please behave yourself and keep quiet, Yuri.' She spoke to him reasonably in Russian. 'You are disturbing the other passengers.' She showed him another of the Hypnos syringes. 'You seem to be a very nice and sensible man and I don't want to be forced to stick one more of these needles into you.' Yuri stopped shouting. 'Thank you.' Nastiya gave him a warm smile. 'I assure you that we have no quarrel with you. I have been told by my boss that if you cooperate you will very soon be released unharmed. In addition you will be paid one year's salary as a compensation for the inconvenience you have suffered, and another year's salary for the loss of your present employment. This goes equally for both Roman and your air hostess. You can tell them that when you have the opportunity.' She paused to let him consider what she had said, and then she continued, 'If you promise not to make any more trouble I will remove your gag so we can talk. But you know what will happen if you start shouting again. Nod your head if you understand and agree.'

Yuri nodded vigorously. When she ripped away the tape, Yuri opened and wriggled his jaws to ease them and restore the circulation. As the same time he was studying Nastiya's face. 'Ah so!' he burst out at last in Russian. 'Now I understand what you are up to. You are going after those two pieces of shit in Kazundu, aren't you?' He used the noun *gavno*, which is a particularly offensive Russian word for excrement.

'Didn't your mother warn you not to talk like that in front of a lady?' Nastiya reprimanded him primly. 'Anyway, I have no idea who you are referring to in such derogatory terms.'

'*Chepukha!* Not half, you don't.' Yuri grinned at her. 'I am talking about his Majesty King John and his prime minister, Carl Bannock. You can do me a big favour and give them a good one from me when you catch up with those two animals.'

Nastiya heard him out, and then she regarded him evenly, before she asked, 'They have treated you badly, these two gentlemen?'

'Gentlemen they are not,' Yuri corrected her passionately. 'They are criminal scum. They treat all of us like shit. They mock and insult me every time they speak to me. They are always cheating me out of my fair wages.' He paused to catch his breath, and to rein in his anger. 'They are perverted animals. If I told you what they

379

are going to do to those passengers in the back of this plane you would vomit.'

'Tell me!' Nastiya invited him.

'They are going to shoot them full of alcohol and drugs, and then force them to perform all sorts of filthy and disgusting tricks. When they are tired of them they will dump them, and fly in another load to break and abuse. I hate both those bastards. I would love to see them go down in flames, I tell you!'

'Why didn't you do something about it yourself?' she asked mildly, and Yuri looked abashed.

'I thought about it often, but they have got so much power and money. What could an old down-and-outer like me do? I need to eat. They are the only ones who would take me on.'

She saw his obvious distress and changed her tone. 'Now that we have become friends and we understand and trust each other, perhaps you will tell me what your radio procedures are on approach to Kazundu airfield,' Nastiya suggested and gave him one of her most seductive smiles.

Yuri chuckled. 'I will help you in any way I possibly can, my darling. As I cross the lake inbound I call the castle on 121.975 megahertz. Then that greasy bastard, Bannock, rants at me for a while. He treats me like his verbal punch bag. After that he gives me clearance, and I overfly the airfield at five hundred feet to check the wind direction from the windsock. I don't trust that slimy swine not to give me deliberate misinformation. Then I turn downwind, cross wind and finals.'

'Do you give a specific call sign to identify yourself?'

'No, Carl Bannock recognizes my voice. He says I speak English like an elephant letting off wet farts.'

'What would happen if you came in to land without clearance?'

'I don't know. I have never tried it. He would probably shoot the living daylights out of me with those fifty-calibre cannons they have mounted at each end of the runway.'

'Thank you, Yuri.' She stood up.

'Now that we are friends and we understand and trust each other, how about you cut these things off my wrists?' he pleaded.

'We don't understand and trust each other that much,' Nastiya told him regretfully.

'Well, at least you could get me something to drink,' he suggested. 'Whatever that drug was you hit me with, it has made me very thirsty.'

'I'll get you a glass of water,' she said.

'I was not thinking about water.' Yuri's tone was aggrieved and she laughed and went to the galley and returned with a bottle of vodka.

'You are the most beautiful and kindest woman I have ever met, but I can't drink unless you free my hands.'

'Yes, I am truly beautiful and kind,' Nastiya agreed. 'But I'm not stupid.' She carried a drinking straw in her other hand, and she squatted beside him and placed one end of it between his lips. Then she dipped the other end into the neck of the bottle. Yuri sucked and swallowed several mouthfuls before she removed the straw from his mouth to allow him to breathe.

'You aren't really married, are you?' he demanded in a voice still hoarse and ragged from the raw spirit.

'Didn't you notice this?' She flirted her ring in front of his eyes.

'*Da*, I saw it, but I hoped that it was just camouflage, to keep the wolves away,' Yuri told her seriously. 'Please tell me that you love me as much as I love you, Nazzy darling.'

Nastiya threw back her head and laughed delightedly. 'Poor Yuri Volkov! You have missed your vocation. You could get a job in the Moscow State Circus. They always need clowns,' she said. 'Here is your reward for trying so hard.' She stuck the drinking straw back in his mouth.

To maintain radio silence, Nella overflew the Zara No. 13 airfield at low level to announce their arrival. By the time she had come around, lined up with the runway and lowered the undercarriage, Paddy O'Brien had paraded the entire Cross Bow contingent on the perimeter to welcome the Condor.

Nella settled the monstrous aircraft onto the landing strip as lightly as a virgin's kiss. Then she taxied back and with a burst of the port engines and opposite wheel brakes pirouetted the gigantic Condor like a ballerina onto the hardstanding, before she dropped the rear loading ramp.

Finally, she shut down all four engines and in the sudden silence Paddy's men burst out cheering and threw their caps high in the air as they swarmed forward to the foot of the loading ramp to welcome the two heroines.

Paddy O'Brien was the first man up the ramp to find Nastiya. Bernie Vosloo was only two paces behind him. The two men embraced their wives with delight and relief. The confused and terrified Thai prostitutes were shepherded down the ramp and in an almost avuncular manner loaded into the back of a waiting truck.

'You have your orders, Sergeant,' Hector warned the non-com he had put in charge of their guard detail. 'If any one of your men interferes with these kids, I'll personally break his balls.'

'I'll see to it they behave themselves, sir.' The sergeant saluted, but he looked wistfully at some of the pretty prisoners before his men whisked them away, still wailing and weeping, to the detention block where they would be placed securely behind bars to keep them out of sight and mind of the fifty or so testosterone-charged young rams that made up the Cross Bow task force. In a fight Hector would not hesitate to place his life in the hands of his boys, but when it came to libidos he would trust none of them even if they were trussed up in a chastity belt.

Hector turned his attention to Paddy and Nastiya, who were still locked in each other's embrace. 'When you come up for air, Nazzy, I would like a word with you.'

She looked at him over her husband's shoulder. 'Go ahead, Hector. I can do two things at once. Talk to me; I am listening.'

'What have you done with the Condor crew?'

Nastiya gave him a long-suffering look. 'Why is always you must pick the wrong time, Hector Cross? Okay, come with me. I show you. But first I tell you that, for money, Yuri Volkov the head pilot will cooperate. He has been badly treated by Johnny and Carl and he strongly disapproves of their sexual orientation.'

The three crew members of the Condor willingly gave Hector

their parole, and he ordered the restraining cable ties to be removed from their wrists and ankles. There was already a dearth of accommodation for the assembled task force. However, the Russian pilots were allocated a tent of their own. It was highly unlikely that they would attempt to escape. They had no inkling of where they were, or in which direction or at what distance their freedom lay. Nevertheless, Hector posted a pair of sentries to ensure that they honoured their promise.

Hector was not prepared to take the same chance with the nubile black air hostess. He wanted her also to be kept out of striking distance of any of his men. He billeted her in a room in the main block, adjoining Paddy and Nastiya's spartan accommodation, where the Cross Bow troops would venture at their peril.

Before Yuri Volkov was escorted to his tent Hector walked with him out into the desert. Out of earshot of his colleagues, Hector negotiated an agreement with Yuri for his full cooperation. Then Hector took him back to the communications room and placed him in front of the radio set. He handed Yuri a typed sheet on which was set out exactly what he had to relay to Carl in Kazundu. Then Hector sat beside him with his hand on the breaker switch, poised to kill the transmission if Yuri deviated in any detail from the script in front of him.

It took almost twenty minutes to raise the communication centre in the throne room of Kazundu Castle, and there was another delay while Carl Bannock was summoned by the duty officer.

He came on the line at last. 'Where the hell are you, Volkov? You are almost six hours overdue, you stupid asshole.'

'I am very sorry, sir.' Yuri's tone was cringing and obsequious. 'We had a total radio failure five hours out from Bangkok, and I was forced to divert to the airport at Abu Zara City to effect repairs.'

'Are you out of your dense skull? Your nearest airport was Male in the Maldives, or even Sri Lanka or Mumbai,' Carl Bannock raged with frustration. 'Why did you wander so far off course, you idiot?'

'Mr Bannock, sir, Abu Zara is the nearest centre in Asia or the Middle East that has spares for our Swiss EX12 AYRAN Transistor.' Yuri knew he could baffle Carl with technical jargon.

There was a brief silence on the air and then Carl snarled the question. 'What is your estimated delay, Volkov, you prick?'

'In excess of seventy-two hours if you want me to wait for the repairs to the radio, sir. That doesn't include actual flying time.'

'Did you pick up those passengers from Bangkok?' Carl went off at a tangent.

'Yes, sir, Mr Bannock! They are all here with me.'

Hector imagined Carl steaming with lust to get his hands on his little sex toys. Yuri was grinning as he also savoured the moment, but he continued in a tone of voice both contrite and eager to please. 'I can fly without radio and be in Kazundu in less than ten hours, if you give the word, Mr Bannock, sir. Naturally I will not be able to initiate the usual radio procedure on my approach to Kazundu.'

'Control will never let you take off from Abu Zara without radio comms, you stupid old bugger!'

'I can arrange it, sir. I have a contact in control, but it will cost some baksheesh. He is asking one thousand dollars US.'

'Okay, Yuri Volkov, pay him and then get your unsavoury Russian buttocks down here pronto, do you hear me? I should fire you, you doddering old fart.' The radio contact was cut abruptly.

'Now I understand why you love and respect your boss so heartily, Yuri.' Hector stood up and patted his shoulder. 'You did a good job of convincing him. I want you and your crew to confine yourself to this base until I return from this mission. Then I will pay you the amount we have agreed on. After that I will fly all three of you to Dubai to catch a flight to wherever in the world you want to disappear. I might even pay for your air tickets.'

Hector and Paddy had planned the complicated loading schedules of the Condor carefully. Those troops and equipment that were to be first out on the Kazundu airfield had to be last into the Condor here at Zara No. 13.

Even so it took almost two hours from when Hector made the 'Go' decision to when Bernie and Nella Vosloo between them lifted the heavily loaded Condor's wheels off the airstrip and she roared up into the moonlit sky. At fifteen hundred feet above the desert Bernie brought her around onto a south-westerly heading, to cut across the Great Horn of Africa and from there to head a touch west of south for Lake Tanganyika and the kingdom of Kazundu on its western shore.

Hector had timed the take-off carefully to ensure their arrival over Kazundu an hour after sunrise. It was a compromise. If they arrived as soon as there was sufficient daylight for a safe landing, then it was highly likely that Johnny and Carl would not leave their beds to come down to the airstrip to greet their Thai guests. The best scenario was to have the two targets standing on the airstrip when the tail ramp of the Condor dropped and the Cross Bow men came boiling down it.

If the Condor arrived much later in the day, and if they then became embroiled in a protracted dogfight with Johnny and Sam Ngewenyama's men, there was a chance that they might find themselves pinned down in a night fight. In the darkness the home side would decidedly have the upper hand.

Now the cards had been dealt and there was nothing left to do but fly on to meet the dawn and the enemy.

Hector was in no doubt as to how he wished to pass the night. However, the only secluded area anywhere on board the overcrowded aircraft was the tiny luggage compartment between the flight deck and the galley in which Nastiya had imprisoned Yuri Volkov. Hector staked this out as his private domain, and as soon as the interior lights were turned down and the men settled for the night he took Jo's hand and led her there.

There was no lock on the inside of the door, but they jammed it closed with their bodies. The partition walls were thin, but they cared not who heard their cries. There was not enough space for them to lie side by side, but that had never been Hector's intention. The floor was hard, but to them it felt as soft as a feather bed. The night was long, but for them it was fleeting. They were heading into the valley of the shadow of death, but they whispered to each other only of a long life shared and love everlasting. In the morning they had not rested but they were refreshed and strong, and they believed they were as immortal as their love for each other.

When the alarm of Hector's wristwatch alerted them they left their hidey-hole and went forward and stood side by side in the doorway of the cockpit. Bernie swivelled around in the left-hand pilot's seat to greet them.

'Sleep well?' He smothered a grin.

'Marvellous,' Hector told him. 'Plain bloody marvellous. How much longer have we got to run, Bernie?'

'Don't ask me.' Bernie shrugged. 'I'm just the driver. Ask your navigator.'

'How are we doing, Nella?' Hector turned to her.

'Forty-three minutes to destination. That big shiny thing out there ahead of us is Lake Tanganyika.'

Hector and Jo stood side by side, leaning on the backs of the pilots' seats and peering ahead.

The sun had almost cleared the horizon on their port side and they were flying down a deep valley of tumbling cumulus nimbus cloud. The peaks reached high above their own meagre fifteen thousand feet of altitude which the instruments on the dashboard were recording. The cloud mountains seemed solid as ice, silver shaded with the blue of bruises.

The rising sun cast the Condor's shadow on the glistening slopes of cloud. Grossly enlarged and distorted, it was surrounded by a gloriole of rainbow colours as it kept pace and station with them.

'Oh, look!' Jo cried aloud and pointed over the Condor's nose. At their own level and directly ahead the dark shape of a fish eagle in flight was backlit by the reflection of the clouds. It was suspended on widespread pinions, seeming to hang motionless. But as the Condor rushed towards it, the bird dropped one wing and plummeted into a slanted dive across their path. It passed so close to their wingtip that they were able to see the glitter of its agate brown eye in the yellow mask of facial skin, and make out the individual feathers in its snowy cap flattened to its skull by the speed of its dive.

'Oh God, what a magnificent creature!' Jo cried with delight as the eagle was snatched from their view and swallowed up by the immensity of space.

Far below them the African savannah and forests were dappled with cloud shadow and brilliant sunlight. Directly ahead the burnished silver surface of the lake dazzled them.

Bernie eased back the throttles to begin the descent, and they dropped towards the earth between the glistening cloud slopes. The needles on the altimeter gauges rotated smoothly anti-clockwise and they crossed the north-eastern shore of the lake at nine thousand feet.

'Twenty-one minutes to destination,' Nella warned them. Hector took the radio microphone from her and held it to his lips. His voice boomed over the Condor's internal PA system. 'Wakey, wakey, gentlemen! Drop your cocks and grab your socks! Twenty minutes to target.'

Below them the lake surface was strewn with thin tendrils of mist. Flights of flamingo hundreds strong flew low over them. The birds followed each other in single file. Upthrusts of warm air lifted them in succession and then dropped them again as they encountered cooler downdraughts, so that they wove undulating pink daisy chains above the lake surface. From the cockpit they watched in awed silence.

'Fifteen minutes to destination.' Nella broke the spell.

Almost immediately after her Jo shouted out, 'There it is! Dead ahead! The castle on the hill!'

Hector unhooked the hand mike of the PA system and spoke into it. 'Okay, all team leaders switch on your Birkin repeater earphones. We are going live with Emma in Houston.' He nodded at Jo to make the contact.

'Do you copy, Emma?' Jo spoke in conversational tones into her Birkin and the response came back immediately.

'I copy you, Jo. I have a live fix on both of the targets. Both Big Boy and Little Boy are in the main bedroom area of the castle. They have company with them as usual. All of them appear to be asleep.' Emma's tone changed abruptly, becoming sharper. 'Hold on, Big Boy is stirring. He is getting out of the bed and now he is crossing the room towards the terrace doors. I have lost him now. He must have exited onto the terrace.'

'Do you think he has heard our aircraft's engines and he is having a look-see?' Jo suggested.

'Yes, that's almost certainly what is happening,' Emma agreed.

'The others are stirring now. Yes, I am picking up the sound of your engines on my headset. Now everybody is climbing out of bed. I haven't seen so much naked flesh on parade since the last time I was in Vegas.'

Carl Bannock opened his eyes, awakened by the fact that Johnny Congo was no longer in bed with him. Over the years that they had been together he had become completely accustomed to the bass rumble and hiss of Johnny's snores. It gave him a comforting sense of security and complete protection. He sat up in the huge rumpled bed and looked around blearily. The bedroom was the size of a ballroom. Counting the one he lay upon, there were twenty-four other beds arranged in the centre of the floor. On all of these, except one, naked bodies of both sexes were sprawled in the same wild profusion as those of the casualties following an epic and hard-fought battle. 'Gettysburg and The Alamo all rolled into one.' He grinned and the image made him feel better. There was a girl lying across his legs, and her skinny posterior reawakened his interest for a brief moment, but then he touched his own genitalia and they were still swollen and inflamed from the previous evening's revelry.

'Get off of me, you pretty little whore.' He kicked her away and she flopped over onto her back without waking, still lost in a haze of drugs and alcohol.

He sat up slowly and rubbed his temples where the pain throbbed dully, and he looked around the room. His attention concentrated on the only unoccupied bed. For a while he was puzzled by the fact that the bed sheets on it were soaked with blood and other bodily fluids. Then slowly the events of the previous evening's entertainment came back to him. He shook his head and frowned, as he began vaguely to recall how at one juncture in the revelry Johnny Congo had suddenly insisted on anally raping the youngest and tiniest of the females. Although her documents proved that she was eighteen years of age, her body was elfin and childlike; which is what had excited Johnny. Up until then she had stoutly resisted all his efforts to inveigle her into the act, even to the extent of offering her an absurd amount of money. However, this was the last evening and Johnny had reached the limit of his patience. Carl chuckled as his memories flooded back in full force. It had taken all the efforts of Carl and two of the strongest ladyboys to hold the girl still for Johnny to achieve his purpose. Her struggles, screams and finally her broken sobbing had been covered by Johnny Congo's roars of abandoned feral ecstasy, and by the shouts and the laughter of the men who held her and the spectators who had gathered around the bed to watch and cheer Johnny on to greater endeavours.

It was only later that Carl realized, despite his drug-befuddled wits, what grievous internal injuries Johnny had inflicted on the girl.

'Shit, Blackbird, you have torn her up something awful. The little whore is bleeding to death. It's soaked clean through the mattress.'

'Well then, you know what we got to do with her, don't you, white boy?' Johnny growled. Without waiting for an answer Johnny picked the girl up from the bed and carried her out onto the ramparts. Carl trailed after them. None of the others were in a fit state of mind to notice them leave the room.

There was a full moon high in the night sky, paling out the stars and bathing the terrace in a pearly luminosity. Carl found himself gripped by a sense of almost religious awe as he followed Johnny down the staircase to the gardens. His gigantic naked form was touched by silver moonlight, like a high priest of some arcane sect, carrying the sacrifice to place it on the altar of an ancient African god.

When Johnny reached the stone retaining wall of the crocodile pen he lifted the girl high over his head. It made such a striking vignette that Carl was moved to tears and the words from a role he had once performed at his prep school in Houston reoccurred spontaneously to him. He fell to his knees and intoned sonorously,

She should have died hereafter;
There would have been a time for such a word.
Tomorrow and tomorrow and tomorrow,
creeps in this petty pace from day to day,
to the last syllable of recorded time;
And all our yesterdays have lighted fools the way to dusty death.

Still holding the girl above his head, Johnny turned back and stared at Carl in amazement. When he spoke his tone was awed. 'Hell, Carl baby! That was real cool. I never thought you could talk that kind of spooky mumbo-jumbo shit, man. What's it mean?'

'It means just drop her over the side, Johnny.'

They both listened to the splash as the girl hit the water far below, and then to the thrashing of the great scaly bodies as the crocodiles fed.

Carl stayed on his knees until there was silence and then he rose slowly to his feet.

'That was beautiful, Johnny,' he said softly. 'That's one of the most beautiful and moving things I have ever watched.'

The memory of it lingered with him now, even though he tried to thrust it aside.

Then he thought of Johnny again and he looked around the dishevelled room. There was no sign of him. Carl swung his legs over the side of the bed and stood up. He started across the floor towards the doors onto the terrace. He stepped warily around the discarded hypodermic syringes and the puddles of vomit, the broken wine and vodka bottles and the abandoned footwear and clothing. He was halfway to the door when he heard Johnny bellow from the ramparts beyond.

'Here she comes. Wake up, everybody. Here comes the Condor.'

Most of the sleeping figures roused themselves, and they followed Carl, trooping out onto the ramparts where Johnny stood, shading his eyes with both hands against the rays of the rising sun as he peered up into the sky. They crowded around him, a plethora of skin colours ranging from Carl's milky white, through the pale yellow and gold of their guests to Johnny's glistening anthracite.

'I was beginning to doubt that oaf Volkov would ever find his way back here without radio contact. But here he comes!' Carl said. 'Let's go down and see what replacements he has brought us for this load of tired yellow whores.' He tweaked the brown nipples of the Thai prostitute at his side, and she shrieked obligingly. Even after such a short acquaintance they had all learned in what direction Carl's fancies lay; and just how much he enjoyed hearing a squeal of pain.

'I am going to give Yuri a real tongue-lashing. I have been thinking up a few more choice insults for him. Come on, everybody, let's go down and meet our new friends, and indulge in a little Yuri baiting.'

Carl led them back into the bedroom where they hastily retrieved last night's clothing that was scattered all about the floor and furniture in wild abandon. They pulled it on as they trooped noisily down the staircase and headed for the courtyard.

The homecoming of the Condor was always a cause for celebration, laden as she was with gifts and luxuries and exciting new faces and bodies. For the guests who had stayed out their time in this strange and frightening place it was the promise of a return to home and safety.

Emma in faraway Houston picked up this concerted movement on her hidden cameras in the main rooms and even the one set atop the tallest minaret rising above the castle walls. She reported it to Jo Stanley in the approaching Condor.

'There are three vehicles leaving through the main gate and heading down the hill in convoy towards the landing field . . .'

Johnny Congo led the convoy. He was driving the white Rover at his usual breakneck speed. Sam Ngewenyama was in the front passenger seat beside him. He was almost as eager as Johnny to get a first glimpse of the latest imports from Bangkok. He knew that they would be passed down to him in due course.

Into the back seat were crammed five of his armed goons. They were clad in ex-US Army issue camouflage and bedecked with bandoliers of ammunition. The barrels of their automatic rifles stuck out of the open windows. Every time Johnny hit a bump in the road they were thrown against each other. Their helmets and weapons clashed together or banged against the roof of the bouncing Rover.

Carl Bannock drove close behind Johnny in one of the Russian amphibious landing craft. He was dressed in a silk dressing gown with a vivid red paisley pattern. His hair was uncombed and it fluttered in the slipstream of the ungainly vehicle as he sat at the driving wheel. Around him Thai girls and transvestites clung onto whatever handholds they could find as the vehicle bounced and bucked over the rough track.

All of them were in the high festive mood induced by cannabis cheroots and other lively substances which Carl had made freely available during the night. Most of them were in a state of rude déshabillé. One of the trannies wore nothing more than a pair of Johnny's voluminous underpants that kept sagging over his hips to expose the crease of his buttocks behind, and much more in front. As soon as he hoisted them up, the shorts immediately began their next downwards slide. One of the real girls stood behind Carl dressed only in his discarded shirt that was unbuttoned down the front and blew out behind her like a cloak. She clapped her hands over his eyes every time Carl raced down towards the next sharp bend in the track. They all squealed and shrieked with laughter as the landing craft careened around the bend with its outer wheels teetering over the drop.

The last vehicle in the convoy was the second amphibian land-ing craft driven by one of the militia sergeants. It had been left far behind the other two. It was carrying a platoon of the castle guard that had been so hastily assembled that most of them were still trying to don their uniforms, and some of them had even forgotten their weapons.

Johnny in the Rover was the first one down the hill and he raced towards the gates in the high mesh fencing that now surrounded the airstrip. He was sounding his horn to warn the airport guards of his approach. Two of them emerged from the guard hut and ran to open the gates. Johnny led the convoy through and turned towards the terminal end of the runway furthest from the lake shore.

They parked beside the sandbagged redoubt which housed the heavy machine guns that protected the landing strip, which was sited in front of other airport buildings. One of these was the barracks that housed Sam Ngewenyama's thugs and their families. The other massive building was the warehouse in which were stored the cargoes brought in by the Condor, as well as the goods awaiting export: the precious coltan and other conflict minerals from the Congolese mines.

To enable the Condor to reach the main doors on the southern side of the warehouse when she was taking on or discharging cargo was a taxi path leading from the runway to the tall sliding ware-house doors.

By this time the rising sun was clear of the horizon. Every head was uplifted and turned to watch the Condor approaching at low level over the lake. As the huge aircraft crossed the narrow brown beach at the edge of the lake and lined up with the runway of the airstrip, Bernie Vosloo at the controls waggled the wings in greeting. The crowd around the waiting trucks at the westerly end of the airfield had the sun full in their eyes, as Hector had intended when he ordered the approach. He didn't want to give them a clear look at the Condor until it was on the ground, and up close at point-blank range.

Nevertheless the welcoming crowds were undeterred. They screamed and danced with excitement. As the Condor howled over their heads some of them ducked instinctively, but most of them caught a glimpse of the lovely women with long dark hair who looked down from the Condor's portholes and waved at them. Even Sam Ngewenyama's machine gunners abandoned their weapons and scrambled up to stand on top of the sandbags to join in the tumul-tuous welcome.

It had taken all Paddy O'Brien's persuasive powers, short of the threat of the firing squad, to induce fifteen of his youngest troopers to don wigs and brightly coloured blouses and to permit Jo and Nastiya to plaster their faces with pancake make-up and lipstick.

Hector was crouched down between the two pilots' seats, where he was out of sight from the ground but able to issue quick commands to Bernie and Nella at the controls. To disguise her femininity from watchers on the ground, Nella was wearing a baseball cap and a pair of dark glasses that she had borrowed from Yuri Volkov. She hoped that the watchers on the ground would recognize these items of apparel.

Both Bernie and Nella were enjoying themselves immensely. They were throwing the massive Condor around the sky with the gleeful abandon of teenagers on a Saturday-night spree. They would never have treated their own cherished Hercules with the same reckless disrespect.

'Okay, bring her up and go around for your final approach,' Hector

393

told them as he clung to the arms of the command seat with both hands. Between them the two Vosloos hauled the nose up into a gut-swooping climb and turned out wide over the forest-clad mountains on the borders of Congolese territory. Then they came around in a wide circle, turning cross-wind and then onto the final approach over the airport buildings. Ahead of them the runway stretched three thousand metres down towards the lake shore. At the eastern end of it stood the second sand-bagged redoubt housing the other battery of fifty-calibre heavy machine guns.

Bernie dropped his wing flaps to reduce the Condor's airspeed and Nella helped him ease back on the throttle handles between the seats. Between them they lowered the aircraft gently onto the red dirt surface of the landing strip, and as soon as she settled they threw the engines into reverse thrust and applied the wheel brakes to bleed the speed off her.

The thrust of the mighty engines ripped a dense and swirling cloud of red dust from the surface of the runway behind the Condor.

'Now hear me, Dave!' Hector spoke over the internal PA system. 'We are eight hundred metres from your drop-off.' He read the distances from the boards that stood along the left-hand side of the runway as they flashed by. 'Five hundred metres, three hundred metres . . .' Dave Imbiss and his Red Team had already left their seats and gone back into the cargo hold. Now they were poised tensely at the head of the rear ramp.

'As soon as the ramp goes down don't wait for my order, Dave, just go for broke!' Hector's voice was raised sharply. They roared over the last two hundred metres towards the armed redoubt from which the twin barrels of the machine guns were trained upon them like the eyes of an executioner. Bernie was gauging the distance to travel with an expert eye.

For a moment Hector thought he had misjudged it, and that they were going to crash into the wall of sandbags at sixty miles an hour. He braced himself and locked his fingers onto the arms of the seats.

At the last moment Bernie pushed the starboard engines of the Condor to full power; at the same time Nella flung the port engines into full reverse thrust. Simultaneously they both stood on the left-hand brake pedals. The condor spun into a violent 180-degree turn and came to a juddering halt with the exhaust nozzles of her four jet engines pointed at the machine-gun emplacement from a distance of only one hundred metres.

For a count of ten seconds Bernie and Nella kept the engines howling at full power, but at the same time they prevented the Condor from moving forward by locking on full wheel brakes. The entire fuselage of the Condor lurched and bucked like a wild animal in a trap, protesting this intolerably harsh treatment. The speed of the gases emitted by her engine nozzles far exceeded that of any tornado; it rocketed up towards the speed of sound. It blew the first row of sandbags off the top of the redoubt wall. The exhaust gases picked up the sand and loose gravel from the surface of the runway and fired it back like tiny bullets into the faces of the gunners peering through the embrasures in the wall of sandbags. It blinded them instantly, scoring their eyeballs, sand-blasting their eyelids and the skin of their faces. Then it hurled their heavy weapons back into their faces, killing or maiming most of them. Their slack bodies were hurled backwards across the interior of the redoubt to smash into the rear wall.

'Shut down power!' Hector shouted at Bernie above the thunder of the jet engines, and he slapped the shoulders of the pilots to re-inforce the order. The engines' roar dropped to a gentle whisper and the Condor ceased her wild gyrations.

'Open the rear ramp!' Hector's voice was loud in the comparative silence. 'Red Team! Go! Go! Go!' The orders were superfluous, but in the heat of the moment he shouted them anyway.

The belly of the Condor cleared the ground by a mere four feet, so the exit ramp did not have far to drop before it hit the ground, and Dave Imbiss led his twelve-man team sprinting down the ramp and across the open ground to the redoubt. They swarmed over the top of the wall and were into the redoubt with the speed and agility of a troop of hungry monkeys climbing a banana tree. Their orders from Hector were to take no prisoners and to leave no live enemy in their rear, but to do it quietly. They found little resistance inside the redoubt.

The gunners and their loaders were blinded and out of the fight. Most of them were already completely quiescent, scattered around the interior of the redoubt like the rag dolls of naughty child. A few were rolling about on the sandy floor, wailing in agony and cupping their ruined faces in their hands. A karate chop with the blade of the hand was sufficient to silence them permanently. However, one of the enemy broke from cover behind the stack of ammunition crates where he had escaped the main rush of exhaust gases through the embrasures.

He reached the narrow doorway in the rear of the redoubt. Dave Imbiss raised the heavy trench knife he was carrying in his right hand. He swung it back over his shoulder, then he whipped his whole upper body into the throw. The ten-inch blade made one and a half revolutions in flight before it struck the running man between the shoulder blades. He lost direction and ran into the wall of sandbags. He slid slowly down the wall, trying to reach over his shoulders with both hands to grip the knife hilt. He coughed once and a spurt of blood hosed from his mouth onto the sandbag in front of his face. His hands dropped to his sides and he doubled up on his knees with his forehead pressed to the floor as if in prayer.

Dave Imbiss stepped up behind him and placed one booted foot on the back of his neck to steady him while he pulled the blood-smeared blade out of his flesh and wiped it clean on the dead man's shirt sleeve. At the same time he spoke quietly into the voice-activated mike of the Birkin.

'This is Red Leader. Target secured.'

It was all over in little more than two minutes from the time they exited the Condor. The runway was three kilometres long. At that distance neither Johnny Congo nor Carl Bannock at the further end had been able to see anything through the dust cloud kicked up by the exhausts, or to hear anything other than the brief thunder of the Condor's engines at full power.

'Okay! Initiating Phase Two,' Hector acknowledged. 'Dave, spike the guns you have captured and then get your arses down the runway to back us up.'

The MGs mounted in the embrasures were all ex-US Army Browning fifty-calibre weapons that Dave knew intimately. He went down the line swiftly and stripped out the sliding breechblock from each of them. He handed the blocks one at a time to the men with him. They ran with them through the rear entrance of the redoubt and threw them far out into the lake. Once the guns were out of action, Dave formed his men up in open order, and led them at a jog trot down the runway towards the airport building three kilometres away. They had covered less than a quarter of that distance when there was the sudden rattle of small-arms fire ahead of them.

The Condor taxied sedately back down the runway towards the main airport building, beside which waited the three parked vehicles and Johnny Congo's reception committee.

Hector stood well back against the rear bulkhead of the cockpit, crouching behind the pilots where he could not be seen through the windshield of the cockpit. With a pair of binoculars he was scanning the layout of the terminal buildings and the sandbagged redoubt.

'Okay, I have a positive ID on Johnny Congo. He is the big black brute on the roof of the white vehicle to the right of the redoubt. Dark-blue shirt and cream-coloured chinos. It's impossible to mistake the swine,' he spoke into his mike for all his team leaders to hear him. 'And there is Carl Bannock standing on top of the wall of sandbags above the MG emplacements. He is doing a war dance and waving an automatic rifle over his head. The little bastard is wearing a long red-patterned robe. It looks like a dressing gown. He is barefooted, as though he has just climbed out of bed. He must be totally out of his mind with giggle juice. Just remember all of you that he is mine.' His tone was fierce. 'There is a crowd milling around the parked vehicles. It's difficult to say how many; maybe fifty or sixty or even a hundred of them; all Johnny's hookers and thugs. His whores are decked out in all sorts of weird gear. Most of them are almost naked and it looks as though a few are totally starkers, letting everything hang out all over the scenery. There is going to be bloody pandemonium when the shooting starts. Don't be too squeamish about peripheral damage when we engage. Better a few innocent bystanders go down than you let a bogey stay on his feet to take us under fire.'

Jo's voice sounded in his ear. 'I didn't hear that. So help me God, I never heard that!'

Hector frowned, and then went quiet as the Condor neared the end of the runway. The range closed rapidly and he was better able to weigh the odds and to make his final decisions. He started speaking again, well aware that he was the only man aboard, apart from the pilots, who could see what was awaiting them.

'The layout of this redoubt looks exactly the same as the one Dave has just silenced. They have the same pairs of twin-barrelled fifty-calibre MGs sited in embrasures and pointed at us. The good news is that the sides of the embrasures are too deep to permit the weapons to traverse to either left or right. The bad news is that we don't have the option of blowing dust into the faces of the gunners. If we try to pull that stunt again, all those goons who are outside the jet blast will throw down a solid sheet of fire on us . . .' Hector broke off suddenly as he felt a light touch on his shoulder and he looked around quickly.

Jo stood close behind him. Up until that time he had been unaware that she had left the jump seat in the galley.

'Hector, listen to me,' she urged him quietly. 'Why don't you use the warehouse building over there as a shield?' She pointed ahead through the windscreen of the cockpit. 'If Bernie takes the Condor down the taxi path on the left-hand side of the warehouse we will be hidden from Johnny Congo for as long as it takes to deploy the rest of your assault teams. Johnny will go on believing you are a bunch of juicy little call girls until you come roaring out from behind the warehouse.'

Hector stared at her for a moment, reviling himself silently for not having seen the answer as quickly as she had. 'Good girl,' he said. 'I owe you another one.' And then he turned back to the pilots.

'Bernie, you heard the lady! Go straight past the redoubt. Tuck us in behind that warehouse as close as you can get. Then immediately drop the landing ramp. Keep all four engines running, and stand by for a quick turnaround and an emergency getaway if things go haywire.'

Then he spoke quietly into the PA system. 'Heads up, everybody! We are only minutes away from Go. We are going to park behind the main airport buildings. We will be protected from hostile fire while we disembark. Both White and Black Teams move back to your exit stations, now!'

He patted Bernie and Nella on their shoulders. 'There is the secure laager for the Condor.' He pointed it out to them. 'Get this old bus into it just as soon as we are clear. Now I am off. Bye-bye! Sit tight! We'll be back.'

'Happy hunting, Hector,' Nella replied and he turned and left the cockpit. He paused only to embrace Jo Stanley and kiss her parted lips. Then he whispered into her mouth, 'I adore you, but for once please do what I ask. Stay here and don't come after me. It's a dangerous world out there. I need you to be with me for another fifty years or so.'

He left her and ran back through the empty passenger cabin. His men had already moved back to their places at the rear exit ramp. He followed them through the open pressure door into the cavernous cargo hold. Paddy's Black Team was drawn up on the starboard side of the hold. Paul had the White Team on the port side.

As Hector hurried down between the ranks towards the rear of the hold he was checking his equipment for the last time.

He wore a camouflage flak-jacket of Kevlar body armour and a helmet of the same material. Both of these were resistant to multiple hits from NATO-standard small arms. In the MOLLE pockets attached to his jacket by Velcro fastening he carried two M84 flash-bang stun grenades and twenty spare magazines each containing forty rounds of 9mm parabellum ammunition for his submachine gun. In the front fastening of the jacket was a tiny hidden pocket. It was just large enough to contain one of the Hypnos knock-down hypodermic syringes from Dave Imbiss's arsenal of dirty tricks.

He carried a Brügger & Thomet MP9 submachine gun as his main weapon. He loved it for its small size, light weight, quick handling and superb accuracy. With a flick of the thumb he was able to change from single shot to nine hundred rounds per minute cyclic rate of fire. Despite its short barrel the top-mounted optic sight allowed him to be certain of hitting a hen's egg-size target with four shots out of five at a range of fifty yards, shooting out of hand.

Hector reached the loading ramp where Paddy and Nastiya waited at the head of the Black Team, and he told them quietly, 'Bernie is going to park us behind the warehouse on the far side of the airport, so initially we will be screened by it from Johnny Congo and his goons. As soon as we disembark we are going to split up. I am going to take my team to the right and come out behind the sandbagged redoubt. You will go the long way round the back of the warehouse and the barracks to get behind them. I will keep them busy on my side until you hit them in the rear. Between us we have to stop them retreating up the hill. At all times bear in mind that we are only here to take Johnny and Carl, not to fight it out to the last man standing. As soon as we have grabbed those two we will get the hell out of here. If we are forced to follow them through the maze of the castle we are going to take casualties.'

'Perish the thought,' Paddy grunted.

'My team will go out first. As soon as we are clear you can disembark.' Hector punched Paddy's arm lightly. 'Break a leg!' He grinned at him. Paddy grinned back. Both of them were high on the fizz of blood in their veins, the heady excitement of mortal danger that kept bringing them back into the fight.

Hector turned away and went to join Paul Stowe at the head of the White Team on the other side of the hold. The Condor jolted to a standstill so abruptly that they were almost thrown off their feet. The rear loading ramp started to drop, but so torturously slowly that Hector could not contain his impatience.

'Follow me!' he snapped at Paul. Then he ran up the moving ramp and dived head-first through the narrow opening. It was an eight foot drop to the ground on the outside. As he fell he flipped his body over to land on his feet like a cat. He absorbed the shock with his legs and then bounded forward towards the corner of the warehouse. He heard his men hitting the ground behind him and pounding after him but he did not spare them a backwards glance.

He reached the corner and flattened himself against the wall. He was breathing lightly but could feel his heart pumping like a well-tuned racing motor. As he glanced around the corner of the wall his vision was as bright and focussed as a gun sight.

Very little had changed in the minutes since he had last seen it; Johnny was still standing on top of the Rover with his hands on his hips. Around the vehicle were clustered the motley horde of militiamen and juvenile whores. Most of them were staring perplexedly towards where they had seen the Condor disappear behind the warehouse. Some of the Thai toys were still dancing and clapping their hands, but one of the semi-naked girls was leaning against the side of the Rover and copiously vomiting up the liquor she had been fed.

The machine gunners in the redoubt had left their weapons and clambered up the wall to peer over the sandbags in his direction. However, what attracted Hector's full attention instantly was the bizarre figure of Carl Bannock still balancing on top of the wall. He was no longer dancing, but unlike all the others his back was half turned to Hector, and he was shouting at Johnny Congo.

'What the hell is that stupid mothering arsehole, Yuri Volkov, playing at now?' he yelled.

He was totally unaware of Hector's gaze upon him. The range was less than fifty yards. In his hands Hector held one of the sweetest little firearms he had ever fired. Before him was the cleanest shot that the fickle gods of war had ever presented to Hector. The man he had come to kill was completely at his mercy.

There was only one consideration preventing him from doing so. He wanted to be looking into Carl's eyes as he died. He wanted to smell the rancid odour of overwhelming terror on his dying breath. He wanted the last thing Carl ever heard to be the name of the woman Hector had loved. He wanted to whisper Hazel's name in his ear at the final moment so that Carl would carry it with him into the flames of hell.

While he hesitated, the moment was passing. He began to lift the weapon, but suddenly Johnny Congo bellowed in a voice of thunder, 'Get down off that wall, Carl, you stupid prick. This is a trap. It isn't Yuri in that freaking plane. It's Hector Cross.' His feral instincts were so critically tuned that Johnny Congo had smelled the danger.

Carl did not react at once to the warning; he remained transfixed. The opportunity was still there for Hector, but now it was fleeting. Swiftly but smoothly he brought up the gun and fired a five-round burst. The recoil was so light that through the magnification of the optical lens he could watch his bullets strike.

He had aimed at Carl's legs to anchor him, but not to kill him. Two of his bullets missed. He saw one kick up a tiny puff of dust way out near the perimeter fence. The second missed shot caught the sick

Thai woman in the background as she leaned heaving with nausea against the side of the Rover. It must have hit her in the head for she went down as though a trapdoor had opened under her feet.

The other three bullets all hit Carl where Hector had aimed. One went into the ankle joint of his bare left foot. Judging by the angle of entry Hector knew that it had shattered the complex of metatarsal bones where they hinged with the descending fibula and tibia bones. The other two bullets went marginally higher as the gun rode up in Hector's hands with the recoil. Carl's legs were directly in line with each other, so when the bullets passed through the left leg they went on to strike the right one behind it, breaking bones in both.

Simultaneously his legs folded up under him and he went over backwards. He tumbled down the far wall of the redoubt and out of Hector's sight.

Just as swiftly Johnny Congo disappeared from the roof of the white vehicle, but he had jumped. Hector could still hear his voice roaring orders at Sam Ngewenyama in Swahili. Hector had been fluent in that language since childhood. He understood that Johnny was ordering Sam and his men to catch the Thai whores and use them as a screen to deter the attackers.

Under cover of the walls of the sandbagged redoubt Johnny ran forward to where Carl Bannock was writhing in a puddle of his own blood on the hardstanding of the runway.

'My legs!' Carl whimpered. 'Oh God help me. Both my legs are broken.' Then his voice changed to a wail of terror. 'Johnny! Please help me. Where are you, Johnny?'

'I am right here with you, Carl baby.' Johnny stooped over him and lifted him against his chest like an infant. Carl squealed again as his shattered legs twisted and swung loosely, bone grinding on shattered bone chips. Johnny ran with him back to the Rover.

Sam Ngewenyama's thugs chased down and rounded up most of the Thai whores, although a few escaped and raced away terrified and screaming amongst the airport buildings. The thugs dragged those they had captured back towards the vehicles. Twisting their arms up behind their backs, they forced them to face outwards towards Hector's men.

As soon as Carl dropped out of sight behind the redoubt wall, Hector ran forward followed closely by Paul Stowe and the rest of the White Team. Hector came around the corner of the redoubt wall, and found Johnny with Carl in his arms and his gang bunched up around him in full retreat back towards the three parked vehicles, dragging their struggling hostages with them.

Johnny Congo's conscripts were all men of the Nilotic family of tribes. They were by their very origins taller than most other human beings. They disdained any man less than six feet in height as a stunted dwarf. They towered head and shoulders over the tiny oriental hostages behind whom they were trying to take shelter. They were also screening Johnny Congo and the body he was carrying back to the Range Rover.

'Go for head shots!' Hector snapped at Paul. 'Keep your aim high, and try not to hit the little yellow buggers.'

In the centre of the retreating line Sam Ngewenyama was the tallest of them all. Hector locked eyes with him and Sam saw the little B&T submachine gun in Hector's hands coming up. He tried to get in the first shot, swinging up the heavy rifle in one hand. The AK-47 is notorious for its tendency to ride up in automatic mode. This is almost impossible to control with a single hand. To exacerbate Sam's predicament the naked ladyboy that he was trying to subdue with his other hand pulled Sam off balance at the critical moment. His first burst kicked up dust around Hector's feet without touching him. A fraction of a second later Hector replied with a single shot that struck Sam in his forehead, a half-inch above the bridge of his nose. He went down in a tangle of lanky arms and legs.

Without lowering his weapon Hector swept it along the line of retreating militia. He fired three more single shots in quick succession, aiming at their exposed heads. As each shot cracked out one of the militia dropped, kicking and twitching convulsively.

The shortest man amongst them was at the end of their line

furthest from Hector. His flat uncouth features were scarred by smallpox. The little yellow girl he was holding as a shield broke out of his grip and raced away, leaving both his hands free for a clean shot. He managed to get off a lucky burst with his AK. The Cross Bow men flanking Paul Stowe were both hit and they went down.

Hector swivelled and fired through the gap they had left. Scarface dropped his rifle and walked backwards, clutching his throat with both hands. Then he fell on his back still clutching his throat. Hector switched his attention to the thugs in front of him. He got off a short burst before the weapon fired its last round. He released the empty magazine, but before he could load a fresh one the line of militiamen confronting him disintegrated and scattered.

Most of them ran straight into Paddy's Black Team as they charged around the far side of the warehouse buildings. Hector smiled grimly at the success of his pincer movement and left the survivors for Paddy to deal with.

He switched all his attention back to the two men he had come to kill. He saw that behind the screen of his retreating men Johnny had run with Carl in his arms to the Rover, carrying him around the far side of it. He threw him into the back seat, then he darted to the driver's side to get behind the wheel.

Hector tried to get a clear shot at him. But now the residents of the barracks behind the warehouse, panicked by the shouting and the gunfire, came swarming out of the building like ants from a nest being attacked by killer wasps. Paddy's men came up hard behind them, driving them to wilder abandon, until they ran headlong into the thugs and the terrified Thai whores trying to escape from Hector's team. This throng of humanity swept across Hector's front, between him and his target, foiling Hector's aim.

Hector ran forward, shoving hysterical tribeswomen and their squalling brats out of his way, but he saw that he was not going to be able to prevent Johnny escaping in the Rover.

Johnny already had the door open and as he ducked his head to climb into the cab Hector shouldered to one side a black woman with an infant strapped to her back. Then he let fly with the machine pistol. He emptied a full magazine at Johnny. He saw his bullets splatter against the side of the Rover, starring the glass of the windows and dimpling the paintwork. But the devil's luck held true. Johnny was behind the wheel and unscathed when the gun in Hector's hands clicked on an empty chamber.

Johnny gunned the engine, spinning the wheels in the dirt and throwing up dust. When the heavily lugged tyres bit the Rover shot away down the road towards the airport gates.

Hector ran to the nearer of the two abandoned amphibious landing craft. He scrambled up the steel boarding ladder onto the boat-deck of this great ungainly machine. Then he ran forward to the pilot's seat in the armoured turret in the bows. With a quick lift of relief he saw that the key was in the ignition switch on the control panel. The powerful diesel engine was still hot and it fired at the first kick. Then it throbbed rhythmically, blowing blue smoke through the elevated exhaust pipe above his head.

Behind him Paul Stowe had led his men up the ladder onto the deck. Hector saw that there were four of them missing, but he had known that casualties were inevitable. He put it out of his mind and jumped up on the driver's seat, waving his arms and yelling at Paddy and Nastiya. They saw him and brought their team at a run, shoving the bewildered black women and children out of their path.

Behind them the remnants of Johnny's routed forces were in full retreat. Most of them had thrown away their weapons and were running for the cover of the jungle. There was only one gateway on that side of the airfield and they jammed the opening in a struggling mass. The range was much too far for the little machine pistol to throw with any accuracy. Nevertheless Hector fired a full magazine at them to help them on their way. He aimed high to compensate for the distance. He saw none of them drop, but there was a sharp increase in their efforts to escape and the volume of their screaming.

Paddy was the first of his team up the ladder and into the landing craft. He shouted at Hector, 'What happened to Johnny and his lover boy? Where did the bastards go to?'

'That's them there!' Hector shouted back at him, and he pointed ahead at the gate in the perimeter fence just as the white Rover sped through it. 'Hurry it up, for Chrissake. They are getting clean away from us.'

There were three of Paddy's men still clinging to the steel boarding ladder when Hector engaged the gears and drove away down the road towards the airport gates. He had seen Dave Imbiss leading his team at a brisk trot up the far side of the runway, heading for the warehouse and barracks. When Hector came abreast of them he swerved off the road, brought the landing craft to a halt and stood up in the control turret. He looked back and saw that Bernie had already started to taxi the Condor towards the laager. He shouted across the runway at Dave.

'Get back there and stand guard over the Condor, until we get back. We are chasing Johnny up there.' He pointed up at the castle. Dave waved and shouted an acknowledgement.

Hector dropped back into the driver's seat, and then he accelerated out through the gates and took the landing craft onto the road leading up to the castle. Ahead of them he saw the dust of the white Rover. It was already more than halfway to the summit.

Cautiously Paddy, Nastiya and Paul made their way forward, clinging to the grab handles as the deck lurched and bounced under them. They clustered behind Hector. The speedometer on the dashboard was reading a reckless forty miles an hour, much too fast for this lumbering behemoth on the narrow twisting track. Nobody protested. They hung on grimly.

'How many casualties did you take, Paddy?' Hector demanded without taking his eyes off the road.

'We had three men down,' Paddy replied. 'There was a bastard behind us in the barracks with an AK. He let us pass and then he opened on us from behind.'

'But, I cancelled him out.' Nastiya's expression was serenely satisfied. 'And none of our casualties are fatal. They are all walkers. I sent them back to the plane.'

'Good girl, Nazzy,' Hector commended her, and then he glanced over his shoulder at Paul Stowe. 'How steep was our butcher's bill, Paul?'

'Higher than Paddy's, I'm sorry to say, sir,' Paul replied. 'Four of our boys went down. One is certainly a goner, maybe two of them.'

Hector ducked down lower in the control turret as a burst of AK-47 fire rattled against the bodywork of the vehicle. The others flung themselves down on the deck and huddled under the shelter of the armoured sides.

'Where the hell did that come from?' Hector demanded.

'There is a bunch of goons up there on the castle battlements,' Paddy replied. 'This old bus should be impervious to small-arms fire. But just pray that they haven't got an RPG or a couple of fifty-calibre cannon up there.'

'I'll leave the praying to you. I never touch the stuff when I'm driving.' Hector kept his eyes on the road as he broadsided the craft around the next turn in a cloud of dust and loose gravel.

'The way you drive the goons don't need an RPG, Hector Cross,' Nastiya told him severely. She crammed her Kevlar helmet down over her blonde curls with one hand and clung to Paddy's shoulder with the other. As always they were using this frivolous banter to mask their essential terror.

Now the automatic rifle fire from the battlements fell on them with the intensity of a tropical monsoon storm. It pounded down on the armour plating like a berserk drummer, and screamed off it in ricochets. It ripped up the surface of the road ahead so they drove upwards through a fog of flying dust and tracer bullets.

Peering through the driver's slit in the landing craft's frontal armour, Hector glimpsed Johnny's Rover disappearing through the castle gates above them. He swore bitterly as he watched the castle gates swing closed behind it.

The next twist in the road cut off his view of the main castle gates, but they were still exposed to hostile fire from the battlements much higher up. In the heart of the storm of flying bullets Hector spoke into the voice-activated mike of his Birkin.

'Jo!' He had to raise his voice to a shout for her to hear him. 'Jo Stanley, are you copying?'

'Affirmative!' she replied immediately. 'But goodness gracious me, what is all that din?'

'Just a whiff of grape, as Bonaparte once remarked. More importantly, do you and Emma have a fix on Johnny and Carl? They have done a runner,' Hector told her. 'They have gone to ground in the castle.'

'Affirmative,' Jo confirmed. 'Emma has a positive on her cameras in the castle. Your two targets have just driven into the courtyard in a white vehicle. Johnny has pulled Carl out of the rear door and is carrying him up the stairs into the main building. Carl seems to be injured. Emma can hear him moaning and she can see that he is bleeding.'

'He is injured all right,' Hector told her grimly. 'I blew his bloody legs off.'

'Oh, my God!' Jo's voice dropped to a horrified whisper. She did not attempt to disguise her shock.

'You didn't think we came here to play gin rummy with him, did you?' he snapped at her. It was the first time he had ever done so, but her squeamishness in the heat of battle, when his own men were being killed and wounded, made him very angry. 'This isn't a game any longer. People are getting hurt out here. Pull yourself together, woman!'

As he was speaking he steered the vehicle around the last tight bend, and as they came out of it he saw the castle keep only three hundred yards ahead of them. The heavy wooden gates were shut tightly.

The road was now running almost parallel to the castle, and so close to the foot of the walls that they were screened from the enemy on the battlements. The barrage of gunfire coming down on them was cut off abruptly.

In the comparative silence Hector spoke again into the Birkin mike. 'Jo, are you still reading me?'

'Yes, sir. I am still reading you.' Her tone was brittle as hoar frost. She had not taken his rebuke lightly.

God save us from amateur sulks and tantrums when we are trying to get the job done! he thought, but kept it to himself. Nevertheless, his tone was as cold as hers as he spoke into the mike.

'Does Emma have a count of the strength of the garrison in the castle?'

'Sir! Yes, sir!' Jo replied. 'Emma confirms the presence of twenty-three hostiles in the castle precincts, that is in addition to Johnny and Carl. Fifteen of them are on the battlements. Five more are defending the main gateway. And then the last three are with Johnny, assisting him to carry the man whose legs you blew off.'

'Message received and understood.' He ignored her gibe. His tone was neutral, but his thoughts were not: *I shouldn't have brought her along on this jaunt. I was not thinking with my head, I was taking orders from much lower down in my anatomy.*

He did not check his speed as he neared the castle gates, instead he jammed his right foot down on the accelerator and the engine bellowed as he drove straight at them.

Now he was so close that he could pick out three gun slits in the gates themselves and two more in the stone jambs on either side of them. From all these openings protruded the black barrels of automatic rifles aimed at him by the guards on the far side. A renewed fusillade of gunfire hammered against the bows of the landing craft and Hector found himself staring through the narrow eye-slit in the frontal armour directly into the blazing enemy muzzles.

He was forced to run this gauntlet for only a few more seconds before he crashed the landing craft headlong into the fifteen-foot-high gates of hewn timber. The huge gates were unable to resist the charge of the massive steel-hulled vehicle. They imploded in a welter of planks and splinters, and came crashing down on the stone cobbles of the inner courtyard. The three riflemen standing behind them and firing through the gun slits were crushed by their weight.

The landing craft climbed over the wreckage and roared into the courtyard. Hector brought it to a standstill in the centre of the open square. The two surviving guards deserted their posts on either side of the demolished doors, and ran back towards the staircase leading into the great hall of the main castle building.

Hector stood up quickly in the turret and fired two quick bursts. The first man went down in a heap at the foot of the staircase and lay without twitching. The second one made it to the top of the staircase before Hector swung onto him and hit him with a full burst. He arched his body as the string of bullets stitched across the back of his camouflage jacket. Then he collapsed and rolled down the stairs, coming to a stop beside his fallen comrade, both of them motionless.

Hector had a fleeting sense of relief that although Emma in Houston might have witnessed the swift execution on her cameras, she would not have been able to share the images with Jo Stanley in the Condor. The two of them were only communicating by short-wave radio. Jo had already endured sufficient to overload her delicate susceptibilities.

'Paddy, did you copy Jo's transmissions?'

'Every word.'

'I am going after Johnny and Carl.'

'Okay, Heck.'

'Take your team up and sort out those fifteen goons on the battlements. They won't stay up there much longer. They might even be coming down to take us on. But most likely they are already running for the trees like their comrades down on the plain.'

'Leave them to me,' Paddy said and snapped an order at the surviving members of his team crouching behind the steel side of the landing craft. 'On me, lads!' They jumped to their feet.

Hector shot a quick grin at Nastiya. 'As for you, my lethal tsarina, don't be greedy. Leave some pickings for the rest of us.'

She flashed him one of her haughty glances. 'Crazy man, Cross. Nonsense you must always talk me, like I am baby.' Under stress Nastiya's English diction crumbled around the edges, and she tended to dispense with all articles and prepositions in the Russian manner.

She turned and vaulted over the side of the craft, landing just behind Paddy. The two of them led the Black Team at a run towards the foot of the staircase where the dead men lay.

Again Hector spoke into his Birkin mike. 'Jo, please ask Emma if she is able to give me another fix on Johnny and Carl. Please note that I said please.' He made a small peace offering.

'Please hold on a moment, Hector, and please note I responded in kind.' There was a trace of a smile in her voice, and she had used his given name. She came back swiftly. 'Hector, Emma has them on camera. They have descended to level Bravo, beneath the main kitchens and storage cellars. They are in the passageway at Bravo Tango 05, moving along it in an easterly direction towards the small postern gate that comes out above the lake. There are still five of them in the group.'

'Thank you, Jo Stanley. We are in pursuit. Standing by.'

'Don't mention it, Hector Cross. Standing by.' At least it was a truce, if not a full peace agreement. Hector brushed it out of his mind. He jumped down from the landing craft and led his team into the castle.

I mmediately as he entered the great hall Hector picked up the blood trail. But there was only a light speckling of drops across the glazed tiles. Johnny would have stemmed the flow with a tourniquet.

'Good!' Hector thought as he followed it. 'I don't want the poisonous little swine to bleed to death before I can get my hands on him.'

Even though Emma had told them that the way down into the dungeons was clear, they fell naturally into the follow-up procedure that was second nature to them. While Hector went forward with a stick of four men, Paul and his stick took cover behind them and screened their advance. When Hector reached a secure vantage point he went to ground and he signalled Paul forward. They leap-frogged swiftly across the great hall and started down the circular stairway that led into the dungeons. When the leading stick reached each successive landing they paused, and allowed the following team to take over the lead from them. They went down through the kitchen area, and kept on down the stairway until they came out at last into the maze of the dungeons.

When they paused there they heard the far-off echo of gunfire coming down to them from the castle battlements high above. It lasted only a short while before the heavy silence fell again.

'Emma reports that Paddy made contact with the hostiles on the battlements,' Jo told Hector over the Birkin. 'Paddy has dispersed them and cleared the area. The survivors have fled in disarray. Your rear area is secured, Hector.'

'Thank you, Jo.' Hector suppressed that last residue of his resentment towards her. 'Please relay this to Paddy. He is to follow us into the dungeons and try to catch up with us as soon as possible. I might need his support.'

'Roger that, Hector!'

'Now please give me an update on my own position.'

Hector had a clear plan of this area in his head from studying the architectural drawings that Ronnie Bunter and Jo had obtained from Andrew Moorcroft. However, they were now fifty feet below ground level and there was not a glimmer of light in this labyrinth of stone. Hector had no reference points to relate to his mental map. He dared not forewarn the enemy of his position by switching on the headlamp that was built into his Kevlar helmet.

He could only scan the way ahead through the black light which was built into the optical sight of his weapon. With it he could pick up the fluorescent glow of the blood trail that Carl had left on the stone cobbles. Finally this petered out, but Johnny and the men with him had Carl's blood on the soles of their boots and they left smudges of it on the stone flooring slabs for Hector to follow.

In the utter darkness his men had closed up behind Hector, keeping contact with him and with each other by a hand on the shoulder of the man ahead.

At her computer in Houston Emma could follow their advance with the cameras she had placed in the dungeons. Each of these contained an infrared eye that clearly reflected the heat emitted by a human body. Through the same device she could also see exactly where Johnny's band were at any time.

Jo's whisper in Hector's earpiece pinpointed his position for him and directed him forward. They gained so rapidly on Johnny that now they could see the beams of his flashlight reflected off the walls of the tunnel ahead of them.

Then suddenly even that glimmering of light was snuffed out.

'Bad news from Emma.' Jo spoke softly in Hector's ear. 'She reports that Johnny has reached the funk hole, and disappeared into it. Emma has lost all contact with them.'

Hector knew of the existence of the funk hole, so he had been expecting this to happen. Nevertheless he felt a flutter of dismay in his guts. They knew nothing about the interior design of the funk hole. Carl and Johnny had built it only after Emma had left Kazundu. Therefore she had not been asked to set up her cameras inside the area. Of course, Emma had overheard Carl and Johnny discussing its construction. That was how she knew the name they had given it. She had listened as they had planned it as their refuge of last resort.

She had even been able to follow the progress of the actual work. One of her cameras was fortuitously placed in such a position that it overlooked the stretch of wall through which Carl and Johnny had excavated the entrance into the bunker.

Judging only by the time it had taken to construct it, and by the amount of earth the workmen had removed, it was obvious that the funk hole must be extensive. Once the work was completed, Emma had been able to watch as the entrance to the bunker was elaborately disguised. However, all that lay beyond that door was still a mystery.

'Okay, Paul.' Hector spoke in a normal conversational voice. 'They have gone to ground behind the secret door. We can switch on head-lamps now. They won't be able to see the light.' They all blinked in the sudden illumination after the darkness.

Hector led them forward again. The soft rubber soles of their combat boots made only a whisper of sound on the stone floor. As Hector rounded the next corner in the tunnel he came to what looked like a dead end. He saw tiny droplets of Carl's blood leading up to the base of the blank wall. He went forward to stand in front of the wall and he examined it closely. He ran one hand lightly over the masonry.

Jo's voice in his earpiece relayed the instructions she was receiving from Houston. 'Emma is watching you. She wants you to move about two feet to your right. Do you see a smaller triangular block of blue stone just below your eye line? Okay, push it in hard. Use the butt of your palm. Put your weight on it and feel for it to give. That's great! Now, still holding the pressure, twist it anti-clockwise.'

As Hector followed these instructions he realized that Emma had often watched Carl or Johnny carrying out this procedure.

Now he felt the block of stone revolve reluctantly under his hand. There was the muffled sound of a locking mechanism releasing within the stonework. Then an entire section of masonry pivoted ponder-ously on a concealed fulcrum. It swung aside to reveal a green painted door.

Hector leaned forward and touched the door. He knew at once that it was metal and not wood. He tapped its surface lightly with his fingertips, judging its resonance.

This was not anything like armoured high-grade chromium stainless steel; the type of material that the doors to bank vaults are made from. It was a low-grade mild steel. The welding was crudely executed, especially around the hinges. It had probably been done by local workmen in Kigoma, across the lake.

'Silly boy, Johnny Congo,' he said softly. 'You are old enough to know that cheap can be very expensive. This bit of slipshod workmanship might just cost you your life.'

'I could not copy that, Hector. Repeat, please,' Jo said.

'I said, happy days are here again.' Hector grinned to himself. Then he beckoned for Paul to come to him.

Two of Paul's men were each carrying a 10kg shaped demolition charge for this very situation. It took Hector less than five minutes to lay the charges to their best advantage against the hinges of the green door.

He ordered his men back behind the bend in the tunnel and followed them, paying out the electrical cable from its reel as he went. His men had already adopted the firing position, kneeling with their backs towards the explosives and both hands covering their ears.

Hector clipped the terminals of the cable to a twelve-volt battery pack. That was all the power required to ignite the primers.

'Fire in the hole,' he warned them and triggered the charge.

The conical shape of the charge concentrated most of the force of the explosives into the metal of the door. The shock wave was relatively mild as it swept over them.

Then they were on their feet and charging back to the entrance of the funk hole. Through the pall of dust they saw that the heavy metal door had been lifted off its hinges and hurled against the facing wall of the tunnel.

Hector looked down a flight of steps into the interior of the funk hole. Electric lights were still burning in the ceiling of the first cell that he could see into.

He was carrying one of the M84 flash-bang grenades in his right hand and the machine pistol in his left. With his teeth he pulled the pin on the flash-bang and hurled it down into the bunker. The flash-bang is designed to temporarily blind and deafen its victims, and to confuse and disorientate them. The blast disturbs the fluid in the semi-circular canals of their ears to the extent that they lose their coordination and sense of balance.

Hector ducked back out of the opening and crouched down, turning his head away, covering his ears and closing his eyes tightly. Even through his closed eyelids he saw the 2.4 million candlepower flash of the explosion and his ears sang with tinnitus as he jumped to his feet again. He found that his coordination was unimpaired as he dashed down the steps into the funk hole with his finger resting lightly on the trigger of the machine pistol. He heard Paul coming down close behind him.

At the foot of the steps he found a large sparsely furnished antechamber. There were three men in the room, all of them Kazundian guards in motley uniform. They had lost their weapons and were rolling about on the floor. Their eyes were out of focus. One of them was trying to get to his feet, but collapsing again with vertigo.

Hector would not waste a bullet on them. He knew he would need every single round when at last he confronted Johnny Congo.

'Take care of them, Paul,' he ordered without looking back over his shoulder. Across the floor in front of him he saw the sprinkling of the blood trail that Carl Bannock had left. It led through the open doorway into the room beyond. With three quick strides he crossed the antechamber, flattened himself against the jamb and then shot a quick glance around it.

Carl Bannock lay huddled on the floor of the inner bunker. A gale of emotion swept through Hector's senses, carrying all reason before it. At last the man who had murdered Hazel was completely at his mercy. His vision narrowed, leaving only a narrow funnel of light, at the end of which was Carl Bannock's loathsome countenance.

Carl's face was contorted with terror. His eyes were wide, staring back at Hector. His mouth lolled open as he tried to speak, but no sound came, and saliva drooled over his lips.

Hector passed through the doorway and went slowly towards him. Carl's shattered legs were twisted under him. They were wrapped in crude bandages through which the blood had soaked. He lifted both his hands towards Hector in a gesture of supplication. Hector tried to say something to him, but his hatred was a thick bitter paste in his mouth that clogged his throat.

Then Hector heard a whisper of sound behind him, and his reason returned to him in full strength. He realized that he had made a fatal error, and that he had placed himself in mortal danger. He ducked and spun around, lifting the machine pistol and pointing it at the source of the sound.

A steel door was sliding across the opening through which he had passed a moment before, cutting him off from Paul and his men in the antechamber.

He knew then that he was facing the wrong way. The danger was behind him. He began to turn back to face it. He was too late.

Something hit him with the weight and force of a speeding steam locomotive. It lifted him off his feet and hurled him head-first into the steel door.

Even though his Kevlar flak jacket had absorbed most of the shock of impact, it felt as though his spinal cord had snapped. The air was driven out of his lungs like a ruptured bellows. The machine pistol spun out of his grip and clattered away into the corner of the room. His ears were ringing from the force with which his head had hit the steel door. Without the Kevlar battle helmet to cushion it, his skull would have been crushed like the shell of a pigeon's egg.

Despite the pain he managed to stay on his feet, and turn back to meet the next onslaught.

Johnny Congo was coming at him again. His face was contorted with a berserker rage. Up until this moment Hector had only seen him at a distance, but now he realized that he had underestimated his size by half. Johnny was a giant of a man. He towered over Hector. His torso and limbs were massive. But he was fast, very much faster than Hector had expected such an enormous man could be. He charged at Hector again.

He lowered his head as he came. Hector saw that the top of his shaven skull was laced with a pattern of scars. Hector recognized this as the trademark of a head-butter. He knew that Johnny would use his head as a lethal weapon, but he realized that he did not have time or space in which to avoid his rush. Hector dropped his own head and met Johnny full on. The tops of their heads clashed together. However, the battle helmet saved Hector again, absorbing some of the intensity of the impact; still he was stunned by the shock. The steel door at his back prevented him from being knocked off his feet.

Hector knew Johnny would come again, and that he could not survive another onslaught. He was outmatched in weight, height and strength. He knew that his only chance was to take the fight to Johnny. He used the steel door at his back as a springboard and launched himself from it.

With his full weight and impetus behind the blow, he swung his right fist into Johnny's face. He felt the cartilage of Johnny's nose collapse under his bunched knuckles, and saw the blood jet out of his nostrils in two bright streams.

Johnny seemed to have barely noticed the blow. He shook his head and came straight back at Hector. But he had given Hector the split second he needed to draw the heavy trench knife from its sheath on his right thigh. He tried to level the ten-inch blade of razor steel at Johnny's chest. But Johnny's long bare arms locked around him, like the coils of a giant boa constrictor. The glossy black muscles bunched and hardened into ropes of steel as he began to squeeze.

Hector's knife arm was pinned to his side. The point of the blade was aimed at the floor, and Hector found that he did not have the remaining strength to raise it. His left arm was trapped against his own chest.

He found his strength receding swiftly as Johnny wrung the life out of him like dishwater from a wet rag. The fingers of Hector's right hand opened of their own volition. The trench knife dropped from them and clattered on the floor between his feet. He felt Johnny lift him off his feet as though he were a child. The great arms tightened around him like an auto-crusher machine compressing the body of an old car. Hector felt his ribs beginning to collapse. He could no longer breathe and his vision began to fade out.

Then through the agony and the darkness he felt a small hard lump under the fingers of his left hand which was still remorselessly locked to his chest. He realized what it was he was touching. He summoned the last kernel of his waning strength. With one numb finger he prised open the Velcro fastener of the pocket in the front of his flak jacket and touched the Hypnos syringe that lay within. Almost of its own accord his thumb moved to pinch the tiny green tube against his forefinger, and to flip open the cover that protected the hypodermic needle. Now his vision had gone completely, but in the despairing darkness he found the strength for one last effort. He rolled the wrist of his left hand. He felt the tiny pressure as the point of the needle touched something.

He did not know what it was, but he probed the needle into it and squeezed. Then he blacked out completely.

When he opened his eyes again he thought that he had been unconscious for hours or even days. Then his nostrils filled with the wild animal stench of Johnny Congo's sweat and he felt his great inert weight bearing down on top of him, pinning him to the ground. He drew a deep breath and then rolled out from under Johnny's body. He sat up groggily. Only then did he realize that he had been unconscious for seconds rather than hours.

He looked down at Johnny's body and saw that the needle of the Hypnos syringe was still buried in the great muscles of his forearm. Johnny was snoring loudly through his open mouth.

Hector heard a scrabbling sound behind him. He turned towards it and saw that Carl Bannock was on his elbows, dragging his lower body across the stone slabs towards him. His crippled legs were slithering along behind him. In his right hand he held the trench knife that Hector had been forced to drop. His expression was as mad and ferocious as that of a rabid dog.

Hector rose to his feet. Carl reared up and threw the knife at him. It was a pathetically inadequate gesture. The knife struck Hector's flak jacket hilt-first and dropped to his feet. Hector stepped over it. He walked slowly to stand over Carl, looking down at him.

'Carl Bannock, I presume?' Hector asked quietly, but there was a world of menace in his tone. Carl's bravado collapsed, and he cowered before Hector, sullen and silent. Hector kicked one of his wounded limbs. It flexed at the shattered joint and Carl screamed.

'I asked you a question,' Hector reminded him.

'Please don't hurt me again,' Carl whimpered. 'Yes. Yes. You know I am Carl Bannock.'

'Do you know who I am?'

'Yes. I know who you are. Please don't hurt me.'

'Who am I?' Hector insisted, and kicked his leg a second time. Carl screamed again.

'You are hurting me,' he blubbered. 'You are Hector Cross.'

'Do you know why I have come to find you?'

'I am sorry. I would change everything if it were in my power. I didn't mean to cause you pain. I am not a bad person. It is all a dreadful mistake. I beg your forgiveness.'

'How do you open that door?' Hector jerked his head towards the steel door behind him.

'I think that Johnny has the remote control in his pocket.' Hector went back to where Johnny lay snoring on his back. He stooped over him and patted his pockets. He found the opener, and he pointed it at the door and pressed the button. The door hissed as it ran back in its guide channels.

Paddy and Nastiya were waiting on the far side, but they pushed their way through the opening as soon it was wide enough to admit them. Paddy's voice was rough with worry and agitation as he demanded of Hector, 'Are you all right, Heck?'

'I couldn't be more all right, my old son,' Hector told him.

'I see you have hit the big bastard with the Hypnos needle.' Paddy looked down at Johnny.

'They work just like Dave said they would. I think he went belly up while I was still squeezing the tube.' Hector nodded. 'But now we have to work fast. We have to get out of here before the enemy regroup. Did you bring the cable ties?'

'No worry, mate.'

'Then give them to Paul. Have him and his boys truss Johnny up good and tight.' Hector touched his bruised and aching chest. 'He is the most dangerous man I have ever met. He is strong as a bloody bull buffalo. I was like a baby in his hands.'

'Why take any more chances? Let's just cancel him out here and now.' Nastiya reached for the holstered pistol on her hip.

'Don't be so soft-hearted, Nazzy. That would be much too kind and easy.' Hector shook his head. 'I am planning something really special for him. On our way home we're going to dump him out through the rear ramp of the Condor at twenty-five thousand feet. He will have two minutes of free-fall in which to repent his sins before he hits the ground.'

'Beautiful!' Nastiya applauded the idea. 'This is the old Hector speaking. The one we all know and love.'

'Paul, get in here with a couple of your lads,' Hector called, and as they came through the door he pointed at one of the heavy teak chairs that stood against the side wall. 'Strap him onto that. We will use it as a casevac stretcher on which to carry him down to the airfield. The bastard must weigh well over three hundred pounds. But the chair looks sturdy enough to hold him.'

As they dragged the chair to where Johnny lay and lifted him into it, Hector turned his full attention back to Carl.

'This is the first prize,' he told Paddy and Nastiya. 'This is the only man I know of who has murdered his own father, his mother, his stepmother and both his half-sisters. He has wiped out his entire family.'

'Worst of all, this piece of stinking excrement was the one who killed my best friend Hazel.' Nastiya glared down at him. 'Also he was trying to kill our baby Cathy. That I don't like too very much.'

'But we must give him credit for one thing,' Hector pointed out. 'He is an animal lover. He is especially fond of pigs and crocodiles; isn't that the truth, Carl? You love to feed them, don't you, Carl?'

Carl stared at Hector dumbly, but gradually the agony in his eyes gave way to terror as he realized in which direction Hector was heading.

'No!' Carl whispered, shaking his head. 'Please don't talk like that. I will give you everything I have. Money? Do you want money? I can give you sixty million dollars.'

'There is not enough money in this world, Carl,' Hector told him regretfully and he turned back as Paul Stowe finished strapping Johnny's huge carcass into the chair.

'You will need all the men with you to help you to carry this great lump of lard down to the airfield. However, he won't wake up for another three hours so you shouldn't have too much trouble with him. Paddy, Nastiya and I will take Carl Bannock where he is going. We will probably catch up with you before you reach the Condor, but if we don't then load Johnny on board and have the pilots wait for us. We won't be far behind you.' He slapped Paul's shoulder. 'Away with you, then!'

He waited while they manhandled the improvised stretcher through the antechamber and up the stairs into the tunnel. Then he went back to where Carl lay.

'What are the names of your pet crocodiles, Carl? Please remind me.'

'No, you can't do this to me. Listen to me. I can explain. You don't understand. I had to do it. Sacha and Bryoni were the ones who sent me to prison. My father deserted me, and so did my mother.' He was gabbling incoherently, a rush of jumbled words. At the same time he was weeping and holding up his hands to Hector. 'Mercy! Please have mercy. I've suffered enough. Look at my legs. I'll never walk again.'

'Hannibal, that's it!' Hector snapped his fingers as he pretended to remember. 'Hannibal and Aline. Shall we go down into the gardens and you can introduce us to Hannibal and Aline?'

Suddenly Jo Stanley's voice spoke over the radio. It was shrill with outrage. 'Hector, I am copying every word of yours. You cannot do this thing you are planning. No matter how guilty he is, you cannot kill him out of hand. You will be sinking to his level. You will be committing a crime against all the laws of God and man. Vengeance is mine, saith the Lord. What you are contemplating is savage and barbaric.'

Hector spoke into his mike and his voice was crisp and sharp as he replied. 'Sorry, Jo darling. We are very busy this end. Can't talk now. Over and out!' He switched off his Birkin and gestured to Paddy to do the same. Once they were both off the air he said to Paddy, 'Let's stop fiddling about, and get the job finished.' He grabbed Carl's wrist and twisted it up between his shoulder blades. Paddy did the same with his other arm. Nastiya squatted down and with a cable tie bound Carl's hands behind his back.

Then the two men lifted Carl onto his knees and dragged him up the stairs into the tunnel. Nastiya followed them, carrying their weapons.

They carried Carl through the labyrinth with his legs swinging under him. Carl kept babbling out his remorse and supplications for forgiveness and mercy, interspersed with shrieks of agony as his dragging feet caught and one of his legs twisted violently, bone grating on bone.

They reached the postern gate and emerged from it. Once more in the sunlight they paused to catch their breath and gaze about them. Hector looked up at the walls of the castle high above them. The tunnel leading out of the dungeons had burrowed under them and they were now in the gardens.

'You and Johnny have done a great job here,' Hector congratulated Carl. 'You have turned this place into a paradise. What a pity that you won't be around to enjoy it much longer.'

The airfield lay below them and they could see Paul and his men carrying Johnny down the winding road towards it.

They turned away and followed the contour of the hillside until they rounded a buttress of black volcanic rock and the water gardens opened out ahead of them. The fountains wove creaming patterns of spray against the high blue of the African sky. And the waterfalls cascaded down the black rock face, spilling into the pools and subterranean funnels on their return to the great lake that lay like a gleaming silver shield far below where they stood.

They went on through stands of giant ferns and strelitzia, festooned with exotic blossoms the colour and shape of birds of paradise. At last they reached the stone coping around the top of the crocodile pen. Carl Bannock's cries of pain and his pleas for mercy and forgiveness dried up as Hector and Paddy laid him over the coping on his belly. Paddy held his legs to prevent him toppling head-first over the wall and falling twenty feet into the green pool below. Hector leaned over the coping beside him.

On the sandbank that curved around the far edge of the green pool the two crocodiles were sunning themselves. Hannibal's huge jaws were opened to their full gape to allow a small white egret to perch on his lower lip and peck greedily at the shiny black leeches that had fastened themselves to his gums. Aline lay close beside him, as motionless as though she were carved from stone. Her eyes were bright and as implacable as polished onyx behind their transparent nictitating eyelids.

'Have you ever wondered what your sister experienced as she was being eaten alive by animals, Carl?' Hector asked quietly. Carl made a choking sound. 'Well, you are about to find out, aren't you?' Hector went on. 'Do you know what it feels like to lose somebody you love, Carl?' Then he answered his own question. 'No, of course you don't. You have never loved anybody but yourself.

'I know what it feels like. I lost my wife. You knew my wife, didn't you, Carl? Yes, of course you did. I want you to tell me my wife's name.' Carl was silent and Hector glanced back at Paddy.

'We have to jog his memory, Paddy. Give his leg a twist, please.' Paddy twisted hard and Carl screamed.

'Let's start again, Carl,' Hector said. 'What was my wife's name?'

'Hazel. Her name was Hazel.'

'Thank you, Carl. Now please don't say anything more. I want that name to be the last word you ever utter.' Hector nodded at Paddy and he seized Carl's ankles and lifted them high, tipping him head-first over the edge of the wall. Carl hit the water and went under. He came up again spluttering and choking.

On the sandbank Hannibal snapped his jaws closed and the egret rose shrieking into the air and flapped away across the tops of the strelitzias. Hannibal hoisted his vast bulk up onto his stubby legs and waddled to the edge of the pool. He launched himself into the turbid water. Aline followed him closely.

'Does this make you feel better, Hector?' Nastiya asked as they watched the carnage from above.

'No, Nazzy. Nothing will ever make me feel better. Nothing will ever still the ache deep down inside of me.' He stepped back from the wall and turned away. The other two fell in on either side of him, and all three of them broke into a run and went down the hill to where the Condor stood at the head of the runway, ready for take-off.

Bernie and Nella saw them coming and started the engines of the Condor. Then they taxied the huge machine up the ramp of the protective laager and stopped at the head of the runway.

As soon as the trio mounted the loading ramp and were safely in the cargo hold of the Condor, Bernie raised the ramp and Nella called over the PA system, 'Welcome back on board, Hector. Please find the nearest seat and get yourself strapped in. We are going for an immediate take-off.'

Hector led the way forward and as he entered the pressurized passage compartment he saw that it was crowded. There were three body bags containing the corpses of the men they had lost laid out on the deck. Beside them were the casevac stretchers with the wounded strapped into them. The mountainous bulk of Johnny Congo was still strapped into the teak chair with his head lolling on his chest. Paul Stowe had taken the precaution of covering him with a nylon cargo net.

'I didn't want to take a chance, sir. I didn't want him to wake up and wreck the plane and all of us in it. But even a bull elephant wouldn't be able to break out of that net.'

'Good man!' Hector voiced his approval.

'I kept those seats for you at the front of the cabin.' He pointed forward.

'Where is Jo Stanley?' Hector asked him.

'I think she is in the galley, in the jump seat behind the toilet.'

The Condor took off and turned onto a northerly heading. They climbed up through the cloud cover to cruise altitude, and Bernie switched off the seat-belt sign. As soon as this happened Hector stood up and went through the curtains into the galley. Jo was sitting alone in the jump seat beside the window. She looked wan and melancholy. She looked up at him and he smiled at her. She turned her head away to stare out of the window. He pulled down the jump seat beside her and sat down.

'Hello,' he said. 'Don't you feel like talking?'

'Not particularly,' she answered, still without looking at him.

'Suit yourself,' he said and folded his arms. They sat for a while, and it was Jo who broke the silence.

'I never want to hear what you did to him.'

'Who are we discussing? Is it the man who murdered Hazel, and who plotted the murder of Catherine Cayla?'

She did not reply, but continued staring out the window. Then he realized she was weeping. He touched her shoulder gently, but she pulled away from his hand.

'Please go away and leave me alone,' she sobbed.

'Do you mean go away, as in go away for ever?'

'Yes!' she said and he stood up and started back towards the passenger cabin.

'No!' She stopped him. 'Don't go.'

He stopped and turned back to face her. 'Yes or no? What is it to be, Jo?'

'You murdered him.'

'Murdered or executed? Our world often hangs on the precise meaning of a single word, Jo.'

'You did not have the right, Hector! You went far beyond law and decency.'

'What law are we discussing, Jo? Is it the law of Al-Qisas, the law of retaliation laid down in the Torah in Exodus and endorsed by the Prophet Muhammad in the Koran?'

'I am talking about the law of America, the law which I practise and hold dear.' She was still weeping, and he had to steel himself to oppose her.

'Yet you call me a murderer. You have judged me already, but the law of America which you practise says that I am innocent until you prove me guilty.'

'Yes, there is doubt. But you are going to kill Johnny Congo next. I overheard you boasting about it on the radio. If you do that, Hector, I will never be able to bring myself to forgive you. I will never be able to stay with you.'

'You want me to turn Congo loose? Is that what you are asking me to do?'

'I did not say that.' She denied it vehemently. 'I want you to surrender him to the law. Hand him over to the American justice system, which has already proven him guilty and passed sentence upon him.'

She jumped to her feet and seized both his hands. 'Please, Hector!

Please, my darling, for my sake. No, do this for both our sakes. Then we can go on together.'

He stared into her eyes for a long time, before he nodded stiffly. 'Very well, then.' But his lips were tight, and his voice was tortured with the effort it cost him to say it. 'I give Johnny Congo to you as the proof of my love. Do with him as you will.'

The US Justice Department sent a Grumman business jet from Washington DC to Abu Zara international airport. There were four US Marshals on board with a warrant for the arrest and detention of John Congo.

By royal dispensation, the handover took place in the hangar in which the Emir of Abu Zara kept his fleet of private aircraft.

The American Marshals were all big athletic-looking men with cropped hairstyles. They were lined up before the open fuselage door of the Grumman. They wore dark civilian suits, but Hector's practised eye noticed the bulges in their left armpits made by the holstered sidearms they carried. He saw the distinctive shape of the steel toe-caps in their polished black shoes.

These are a bunch of tough cookies, Hector decided as with Paddy and eight of the Cross Bow operatives they marched Johnny into the hangar. Johnny shuffled along in leg irons and his arms were secured behind his back with steel handcuffs. The handover was quick and unceremonious. The head Marshal handed Hector an official US Government receipt, then shook his hand and murmured a few words of thanks. He nodded at his colleagues and two of them stepped forward and seized Johnny's elbows. They dragged him towards the open door of the jet.

Suddenly Johnny turned and started back to confront Hector. Despite the handcuffs and the leg irons, the two burly Marshals were unable to restrain him. Johnny dragged them along with him. He was bellowing a stream of such filthy language as impressed even Hector and his hard-boiled Cross Bow operatives.

He came straight at Hector. His nose was still swollen and distorted from the punch that Hector had given him.

'It was me gave the order to kill your fucking whore wife . . .' he shouted, and he was close enough for Hector to feel his spittle on his cheek. He dropped his head to smash it into Hector's face. Hector was anticipating just this. He was balanced on his toes; it was the perfect set-up. He put all his weight behind the blow. He knew before he even made contact that it was the best punch he had ever thrown. It landed on the precise point of Johnny's jaw.

Even Johnny's massive neck muscles could not prevent his head being snapped around to the full extent of its rotation. He went down like a black avalanche and lay motionless on the hangar floor. There was a sudden and complete silence. It was broken by the senior US Marshal.

'Holy cow, mister. You're good! That was one of the best shots I've ever seen,' he said and came to shake Hector's hand again, but this time with feeling.

'Take him away, and give him the hot needle,' Hector told him.

'That is the plan, sir,' the Marshal agreed.

Five days later Hector received a phone call from Ronnie Bunter to let him know that the new date that had been set by the high court for Johnny Congo's execution was 15 October, three weeks ahead.

The threat to Catherine Cayla's life had been completely removed at last. They could return to normal life. Hector and Jo took Catherine and her nurses with them when they left Abu Zara and flew back to London.

The mews house was perfect and London was even better. There were restaurants and clubs that Jo had only read about, so she had to be educated. She had very few clothes with her, so they did not need an excuse to go shopping for her in Bond Street and Sloane Street. Jo had never even held a fly rod in her hand before. She had heard about Atlantic salmon, but as a Texan she had never seen one.

Hector drove Jo and Catherine Cayla north to Scotland, where they spent three days as the guests of a noble duke at his castle on the Tay river.

427

Jo and Catherine watched from the bank as Hector waded out waist deep into the river, and Spey cast with a fifteen-foot rod.

That evening, while they were changing into black tie and dinner dress, Jo gave her opinion of his day's performance. 'It's very beautiful to watch. It's like a ballet, so graceful and skilled.'

'So tomorrow I will teach you to Spey cast,' he offered.

'No thank you,' she declined. 'It's pretty but it does seem rather a plentiful waste of time.'

'What do you mean by that?' he demanded.

'Well, you didn't catch any fish, did you?'

'It's not the catching that's important, it is the fishing in itself.'

'It all sounds a bit daft to me,' she said. It was heresy, but Hector let it pass. The rift between Jo and himself was now healed and forgotten, and he was happy. He did not want to open it again.

By the third day the two girls had lost interest in the proceedings. Jo had her book and Catherine had her dolls. When those palled they went for short walks, holding hands and telling each other wonderful stories that neither of them understood. When Catherine tired, Jo carried her on her hip, and Catherine tried to make Jo share her dummy with her.

They returned from one of these walks to find Hector still in the middle of the river, but now he was no longer casting and his rod was bent almost double. He was uttering strange cries that really caught their attention. They stood hand in hand and watched with curiosity. Then the salmon jumped. It erupted out of the water, bright silver in the sunlight, and fell back with a mighty splash. The two girls shrieked with sudden excitement.

Fifteen minutes later Hector waded ashore carrying a gorgeous twenty-pound salmon in the landing net. He laid it on the grassy verge, and removed the hook from its lip. Then he lifted it out of the net and, holding it gently in two hands, offered it to Catherine to touch. She hurriedly removed her thumb from her mouth and pressed her face into Jo's bosom.

Hector looked at Jo. 'What about you? Would you like to touch a real live Scottish salmon?'

Jo thought about the offer for less than a second and then she shook her head. 'Perhaps next time,' she said.

Still carrying the fish, Hector went back into the river. He held the fish up and kissed its wet cold nose, and then he lowered it into the water and held its head facing into the current. It lay quiescent in his hands for a while, pumping its gills, recovering its balance and its will to live. Then it shot away into the tea-coloured waters.

That night after they had made love and were settling down to sleep in each other's arms, she whispered drowsily, 'You are a strange man, Hector Cross. You kill men without the least compunction. On the other hand you go to infinite pain and expense to haul a fish out of the water, and then you let it go again.'

'I only kill those who deserve to die,' he replied. 'That fish had twenty thousand eggs in her belly. She didn't deserve to die. She and her babies deserved to live.'

The next day they drove back to London. It was a long road and they arrived back at The Cross Roads and watched Catherine Cayla devour most of her dinner of minced chicken and squash. What she didn't swallow dribbled off her chin onto her bib.

Afterwards they were invited by Bonnie to attend the complicated ritual of putting Catherine to bed in the nursery with all her bunnies and teddies arranged around her cot in their correct order.

'But, how do you know the correct order?' Hector asked.

'She lets us know,' Bonnie explained. 'I know you think we are just making noises, but it's a secret language. You will only learn it if you spend more time with us.' It was a rebuke, and he knew he deserved it.

Later that evening, when Jo had finished her pre-bedtime routine and emerged from her bathroom glowing with unguents and redolent and lovely as a spring garden, Hector lifted the covers on her side of the bed to make room for her. She snuggled down in the circle of his arms making soft comfort sounds, not unlike those emitted by Catherine Cayla settling down for sleep.

'May I consult you on a client–attorney basis before we move on to more important matters?' Hector asked her.

'You pick the damnedest times, don't you?' she murmured. 'But ask away if you must.'

'If Carl Bannock were dead, then what would happen to the assets of the Trust?' She went silent for a while, and when at last she spoke her tone was distant.

'I have no reason to believe that Carl Bannock is not in blooming health.' She looked him unashamedly in the eye as she made this hypocritical denial, then she went on. 'However, if one were to assert the contrary then the law of the State of Texas is quite clear.' She sat up and hugged her knees, considering for a moment before she continued.

'Any person claiming that Carl was dead must be able to lay before the court irrefutable evidence of his death, such as a death certificate issued by a medical practitioner or a sworn statement by a credible eye witness of the death. Hector, are you able to think of anyone who would be prepared to stand up in court and swear under oath that they witnessed the death of Carl Bannock?'

'Not off hand,' Hector admitted.

'Well then, failing irrefutable evidence of death, the law states that a period of seven years must elapse before interested parties may petition the Texas High Court for a Presumption of Death Ruling. Evidence presented to the court must show that there has not been any reason to believe the subject is still alive, such as a reliable sighting of the subject or any contact with him by persons who might reasonably expect such contact. In our case the trustees can reasonably expect Carl to contact them to demand the benefits owing to him by the Trust, such as quadrupling any funds that he earns on his own behalf. If Carl does not do so, it would be strong evidence that he is dead. Are there any more questions? Or can we get on with the main business for which we are gathered here tonight?'

'I have no more questions, but I do have just one comment: it's a bitter hard world if my poor helpless little waif has to wait until she is almost eight years of age before she can afford to buy her first Ferrari.'

'Oh! You!' she exclaimed. She picked up a pillow and hit him with it.

Their lovemaking that night was especially intense and satisfying to both Jo and Hector. Afterwards he fell into such a deep and dreamless sleep that he did not hear Jo leave the bed.

When he woke again he heard her in her bathroom. He checked the bedside clock and found it was not yet five a.m. He roused himself and went for a short walk to his own bathroom. On his way back to the bed he paused at her door and heard her speaking on the phone. She was probably calling her mother in Abilene. Sometimes he wondered what they still had to talk about after all these years of phoning each other almost every night. He returned to the bed and drifted off into sleep once more.

When he woke again it was seven o'clock. Jo was still sequestered in her dressing room behind the closed door. Hector put on his dressing gown and went to the nursery. He came back to bed with Catherine in his arms, clutching her morning bottle. He propped himself up on the pillows, and held her in his lap. While she sucked away at the teat of the bottle he became enthralled by her face. It seemed that she grew more beautiful, and more like Hazel with every passing day.

At last he heard the door to Jo's dressing room open. When he looked up smiling, she was standing in the doorway. The smile slowly faded from his face. Jo was fully dressed and she had her small travelling valise in her hand. Her expression was sombre.

'Where are you going?' he asked, but she ignored the question.

'Johnny Congo has escaped from prison,' she said. He stared at her and he felt the ice forming around his heart. Jo drew a deep breath before she went on speaking. 'He killed three of his guards and got clean away.'

Hector shook his head in denial. 'How do you know this?'

'Ronnie Bunter told me. I have been on the phone to him for half the night, discussing it with him.' She broke off to clear her throat. Then she went on softly. 'You will blame me for this, won't you, Hector?'

He shook his head, but he could not find the words to deny it. He knew what she had said was true.

'You will go after Johnny Congo again,' she said with quiet certainty. He did not answer her immediately.

'Do I have any other choice?' he asked at last, but the question was rhetorical.

'I have to leave you,' she said.

'If you truly love me, you will stay,' he protested, but quietly.

'No, because I truly love you I must go.'

'Where to?'

'Ronnie Bunter has offered to give me back my old job at Bunter and Theobald. At least there I can do something to protect Catherine's interests in the trust.'

'Will you ever come back?'

'I doubt it.' She began to weep openly, but she went on speaking through the tears. 'I never imagined there could be any other man like you. But, being with you is like living on the slopes of a volcano. One slope faces the sun. It is warm, fertile, beautiful and safe there. It is filled with love and laughter.' She broke off to choke back a sob, and then she went on. 'The other slope of you is full of shadows and dark frightening things, like hatred and revenge; like anger and death. I would never know when the mountain would erupt and destroy itself and me.'

'If I cannot stop you going, then at least kiss me once before you do.' But she shook her head again.

'No, if I kiss you it will weaken my resolve, and we will be stuck with each other for ever. That must not happen. We were never meant for each other, Hector. We would destroy each other.' She gulped another breath and then she looked deeply into his eyes and said, 'I believe in the law, while you believe you are the law. I have to go, Hector. Goodbye, my love.'

He knew in his heart what she had said was true.

She turned her back on him and went out through the door. She closed it softly behind her. He listened for the last sounds of her departure but the house remained silent.

The only sound was Catherine suckling on the teat of her bottle.

He looked down at her and said softly, 'Now it is just you and me, baby.'

Catherine popped the teat out of her mouth. She reached up to his face to touch with one chubby pink finger the single tear on his cheek. She had never seen anything like that before and her eyes were huge and awed. She said softly but clearly, 'Good man, Baba.' And he thought his heart might burst.